KATHRYN GAUCI was born in Leicestershire, England, and studied textile design at Loughborough College of Art and later at Kidderminster College of Art and Design where she specialised in carpet design and technology. After graduating, Kathryn spent a year in Vienna, Austria before moving to Greece where she worked as a carpet designer in Athens for six years. There followed another brief period in New Zealand before eventually settling in Melbourne, Australia.

Before turning to writing full-time, Kathryn ran her own textile design studio in Melbourne for over fifteen years, work which she enjoyed tremendously as it allowed her the luxury of travelling worldwide, often taking her off the beaten track and exploring other cultures. *The Embroiderer* is her first novel; a culmination of those wonderful years of design and travel, and especially of those glorious years in her youth living and working in Greece – a place that she is proud to call her spiritual home.

For more about Kathryn and her work, you can visit her website at www. kathryngauci.com

D1108709

CONSPIRACY
of Lies

KATHRYN GAUCI

The love that lasts the longest is the love that can never be.

Somerset Maugham

Prologue

Côte d'Émeraude, Brittany, 13th May 1940

When Claire heard the news her heart sank. She turned the radio up louder.

'In the early hours of the morning, German forces smashed their way through the Ardennes onto French soil...' The news broadcast abruptly ended and was followed by the Marseillaise.

It was the news she had dreaded. After seven months – seven long months of waiting and watching – the inevitable had happened: the Phoney War had ended, the real war had begun and France appeared destined to suffer the same fate as her neighbours, Belgium and Holland. Half-dressed, she ran outside and across the courtyard to the studio. Marcel was sitting at his desk typing.

'It's happened,' she said matter-of-factly. 'The Germans have finally attacked.'

Marcel stopped typing and stared at the half-finished sheet in front of him for a few moments, deep in thought.

'Damn!' he said under his breath. 'Damn, damn, damn!'

'We should leave,' Claire continued. 'Go back to Paris straight away. Don't you agree?'

Instead of answering, he pulled her to him and began to kiss her, softly at first and then more violently. Pushing aside the typewriter, he sat her on the desk, pulled down the shoulder straps of her silk petticoat and smothered her body with kisses, making love with a passion so intense it seemed as if her whole body was on fire; a delirious culmination of pleasure and pain that caused her to cry out in ecstasy. When it was over, he stood by the window, looking across the fields towards the English Channel.

'I'm sorry,' he said in a soft voice. 'I shouldn't have done that. I don't know what came over me.'

Claire pulled her slip back down, placed the delicate ribbon straps back over her shoulders and went over to him, burying her cheek in the small of his back. His skin glistened with sweat. She traced the outline of his spine upwards with her manicured red nails and tenderly touched the long scar that cut across his lower cheek at an angle to the bottom of his earlobe. It pulsated with the rush of blood from their lovemaking.

'It's alright,' she replied.

He turned to face her, brushing the soft strands of honey-blonde hair away from her flushed cheeks.

'Darling Claire, these are uncertain times but whatever happens I always want you to remember that I love you.'

His eyes had a look of anxiousness she had not seen before. It was a strange comment to make after two weeks of bliss and she quickly brushed away any negative thoughts. She nestled into his arms, telling him she loved him too.

After a few minutes, he pulled away. 'But you're right – we should leave as soon as possible. Why don't you go back to the house? I have some things to finish off here first. I'll join you later.'

Claire returned to the cottage, pulled out the suitcase from under the bed and began to pack. The bedroom looked out across the courtyard towards the outhouse that had once been a painter's studio. Occasionally she glimpsed Marcel pacing the floor. Sometime later she saw him leave and head towards the gate. He looked up and saw her watching him. Slinging his beach towel over his shoulder, he waved and then continued down the pathway towards the sea. She returned to her packing.

When he failed to return a few hours later she became worried. The sun was beginning to set on what had been another beautiful warm day and she was looking forward to one more evening together – moules marinière on the promenade overlooking the cliffs. She looked at the bruises that blossomed on her body and thought about their lovemaking earlier. It had always been intense, a dangerous drug that she had become addicted to, yet this afternoon had been different; his passion had frightened her and it bothered her that he had chosen to go for one last swim alone instead of together as they had done every afternoon for the past two weeks – today of all days, when she needed him so desperately; needed to savour every second that remained of this holiday. Her thoughts were interrupted by a loud hammering on the door.

'Come quickly,' a man's voice shouted. 'There's been an accident on the beach.'

The sun was already setting over the English Channel and the tide was steadily creeping in when she made her way down the steep cliff steps. The small crowd of onlookers moved aside as Claire approached. On the sand lay a striped beach towel and a pair of light blue trousers.

'He was here for a while,' a woman said. 'Someone saw him wade into the water. The next thing we knew, he seemed to be in difficulty – out there, past the rocks. And then he disappeared.'

Claire's heart raced. The warm sea breeze turned icy on her cheeks. She simply could not comprehend the situation.

'It can't be,' she cried, looking at the men scouring the rocks with their torches. 'It's impossible. Marcel is a strong swimmer, and the sea – it's so calm.'

Kerosene lamps dotted the beach and searchlights scanned the area all night. Everyone turned out to help, but it was no use. After a few days, the search was called off. Marcel was pronounced missing, presumed drowned. What had begun as a summer of joy had now turned into a nightmare. For Claire, Marcel's death was the first casualty of the war.

Chapter 1

Kibworth Harcourt, Leicestershire, May 2001

It was almost 2.30 in the afternoon when Sarah turned into the driveway of Grange House. Mrs Prescott, her mother's housekeeper, was just leaving.

'I'm sorry, Mrs P,' Sarah said, winding down the car window. 'It took longer than I expected.'

'Messy business, divorce,' replied Mrs Prescott. 'I'm only glad my George passed away before I could divorce him.' She laughed.

Sarah smiled; her first smile all day. Mrs Prescott spotted the shopping bag and a bottle of wine on the passenger seat, along with a bunch of flowers. Nothing escaped her attention.

'No time to bake a cake today, I'm afraid. The market was still open when I left and I thought I'd buy lunch instead – pheasant pâté and a local cheese.' Sarah patted the bottle of red wine on the seat. 'And something to celebrate with.'

'Don't you worry yourself about your mother,' sniffed Mrs Prescott. 'When she told me you might be late, I prepared lunch myself. Turkey sandwiches, *and* I baked a cake – your mother's favourite: devil's food cake with a chocolate buttercream icing.'

Sarah thanked her. Her mother was a no-fuss 'Victoria sponge with a plain iced topping' woman, but Mrs Prescott always liked to think her cakes were her mother's favourite and no one had the heart to tell her otherwise.

'By the way,' said Mrs Prescott before leaving. 'The postman arrived late today and I put the letters on the table in the hallway. Can you make sure your mother gets them?'

Claire Bradshaw was sitting in the garden reading a book when Sarah arrived. Rusty, the golden retriever, was lying by her feet. When he heard Sarah's voice, he bounded towards her, wagging his tail. Not far away, Jack Hibbert, the gardener, was mowing the lawn. He doffed his cap when he saw her.

'How did it go?' Claire asked. 'Not very well judging from the look on your face. Come inside and tell me all about it. Mrs P has prepared lunch.'

Sarah took out the pheasant pâté and cheese and placed them on a platter next to the turkey sandwiches and Mrs P's devil's food cake that sat, centre stage, in the middle of the table on a pretty Royal Worcester cake stand. While her mother arranged the flowers in a vase, Sarah took out two glasses and poured them both a glass of wine.

Claire looked at the label. 'Château Margaux – a *grand cru*! My, that must have set you back a pretty penny.'

'You taught me well, Mum,' replied Sarah. 'Only the best.'

Claire savoured the first sip. 'It's a long time since I had a fine Bordeaux and I remember the occasion well: when the twins graduated. How are they, by the way? How are they coping with the divorce?'

Sarah helped herself to a turkey sandwich. 'Fine,' she replied. 'In fact they said we should have parted earlier. They were sick of all the arguments I suppose.'

Claire felt a great sadness for her daughter. She had had such high hopes for her and she hated to see her like this – beaten and dispirited.

Sarah read her mother's thoughts. 'I've made a real mess of things, haven't I?'

Sarah Carrington was forty-eight years old, nine years younger than her brother Peter. But unlike Peter, a successful banker in London with a large Regency home in the affluent and fashionable area of Holland Park, a happy marriage and three children set to follow in his footsteps, Sarah had little to be happy about. At that moment, sitting in her mother's kitchen, she wondered what else life had in store for her. She certainly had no desire to get married again, even if all her friends told her she would.

Sarah and Alistair had met at university. It wasn't exactly love at first sight, she thought afterwards, but they had been good for each other. They were both ambitious – that is, until the twins, Christopher and James, came along and Alistair persuaded her to put her career on hold and stay at home to bring up the children.

'You can always go back to teaching when the children are older,' he told her. In the meantime, Alistair's career as a lawyer forged ahead and Sarah felt resentful. When she was ready to join the workforce again, she found herself overlooked for younger and brighter candidates.

That was when the affair started: a string of affairs to be exact. The first one – Michael – began as an innocent flirtation. He was a teacher at the twins' school. The affair lasted less than a month but it was enough to set her body on fire again. For the first time in more years than she cared to remember, Sarah felt wanted – desirable was how she explained it to herself; a real woman made of flesh and blood. Something she had almost forgotten existed. Then there was the microbiologist she met by accident at a university reunion dinner. When she thought about it, they had little in common except good sex, and as usual, he filled a void. The last one was an architect who worked in London. At the time she even considered leaving Alistair for him – until she discovered he was a serial philanderer and already married.

And then, just when she thought it might be better to reconcile her relationship with Alistair, he surprised her with the news that he was leaving *her* for his secretary Emily, a petite blonde and a good fifteen years younger than Sarah. Worse still, he was filing for a divorce: he and Emily were going to be married and he needed the money from the house to start a new family.

Sarah was shocked. That Alistair had beaten her to it was the last thing she had expected: staid, dependable Alistair, who had never looked at another woman in his life, or so she thought. Most hurtful of all was the twins' reaction. They were both at university and let her know in no uncertain terms that half of their holidays would now be spent with their father and Emily.

'We like her, Mum,' Christopher had told her. 'And she makes Dad happy.'

With little hope of rekindling the fractured relationship, Sarah agreed to the divorce because, as Alistair pointed out on more than one occasion, it was she who had gone astray. *Gone astray!* His words made her sound like a stray tomcat.

'If you'd paid attention to my needs, I would not have *strayed*,' she retaliated.

'You'll find someone else,' he told her. 'You always do.'

And now, here she was, living in a nondescript semi-detached in a nondescript area of Northampton whilst Emily and Alistair settled into a Georgian townhouse not far away from his business in Market Harborough. Pouring another glass of Château Margaux, Sarah had never felt so unsure of herself in her life.

Claire listened to her daughter's woes with the patience that only old age brings. She helped herself to a piece of cheese and took another sip of wine.

'You'll find someone else. Give it time.'

Sarah shrugged. 'Tell me something, Mum. Why did you never like Alistair? After all, he was – *is* a good man, when all is said and done.'

Claire wiped the corner of her mouth with a white linen serviette. 'It's not that I didn't like him. He just wasn't for you.'

'What do you mean?' Sarah asked, swirling the wine around her glass.

'It's difficult to explain. You were always a vibrant child, headstrong and with a zest for life. You needed someone like you. Alistair – well, to put it bluntly, simply lacked passion. Milk flowed through his veins, not blood.' Claire looked her daughter squarely in the face. 'To be quite honest, I'm not surprised you had affairs. You should have left him earlier…so stop feeling sorry for yourself.' She sat back in her chair. 'There, I've said it,' she said with a loud sigh.

Sarah sat dumbfounded. For years she had nursed the guilt that it was she who had destroyed the marriage. Now here was her mother, telling her that it was fine: she had done nothing wrong.

'Why didn't you say something before?'

'My dear, you wouldn't have listened to a word I said. The young think they know it all. I am afraid you are like me. You have to find out the hard way.'

Sarah was just about to ask what she meant when the gardener walked into the kitchen.

'Be a dear and prepare Jack a plate of turkey sandwiches, will you?' Claire said to her daughter. 'And a generous slice of Mrs P's devil's food cake. We'll have tea in the garden and enjoy Jack's handiwork. The garden is looking wonderful at this time of the year – the delphiniums and foxgloves look a picture.'

Sarah picked up the tray and followed them into the garden. The sky was a cloudless pale blue and the scent of freshly mown grass filled the summer air. She felt grateful for Jack's presence; he had been the gardener at Grange House for as long as she could remember. It was her father who had hired him after Claire heard of his prowess at the local horticultural shows, and it was Jack who kept the lawn in tip-top condition for her mother's garden parties, who tended the herbaceous borders with their scented flowers and who kept the fruit orchard and vegetable patch productive. When John Bradshaw died, Claire asked him to stay on and over the years she had come to rely on him more and more. As for Jack, Grange House became his second home after his wife Molly passed away shortly after John Bradshaw's death, and he was only too happy to be at Claire's beck and call.

Since her heart attack just over a year earlier, the doctor had warned

15

Claire that she if she didn't slow down she would not reach the ripe old age of one hundred as she always predicted. Claire Bradshaw had always been a fit and healthy woman who enjoyed the pleasures of life: afternoon tea parties with her friends, attending the local hunt get-togethers long after she was able to ride, playing bridge once a month and helping out with the Women's Institute, to name but a few. The heart attack came as a shock and she was suddenly aware that she was not invincible. After much badgering from everyone around her, Claire took their advice and began to take life more slowly. Apart from reading, her garden had always been her pride and joy and she was now devoting the last few years of her life to enjoying it.

Sarah listened as her mother and Jack discussed the plants for the new garden bed. Claire's enthusiasm for life was now concentrated on her home.

After consuming a large slice of devil's food cake, Jack returned to his gardening and Claire to her book.

'Is there anything I can get you before I leave, Mum?' Sarah asked.

'Another pot of tea would go down a treat,' Claire replied.

Sarah returned to the kitchen and put the kettle on. Waiting for the tea to brew, she suddenly remembered the post in the hall and went to collect it. Along with the usual advertisements for double glazing and a new pizzeria in Market Harborough, a gas bill and a notice from the council about a rate increase, was a handwritten envelope from France addressed to Madame *Claire Bradshaw*. Sarah turned it over. She didn't recognise the handwriting and there was nothing to say who the sender was.

She returned to the garden with the pot of tea, and after asking if there was anything her mother needed, told her she would call by in a few days' time.

'Oh, by the way,' she said, placing the letter on the table, 'this came for you. It appears to be from France.'

Sarah noticed her mother's reaction. It was only for a brief moment, but the look on her face appeared to be one of shock. Almost instinctively Claire pulled herself together and smiled.

'Thank you, dear,' she said, slipping the letter into her pocket. 'I shall look forward to your next visit.'

During the drive back to Northampton, Sarah thought about her mother's reaction to the letter. She had certainly not wanted to open it in front of her. After a while, she managed to convince herself it was probably nothing of importance. Goodness knows, what with the divorce, her emotions were all over the place. She had better pull herself together.

When Sarah arrived home the message light on the answerphone was flashing red. After pouring herself a stiff drink, she kicked off her shoes and sat back to listen to her voicemail. The first call was from Alistair saying thank you for not making a scene at the solicitor's, and he hoped they could still be friends. She was in no mood to hear his voice, and quickly erased the message. The next was from Peter congratulating her on her newfound freedom, and also informing her that he was going to New York on business. The last three were from the same caller – Jack Hibbert.

'Your mother suffered another heart attack not long after you left. She has been rushed to the hospital. It doesn't look good – I think you'd better get yourself there as soon as possible.'

Sarah grabbed her keys, and before leaving for the hospital, made a call to Peter. 'You might have to put the New York trip on hold,' she told him. 'Mum's in hospital. It appears she's suffered another heart attack.'

Sarah was still in a state of shock when she arrived at the hospital's accident and emergency department. Jack Hibbert, still dressed in his gardening clothes and mud-splattered boots, was waiting for her.

'I followed the ambulance,' he said glumly. 'I thought it best someone stay with her until you arrived.'

'What happened? She seemed fine when I left.'

'After you left she continued reading for a while. Every now and again I looked up and caught her deep in thought. She had a faraway look on her face and I thought she might have been thinking about you and the divorce. Your mother doesn't say much but she has been worrying about you of late, you know. Anyway, I was just about to leave for the day when she asked if I would pick her a lettuce and a few tomatoes for her tea. As I headed for the vegetable patch, I saw her head towards the greenhouse. I thought nothing of it as she spends quite a bit of time there most afternoons, tending her plants in readiness for the local horticultural society show in August. Several minutes later I heard a loud crash and Rusty barking. When I went to see what happened, I found her lying on the floor. It must have been a heavy fall because she knocked over a bench. The place was a mess – broken plant-pots everywhere. Her head was bleeding badly and I presumed that a pot must have landed on her after she fell. It was an awful sight. And all the time, Rusty sat beside her, whimpering. It's at times like that when you wish animals could talk.' Jack pulled his shoulders back and sighed. 'I called the ambulance straight away and then called you.'

Sarah was still trying to take it all in when a doctor came over.

'Sarah Carrington? You're Mrs Bradshaw's daughter, I presume.'

Sarah nodded. 'How is she? Can I see her?' she asked anxiously.

'She's just out of surgery and sleeping now.'

'Can I see her for a few minutes – just to put my mind at rest?'

The doctor ushered her to a small room. Seeing her mother connected by tubes to fluid bags and monitors displaying an array of graphs, Sarah struggled to fight back the tears. A monitor emitted a series of high-pitched beeping sounds and a nurse quickly arrived to check that all was well. After conferring with the doctor, she made copious notes on the pad hanging from the end of the bed and left.

'I'm afraid she's heavily sedated at the moment. She's very weak and could be like this for a few days. It was a serious fall, and the trauma to her head didn't help either. We have taken several scans but at this point we don't know if there is any brain damage. The left side of her skull was badly fractured and she has had fifteen stitches.'

Sarah sat down in the chair beside the bed and gently held her mother's hand. Claire Bradshaw's head was covered in bandages and her face was swollen black and blue. She hardly recognised her.

'Oh, Mum,' she said softly. 'What happened to you?'

Sarah was still asleep in her old bedroom at Grange House when Mrs Prescott entered carrying a tray. Rusty followed her, jumped onto the eiderdown at the foot of the bed and manoeuvred himself into a comfortable position against Sarah's feet.

'I thought I'd bring you breakfast in bed. From what Jack tells me, it was a long night.'

Sarah stretched out her arms and gave a long yawn. She had not eaten since the turkey sandwiches the previous day, and the aroma of fresh toast made her realise just how hungry she was. After she'd propped herself up against her pillow, Mrs Prescott placed the tray on Sarah's lap and sat down on the edge of the bed, smoothing the creases of her spotlessly white apron.

'I couldn't believe it when I heard,' Mrs Prescott said. 'She has been so well.'

'Yes, that's what I thought, but something must have triggered the heart attack.'

'Well, they do say these things can come out of the blue. My George, for instance – never a day's illness in his life, and then gone, just like that: stroke, they said. They told me there must have been warning signs but I didn't see any.'

Sarah smeared a thick layer of marmalade on a slice of toast and poured herself a cup of tea while Mrs Prescott chatted dolefully about other people's ailments and whether or not they could have been prevented.

'I wonder if it had anything to do with that letter?' Sarah asked.

Mrs Prescott looked at her for a moment. 'You mean that letter from France?'

Sarah smiled to herself. The postman may have arrived late but that didn't stop Mrs Prescott from going through her mother's post.

'Yes, that one,' she replied.

Mrs Prescott pinched her lips together and tried to think. 'I don't know about that. I mean, it's not as if it's the first letter from France, is it?'

Sarah put down her cup and looked at her. 'You mean there were others? When?'

'Oh, sometime ago now — it's hard to recall. Your mother gets so many, what with all those societies she belongs to and all.' Mrs Prescott looked puzzled. 'Do you really think that was what brought on the attack?'

'I don't know, but something tells me it might have had something to do with it.'

Mrs Prescott got up to leave. 'Perhaps we should just be patient and wait to see what the doctors say. When are you going back to the hospital?'

'This morning: Peter is driving down from London. We arranged to meet at the hospital and see the doctors together.' Sarah handed the tray back to Mrs Prescott. 'All the same, Mrs P, if you do manage to remember anything about the other letters, please let me know.'

Mrs Prescott nodded.

'And thank you very much — it's a long time since someone brought me breakfast in bed.'

Peter and Sarah sat beside their mother's bed for what seemed like an interminable amount of time before the doctor called them into his office. After offering them a seat he sat at his desk and consulted his notes. Sarah's heart was pounding with apprehension.

'Mrs Bradshaw has suffered a very bad fall,' the doctor said, his voice taking on a serious tone.

Sarah wished he would get to the point as soon as possible instead of stating the obvious.

'At first we thought she may have had a major heart attack and need bypass surgery, which at your mother's age would be a risky procedure, but it now appears that is not our primary concern.'

The doctor leaned back in his swivel chair and locked his fingers together with the dignified air of a man clearly accustomed to dealing with bad news. 'According to the results of the tests, it was the trauma to the head – most likely from the heavy pot that cracked her skull – which caused the most damage. There is fluid on the brain and she must be kept under strict supervision in an induced coma for a few days longer. This sort of thing often causes severe memory loss.'

He paused for a moment, bowing his head to look over the rim of his glasses to gauge Peter and Sarah's reaction. 'If that is so, it may be that the loss of memory is irreversible.'

Sarah started at his words.

'Only time will tell,' he added. 'For the moment we must wait and see. The main thing now is to drain the fluid and keep an eye on the stitches: we want to avoid any infection. We will know more in a week or so when the swelling goes down.'

'Are you trying to tell us that there is no chance of a full recovery?' Peter asked.

'Certainly not, Mr Bradshaw, but it is my duty as a doctor to inform you of the facts as we see them. These things are unpredictable and I'm afraid your mother doesn't have age on her side.'

'My mother is a very strong woman,' Sarah blurted out, her eyes wet with tears. 'She recovered from the last heart attack in no time at all.'

'That is indeed so, in fact the notes here do state your mother's apparent good health, so let us hope that the outcome will be positive this time. That is what we all want for her. For now we must be patient.'

After the meeting, Sarah and Peter made their way to the hospital cafeteria to collect their thoughts. There was much to discuss.

'How long do you intend to stay?' Sarah asked her brother.

'As the doctors are going to keep Mum in an induced coma for a while, I thought I'd go back tomorrow: get the New York trip over with. There seems little point in hanging around here. I'll come back as soon as I return to England in a week's time. By then we will know more.'

Sarah looked disappointed. 'She may be in an induced coma, Peter, but I am sure she will benefit from having you near. After all, the two of you are very close. We might not see you as regularly as we should, but you are still her favourite, you know.'

Peter laughed. 'Mother doesn't have favourites, you know that. She abhors that kind of thing.'

Sarah didn't reply. She loved her brother deeply, but in her eyes, Peter had always been Claire Bradshaw's favourite. She often wondered if it had something to do with the age difference. Peter being the only child for nine years meant all Claire's attention had been focused on her son until Sarah was born. Consequently, the two had formed a close bond which Sarah sometimes looked on with envy.

'What about you?' Peter asked. 'Will you stay at Grange House for a while?'

'With the situation as it is, I couldn't contemplate leaving her and going back to Northampton at the moment. I'll stay at Grange House for as long as she needs me.'

'That's a good idea. It might take your mind off the divorce as well. How is Alistair, by the way?'

'Fine – in fact, not missing me at all. He has Emily in his life now. She's young and by all accounts, the kids love her. Funny how life works out, isn't it?'

'Poor Alistair,' Peter replied.

'Poor Alistair?!' Sarah exclaimed in disgust. 'Poor Alistair did quite well out of the settlement. He is a lawyer after all.'

Her thoughts turned to the letter. 'I have no way of knowing for sure – at least not until she comes out of the coma – but I have a sneaking suspicion that the heart attack may have been brought on by a letter from France that arrived in the post yesterday.'

Peter looked slightly amused. 'Why would a letter from France cause a heart attack? Your imagination is getting the better of you again.'

'Mrs Prescott said there had been others but she couldn't remember when.'

'There you are: if there were other letters – and I don't doubt for one minute that there were, knowing Mum's wide circle of friends – why didn't they cause her to have a heart attack before? You're not making any sense.'

'Think about it, Peter. The last heart attack was over a year ago – what if that was caused by one of those letters?'

'I think this divorce has placed pressure on you,' Peter replied with a smile. 'You are tired and not thinking logically.' He looked at his watch. 'Come on, there's nothing we can do here at the moment. Let's go back home. I'll take you into Market Harborough for a meal tonight, for old times' sake. It will take your mind off things. What about the Coach & Horses? They still serve a good roast duck, I believe.'

*

21

After Peter left for London the following day, Sarah made her way to the greenhouse to see if she could locate the letter. According to Mrs Prescott, she had not laid eyes on it since the morning it arrived, and it was not in any of Claire's pockets when she was taken to the hospital: Sarah had already checked. The only place it could be was the greenhouse.

Jack Hibbert ambled towards her with the broom. 'I thought I'd better clean the place up,' he said. 'And fix that bench. Your mother won't take kindly to seeing it in that state when she returns.'

The place certainly was a mess. Dozens of plant-pots, all filled with carnations, lay smashed on the brick floor.

'That's where I found her,' he said. 'Just over there.'

Blood-splattered shards lay near where Claire Bradshaw's head had lain. Petals, torn from red and white carnations, lay scattered over them like a fragment of a Jackson Pollock canvas. Sarah's eyes scanned the debris. There was no sign of a letter. She began to pick up the broken pots whilst Jack tried to salvage what he could of the plants and repot them.

'Your mother's carnations were always best in show,' Jack told Sarah. 'Pink, white, red: it didn't matter which colour, they were all spectacular blooms.'

'Why did she cultivate carnations?' Sarah asked. 'Wouldn't it have been better to cultivate something showier – like orchids for instance, or even dahlias? I don't know why, but I associate carnations with death.'

'I can see you're not a gardener,' Jack laughed. 'The scent is wonderful.'

After they'd finished cleaning the floor, he asked if she wouldn't mind helping him with the bench. 'Pass me that hammer and those nails and help me prop this up while I nail it back in place.'

The bench was heavy but between the two of them, they managed to get it back into its rightful position.

'If you don't need me for anything else, Jack, I'll go back to the house. I want to visit Mum this afternoon.'

Sarah turned to leave, and in doing so noticed a crumpled envelope amongst the remaining shards that had lain hidden under the bench. She bent over and picked it up.

'This is what I was looking for,' she said.

A large patch of blood had seeped into the folds, making it difficult to open without damaging it further. When she did finally open it, she was surprised to find there wasn't a letter inside after all, only a newspaper cutting. The frown on Sarah's face told Jack it wasn't what she was expecting to find.

'No letter?' he asked.

Sarah looked puzzled. 'Only this.'

A cutting from a German newspaper was the last thing she had expected to find. Worse still, it too bore the bloodstains. Her command of the German language was basic, the result of spending four weeks in Hamburg as a school exchange student during the last summer before she entered university, but it was enough for her to realise that the cutting was from the *Badische Zeitung* of 3rd April 2001, and that it was a death notice.

She quickly returned to the house. In the sitting room, with its French windows and expansive view towards the lawn and across the garden, was the family library. Claire Bradshaw had always been an avid reader, and as she was fluent in both French and German, many of the books were in their original language. Sarah pulled out a large, well-used German-English dictionary and began to work on the translation.

The article showed a photograph of a distinguished gentleman wearing steel-rimmed glasses. Sarah surmised that he was about seventy when the photograph was taken. His hair was silver-grey and his face and dark eyes bore the look of a man who had been handsome in his youth. Underneath was written:

Von Rosenkranz died peacefully in his sleep at his home in Schluchsee on 2nd April 2001. He is survived by a son... A private ceremony will be held at the family estate in Schluchsee on 7th April.

Unfortunately the blood had seeped onto part of the man's name and that of his son, making most of it impossible to read.

After a week, the doctor informed Sarah that the swelling on her mother's brain had subsided and they would be bringing her out of the induced coma. All that remained now was to see if there was any long-term brain damage. Sarah and Peter waited anxiously in the hallway whilst the doctor finished his examination.

'I'm so glad you could make it,' Sarah said. 'I sat by her bedside every day, never knowing whether she would pull through or not. It's been such an emotional roller coaster.'

'Well, the worst is over now. At least she's back on the road to recovery.'

'You won't mention the newspaper cutting, will you?'

'I can assure you of that,' Peter said with a smile. 'You're probably barking up the wrong tree anyway. It may have been just a coincidence that

23

it arrived the same day as the heart attack.'

'I've been racking my brains to remember if Mum knew any Germans. I know she taught German in Paris for a while — until the war disrupted their lives, that is — but I can't recall either her or Dad having any German friends apart from the old couple who lived in the next village, and Dad said they were interned during the war along with others deemed to be a risk to the country. The only foreign friends they spoke about were the French ones — mostly people they met in France — and I do recall one or two Italians, but not one German.'

'Mum and Dad had lots of friends, Sarah. What about the Polish crowd she used to visit when she went to see her old friend Violette in London?'

'Ah yes, Violette. Funny how we always called her Madame Violette even though she married an Englishman. Violette Hamilton, wasn't it?'

'Actually, he was Canadian,' Peter replied. 'But they decided to live in England after the war. I think he was offered a position with the War Ministry. According to Dad, Roger Hamilton was an ace pilot in his time and was made squadron leader just before his plane was shot down in Normandy.'

'Wasn't Dad's plane shot down around that time as well?'

'Yes. Dad said Roger and he met when they were recuperating in the same makeshift hospital somewhere near Bayeux. By all accounts the battle for Normandy was a nasty affair and they were both lucky to be alive. Mum and Violette were both nurses there.'

'A wartime romance.' Sarah smiled. 'Violette and Mum are still friends, you know — perhaps we should let her know about Mum being in hospital? She still lives in London, doesn't she?'

Peter thought for a moment. 'I believe she's somewhere in Belgravia: the address and phone number are bound to be in Mum's address book.'

Their conversation was interrupted when the doctor called them into the room. 'We are very pleased with her progress,' he told them, 'although she's not out of the woods yet so it might not be a good idea to stay too long.'

Sarah breathed a sigh of relief when she saw her mother. The swelling and bruising on her face had subsided, and with most of the tubes gone, she looked as though she was sleeping peacefully.

'She certainly looks a lot better than the last time I saw her,' Peter remarked. 'I must admit, I was afraid that this time she wouldn't pull through.'

'Mum doesn't give up easily,' Sarah replied.

They sat by their mother's side for over an hour and were almost ready to leave when they saw her eyelids flicker and open. Claire didn't speak, but the look in her eyes told them their mother knew who they were. They were elated; it was more than they could do to contain their emotions. Within minutes the doctor was back at her bedside.

'Hello, Mrs Bradshaw,' he said, shining a small torch into her eyes and checking her pulse. 'You have visitors.'

Claire drowsily closed her eyes again, retreating back into a deep sleep.

'It's to be expected,' the doctor told them.

It was not until several days later that Claire Bradshaw uttered her first word, and when she did it was to Peter. She lifted her hand towards him.

'Marcel,' she murmured. 'Marcel...'

Peter stroked her hand. 'It's all right, Mum, everything's going to be fine. Sarah and I are here for you,' he said reassuringly.

Claire looked into her son's eyes and smiled – a tired, sad smile. Then the smile faded and she closed her eyes again.

Sarah could not help feeling a deep sense of disappointment. It was she who had sat by her mother's bedside day after day; she who was prepared to put her life on hold and take care of her should the need arise, and yet it was to Peter that Claire looked for reassurance. The fact that her mother had called Peter 'Marcel' did not concern either of them. After all, the doctor had warned them that she would feel disoriented for a while; it was one of the side effects of the drugs.

It would take a few more days before Claire Bradshaw fully came to terms with what had happened, and when she did, her face bore a look of unease. In that moment, Sarah knew her mother had changed and she wanted to know why, but for the time being, all that mattered was that she made a full recovery.

Chapter 2

It had not been difficult to find Violette Hamilton's telephone number; Claire had underlined it several times in her address book. Sarah decided to give her a call to tell her about her mother. With time on her hands, she also asked if she could come down to London and pay Violette a visit. Violette was more than happy to see her.

A stone's throw from Buckingham Palace, 19 Wilson Place, in the exclusive residential district of Belgravia, was the last house in a crescent of white stuccoed townhouses built in the classic Regency style. Four storeys high plus an attic and basement, it was the epitome of elegance and wealth.

Sarah stood inside the grand portico entrance with its Ionic columns and rang the doorbell. It was answered almost immediately by Gabrielle, Violette Hamilton's maid, a slim young woman in her mid twenties. With a small, dainty white apron and cuffs over a neat black dress, her blonde hair fastened back in a roll, Gabrielle looked every part the maid of a house of distinction. A faint smile crossed Sarah's lips when she contrasted Gabrielle with Mrs Prescott, a woman of generous proportions whose preference for design in 'pinnies', as she called her aprons, was for overblown florals.

Inside the entrance hall, Gabrielle relieved Sarah of her jacket and went to inform her mistress of her arrival. Sarah surveyed the spacious hall in admiration. Mahogany French Empire consoles stood against the pale lemon walls, contrasting tastefully with the large, black-and-white diamond-shaped floor tiles. In the centre of the hallway, underneath a crystal chandelier of graceful proportions, stood a circular marble table with an enormous nineteenth-century French vase filled with white oriental lilies. Their scent was exquisite. Moments later a door on the far side of the hallway opened and Gabrielle ushered Sarah into the drawing room where a table had been prepared for afternoon tea.

It had been almost ten years since Sarah last saw Violette and she was still as she remembered her: warm, vivacious and still with a thick French accent despite the fact that she had lived in England for over fifty years. Kissing Sarah on both cheeks in the French manner, Violette expressed her great delight in seeing her again.

'My dear, it has been too long,' Violette said, handing Sarah a napkin and a small white plate and offering her a silver tray of delicate confections: scallop-shaped madeleines dusted with icing sugar, *visitandes*, macaroons and an assortment of fresh fruit tartlets. 'Finally, I found a chef who is also a fine patissier,' she added. 'Does your mother's housemaid still bake those enormous cakes – the ones with the mounds of icing?'

Sarah thought of Mrs Prescott's devil's food cake and how out of place it would look amongst such fanciful morsels.

'And now,' Violette continued, settling back on the couch and taking the tiniest bite of a *visitande*, 'please tell me about your mother. When do you expect her home?'

'The doctors said it could be as early as next week. The stitches are healing well and she's sitting up now. Thankfully there are no signs of long-term damage and her memory is improving, although she has no memory of the fall.'

'And you say this is the second heart attack?'

'Yes – didn't she tell you about the other? It happened just over a year ago.'

Violette twirled a pearl of her necklace between her beautifully manicured fingers and gave a little sigh. 'This is the first I've heard about it, when you called me yesterday. If I had known, I would have paid her a visit. We do exchange greeting cards but I'm afraid to say that we haven't spoken for a while – perhaps three years or so.' Violette thought for a moment. 'And if my memory serves me well, the last time she came here was over six years ago. She came for the weekend and promised to come back to London again and I said I would come to Grange House, but you know how it is when you get older, my dear   time passes. *C'est la vie.*'

Sarah was astounded that her mother had not told Violette about the first heart attack, especially as Claire had always said Violette was her closest friend.

'Perhaps Mum never told you because she didn't want to worry you,' she said with a lack of conviction. 'After all, it was only a minor attack and she wasn't even aware it had been a heart attack until the doctor told her.'

Violette picked a crumb of *visitande* off her immaculate pale blue-and-pink Chanel tweed skirt and put it on the plate. 'Do the doctors know what brought this on?' she asked.

'No, but I can't help feeling that it has something to do with letters she's been receiving from France.'

'From France! What makes you say that?'

Sarah picked up her handbag and took out the blood-splattered envelope with the newspaper cutting. 'This arrived the morning Mum suffered the attack. It was posted in France but inside was this death notice from a German newspaper. Unfortunately part of the name is undecipherable but I wondered if by any chance you might know who this man is?'

Violette reached for her reading glasses and looked at it carefully. At one point, she brought the cutting closer to her face, squinting at it for quite a few seconds. 'I have no idea who he is. I've never seen him before. I'm sorry, I can't help you.'

Sarah was not entirely convinced. She could have sworn she saw Violette flinch for a split second before giving it back.

'And these other letters you say she received – the ones from France – who are they from?' Violette asked.

'I'm afraid I don't know. I only have Mrs Prescott's word for that. She said Mum received quite a few but she can't remember when. I looked in the writing bureau where Mum keeps her correspondence but could find no trace of them.'

Violette picked up the teapot and offered Sarah more tea. 'So I take it you haven't asked your mother about this?'

'Not at the moment. When she's well, I might. Anyway, it's probably nothing. Peter thinks it's just a coincidence.'

'He's probably right.'

'All the same, it's not every day someone gets a German newspaper cutting in the post, is it?'

Violette sat back and studied Sarah for a few moments whilst she sipped her tea. 'If you want my advice, *chérie*,' she said, her voice taking on a serious tone, 'I would let sleeping dogs lie.'

Sarah looked shocked. She had the distinct feeling that for whatever reason, Violette was warning her not to pursue this.

A clock decorated with a gilt scene depicting Orpheus in the underworld, sitting on a nearby dresser, chimed three o'clock. Next to it stood a cluster of framed photographs. One was of Claire and Violette in their younger days, their arms linked together, standing on a bridge over the Seine with the Eiffel Tower in the background. They couldn't have looked happier. Violette, the petite French woman with the sultry dark eyes, her thick black hair in a sharp, tidy bob, was wearing a white cotton shirt and a slim pencil skirt, and Claire, her honey-blonde hair cut just above the shoulders, was stylishly dressed in a pale dress belted around the waist, over which hung a long, single strand of pearls.

'When was that taken?' Sarah asked.

At the mention of the photograph, Violette's face brightened again. 'Sometime in 1936 after we graduated from the Sorbonne. Your mother studied languages and for a while had plans to become a journalist. I was a follower of Freud and wanted to study psychoanalysis. We were both full of ambition in those days.'

'Mum always seemed happy to be a wife and mother – I never thought of her as being the ambitious type.'

Violette laughed. 'My dear, sometimes fate takes us on a path we don't anticipate. Dark clouds were gathering across Europe and the future was uncertain. When she graduated, your grandmother became ill and Claire took it upon herself to look after her. That's why she only worked part-time.'

Sarah sensed that Violette was in the mood to talk, and she was eager to listen. Claire Bradshaw had often talked about growing up in Paris. By all accounts, she had led a happy and privileged childhood. Her mother, Gertrude, was English and had married a Frenchman, Henri Bouchard, prior to World War I. At first, Henri's family were unimpressed by their son's choice of a wife as they had hoped he would choose someone more suitable from the upper echelons of French society. But Gertrude was a clever woman and she knew how to win them over. Gertrude and Henri's first child – a boy named Jacques after his grandfather – was born in 1913. Then war broke out, and Henri was made an officer and sent to the front. He was there for almost a year but returned home to recuperate from the effects of chlorine gas unleashed on the Allied troops by the Germans during the Second Battle of Ypres in 1915. After he recovered, Gertrude begged him not to go back, but Henri was a fierce patriot and not wanting to face Gertrude's tears, left one morning without saying goodbye. When Gertrude found out, she broke down in tears; she had not told him that she was carrying his child again. Henri died during the first days of the Battle of the Somme, never knowing that his wife had given birth to a daughter one month earlier.

After the war another tragedy befell the family. Henri's elderly parents and Claire's elder brother, Jacques, their immune systems already weakened by malnutrition due to the war, succumbed to the Spanish flu epidemic sweeping the continent and died within a week of each other.

Now Gertrude found herself alone in a country ravaged by war and with a small child to look after. Luckily, Henri and the Bouchard family had provided well for her. Gertrude was left the house in Paris and a small allowance to enable her to live modestly for the rest of her life. With only a daughter to dote on, Claire was the apple of her mother's eye. She was sent to a good school run by nuns, and when she was accepted into the Sorbonne, Gertrude could not have been happier.

Violette recalled meeting Gertrude for the first time. 'Gerty terrified me,' she said. 'Such an indomitable character, and she wanted to know everything about me. What I didn't know then was that she was suffering from cancer and refused to acknowledge it. No one was allowed to mention the illness at all. We watched her slowly deteriorate. After your mother graduated from the Sorbonne, she put any ideas of pursuing a career in journalism on hold to work as a part-time teacher at a girls' school, just to be near her. Your mother also loved dancing but it took us all our time to persuade her to leave Gerty's side and join us in the nightclubs.'

'Mum said her mother died just before the war,' Sarah said.

'That's right, not long after the Czech Crisis. I recall that she and your mother used to read all the newspapers. At the time there was a loud hue and cry about Hitler wanting to seize that part of Czechoslovakia known as the Sudetenland. Rather than face another war, France, Italy and England signed an agreement with the Nazis allowing him to annex it. Gerty blamed the British, and in particular, Neville Chamberlain. "Can't they see what this dictator is doing?" she used to say angrily. "Even Winston Churchill says they have behaved dishonourably." Goodness knows what she would have said a year later.'

'Well I can see where Mum gets her strength and social conscience from,' said Sarah. 'All those societies and charities she belongs to. She has inherited Grandma's resilience.'

She looked at the time. It was getting late, but she was becoming too wrapped up in her mother's past to leave. 'And when grandmother died, what happened then?' Sarah asked. 'Did Mum manage to get her life back?'

'Those last few months before the war were wonderful. We tried not to dwell on the political troubles and have a good time. It wasn't difficult, you know, Paris had much to offer: dances, jazz clubs, the theatre. Your mother and I particularly liked the bal musette. On a Saturday afternoon, we often took ourselves off to the outdoor cafes in the 5th arrondissement not far from the university, whiling away the hours dancing to the accordion. The tango, waltz, foxtrot – we loved them all. Your mother was a good dancer and was never short of a partner. She loved life, that's what I remember most about her. Playing Chopin and Schubert for Gerty whilst she was ill was all well and good, but it was too dreary for a young woman, at least I thought so at the time. After she died your mother started to live again.'

Sarah recalled with fondness the evenings her parents went to dances in Leicester. In those days the big-band orchestras were still popular and they never missed a chance to see the great bandleaders of the time – Victor Silvester, Ted Heath, Bert Ambrose and the highly acclaimed Gerald Walcan Bright, better known as Geraldo, to name just a few. With her clothes purchased from the best dress shops in London and wearing her favourite French perfume, Sarah's father always commented on how glamorous her mother looked.

'Sadly I don't recall her going to another dance after Dad died, but she still played the piano, and now that you mention it, she did play a lot of Schubert and Chopin. I always thought it seemed to ease her loneliness. '

'When the war came we lost touch for a while,' Violette said with a heavy sigh.

'Mum said she managed to get out of France as the Germans were heading towards Bordeaux, and that you got out sometime later. Did you manage to meet up in London?'

'I left a few months later. France was divided then into the occupied and unoccupied zones. It wasn't easy for me to leave – I needed certain documents, which were not easy to get. I left my family behind not knowing if I would see them again. I found work as a part-time French teacher. I did try to find your mother but unfortunately the bombing caused havoc and I didn't meet up with her again until we were back in France in 1944. We had both joined the Women's Auxiliary Nursing Unit.'

'When you were in Normandy?' Sarah asked.

'Yes. At the time, I had no idea your mother was there. Can you imagine my delight when I found out we were working at the same hospital?'

The clock chimed again and Sarah reminded herself she had a train to catch. Violette rang a tiny bell and Gabrielle entered the room. 'Call a taxi to go to St Pancras Station, please, and then wrap a parcel of cakes for Sarah to take back with her.

'I have enjoyed our little chat,' she said to Sarah. 'Please keep me informed of your mother's progress. When she is well enough to receive visitors I will come to see her. And if I were you, I would throw that cutting away. Take my advice, my dear: leave well alone. Don't pry into the past. It is not a wise thing to do.'

31

During the journey back, Sarah thought about their conversation. On the surface Violette had been only too happy to talk about her early friendship with her mother, yet underneath it all, Sarah couldn't shake off the feeling that it might have been a diversion, and that Violette *had* recognised the man in the newspaper cutting. In the end, she was no closer to finding out who he was than when she first found it. One thing was for sure: she was not going to do as Violette suggested and throw it away.

Two weeks after Sarah's visit to London, the family gathered together to welcome Claire Bradshaw back to Grange House. Peter had driven down from London with his wife, Jayne and the children, and in an effort to show there were no hard feelings, Alistair arrived with the twins. Sarah sighed when he placed two bottles of Clos Vougeot Grand Cru on the dresser alongside the gifts of flowers and cards from well-wishers; they were worth a small fortune.

'Only the best for my favourite mother-in-law,' he said to Claire, giving her a familial peck on the cheek. 'I know how you like a good red.'

Alistair's thoughtfulness made Sarah catch her breath. A pang of nostalgia made her realise how much he could rise to the occasion when necessary. 'Thank you,' she said, 'and for bringing the boys over as well. It means the world to us.'

For the moment Sarah was prepared to accept him back into the fold again, although she stopped short of enquiring about Emily. One of the grandchildren pulled out a chair for their grandmother at the head of the table whilst Peter popped the champagne and began to pour everyone a glass.

'And now, everyone, I'd like to propose a toast,' he said, putting his arm around his mother's slender waist and raising his glass. 'To my darling mother, it's wonderful to have you back where you belong.'

A chorus of 'hear, hear' filled the kitchen as everyone followed suit and drank to Claire's health.

Much to everyone's delight, Claire said she wanted to make a little speech of her own. Peter refilled the glasses.

Still weak, her words were slow and deliberate. 'You cannot imagine how happy I am to be back at Grange House again. I am touched by your love and generosity.' She reached for Peter's hand. 'It has been my family that kept me going. Dear Sarah, who is always there for me when I need her – a big thank-you, and…' She turned to Peter, squeezing his hand. 'And my dear Marcel. Words cannot express what it means to have you by my side again.' Claire brought his hand to her lips, closed her eyes and kissed it – a long, lingering kiss, as if she were afraid to let it go. When she opened her eyes again she appeared confused.

A hush descended over the gathering. Peter glanced across at Sarah, who stood with her hand clasped over her mouth.

'Well done,' Jayne said, applauding Claire's speech and at the same time attempting to defuse the confusion.

One by one, everyone started to clap. Mrs Prescott handed round an assortment of sandwiches and in the excitement of the afternoon, Claire Bradshaw's momentary confusion was forgotten by everyone except Peter and Sarah.

After everyone had left and Claire had retired to bed, Sarah made a call to Violette Hamilton.

'Does my mother know anyone called Marcel?' she asked.

There was a silence at the other end of the phone. For a moment, Sarah thought she had been cut off.

'Violette, please, if you know, please tell me.'

It was impossible for Violette to ignore the distress in Sarah's voice.

'Did you say Marcel?'

'Yes.'

Violette began to speak rapidly in French. '*Mon Dieu, je le savais. Rien de bon ne sortirait de cette indiscrétion. On doit laisser le passé dans l'histoire.*'

'Violette,' Sarah interjected. 'Please speak English.'

Clearly Violette was not in the mood to pursue this. 'I knew no good would come of this. The past should be left alone. I warned you not to pry.'

Sarah was hurt. 'I didn't. It's just that Mum seems confused. This afternoon she called Peter "Marcel". And then I suddenly remembered she did it in the hospital too – the day she came out of the coma.'

'*Bien*,' Violette replied after a while. 'Please tell your mother that I will come down to Grange House in the next few days: we have much to talk about. In the meantime, take good care of her. I fear this fall has affected her more than you think.'

Sarah put down the receiver, went into the drawing room and took the cutting out of the writing desk. She poured herself a brandy, sat in the armchair, swung her legs under her and quietly studied it, looking for clues.

'Who are you?' she asked aloud to herself. 'And who is Marcel?'

*

The next morning, Sarah woke to the sound of voices in the garden. She could hear her mother talking to Jack Hibbert about a new vegetable garden. The comforting smell of baking wafted up from the kitchen towards her open window. Minutes later the two of them headed along the gravel path towards the greenhouse, followed by Rusty, who had not left Claire's side since she returned.

Throwing on her clothes, Sarah hurried downstairs to follow them. As she neared the greenhouse she overheard their conversation. Jack was showing Claire the carnations that he had managed to salvage. The blooms were enormous and they smelt wonderful. Claire appeared distracted, and anxiously started to cast her eyes around the greenhouse.

'Did you find anything when you cleaned up?' she asked.

'Like what?'

'It's just that I seem to have mislaid something – an envelope. For the life of me, I cannot imagine what I did with it. My memory is still playing havoc with me.'

Jack was in a dilemma. It was impossible for him to lie to her after so many years of friendship.

'Well, let me think…' he said, stalling for time.

Claire bent down and scoured the floor.

'Is this what you're looking for, Mum?' said Sarah, standing in the doorway and holding out the envelope.

Claire swung around. The shock of seeing Sarah holding the newspaper cutting made her clutch the bench. Fearing another attack, Jack quickly unfolded an old wooden garden chair for her to sit on.

'Will you leave us for a moment, please?' Sarah said. 'Mum and I have a few things to discuss.'

Jack straightened his cap and gave her a disapproving look. 'Did you have to?' he said in a low whisper as he left. 'Now of all times.'

After he'd gone, Sarah gave her mother the cutting. 'I found it when we were cleaning up and I was curious to know what it was, so I used your dictionary to translate it.'

Claire's hands begin to tremble as she took the cutting and looked at it.

'Would you like to tell me who he is?' Sarah asked. 'It's just that I didn't think you knew anyone in Germany.'

Claire smiled – that same sad smile Sarah had seen in the hospital. 'I did know him once,' she began. 'A long time ago, during the war.'

Sarah looked confused. 'What do you mean, Mum? I thought you

34

went back to France to fight them. You're not making any sense.'

A tear rolled down Claire's cheek, and Sarah began to wonder if Violette and Jack had been right. Perhaps she should have left well alone.

'My dear Sarah, I tried to put those days behind me. You cannot possibly understand what war is like. You see many things – terrible things that never leave you – and yet amidst it all, certain things happen and you know the human spirit will never be destroyed, no matter what. Forgive me if I cannot share everything with you. Some memories are too painful. Please understand.' She put the cutting in her pocket. 'And now, if you don't mind, I would like to go back to the house. I shall lie down for a while.'

Jack Hibbert and Mrs Prescott sat at the kitchen table, talking in low voices.

'Mrs P, would you be so kind as to take a cup of tea to my mother's room?' Sarah asked, noting their sudden silence when she walked through the door. 'She will take a nap until lunchtime.'

Upstairs, she helped her mother onto the bed, took off her shoes and covered her with a blanket. Within minutes, Mrs Prescott brought in a cup of steaming hot tea and a chocolate biscuit and placed them by the bed.

Sarah handed her mother a sleeping pill to take with her tea. 'By the way,' she said, 'Violette Hamilton telephoned to say she is coming to see you in a few days' time. She's extremely concerned about you.'

She sat on the side of the bed until her mother drifted off to sleep. Claire looked much older and so very vulnerable. She promised herself never to mention the matter again, and reconciled herself with the fact that if her mother chose not to talk about it, then she had a good reason for it.

In order to give Claire and Violette time together, Sarah spent the day in town. When she returned, Violette had gone back to London. Mrs Prescott pressed her fingertips to her temples theatrically, complaining bitterly that after listening to French all day she now had a splitting headache. Sarah smiled to herself. Her mother and Violette always conversed in French, partly because it was their first language and partly because Claire Bradshaw was aware of Mrs Prescott's habit of eavesdropping.

Sarah found her mother at her writing desk in the drawing room, leafing through an old photograph album. An empty bottle of Alistair's Clos Vougeot and two glasses stood on the coffee table next to the remnants of a chocolate cake. The pungent smell of French cigarettes filled the room, forcing Sarah to open the windows to let in some fresh air.

Claire beckoned Sarah to come and sit by the desk. The late-afternoon sun streamed through the French windows, drenching the room in an ethereal golden rose. Sarah breathed a sigh of relief when she saw her mother smile. A part of her had feared her recent conversation with Violette had opened a can of worms. Whatever had taken place between the two of them, she had no idea, but the look of perpetual sadness her mother had worn since coming out of the coma had gone.

'It was good to see her again,' Claire said. 'We have let too many years pass.'

She turned back to the album. Sarah saw it was the one containing photographs taken in Normandy. 'Can I see?' she asked.

Claire slid the album over. 'This one is taken at the abbey. We had just set up a temporary hospital. That's Violette, the one flanked by several airmen. Men always fell for Violette's charms,' she said. 'And that's me, standing behind your father.'

Sarah looked closely. Her father was lying on a makeshift bed, his legs bandaged and his arm in a sling.

'We had just met,' Claire continued. 'It was shortly after the Battle for Caen. *Mon Dieu*, darling, you cannot imagine how terrible it was. The SS panzer divisions were relentless in their counter-attack. A few weeks after this picture was taken and Caen was secured, we moved further south near Falaise. The fighting was still fierce and the roads and fields were littered with the dead and wounded – thousands of them. The sickening stench of death seeped into our very bones.'

During the next hour, Claire continued to talk about Normandy: of the terrible sights she had witnessed and of the bravery of the people themselves.

"War brings out the best and the worst in us,' she said.

After listening to the heart-wrenching stories, Sarah felt as if her mother had unloaded a great burden that had remained silent all these years and she was much more optimistic about her recovery. Later that evening Peter telephoned to see how the meeting had gone.

'Violette's visit has done her the world of good,' Sarah told him. 'It was just the tonic she needed.'

'And the mystery men, any mention of them?'

'Not a single thing. We are just going to have to forget it.'

Towards the end of August, Sarah drove Claire to the hospital for a final check-up. Proclaiming her to be fit and well, the doctor told her that he didn't need to see her again for another six months. During the drive back to Grange House, Sarah thought her mother was unusually quiet.

'What is it, Mum, everything all right?'

'I've been thinking. Now that I'm well again, I would like to take a little holiday. It's been years since the last one.'

'I agree,' said Sarah. 'Where would you like to go? Bournemouth, Cornwall...perhaps the Yorkshire Dales? Tell me and I'll arrange it.'

'Oh no, my darling, nothing like that. I'd like to go back to France.'

Sarah was so taken by surprise she almost missed a sharp bend. 'France!' she exclaimed.

Claire Bradshaw clasped her hands firmly on her lap and took a deep breath. 'Yes,' she said, almost defiantly. 'France – and I'd like you to come with me.'

Chapter 3

Falmouth, Cornwall, 1943

At around midnight on a moonless night in summer, Claire Bouchard – aka Secret Agent Manon; cover name, Marie-Elise Bouchard – rugged herself up against the cold, biting winds from the Atlantic and boarded the darkened motor-gunboat waiting to take her across the English Channel. The captain passed her his flask of brandy, turned the throttles fully open and headed out of Port Pendennis. Taking several long swigs, Claire was grateful for the immediate warmth that radiated though her body. A thick fog soon enveloped the boat, and out at sea a fierce storm gathered; only a madman would venture out in this weather. It was going to be a long night.

Destructive gale-force winds threatened to capsize the boat time and time again, but the captain doggedly refused to turn back. Huddled below deck, Claire clung to a rail for dear life, occasionally clutching the silver crucifix around her neck and murmuring prayers to God and Saint Nicholas, patron saint of seafarers.

After what seemed like an eternity, the boat neared the French coast and the captain turned off the engines. With no silvery moon to light up the water and the only sound that of the stormy sea, they waited until, out of the blackness, the dark shape of a small motorised fishing boat appeared and drew up against the bow. Along with several large containers of supplies, Claire was hastily transferred onto the boat. His mission complete, the captain wished his anonymous passenger good luck and returned at full speed back to the relative safety of the English coast.

The weather worsened and the rain came down in torrents. Claire was violently sick and she had no idea where she was. All of a sudden a light flashed and the fisherman skilfully manoeuvred the boat towards a rocky inlet. Treacherous waves dashed them against the rocks, almost smashing the boat into pieces. Two men appeared out of the darkness.

'*Allez, rapidement!*' a voice shouted. 'Jump quickly before it's too late.'

Claire strained to get a foothold on the rocks, twisted her ankle and slipped. Seconds before a foaming wave threatened to engulf her and hurl her back out to sea, a man reached out and grabbed her. Soaked to the bone and unable to walk, she was deposited like a sack of potatoes onto higher ground.

'*Bienvenue en France*,' the man said with a grin. 'Welcome to France.'

Saint-Malo, Côte d'Émeraude, Brittany, September 2001

'Mum! You've not heard a word I said,' said Sarah.

Claire Bradshaw turned to face her daughter. 'I'm sorry, darling, I was miles away. What did you say?'

Sarah sighed. For the last ten minutes she had leafed through a mound of brochures from the tourist office in Saint-Malo, commenting on the various sites in the area.

'You've been staring at that beach for ages. A penny for your thoughts?'

'It's nothing. I was just thinking what a perfect day it is for a swim. Not a cloud in the sky and the water looks so inviting.'

Sarah took off her sunglasses, called the waiter over and ordered from the menu. '*Soupe de palourdes à la fleur de thym, s'il vous plaît, et deux verres de Muscadet.*'

She leaned back in the chair and breathed in the salty sea air. 'It certainly is a beautiful place. I think I'm going to like it here, although it did come as a surprise when you said you wanted to come here and not Paris.'

When Claire announced her desire to return to France, Sarah naturally assumed it would be to Paris — after all, that was where her mother grew up — and so she was enthusiastic about the idea. It had been years since she was there herself — the year she married Alistair. Young and in love, they had spent most of their time making love in a seedy hotel in Montmartre. When she returned to England, her mother had asked her what she had seen. Sarah remembered feeling embarrassed; she had hardly seen anything except for Notre Dame and the Eiffel Tower.

'And the house on Rue de Bagnolet where I grew up, did you go there?' Claire asked anxiously.

'No, Mum — the next time,' Sarah replied apologetically. Claire had not been able to hide her disappointment.

The years slipped by, and with them her mother's stories of Paris faded. With the opportunity to return to France, Sarah would redeem herself. So it came as a shock when her mother announced she no longer had a desire to go back to Paris. Instead she wanted to go to Brittany.

'Brittany?!' Sarah echoed. 'Why Brittany? You never mentioned it before. Why not Provence, the Loire, or even Bordeaux where we could visit the vineyards?'

Claire muttered something about it being a beautiful place and not too far away should something happen – the *something* presumably being another heart attack.

Sarah threw her hands up in a gesture of capitulation. 'Fine, whatever you want. We'll go by car.'

The waiter arrived with the clam soup. 'It's wonderful,' Sarah said, after savouring a mouthful, 'and the fruitiness of the wine complements it well. A perfect choice.'

'With an abundance of fresh seafood, it would be a sin to order meat. I am afraid that we're just a little too early for *coquilles Saint-Jacques* though. The rule of thumb is that oysters are best harvested when there is a letter R in the month.'

'There's an R in September,' Sarah replied.

'Of course, but it's still best to wait a few weeks.'

Sarah took another sip of wine, pulled out the map and ran her finger over the winding yellow line that signified the coastal road from Saint-Malo to Saint-Brieuc.

'Another hour at the most and we should be there – that is if the roads aren't clogged with holidaymakers. Are you sure the address is correct?' Sarah asked. 'It's not much to go on.'

Claire broke off another piece of crusty bread, dipped it into her soup and took a bite before answering. 'I've told you, we're not going to get lost. Just follow the road towards Saint-Brieuc. About ten kilometres before, we will see a signpost pointing to La Forêt de la Sevigny. There we turn off and follow the road inland for about a kilometre. At this point, we will come to a fork in the road. We take the left turn, which leads us to the cottage – it couldn't be simpler.'

'Well, I must say, Mum, you seem to have the directions off pat. Anyone would think you'd been there before.'

Sarah folded up the crumpled map and called the waiter over to pay the bill. 'Perhaps we should buy a few groceries before we leave, just in case there are no shops nearby, although Mrs P did insist on packing a few things: a fruit cake, rhubarb jam and of course English tea. Apparently she thinks it might be hard to find here.'

Claire rolled her eyes.

'And you're sure there's not a telephone in the cottage?'

'The owners live in England. What need would they have for a telephone?' Claire replied as she paid the bill and tipped the waiter handsomely, commenting on the excellent food.

The waiter bowed graciously, exchanging a few pleasantries with his satisfied customer. It dawned on Sarah how at ease her mother seemed here. It was hard to believe it had been fifty-seven years since she was last in France, and Sarah had often wondered why she never wanted to return. It was as though she purposely chose to put that part of her life behind her. 'There's nothing left of my old life,' she used to tell her children. 'The war ruined it.'

'It's just in case we overshoot the turn-off or can't find it for some reason or other...' Sarah stopped talking. Her mother wasn't listening. Instead she seemed preoccupied with something on the other side of the square. 'What is it? What are you looking at?'

Claire pushed her chair back and stood up. 'Just a moment, there's something I have to do before we leave.'

Before Sarah could utter a word, Claire was making her way across the square towards a large stone monument topped with a cross. An old woman selling flowers sat on the nearby wall. Claire took out some money from her handbag and bought a bunch of red carnations. Sarah followed her. By the time she got there, her mother had already laid the flowers at the base of the monument and was reading the names on it. In all there were one hundred and fifty-six, among them twenty-five women. It didn't take long for Sarah to realise that that the monument was dedicated to members of the French Resistance.

'There was hardly anything left of Saint-Malo after the war,' Claire told her daughter. 'The Germans dug their heels in but in the end, the commander capitulated to General George Patton. Shells, rockets, bombs... Saint-Malo took it all. Much of what you see now was rebuilt – a medieval illusion. And these brave people,' she continued, meditating on the names, 'they belonged to the Maquis. They were executed a few weeks before the town was liberated. This monument marks the place where they were shot.'

Sarah touched her mother's arm to comfort her. A part of her had feared that sooner or later, memories of the war would come flooding back to her, and she wondered if it had been a wise decision to return.

'Come on, Mum,' she said tenderly. 'Let's get going or we'll be late.'

During the drive, Sarah thought about her mother's reaction in Saint-Malo. Until that point, she had been fine. Now she was brooding and distant again, and the thought of spending two weeks with her while she was in this mood was not a particularly appealing one.

From the very beginning, Sarah had thought a trip back to France would be unwise, but after consulting the doctor, he assured her that her mother would be fine and this could be just the tonic she needed. Furthermore, Peter agreed with him. A splendid idea, he had said, but then he would, wouldn't he: he wasn't the one who had lived with Claire's mood swings for the past few weeks. More than anything else, Sarah couldn't help wondering why her mother had chosen to visit Brittany, and more to the point, why she had shunned her suggestions of recommended hotels in favour of a cottage in the middle of nowhere. When pressed as to how she found out about the cottage, Claire merely said that a friend of a friend owned it and Sarah didn't know her.

'Anyway,' her mother had said, 'it will be a good place to get away from everything.'

Get away from what? Claire Bradshaw had never been the sort of person who needed to get away from anything. She had it all: a beautiful home, a husband who, when he was alive, had doted on her and given her two children, and now the grandchildren. Indeed, her personality was such that she embraced life and revelled in the company of others. When Sarah voiced her concerns to Peter, he merely laughed and said she was being overly sensitive and that she should trust their mother's judgement.

It took just over an hour to reach their destination. The wooden signpost pointing to the turn-off to the Forêt de la Sevigny was partially hidden behind an old beech tree, and had it not been for a sharp bend in the road forcing them to slow down, they would have overshot it. It was Claire who spotted it.

'We're here,' she said, regaining her earlier enthusiasm. 'Look, there's the road.'

Sarah backed up the car and turned into the road, which, after a few metres, petered out into a narrow, rough track bordered by a dense hedgerow of blackthorn bushes laden with sloes – tiny fruits which in a month's time would ripen to a deep black with a waxy, purple-blue bloom. The car bumped its way over furrows of tractor tracks hardened by the summer sun, leaving a cloud of dust in its wake. Sarah was thankful it wasn't raining. Two rabbits ran across the road, momentarily stopping to look at the car before disappearing into the ditch.

'We should have brought Jack with us,' Sarah said with a smile. 'He would have had them bagged in no time.'

When they came to the fork in the road, the signpost pointed to La Forêt de la Sevigny to the left, and below it, to Sarah's great surprise, pointing in the same direction, was a smaller sign – Manoir de Sevigny.

'You never mentioned a manor house, Mum. Perhaps that's where we should be heading – to the right.'

'No,' Claire replied, rather forcefully. 'The cottage is definitely to the left.'

Sarah was in no mood to argue and took the road to the left. After a few bends, the road opened out into what passed for a gravel car park, and there, behind a low granite wall, she caught a glimpse of the slate-grey rooftop of a cottage peeking out from behind hedges of escallonia.

She breathed a sigh of relief. 'I thought we'd never make it.'

Built in a mixture of traditional stone and wood, the cottage was set amidst a beautifully tended garden: camellias, hydrangeas and beds of lavender lined the pathway. The cottage itself, with its bright blue shutters, was separated from several outhouses by an informal cobblestoned courtyard surrounded by containers of vivid red geraniums, in the middle of which stood an outdoor table setting underneath a yellow-and-white striped umbrella. Clinging to the stone walls of the cottage was a white wisteria, its pendulous bunches of delicate flowers tinted a pale pink in the late-afternoon sun. The scent was exquisite. And across the courtyard, the outhouses were covered in ivy and honeysuckle.

Sarah gazed in astonishment. Remembering Peter's words about trusting their mother's instincts, she now felt rather foolish for doubting her in the first place.

'I must say, I wasn't sure what to expect after such a bumpy ride, but it's delightful. From the road, no one would suspect it was here.'

'*Bonjour,*' a voice called out. The women turned to find an elderly man with a walking stick ambling towards them from a pathway which led to the back of the house. In his other hand he carried a basket with a loaf of bread poking out from under a red-and-white checked tea towel. When he reached them, he took off his cap and introduced himself as Monsieur Leroux. His face bore a kindly expression. Sarah took an instant liking to him. Except for the large moustache, he reminded her of Jack Hibbert.

'And this must be Madame's daughter,' he said to Sarah. 'Is this your first time to France?'

Sarah told him that she had been to Paris, but that was years ago.

'Your first time to Brittany, then?

'I'm afraid so, yes – my mother's also, and I have a feeling we're going to enjoy it here.'

The man glanced back at Claire, who stared impassively at his face.

'*Bien!*' he replied, picking up the basket. '*Bien!* And now, if you'll follow me, I'll show you your accommodation.' Monsieur Leroux took the key out of his pocket and unlocked the door.

'You go inside, Mum – I'll collect the suitcases from the car.'

Inside the cottage, the old man put the basket down on the table, took a quick look out the window to check Sarah was well out of sight, and then turned to face Claire. Taking both her hands in his, he squeezed them tightly and looked closely at her face for a few seconds. His eyes were moist with tears.

'Welcome back to France. *Mon Dieu*, it's good to see you again. How long has it been?'

'Fifty-seven years, to be exact,' Claire replied, fighting back the tears.

He touched her cheek tenderly. 'I thought I'd never see you again.'

'Like most of us, I tried to put it all behind me.' Claire hesitated for a moment. 'As you see, I married – an Englishman. We met in Normandy, soon after—'

The sound of Sarah's footsteps coming across the yard brought the conversation to an abrupt end. Monsieur Leroux turned to the basket and took out its contents.

'I thought you might like these,' he said. 'A few eggs, butter, local honey, a baguette and…' He took out a bottle of wine and held it in the air. 'Something to welcome you both to France.'

Sarah looked at the label. 'Is it a *vin locale*?'

'A superior Chenin Blanc from the Loire,' Claire replied.

'My mother knows her French wines.' Sarah smiled. 'She has tried to teach both my brother and I about them. We're eager learners but I am afraid we will never surpass Mum. She's a connoisseur.'

Monsieur Leroux deposited their suitcases upstairs, picked up the empty basket and bid them farewell. 'If you need anything, you can find me at the farm. It's not too far away. Oh, and there's a few restaurants and a bar several kilometres from here, overlooking the cliffs. During the summer they're open late for the holidaymakers.'

After he left, Sarah saw her mother was shaking like a leaf.

'What is it?' she asked anxiously. 'You're as white as a sheet. Where are your tablets?'

She quickly gave her mother two tablets prescribed for her heart condition by her doctor and a glass of water. After a few minutes, the colour returned to Claire's face.

'Do you mind if I have a lie-down for a while? All this travel has exhausted me somewhat.'

The upstairs part of the cottage had a tiny bathroom, which Monsieur Leroux explained had only recently been put in, and two bedrooms decorated in the rustic style with whitewashed walls and a low ceiling criss-crossed with dark wooden beams. The decoration was simple and restrained but comfortable and intimate, and someone had thoughtfully placed a vase of wild flowers in each room. The larger of the two had a panoramic view across the pale green fields with the Atlantic in the distance; the smaller one, with a single gabled dormer window, overlooked the pretty courtyard, outhouses and garden, and part of the lane they had driven along. Claire said she preferred the smaller one. Sarah pushed back the shutters and opened the windows as her mother settled herself on the bed. The heady scent of wisteria drifted into the room. By the time Sarah had emptied their suitcases, Claire was fast asleep. She pulled a blanket over her, pushed back a few strands of hair from her forehead and gave her a kiss. For the second time in the last few months Sarah noticed how much older her mother had become.

While her mother slept, Sarah made herself a coffee in an old percolator which looked as if it had seen better days, cut herself a large slice of Mrs P's fruit cake, scooped up the brochures she had picked up from Saint-Malo and went outside to sit in the garden. Amidst the sweet-smelling air and soothing sounds of the countryside, she was secretly glad they hadn't booked a smart hotel on the seafront after all. Perhaps this is what we both need, she thought to herself – to escape civilisation for a while. Here she would be able to unwind and think about her future. She thought about her mother's remark about Alistair: 'He wasn't for you – he has no blood in his veins.' Why hadn't she realised this sooner? It would have saved all the heartache.

She flicked through the brochures looking for the Manoir de Sevigny and found no mention of it. Like this cottage – how much more of Brittany lay hidden from the outside world? Her thoughts turned to Monsieur Leroux; didn't he say he lived in a nearby farm? She hadn't seen that either.

She looked at her watch. After such a tiring day, her mother would be asleep for at least another hour and she decided to fill the time by taking a walk. She would start with locating the farm; surely it couldn't be that far away.

Sarah followed the footpath around to the back of the house and found that it passed through a narrow opening in the hedge, beyond which was a serenely rural scene of undulating fields. Not far away was what appeared to be the beginning of a forest, which she presumed to be La Forêt de la Sevigny. The path veered right along the hedgerow towards the forest where it quickly became obscured by swathes of grasses, silvered in the soft breeze. At the edge of the forest was a steep embankment covered in a carpet of lichen and bright yellow marigolds, and at the bottom was a winding stream. Across the stream, she could just make out a trail that disappeared amongst dense ferns and woodland. Sarah stopped and looked around. Surely Monsieur Leroux − an old man with a walking stick carrying a basket of food − could not have come this way to the cottage, she told herself. Yet there was no other path and the long grass showed no signs of being disturbed.

Sarah's curiosity was getting the better of her. She slipped precariously down the embankment to try and cross the stream and was pleasantly surprised to find a series of natural rock formations in the water, which made it easy to cross. Making her way through the ferns, she came across a sign nailed to a tree.

Forêt de la Sevigny
Propriété privée

She pressed ahead at a brisk pace until the woodland thinned out into a meadow separated by a road from a cluster of farm buildings. Behind it, set in acres of beautiful parkland, was a gracious stone building, which she presumed must be the Manoir de Sevigny. In the farmyard, two men stood deep in conversation. The one leaning against a tractor, she recognised as Monsieur Leroux. Her curiosity satisfied, Sarah made her way back to the cottage via the road, which she deduced would take her back to the intersection. She was almost at the point where the road split into two when an old green Citroën hurtled past her, covering her in a cloud of dust. She had no time to see the driver's face, he was going so fast.

*

Refreshed and relaxed, Claire was sitting in the garden when Sarah arrived back at the cottage.

'I finally found it,' Sarah said, kicking off her dusty shoes.

'Found what?'

'Why, the farm of course. You would never believe the route Monsieur Leroux must have taken to get here – and carrying eggs into the bargain. Why he didn't simply get in the car and drive here, I'll never know.'

She started to tell her mother about the footpath that led across the stream and through the wood.

'And another thing – it might be quiet around here but there are some crazy drivers. I almost got run over by an old Citroën. The driver was going so fast. I hardly had time to register his face.'

Claire listened whilst her daughter chatted on about her walk.

'Anyway, did you manage to have a good sleep?' Sarah asked.

'Like a baby,' Claire replied.

In the soft, warm glow of a perfect summer evening, Sarah laid her head back on the chair, breathing in the fragrances of wisteria and honeysuckle. 'Where would you like to eat?' she asked. 'I thought we might go to one of those restaurants that Monsieur Leroux mentioned. They're not too far away and then we can get an early night in readiness for sightseeing tomorrow.'

'I thought we might open his wine first – have a little celebratory drink. It's been in the refrigerator for a few hours and should be just right. What do you think?'

'A good idea   I'll go and get it.'

Sarah picked up her dirty shoes and returned to the house. Some minutes later, she returned carrying the wine, two glasses and an old corkscrew, and a small platter of biscuits and leftover cheese and pâté from a market on the way to the house. She poured them both a glass and proposed a toast to their holiday. As she swirled the wine around a heavenly bouquet of honey and apricot soared from the glass. How different to the cheap rosé she drank on her last trip to France, she thought to herself; there was nothing unforgettable about that.

'Just what I needed,' she remarked after taking a long sip. It's a very good wine, just the thing for a lazy summer evening. I'm relaxed already.'

She leaned back in the chair and thought back to that terrible evening three months earlier. The picture could have been very different; her mother could have died. At the very least she could have suffered major brain damage, as the doctor thought was likely. Instead, here she was, looking relaxed and enjoying two of her favourite things – drinking French wine and sitting in a garden in the country of her birth.

'How does it feel to be back on French soil,' Sarah asked, 'after all these years?'

Claire deliberated over her answer. 'I should have come back earlier.'

'Why didn't you? After all, Dad offered to bring you back many times.'

'I supposed I was scared – it just didn't seem right.'

'But what on earth was there to be scared of? You loved France.'

Claire took a sip of the wine. 'I agree with you. It is rather a good wine,' she said, ignoring the question.

'How did you become such a connoisseur of French wines? I know you used to bring a couple of bottles back from your visits to Violette's. Was it there? I imagine with Violette's style – not to mention her money – only the best would have been in order.'

'It's a long story, and you're right, one can't accuse Violette of lacking good taste.'

The pair sat in silence for a while, soaking in the warmth of the late-afternoon sun. The sun was beginning to sink over the cottage, bathing it in a light that reminded Sarah of the dappled texture of an Impressionist painting. Monet – or was it Seurat? She couldn't remember which.

'You didn't answer my earlier question, though. Why were you afraid of coming back?'

Claire let out a deep sigh and looked directly into Sarah's eyes. 'There was a reason – something I'd always intended to keep to myself until now.'

Sarah looked shocked. Her mother had never been the sort of person to keep secrets. 'And this something…did Dad know? I thought you two were close.'

'We were, it's just that…well, you know what it's like: sometimes people keep a few secrets to themselves, don't they? I'm sure you understand what I mean.'

What was her mother alluding to? The Bradshaws had always been a happy family, her parents the ideal couple. Even amongst their friends everyone commented on their happy marriage. Was she now going to tell Sarah after all these years that this was not so? Had one of them been unfaithful – surely not? Sarah braced herself for bad news.

'I loved your father,' Claire said. 'He was a good man and we were very happy, but no, I'm afraid I couldn't share my secret with him, it would have broken his heart.'

Sarah rubbed her temples. 'Mum, I'm confused. If you loved each other as you said you did, surely you could have told him anything. Dad was a kind and gentle man. If you did something wrong – which at this point, I cannot even begin to imagine – then he would have forgiven you.'

Sarah's eyes had a pleading look. She wanted this so-called 'secret' to be nothing at all. In her nervousness, she reached for the wine and poured herself another glass, spilling some in the process.

'I brought you here to tell you something,' said Claire, matter-of-factly. 'No one knows more than me how severe the heart attack was, and if I have another one, I probably won't survive it. It's been years since you and I were together, I mean truly together – as we have been since I was in hospital. We both needed each other's support, I'm afraid. You with the misery of your divorce, and me, well...I couldn't have done without you. The thing is, I know you've been concerned about me – about my little lapses of memory.'

'What do you mean?'

'I know my mind has been a little scrambled just lately. As we get older our memory blurs – old acquaintances shoot out of nowhere to remind you that you had another life.' Claire smiled. 'Some are good memories, some less so. In my case, the shock associated with the fall unleashed memories I would have preferred to have forgotten.'

Emboldened by the wine, Sarah asked why her mother had brought this up now.

'Something happened when I was young – something I tried hard to put behind me. For years I thought I'd succeeded but the events of the last three months told me I hadn't. The time has come for me to lay the past to rest. The thing is, Sarah, I've been here before.'

Sarah looked even more confused. 'You mean here – France?'

'I mean here in Brittany. The truth is, I was here well before I met your father, long before D-Day and the final days of the war.'

For a moment, Sarah felt as though she was sitting in front of a stranger, and she struggled to find words to say. This was not her mother talking, dependable Claire Bradshaw, a woman who abhorred lies and deceit of any kind.

'Does this have anything to do with that newspaper clipping?' Sarah asked.

Claire found it difficult to answer the question. 'I owe it to you to tell you the truth. I couldn't do it in England – I had to come back to where it all began.'

Sarah saw that her mother suddenly looked frightened. Her bottom lip trembled and her eyes glistened as she tried to fight back the tears. In that moment she knew that whatever it was her mother wanted to tell her, it was not going to be easy and she had to be strong for her. She reached over and took her hand.

'Whatever you want to tell me, Mum, I am here for you no matter what.'

And then the words tumbled out.

Chapter 4

Paris, Autumn 1939

After Hitler's blitzkrieg attack on Poland in September 1939, France and Great Britain declared war on Germany. Gerty Bouchard had been dead for almost six months, and Claire was relieved her mother was not alive to hear the news. Like many of her generation who had lost their menfolk in the Great War, Gerty had harboured a deep mistrust of the Germans, but whilst the majority of the French population wanted Germany to pay dearly for that war, Gerty had been astute enough to recognise that the harsh conditions imposed on the German people under the Treaty of Versailles would have dire consequences. She had followed Hitler's rise to power with more than a passing interest and the Anschluss with Austria and subsequent occupation of Czechoslovakia came as no surprise to her. Czechoslovakia had been created in 1919 out of the old Austro-Hungarian Empire and it contained numerous nationalities, 3,200,000 of which were German.

'If he takes Czechoslovakia, he will take Poland,' Gerty warned her daughter. 'And then he will want Alsace. Mark my words, I can feel it in my bones.'

Now Gerty's bones were at rest and France was at war. A few German planes flew over Paris in September, more as a show of strength than anything else, and troops were dispatched along France's northern borders, but for most people it was business as usual. The French people called it the Phoney War, Winston Churchill referred to it as the Twilight War, and the Germans called it a *Sitzekrieg* – Sitting War. Whatever it was, Claire felt a huge void in her life. The past few years spent caring for a sick and demanding mother had depleted her energy and she was at a loss as to what to do with her life.

It was Violette who came up with a solution to snap her out of her malaise.

'Why don't you try your hand at journalism?' she suggested. 'It's what you always wanted to do.'

'Who would be willing to hire me now, with the situation as it is? I have no experience and the French newspapers are careful about what they report.'

'Not the foreign press. From what I gather, they are extremely hungry for news and I know just the right person – the editor-in-chief of a London newspaper. He's a friend of my father's.'

Violette's powers of persuasion had the desired effect and a few days later, Claire found herself sitting in a bistro in the Latin Quarter with the editor-in-chief of the French office of *The Times*, Hugo Manning. Suitably impressed with her credentials and above-average knowledge of politics, he offered her an assignment.

'Nothing difficult,' he assured her, 'but it does mean moving out of Paris for a week or two.'

Claire asked what the assignment was.

'You're aware that we have troops stationed along the border with Germany, just in case Hitler decides to do the same to us as he's done to the Poles?'

'You mean along the Maginot Line?'

'That's correct. The area close to the German border is heavily secured, concrete fortifications that run all the way to Switzerland, but the border with Belgium is weakly protected. The British have sent an expeditionary force there, so it would be good if you could visit there, move around a bit, keep your eyes and ears open and report back to us. Anything – gauge the morale of the people... You know the type of thing.'

Claire thought it a strange request. After all, it was common knowledge that the city of Strasbourg had been evacuated and thousands were fleeing Northern France on a daily basis. Surely that should tell him something. But any doubts she had were quickly laid to rest and the following week, she boarded a train to Reims, where she was to be based for a few weeks. During the first week she moved from town to village along the border: Amiens, Lille, Valenciennes, Charleville, Verdun, Metz. In some places it was so quiet that restless soldiers took to playing soccer or cards all day to occupy themselves. In one area she even found them gardening. Everywhere the men said the same thing: 'We wish something would happen – anything to relieve the boredom.'

Disillusioned that she could find nothing of consequence to report, Claire thought about returning to Paris. At the back of her mind she wondered if Hugo Manning hadn't given her the assignment as a favour to Violette's family. Perhaps she wasn't suited to journalism after all, and she certainly couldn't go on spending his allowance for nothing.

In desperation, she made a call to Paris and told him of her decision to return. It was a brief conversation in which he persuaded her to give it another week. This time she might like to go to the villages around Reims; visit the champagne producers. He would organise for someone to pick her up in the morning. In the meanwhile, she was to book herself a table at a fine restaurant that evening and enjoy herself.

'Spoil yourself, old girl,' he told her. 'I'll pick up the tab.'

Claire hated the way he referred to her as 'old girl', but reminded herself that Violette had told her it was an affectionate expression he used with women he liked.

An hour later, refreshed and wearing a pretty salmon-pink dress, Claire arrived at a nineteenth-century property on the outskirts of Reims. After receiving a warm welcome from the maître d', she was shown to a well-appointed table in a restaurant whose atmosphere and elegant sophistication rivalled the best restaurants in Paris. The sommelier came over and handed her the leather-bound wine list consisting, amongst other great wines, of over three hundred vintages of champagne. She settled on a Pol Roger, a vintage which the sommelier assured her was one of the best. Settling back and savouring the luxurious elegance of her surroundings, she couldn't help thinking about the plight of the soldiers she'd seen over the past two weeks, and was racked by pangs of guilt. She mulled over her telephone conversation with Hugo Manning.

'Never ignore how important wine is to France,' he told her. 'Above all, the Germans recognise the economic and symbolic importance of France's wine industry. Should things take a turn for the worse, a German-dominated France will be milked for all it's worth. They will systematically strip France of her bounty and champagne will be high on that list. It doesn't bear thinking about.'

The waiter brought her an amuse-bouche of a single langoustine in a lemon cream with a touch of Iranian caviar. She thought of the soldiers again. Winter was almost here; the days were getting shorter and their spirits would sink further. France was at war, even if many doubted the inevitability of a real war, and in this moment, sitting at this table, enjoying the best life had to offer, none of it seemed real. In a few days she would be back in Paris and the uncertainty of life would continue much as it had before.

Magically, and as if on cue, her glass was replenished. Lifting the pale gold liquid to her lips, she savoured the sensation. It was the first time she had tasted something so exquisite and whatever happened in the future, she would always remember the luxury of this evening. Before it was over, she silently thanked Hugo Manning for persuading her to stay.

She was up bright and early the next morning. A man who she estimated was of a similar age to Hugo Manning, probably in his late thirties, was already waiting for her in the lobby. He introduced himself as John Dufour, an old friend of Hugo and part-time journalist for Reuters.

'How was your evening?' he asked.

'I can't recall ever having such a wonderful experience,' she said with a smile. 'It was simply marvellous.'

'Hugo must have a soft spot for you to have sent you there. It's as much as we can do to get a baguette out of him. He runs a tight ship.'

Claire didn't reply. To her way of thinking, she had done very little so far. 'Where are we going?' she asked as he started the car.

'We're going to visit one of the champagne houses. I have a list drawn up. There's about twenty in total. And by the way, we're here on behalf of Le Saint-Pierre.'

Claire had heard of it but had never visited it; it was well out of her league. Frequented by the rich and famous, it was one of the most famous restaurants in Paris. Newspaper journalists clamoured around the doorway each day in the hope of getting a shot of someone famous.

'I know even less about champagne than I do about journalism,' she said with a heavy sigh. 'So I don't see how I can be of much help to you.' She turned to look at him and caught him smiling. 'And I thought you said you were a journalist?'

'I am, but I do know something about champagne,' he answered. 'My father was a wine dealer in Bordeaux, and my mother was English, like yours.'

Over the next few days, Claire's knowledge of champagne improved enormously, aided in part by the fact that she had never forgotten her first taste of the fine champagne almost a week earlier, and searched to replicate it. Each evening, John Dufour would drop her off at her hotel where she would dine alone and write up her notes for the day. And each day he gave her a bottle of champagne from their purchases, which he always said was courtesy of *The Times*, and he drove away with the rest. What he was going to do with it all, she had no idea.

Much to her surprise, what had at first appeared to be a fruitless exercise was now beginning to bear fruit. A militant mood prevailed in the region. It was as Hugo Manning had thought – the champagne makers were not taking any chances and were gearing up for the real war. Almost all the families had connections with Germany in one way or another. For some, the connections went well beyond commercial ventures; they were godparents to each other's children. During the visits, John Dufour carried on seemingly routine business meetings while Claire managed to engage others, particularly the women, in everyday chit-chat. On hearing it was her first time to the region they told her about how bad things had been during the Great War.

'You people in Paris, you didn't experience what we did. The battles rendered our vineyards useless. Mortar shells and artillery blew everything up and it took us years to clean up the soil due to chemical poisoning. After that there was the Great Depression. It took years to build it all up again, and then you see what happens – we have one of the worst harvests in years, there are hardly any grapes to pick. Harvest-time is the happiest time of year, a magical time, but 1939 is a year we will all remember.'

Claire commiserated with them. She certainly knew how bad the autumn had been from her few days traversing Northern France. Rain, snow; it was terrible. To most, it seemed that the peasants' legend about war was coming true.

'To announce the coming of war, the Lord sends a bad wine crop,' they told her. 'While war continues, he sends mediocre ones. To mark its end, he sends a fine festive crop.'

As their work drew to a close, both Claire and John Dufour had little doubt that in the minds of the people of the champagne region, war was just around the corner. They had both noticed the amount of 'repair work' going on.

'The cellars need repairing,' someone had said when Claire commented on the amount of concrete being delivered throughout the villages. But there was little doubt in Claire's mind that the champagne houses were not taking any risks; they were discreetly barricading their best vintages behind walls. Sections of labyrinthine caves were quietly being closed off, and she had a strong suspicion that should things take a turn for the worse, it would not only be champagne that would be hidden in those caves.

A week later John Dufour accompanied Claire to the railway station in Reims. He was not going with her as he had work to do elsewhere. They shook hands and he thanked her for her company, which he said he had enjoyed immensely as much of his time was spent travelling alone. He was not forthcoming about his work, and Claire had never bothered to ask. She was just grateful to have had company for a change. A porter picked up her suitcase and pushed his way through the gathering throng of soldiers heading home on leave to an empty first-class compartment. She took her seat next to the window, leaned back in the plush velvet seat and gave a deep sigh. In just over an hour she would be back in Paris and her life would continue much as it had before.

The engine let burst a roar of steam and the train slowly pulled out of the station. She opened a copy of *Paris Match* that John Dufour had purchased for her on the platform and flicked through the pages. Several minutes later, the door opened and a smartly dressed man popped his head inside the compartment.

'Mind if I join you?' he asked.

Claire nodded her approval and continued to read her magazine. The man placed his luggage on the overhead rack, took off his overcoat and hung it neatly on one of the brass hooks that lined the dark wood panelling, and seated himself in the opposite seat. She lifted her head momentarily to observe him. Everything about him registered immediately. The light from the window caught his dark brown hair, lustrous and slicked back, parted with precision to the left. He had hazel eyes and a strong facial structure emphasised by the healthy, tanned glow of an athlete in his prime. It was hard to tell, but she guessed him to be in his mid-thirties. From his honey-coloured cashmere overcoat to his tailored dark blue suit, he oozed style and confidence. She noticed his smooth hands and long fingers as he carefully folded his nut-brown leather gloves and laid them next to his briefcase on the seat beside him – expressive hands that had never known the pain of hard manual labour, Claire thought to herself. Her eyes strayed to his shoes – a rich nut brown to match the gloves, and highly polished. Everything about him spoke of a man of means, but there was something else that Claire noticed – something that marred the otherwise perfection of the man. A scar cut across his lower left cheek, clipping a part of his earlobe; a pinkish streak against the tanned skin.

He caught her looking at him and smiled. Her face flushed and she quickly resumed reading the magazine.

'I saw you at the hotel,' he said after a while. 'Last night. I was in the bar when someone dropped you off at reception.'

Claire looked up and examined his face. 'I'm sorry, but I don't recall seeing you,' she answered, knowing that if she had, he was not someone she was likely to forget.

'I didn't mean to interrupt. It's just that I don't forget a pretty face.'

Claire's cheeks reddened. She smiled, thanked him for his flattering comment and turned the page of her magazine, realising that she had not read a word of it since he entered the compartment. He pulled out a newspaper from his briefcase and much to Claire's relief, began to read. He did not utter another word until the train stopped at a station on the outskirts of Paris. More people clambered aboard. This time they were joined by an elderly couple on their way to visit their daughter in Marseilles. The man struck up a conversation with them immediately. It seemed he was from Alsace. The elderly man commented on the evacuation of Strasbourg, to which the younger man replied that he was sure it would be short-lived as he thought the Germans had no intention of attacking France. Claire considered entering the conversation and asking how he could be so sure, but decided not to get involved. At that point, the man pulled the window down and asked a guard how long they were likely to be there. When he replied, 'At least ten minutes', the man said he was going out for a moment, and would they kindly look after his luggage; he would be back shortly. Claire watched him battle his way through a group of people to a cafe on the platform.

Just minutes before the whistle sounded, he reappeared carrying baguettes and hot coffee, which he offered to everyone in the compartment. The elderly couple thanked him profusely.

'And you, Mademoiselle,' he said to Claire, 'will you partake in a light lunch with us?'

She put away her magazine, took out a fresh linen handkerchief and laid it on her lap, and took the baguette.

'Ham and cheese,' he said. 'I hope it's to your liking.'

Claire was hungrier than she thought, and the snack went down a treat.

'Heading to Paris as well?' he asked her.

Claire replied that she lived there. It was clear he wanted to engage her in conversation, and after accepting his food, she couldn't turn away. He told her that he had been to Paris several times in the past, but this was the first time he would be living there.

'I will be living near the Champs-Élysées,' he said. 'My work is close by. Avenue Gabriel, perhaps you know it?'

Claire acknowledged that she did indeed know it. Such a prestigious address was only for the wealthy and well-connected, which she had come to assume her fellow traveller was indeed one of.

'I am afraid we will not be neighbours,' she replied. 'I live in the 20th arrondissement near the Cimetière du Père-Lachaise.'

Half an hour later, the train pulled into the Gare du Nord. The man offered to help Claire with her luggage. When they stepped off the train, she saw Violette coming towards her. The two embraced warmly.

'I was beginning to think you'd never get here,' Violette said. 'How was it?'

Then she noticed the man standing behind her. Claire thanked him for helping her with her suitcase.

'It was a pleasure, Mademoiselle,' he replied. 'Perhaps our paths may cross again?'

'Well, well,' Violette said, after he'd gone. 'You are a dark horse. Where did you pick up such a good-looking man as that? What was his name?'

'Do you know, I haven't got a clue, but he was rather handsome, wasn't he?'

The two girls linked arms and laughingly walked away.

Despite any misgivings Claire had about journalism, Hugo Manning assured her that she had done an excellent job and offered her another assignment. She thanked him for his belief in her abilities, but told him she had decided to go back to teaching. By the spring of 1940, Claire had settled back into the familiar routine of teaching languages at a girls' school near the Parc des Buttes Chaumont, not far from her home. Teaching provided stability, yet she was restless and at a loss for what to do with her life. Those few weeks in Reims had opened her eyes to another world. That world – one of elegant dining and fine wine – belonged to Violette, not her. Violette, whose family boasted an aristocratic lineage and whose parents socialised in the right circles. Violette, whose connections had made Hugo Manning offer her a job she was not equipped to do. Now it seemed that Violette's star was on the ascent and she was pursuing her dream of becoming a psychoanalyst and studying with a colleague of Freud, whilst Claire's life was doomed to tedium. She had to snap out of it.

With the arrival of spring, the morale of the people, which had been low throughout the winter, lifted. Parisians began to take strolls in the parks once more and the outdoor cafes were filled to capacity. Violette suggested she and Claire visit some of their favourite bookshops along the Left Bank. Already laden with armfuls of purchases, they made one last stop at their favourite bookstore, Shakespeare & Company in the Rue de l'Odéon

Whilst Violette scanned the shelves for anything on psychoanalysis, Claire perused books on Hemingway, Fitzgerald and Ezra Pound. She picked up a copy of *The Sun Also Rises* and started flicking through it; she might add it to *The Great Gatsby* for her students to study.

At that point she became aware of someone standing behind her. Instinctively she swung around and was confronted by the man who had shared the same train compartment with her almost six months earlier. Once again, he was smartly dressed, this time having replaced his well-cut suit for a pair of casual cream-coloured trousers and a pale blue ribbed pullover, under which he wore a matching open-necked shirt with a cream silk cravat covered in the smallest of blue dots. With her olive-green skirt and sensible walking shoes, Claire felt rather dowdy in his presence.

'Well, I was right after all, Mademoiselle,' he said. 'Our paths have crossed again. His eyes scanned the book in her hands. 'Hemingway – a good choice.'

'It's for my students,' Claire stammered. 'I teach languages.'

'I knew from the moment I saw you that you were not just a pretty face.'

Claire's eyes flitted nervously from his eyes to his mouth with its infectious smile. She glanced across the room and saw Violette heading towards them.

'Ahhh!' exclaimed Violette in a coquettish manner. 'How lovely to see you again. I'm afraid we were never introduced before. My name's Violette.'

The man shook her outstretched hand firmly. 'Marcel,' he answered, and turned back to Claire. 'I'm sorry, I should have introduced myself when we first became acquainted.'

'Claire,' she said, extending her hand also. 'How are you finding Paris?'

'I'm enjoying it very much.'

'If it's not a rude question, Monsieur, what is it that you do?' Violette asked.

'I'm a lawyer,' he replied, and taking Violette's friendly manner as a sign of acceptance, asked if they would care to join him for an aperitif. 'There's a wonderful little cafe not far from here and I'd be delighted if you two charming ladies would join me.'

'We'd love to, wouldn't we, Claire?' Violette replied.

Swept along with their enthusiasm, Claire paid for her purchases and the three made their way along the Seine to the cafe where Marcel ordered three *Lillet Blancs*. For the next half-hour Marcel and Violette chatted away

– she about her work at the clinic and he about how much he liked Paris. Claire remained uncharacteristically quiet.

'Well,' said Violette, after they parted ways. 'He's sweet on you, that's for sure. And if I'm not mistaken, you like him too.'

Claire was surprised by Violette's remark. 'I thought it was you who held his attention,' she replied.

Violette rolled her eyes. 'Dear Claire, I'm not blind, you know. You hardly said a word, and when he looked at you, you blushed.'

Claire knew she was right. There was something about him that set her heart racing, and if she was truthful with herself, it had happened the first time she laid eyes on him.

'He's out of my league. Look at the way he dresses. He's immaculate.'

Violette sighed. 'And look at you: you're beautiful – *and* you have a brain. What a combination. You could have any man you wanted if you set your mind to it. You need to get out more, stop being such a recluse – have a good time like you used to.'

Several days later, Claire arrived back at her apartment and was greeted by the concierge holding an enormous bunch of red roses.

'A gentleman called by earlier this evening and when I told him you were not at home, he said I was to see that you got these personally. There's a note with them.'

In the privacy of her apartment, Claire laid the flowers down on the hallway table and eagerly opened up the envelope.

I have booked a table for two on Saturday at Le Saint-Pierre. I will pick you up at 7pm.

Marcel.

She read it several times before it finally sunk in. Le Saint-Pierre – the exclusive restaurant she had heard so much about. It didn't seem real – and the audacity of the man! How could he be sure she even wanted to go? But she did – more than anything in the world.

The telephone rang. It was Violette.

'Well,' she said, 'what did I tell you? Your admirer obviously remembered the place where I told him I worked and looked up the telephone number to say he wanted to take you out. He asked for your address.'

Claire could hardly contain her excitement. 'He left the most beautiful bunch of flowers with a note saying he wants to take me to Le Saint-Pierre on Saturday.'

Violette let out a squeal of excitement. 'My, my, he's definitely trying to make an impression.'

The following day, Claire took all the money she had put aside from her work in Reims and visited the exclusive dress shops on the Rue du Faubourg Saint-Honoré. They were all far too expensive for her. In the end she found a small, stylish boutique not far away in a side street with evening dresses at half the price and bought a claret satin-and-velvet evening dress with a low-cut neckline in claret chiffon. With the little money she had left over, she also bought a pair of shoes, a matching bag and a pair of elbow-length gloves.

For the next few days, Claire's emotions oscillated from elation to fear and back to elation again. Perhaps she was making a grave mistake by allowing herself to hope that anything might come from this date. It troubled her that Marcel appeared to be a man of high status with high expectations and she simply did not have the means to be the sort of woman someone like him would aspire to. What if she never saw him again – well, then there would be no need to worry, would there? Violette was right; she would have a good time while she could. No harm done, just a small fortune spent on a new wardrobe that no doubt she would wear again sometime in the future.

Chapter 5

It could not have been a more perfect evening. The warmth of a beautiful spring day still lingered in the air and the lights of Paris danced on the Seine and twinkled through the blossom-filled trees that lined the grand boulevards like tiny lights on a Christmas tree. Springtime in Paris was for lovers; the outdoor cafes were filled with them, their eyes and body language eager with expectation. In the back of a chauffeur-driven car, sitting next to a man she knew nothing about, Claire felt that same sensation; the frisson of excitement that accompanied a leap into the unknown. She smoothed down the folds of her dress in an attempt to calm herself.

'You look wonderful,' Marcel said for a second time that evening.

Claire smiled. She was already falling under his spell. From the moment he sent her the flowers, she had thought of nothing else. She had looked forward to this moment with a mixture of fear and joy. And as soon as she laid eyes on him again, the fear dissipated, replaced by an intense desire that she had purposely tried to avoid on their first meeting.

'I was afraid you wouldn't come,' he said. 'After your apparent coolness towards me on the train, I thought you didn't like me.'

Claire apologised for her rudeness, claiming that she had other things on her mind at the time.

'It's been rather a difficult year. My mother died after a long illness and I was at a loss about what to do with my future.'

'I'm sorry, the loss of a parent is never easy. And your future – have you sorted it out? I would imagine that you are an excellent teacher.'

She was about to tell him about her thoughts of becoming a journalist but quickly decided there was nothing to tell; she had long given up that idea.

'I do enjoy my work, very much in fact, and I'm so grateful to have a job at all. It takes my mind off things. Everything seems so uncertain, what with the war and everything.'

'Ah yes, the war.'

She looked at him for reassurance. 'Do you think there will be a war – I mean a *real* war, on French soil? This Phoney War has been going on for so long now, it all seems so unreal.'

'I don't know. Let's hope not. France and Germany would make a good alliance – if it weren't for the British being so obstinate, getting into the ears of French politicians. Why should we go to war over Poland? After all, it was they who broke the peace and attacked Germany. It was only natural that the Germans would retaliate.'

His words shook her.

'I'm not sure that I would agree with you there,' she said rather tersely. 'Or that a few million others would either. It was a pretence to get what they wanted, a poor pretence at that. We all know the Third Reich wanted Danzig as much as the Sudetenland. And by the way,' Claire continued, 'my mother was English so I do have some sympathy for them. They are our allies. Who else will come to our aid?'

Marcel leaned a little closer and put his finger on her lips. 'Shush, I didn't mean to upset you. Let's not sully the evening with talk of the war. I'm glad that you're here. That's all that matters.'

Claire agreed wholeheartedly.

When they arrived at Le Saint-Pierre, a group of photographers had already gathered around a car waiting for the occupants to alight. For their patience they were rewarded with a glimpse of one of France's most famous stars.

'Look, isn't that Maurice Chevalier?' Claire said. 'And that must be his new wife. I hear he's back from America for good.'

After the couple entered the restaurant, the photographers turned their attention towards Marcel's car, hoping to snap another famous face. The driver waved them away and in a matter of seconds they were inside Le Saint-Pierre, where Marcel was greeted with the familiarity of an old customer.

Marcel placed his hand on the small of Claire's back and ushered her between two marble Ionic columns, in front of which were two enormous potted palms. The sumptuous decor of Le Saint-Pierre took her breath away; she felt she'd entered another world. Antique oil paintings, tapestries and gilded mirrors graced the walls and next to them stood some of the finest pieces of furniture she'd ever seen, the sheen of which gleamed like mirrors under a row of multi-tiered chandeliers. A discreet table for two had been reserved for them at the far end of the room, strategically placed near a window to give a clear view of the Eiffel Tower. The sommelier brought over an ice bucket and stand, pulled out a bottle of champagne, wiped it with a starched white cloth, and with a proud flourish of one who took his work extremely seriously, showed it to Marcel. Claire noted the label. The sommelier popped the cork and proceeded to pour.

'Krug 1928,' said Marcel. 'One of the finest champagnes ever made.'

After Reims, Claire was impressed.

He raised his glass to her. 'Thank you for coming. I hope you won't be disappointed.'

'I hardly think that will be the case. You have excellent taste,' Claire said with a smile. 'It seems that you have been here before.'

'Quite so — on several occasions in fact. My work requires that I occasionally entertain important clients.'

'And tonight, am I one of your important clients?' she asked mischievously.

Marcel leaned forward and smiled — the same alluring smile he had given her on the train to Paris. 'The most important,' he replied in a soft, deep voice that took her breath away.

He turned his attention to the menu. 'And now, can I recommend the *carre d'agneau Provencal* with *petits legumes farcis?*'

'I am in your hands tonight. If the food is as good as the champagne, then I am guaranteed a memorable evening.'

'Tell me something,' Marcel said after the waiter had taken their order. 'Is there a man in your life — a lover perhaps?'

He held her gaze, waiting for an answer.

'No. There is no one. And you, is there a woman in your life?'

'No.'

Claire studied him for a moment, surprised that the conversation had taken such an intimate turn so quickly. He mesmerised her, and his aura of power and wealth excited her.

'Forgive me, but I find that hard to believe. I would have thought a man like you could have any woman he liked. You don't exactly strike me as being the shy, laid-back type.'

He laughed. 'That, I am not, but when it comes to women, I am hard to please.'

The conversation was interrupted by a bevy of waiters bringing their meal, the last one pouring a rich, dark trickle of sauce from a silver jug onto her plate next to the lamb and then placing it on the table. Claire caught a glimpse of Marcel's reflection in a large mirror ornately framed in garlands of flowers festooned with cherubs and doves. The light from the chandelier on the mirror highlighted his scar. Her heart raced. She had never met a man quite like him before.

'How did you get the scar?' she asked.

'Fencing – I took it up in my teens.'

'Didn't you wear the protective mask?'

'On that day, I am ashamed to say, no. It was a dare from a rival fencer. I lost.'

'I see. A duel with a jealous lover,' Claire smiled, imagining him competing for the attention of a beautiful woman.

Marcel laughed. 'I was young and impetuous – easily aroused. Since then I've learnt to be sure of the outcome before committing myself. I'm a bad loser.'

He wanted to know more about her, and they found that they shared similar interests – literature and the arts. He told her that he would have liked to have been a writer but his father wanted him to study law.

'He sent me to study in Berlin,' he told her.

'Why Berlin and not the Sorbonne?'

'My uncle was a professor there.'

'I also teach German,' Claire said. 'Although because of the war, those classes have been cancelled in favour of more English classes. It's a pity – my students like Hesse, and of course, Goethe. I believe *The Sorrows of Young Werther* had a profound influence on Scott Fitzgerald, although I must confess to never having read it. As for myself, I rate Thomas Mann's *Death in Venice* as one of my favourites.'

Marcel acknowledged her good taste in literature. 'Anyway,' he continued, 'I stayed in Berlin for a few years and returned to take up a position in the family business in Alsace. Then I decided to come to Paris.'

'And what were you doing in Reims?' she asked. 'Was that also for business?'

'I was there on behalf of a client, but I took a few days extra for a little sightseeing. And you, what were you doing there?'

Claire decided not to muddy the water with talk about the work for Hugo Manning. 'I needed some time to myself to decide my future,' she replied.

On the other side of the room, Maurice Chevalier and his wife were joined by a group of dancers from the Folies Bergère.

'She's certainly beautiful,' Claire said. 'I believe she's Russian.'

'And Jewish,' Marcel replied.

Claire stiffened, surprised at his remark. 'Perhaps you were in Berlin too long. Such a remark does not do you justice.'

'Simply a statement of fact, that's all. And I agree with you, she is rather beautiful.' He reached across the table and took her hand. 'But I'm afraid not as beautiful as you.'

His eyes flirted with her and she relaxed a little, desperately wanting to believe him. In that moment his comment was brushed aside. She was under his spell.

During the drive home, Claire asked Marcel if he would care to join her for a nightcap and he accepted. A year ago, this would have been unthinkable; Gerty would not have approved of her actions. In her mother's book, inviting a man she barely knew back to an empty apartment after midnight would have spelt trouble. Since her death, the thought of going home to an empty house had filled Claire with dread, yet tonight, emboldened by too much champagne, she understood that living alone also had its advantages – she could do just as she wanted. Nothing in the world would have stopped her prolonging the magic of the evening.

The air in the apartment was stifling and she opened a window in the drawing room a little to let in some air. The sounds of the night grew fainter by the minute. Somewhere down the road, the door to a bar opened and a burst of piano music momentarily drifted into the street. Marcel declared that a cognac would finish the night off perfectly. Claire went to the kitchen to fetch a couple of glasses, leaving him alone, looking through a pile of gramophone records.

The gramophone started and the voice of Lys Gauty singing 'Le Chaland Qui Passe' filled the apartment. It was a song that always moved Claire, and tonight was no exception. As she reached for the glasses she caught sight of herself in the small wall mirror. Her face was flushed with a mixture of happiness and champagne. With the music playing softly in the background, Claire realised she had never been so happy. The lyrics haunted her: 'Do not think of anything… The current makes us wander.' She gripped the side of the table momentarily to catch her breath. This couldn't be happening to her. It was too good to be true.

When she returned to the drawing room, she found Marcel had turned off all the lights except one and was sitting in her mother's old armchair next to the fireplace. The music stopped and she put the glasses down to play another record.

'Stop,' said Marcel, in a low voice. 'Stay where you are.'

Claire turned to face him, and in doing so, realised that she stood in a pool of moonlight streaming through the window. She looked down at herself. The claret dress appeared to be on fire. She touched the ruched chiffon neckline that emphasised her cleavage with her fingertips and saw that her skin looked a warm, pale gold in the light.

'I cannot remember the last time my eyes saw such a beautiful sight,' Marcel said.

With the room in near darkness, Claire could just make out his silhouette. His voice, commanding and persuasive, filled every inch of the room.

'Take it off,' he said. 'Take the dress off – slowly.'

As if hypnotised, she did exactly as she was told. Her hands reached for the clip at the back of her neck. It snapped open, allowing her to unzip the dress. Slowly, she kept telling herself, ever so slowly. The chiffon neckline slid down her arms, baring more of her cleavage, which rose up and down steadily with her breathing. Strangely, she was calm. It all seemed so natural. And as much as she was aware of his eyes watching her every move, Claire was even more aware of her own sexuality. The dress slid down a little more, exposing her ivory silk bra. She let the dress go and it slipped to the ground in soft folds around her feet. Unabashed, she stepped out of it and stood proud, clad only in her lingerie. The room was strangely silent and in the shadows she was aware of his eyes on her.

Her hands reached around her back and she unclasped the bra, exposing her breasts. The bra fell onto the floor next to the dress. She bent forward to step out of her panties and saw that her nipples were hard and erect. It excited her. Wearing only her suspender belt and silk stockings and illuminated by the moonlight, Claire had never felt like such a sexual being as she did at that moment. Her whole body was on fire. She stooped to undo a stocking and saw that Marcel was coming towards her. He put his hand out to stop her.

'No. Let me see you as you are.'

Slowly he walked around her, studying every part of her body as an artist studies a model before he decides in which position to paint her. He reached for her face, gently stroking every part of it, like a blind man seeking to imprint the impression in his mind. Slowly and deliberately, his hand moved down her neck and over her shoulders and down the curve of her breasts, momentarily stopping when he placed it over her heart, which beat like a drum underneath the soft, bare skin. Claire closed her eyes, savouring the pressure of his hand as it moved over her. When his fingers moved to her nipples, she could hardly contain herself. She tipped her head back and uttered a long, low moan. He leant towards her, kissing, pulling and squeezing them between his lips until she felt a warm, throbbing sensation in her groin that was impossible to bear.

'A woman like you was made for loving,' he whispered.

At any minute, Claire thought she would burst; every nerve in her body was aroused. Never before had she wanted to make love as she did now. There were no thoughts – only wild, primordial emotions kindled by his erotic teasing, she savoured every moment of him caressing her body, one minute with his hand, the next minute his tongue. With her eyes still closed, she felt him unclip her stockings and slide them down her legs. Lastly, he removed her suspender belt. He knelt in front of her and gently pushed her legs apart. Her flesh was moist with desire and he indulged himself, inhaling the sweet smell of her sex and stroking his cheeks against the softness of her pubic hair that glistened in the moonlight. Instinctively, Claire put her hands on his head and pulled him to her. She felt his mouth covering her, parting the tender area between her legs as though they had all the time in the world. This intense sensation of his tongue exploring her was more than she could take and filled with passion for him, she cried out in a delirium of desire, pleading with him to take her. And then, when she thought she could not bear it any longer, he stopped.

For a brief moment Claire felt light-headed and confused. Why had he stopped?

He picked up her dress. 'Put it back on,' he said, kissing her on her neck. 'Not tonight, my darling. I want everything to be perfect when it happens.'

Claire wanted to protest but she was at a loss for what to say. She stood for a moment to catch her breath whilst he fastened the back of her dress. Her underwear was still scattered on the floor. He picked it up and placed it on the chair.

'There will be another time,' he said, drawing her to him. 'You will thank me for waiting. Making love is not something that should be rushed. I want you to remember it for the rest of your life.'

He kissed her goodnight – a long, lingering kiss that began to arouse her once more. His tongue tasted of her body and drove her wild with desire again.

After he had gone, Claire slumped in a chair, mulling over what had just taken place. The moon had moved across the night sky and its golden beam no longer shone into the room. She looked around. All that remained of that evening was a crumpled pile of lingerie and two unused glasses. He had lit a fire in her like no man had ever done before. They had talked about many things that night, but she still had no idea where he lived or worked and he hadn't given her a phone number. Now all she could do was wait.

Violette was already at the bistro when Claire arrived and she was anxious to hear all about her date. One look at Claire's face and Violette knew it had gone well.

'Well? Do tell me about it. I can't wait to hear,' she said before Claire had even had a chance to sit down. 'I must say, my dear, you look radiant so I take it the evening was a flying success.'

Claire leaned back in the high leather seat and smiled. 'You wouldn't believe me if I told you,' she replied. 'I never knew such a man existed. He was more – much more than I ever dared hope for. And what's more, I believe he really does like me.'

'When are you seeing him again?'

Claire let out a long sigh. 'I don't know, but after such an evening I am sure it will be soon.'

'Did you find out anything else about him? His wealth, for instance – did he say where he worked?'

'Well, not exactly. We didn't get to talk about that. I only know that he studied and worked in Berlin for a while. Then he came back to join the family business before coming to Paris. It seems that he is a regular at Le Saint-Pierre – he takes his clients there.'

Violette chastised her playfully for not asking more about him, and Claire did confide to her that she had invited him back to her apartment but stopped short of mentioning the amorous ritual that had taken place. Violette listened attentively and then laughed. She was a woman of the world – there was no need to say anything; she understood something momentous had taken place and was only too happy to see her old friend in high spirits again.

Claire was the happiest she had been in a long time. In fact she couldn't remember ever being as happy as this. There had been the odd flirtation, stolen kisses after a dance and the occasional fondling of her breasts by inexperienced lovers, but it all paled into insignificance when she thought of Marcel. He had kindled a fire in her that now raged and enveloped her whole being.

But after a week that happiness began to fade. There had been no contact from him at all; not even a telephone call, and she began to panic.

Surely he would not have said and done those things if he had not meant them. Violette assured her that it was nothing to worry about; that playing hard to get was a man's prerogative as well as a woman's, and anyway, he was probably busy with his work.

Another fortnight passed and Claire's high spirits deteriorated into a depression she found hard to shake off. She couldn't concentrate on her work, found it hard to sleep and spent most of the evenings playing records, in particular, *Le Chaland Qui Passe*, until she accidentally dropped it after drowning her sorrows in cognac.

And then, one month later, when she had just about given up all hope of ever seeing him again, he sent her another bunch of roses and a small package wrapped in brown paper and tied with string. Her heart leapt with joy. She ripped open the envelope, and with shaking hands, read his note.

Mon amour Claire,

Meet me by the Carpeaux Fountain in the Jardin du Luxembourg on Sunday at 2pm.

Marcel

That was all. No mention of why he had not contacted her; no florid declarations of love – nothing. And also, like before, there was no telephone number. He just assumed she would do as he asked. But he *had* called her *mon amour*, and that made her heart race. Her attention turned to the package. It contained a book – *The Sorrows of Young Werther*, which he had evidently noted she hadn't yet read. Claire held it to her breast. He had thought of her after all.

I knew it, she told herself. I knew he wouldn't forget me.

When Sunday came, Claire dressed with great care; a figure-hugging, ribbed lilac sweater over a chocolate-brown pencil skirt. A simple, stylish look she had perfected from skimming the fashion magazines. Her hair was swept up in a roll but at the last minute, she undid it, letting it tumble around her shoulders. He would like it better this way, she told herself, and today she wanted nothing more than to please him.

On such a splendid day, the Jardin du Luxembourg was filled with people. Situated on the fashionable Left Bank, it was Paris' most romantic park. The lovers' park, they called it, and the fact that Marcel wanted to meet there, Claire read as a good omen. Her stomach full of butterflies, she made her way along the tree-lined pathway towards the Carpeaux Fountain. She was early but he was there already, sitting on a bench observing the four nude sculptures of women supporting the globe that represents the four continents of classical iconography. When he saw her he jumped up and held out his arms. Without as much as a word, he seized her and pulled her to him, kissing her hard on the lips.

'Let me look at you,' he said, whirling her around. 'You've lost weight.'

Claire wanted to tell him that she'd had no appetite due to worrying if she'd ever see him again. Instead, her emotions caught up with her and she collapsed into his arms, sobbing.

'I'm sorry,' she said, trying to gain her composure. 'It's just that…well, when I didn't hear from you, what was I to think?'

They sat down on the bench. He put one arm around her shoulder, and placing his other hand under her chin, forced her to look at him.

'I had to go away on business. Something urgent came up. It couldn't be helped. If only you knew how much I wanted to see you again, how much I wanted to make love to you – to finish off what we began.'

He kissed her again, a kiss full of longing and desire. Hungry for his affection, Claire reciprocated with equal intensity.

'I have a surprise for you,' he said after a while. 'I want you to come away with me. I've rented a cottage for two weeks by the sea, in Brittany.' He leaned closer and whispered in her ear. 'Remember what I said. Making love is something that should not be rushed, and we will have all the time in the world. I know your feelings are as strong as mine, so what do you say?'

'When?'

'This weekend.'

'But my work – and the war!'

'France is still free, and you can make an excuse at the school.'

His eyes flashed with mischief and he covered her face with kisses, oblivious to the people passing by. His kisses excited her. She marvelled at how powerfully persuasive he could be without trying.

'Fine,' she answered with a smile. 'I agree.'

Côte d'Émeraude, Brittany, 12th May 1940

The tide was steadily coming in, lapping gently over the nearby rocks. Claire adjusted the straps of her bathing costume and rubbed more oil into her reddened shoulders. She turned and looked admiringly at Marcel dozing peacefully next to her on the striped beach towel. Sand clung to his tanned skin, and his hair, dishevelled from their last swim, glistened in the afternoon light. She pulled a book out of her bag and lay back on the towel to read. A gentle sea breeze caressed their bodies. In a few days they would be back in Paris and all this would be a dream. She didn't want to think about it. All she wanted to do was savour the moment. The pent-up force of desire had brought out emotions she never knew existed. She had left Paris a virgin, inexperienced in the art of lovemaking, and she would return a woman – a woman who had abandoned herself to her sexuality.

Marcel's appetite for sex was insatiable and his lovemaking was tender one minute, violent the next. They couldn't get enough of each other. Such happiness could not be surpassed, and yet it was – time and time again. It was all too good to be true. She moved closer and kissed him lightly on the cheek next to the scar that was so much a part of his handsome features. He opened his eyes and smiled lazily.

'I hope I haven't disappointed you.'

Claire cuddled up against his bare chest. The saltiness of his scent filled her nostrils.

'No, my love, you haven't disappointed me. You were right, lovemaking shouldn't be hurried.'

And then, as abruptly as it started, it ended. The news that the Germans had finally attacked brought it all to an end. When she delivered the news to him in the outhouse where he had spent a few short hours each day trying to write poetry, they made love for the last time. Passionate, frenzied and violent, it was as if he never wanted her to forget the moment. They would return to Paris straight away, back to the unknown. Shortly after, when she was packing their suitcases in the bedroom, she looked out of the window and saw him cross the courtyard towards the gate, his striped beach towel slung over his shoulder. He saw her watching him as he closed the gate and waved before heading for the beach. He was going for a swim, and it disappointed her that he was going alone. It was something they had done together every day.

When he failed to return a few hours later she became anxious. Perhaps he'd gone for a walk, she told herself. After all, that was something he occasionally did in the mornings before lunch. But he was never gone longer than two hours. As the sun began to set, her thoughts were broken by a loud hammering on the door.

'Come quickly,' a man's voice shouted. 'There's been an accident on the beach.'

Claire's heart raced and she began to panic. She grabbed her shawl and followed him back to the beach. The sun was already setting over the English Channel and the tide was steadily creeping in when they made their way down the steep cliff steps. A group of people had already gathered around Marcel's striped beach towel and pair of light blue trousers. Claire stared at them as if it was all a bad dream.

'Someone saw him wade into the water. The next thing we knew, he seemed to be in difficulty,' someone said. 'Over there, past the rocks. That's the last we saw of him.'

'Try not to worry,' a woman said, putting her arm around Claire's shoulder. 'We're doing our best to find him. I'm sure everything will be fine.'

Claire watched the men scouring the rocks with an overwhelming pain in her heart.

'It's impossible,' she cried. 'Marcel is a strong swimmer, and the sea — it's so calm.'

Yet despite her hopes, her instincts told her something had gone terribly wrong and she knew she would never see him again.

What had begun as a summer of joy had now turned into a tragedy. Without him by her side, she simply did not know how she would face the prospect of war.

Paris, 1940, Three Weeks Later

Paris was seized by panic. It was a nightmare. When Claire heard that millions of French men, women and children were fleeing south, and that British and French troops were evacuating from the northern beaches at Dunkirk, she knew the situation was hopeless. The headmistress at the school sent word that her services would no longer be required as the school was officially closed and no one knew when it would open again. All she could do was sit at home and listen to the radio. Violette joined her. Communications had been cut but they still had a good idea what was going on. After the initial exodus, an eerie quiet descended over Paris. Shops were boarded up and those who stayed prayed the city would be safe. Surely, even the Germans couldn't bomb the city of Paris — it wasn't possible. Yet on the outskirts of Paris, the Citroën and Renault factories were bombed and nightly air raids and the sounds of anti-aircraft fire grew more frequent by the day.

On Monday 10th June, the government officially left Paris for the Loire Valley. The following day, Winston Churchill and a small delegation flew to France to urge the French government to fight, but the government was in turmoil and Prime Minister Reynaud and his deputy, eighty-four-year-old Marshal Pétain, hero of Verdun in World War I, no longer believed the Germans could not be repulsed. They were already heading towards Paris.

'You must leave,' Violette told Claire. 'Get out while you can. Go to England.'

'But I'm French,' Claire protested. 'What will I do in England? I don't even know if I have any living relatives there any longer.'

'You are part English. The Germans may not look favourably on that. Besides, there's nothing to keep you here.'

'And there's nothing for me in England either. I don't even have a passport.'

'Sometimes you can be so stubborn,' Violette replied caustically. 'You know as well as I do that the Germans mean to stay. Life will never be the same. At least England is still free.'

'For how long?'

The two sat in silence for a while, mulling over what to do next.

'I can get you a passport,' Violette said after a while.

'And how do you propose to do that?'

'From Hugo Manning.'

'Hugo Manning!' Claire stammered. 'How on earth can he help?'

'He has people working for him that can pull a few strings. Besides, he already has your details and a photograph on file from your time in Reims.'

Claire put her head in her hands and sighed. 'Please don't do this, Violette,' she urged.

But Violette's determination refused to be shaken. A few days later she was back at the apartment, waving travel documents and a British passport in the air.

'There,' she said, 'what did I tell you? He knows how to pull strings. But one thing's for sure: had I left it any longer, it would have been impossible. He's leaving for Bordeaux this evening. Unfortunately he can't take you with him, but he informed me that there are still trains leaving from Gare d'Austerlitz.'

'And you? What will you do?'

'Don't worry about me. God willing, I'll be fine. Now hurry. I have just enough petrol to take you part of the way there and you'll have to walk the rest.'

Claire pulled out her sturdy suitcase – the same one she'd taken to Reims, and more recently to Brittany, and stuffed it full of clothes and a few photographs.

She locked the apartment door behind her and headed downstairs to Violette's car. She suddenly remembered she'd better inform the concierge, and turned round to go back.

Violette stopped her. 'No. Don't tell anyone, it's better this way. I'll keep an eye on the place for you.'

Claire's mind was in turmoil but she knew Violette was probably right and handed her a spare key. Violette dropped her off about two kilometres away. The pair held each other in an emotional embrace. They had been friends for years, shared so much and been there for each other in adversity. The future had never looked so uncertain and neither knew if they would ever see one another again.

'New adventures,' Violette shouted through a mist of tears as she got back into the car. 'God go with you.'

Gare d'Austerlitz was a seething mass of people, pushing and shoving each other in sheer desperation. It was impossible to get anywhere near the ticket office. Fearful she would miss the train, Claire pulled a guard away from his duties, stuffed a wad of notes in his hand and asked him to get her a ticket. He looked at the notes, astounded, told her to wait and not to move. When he disappeared into the crowd, Claire had no idea if she had just thrown her money to the wind. Through the din she could just make out the final announcement for the departure of her train. Her heart sank. At that moment, the guard appeared, picked up her suitcase and told her to follow him. The whistle sounded and with only a minute to spare, he threw the suitcase onto the train, handed her the ticket and helped her up the steps.

'Your change,' he shouted as the train slowly began to shunt along the track.

'For you, my saviour,' she shouted from the window, and blew him a kiss.

The train gathered speed and Claire looked for somewhere to sit. It was impossible. The compartments and the corridors were filled to capacity. She would have to spend the journey sitting on her suitcase. She sat next to an elegantly-dressed woman wearing an expensive fur, who stared listlessly out of the window, her eyes red and swollen from crying. In her arms she rocked a small girl to and fro. The child stared at Claire with wide, frightened eyes. It was strangely silent, as if it instinctively knew that crying would not help the situation.

After the train left the outskirts of Paris and began to head south through the countryside, Claire caught her first sight of the utter desolation and chaos of the past few weeks. The main roads were clogged with a never-ending procession of people heading south; like her, fleeing to goodness knows where. With no petrol available, abandoned vehicles filled with cherished possessions lined the roadsides in their hundreds, and carts, their wheels groaning under the enormous weight of household goods, on which were often seated small children and the elderly, trundled by, drawn by tired farm horses that looked as if they would collapse at any moment.

She took a few biscuits out of her bag and offered one to the woman and child. The woman declined but the child took one eagerly and gave her a smile. Claire sat with her back against the wall of a compartment, watching the countryside pass by. The events of the past few weeks caught up with her and tears began to trickle down her cheeks. In the turmoil, she had had no time to mourn Marcel's loss. Survival had taken precedence over love. Perhaps it was better this way. There would be time for grieving later. She wiped away the tears and looked at the woman beside her. Where was her man – had she lost her love too? The small child sat up on her mother's lap, and held out her tiny hand for Claire to hold. Claire clasped both hands around it. What was it that could make a child old beyond its years, she asked herself?

Chapter 6

Côte d'Émeraude, Brittany, September 2001

The sun had long sunk beyond the horizon by the time Claire and Sarah reached the restaurant. Even at such a late hour it was still busy with sun-bronzed holidaymakers, but the owner managed to find them a table overlooking the clifftop. Tiny lights from the numerous small fishing boats flickered on the dark, satiny water that glistened in the moonlight. A soft, salty sea breeze enveloped them, bringing on a hunger they had not realised they had until now. It was a romantic setting, and Sarah wondered if her mother had shared such a night with Marcel.

They ordered moules marinière and local wine and ate without uttering a word, both wrapped up in their own thoughts. After they'd finished, the waiter brought over two complimentary glasses of apple brandy.

'I'm afraid I've shocked you, haven't I?' Claire said after a while.

Sarah looked towards the clifftops and noticed steps leading to a cove somewhere below. She thought of Marcel, towel slung over his shoulder, heading to his death, and turned her gaze towards her mother's familiar face, which suddenly no longer felt familiar. Hearing her talk unashamedly about sex – well, it just wasn't her mother. Mothers weren't supposed to be interested in sex, let alone enjoy it. Listening to the story of this intense, albeit brief affair, Sarah couldn't help feeling a twinge of jealousy. She'd never experienced such profound intimacy with any of her lovers, least of all Alistair. That kind of love was rare; something you only read about in books.

'What happened next? Did you meet Hugo Manning in Bordeaux?'

'As with even the most well-organised of plans, things didn't quite work out as expected. Every now and again, the train came to a standstill. German Stukas appeared out of nowhere, their sirens shrieking, indiscriminately dropping their bombs on innocent people and disappearing as fast as they came. We were like sitting ducks. Two of the carriages were strafed and I heard that several people were killed. It was worse for those on the roads. God knows how many perished. When I eventually arrived in Bordeaux, I was too late. Hugo Manning had left. He did leave a note at the reception desk though, apologising for missing me and telling me that I was to contact the owner of the Brasserie Lion d'Or. I was to peruse the menu and tell him Mr Manning suggested I have whatever the dish of the day was. He also told me he'd paid for my room for a few days. In the meantime, the Germans had taken Paris.

'I was so exhausted and the last thing I wanted was food, but the following day, I did locate the brasserie and the owner showed me to a table. He told me that rabbit in white wine was the dish of the day – the brasserie was famous for it. It was the code phrase he used for those he was trying to help evacuate. He did indeed bring me a dish of rabbit and whispered that I was to be ready to leave in a few days. Someone would let me know the night before.'

'How long did you have to wait?' Sarah asked.

'Thankfully only a couple of days. The Germans were beginning to make headway throughout France and Bordeaux was chaotic. We had to get a move on. I was to wait at the Pont de Pierre on Quai Richelieu where someone would pick me up. I was half an hour early. A man stood nearby, also with a suitcase. Neither of us spoke but it was obvious we were both there for the same reason. Our pick-up was late and I could see the man beginning to panic, lighting one cigarette after another. Then a black Citroën pulled up and a young woman got out of the passenger side and hugged us both as if we were long-lost friends whilst the driver unceremoniously flung the suitcases into the boot of the car.

'An hour later we arrived at a farmhouse on the outskirts of Bordeaux where four other people were also waiting to leave. Someone turned on the radio and we heard the voice of Marshal Pétain. In his thin voice, he feebly announced, "It is with a heavy heart that I tell you today that we must cease hostilities. The fighting must stop." Pétain was now one of Hitler's stooges.

'Shortly after, we left for Biarritz where we split into two groups. The man on the quayside, who I discovered was also from Paris, stayed in our group, along with a German Jewish lady who had fled Nazi Germany in 1935 when her husband was sent to one of the labour camps. For days all she did was cry and warn us of the consequences for Jews in France until in the end someone told her to be quiet or we'd have to leave her behind.

'We crossed the border into the Basque country and parted ways. I made my way to Portugal. There I heard that the government had moved to Vichy and that counter-intelligence services were now deployed against anyone who disagreed with the new regime. A month later I left Lisbon for England.'

It occurred to Sarah that she'd never thought to ask how her mother arrived in England. In hindsight she couldn't understand why. Claire Bradshaw had rarely talked about her past. The only things she ever mentioned were growing up in Paris and then meeting her husband in Normandy. Now it dawned on Sarah that there was a missing piece to this jigsaw puzzle. Seeing her mother was in the mood to talk, she continued with her questions.

'What did you do after that?' she asked.

'When I arrived in London, I was alone and knew no one. I didn't have any relatives – or at least if I did, I didn't know who they were. I just remember it being so cold, so depressing, what with the bombing and all that, and I felt so low. I found a room in a lodging house in Notting Hill run by an elderly widow. It wasn't anything flash but I was running out of money. There were three other boarders, all from Poland. Mrs Wallace was the landlady's name. She took a liking to me, and sensing that I was in desperate need of money, put me in touch with her daughter, Grace, who ran a small, bespoke milliner's – shop just off Bond Street.'

Sarah thought back to her youth. She didn't remember her mother being a hat person.

'Grace was a very creative person and as she had just lost one of her workers, she decided that rather than take on someone else, she would do the work herself. My job was to look after the customers, most of whom came through word of mouth via her contacts in Bond Street. She liked the fact that I was Parisian – apparently I would give her shop a French touch. The pay wasn't much but at least it covered my board and lodgings.'

Claire became despondent. Clearly, thinking about that time brought back memories she had tried hard to forget. She spoke about the relentless bombings, of air-raid sirens and the nights spent in air-raid shelters, never knowing if the house would still be there afterwards.

'Everything smelt of smoke,' she continued. 'I'd almost forgotten the sweet smell of the trees in blossom along the Seine. It all seemed so long ago – another world. In six short weeks, the French Army had been swept aside by the Germans. I grieved for France and wondered if I'd made the right decision to leave, especially after the Royal Navy bombed the French fleet at Mers El Kébir. The Poles were the same. They wanted to go back and fight. Mrs Wallace tried to liven up the evenings with music – Glenn Miller and Vera Lynn were our favourites. And of course, we listened to the radio broadcasts, all of which seemed to bring nothing but bad news. The Germans seemed undefeatable.'

'And did you work at the milliner's until you went back to France after D-Day?' Sarah asked.

Claire lifted her shoulders and let out a long sigh. She asked the waiter for another apple brandy. Sarah understood that she was plucking up the courage to tell her something else.

Claire took a deep breath. 'No.'

'Then you must have found other work?'

When Claire didn't answer, Sarah looked worried. Why had her mother never told her of the job at the milliner's? After all, it wasn't anything to be ashamed of. What else had she done? Why was she suddenly reluctant to talk? She sat back in her chair, took a sip of apple brandy and waited for her answer.

Seeing her daughter's determination to hear the truth, Claire continued. 'One of my jobs at the milliner's was to pick up fabric and accessories from the wholesaler's. I was out one day when I bumped into her.'

'Who?' Sarah asked. 'Bumped into *who*?'

'Violette.'

Sarah's jaw dropped. 'But I thought you met up with her again in Normandy.'

'That's not exactly true,' Claire replied. 'I had to pass Bond Street, and on my way back I saw her step out of a dress shop.'

'Go on,' said Sarah, remembering Violette's conversation in London. She now understood that they had both colluded to hide the fact that they *had* met up before 1944. Why?

'I'd often thought of her but until then I had no idea if she did leave Paris as planned. All I know is my heart lifted when I saw her. We embraced in tears, neither wanting to let go of the other. I learnt that she almost didn't make it. She followed a similar route to me but a border guard became suspicious of their documents and was about to call his superior when the leader of the group pulled out a gun. They tied him up and left him, but not before stripping him naked. Violette laughed when she told me, but I shuddered to think what could have happened to her.

'We arranged to meet the following day at Lyons' Tea House on the Strand. She told me she lived in Pimlico. When I asked her what she'd been doing, at first she was elusive, but when pressed, she eventually told me she worked for de Gaulle's Free French Army – some sort of secretarial work. She pointed to the cross on her lapel. "The Cross of Lorraine," she said, giving it an affectionate pat. "The symbol of Joan of Arc, and now of the Free French."'

Sarah smiled to herself. So Violette's teaching work had been another lie.

'I'd heard about de Gaulle setting up headquarters in London. In fact, I'd even heard some of his broadcasts but I had no idea how established his network really was. All I knew was that at first he had been a lone voice in the wilderness, but at least he offered the only alternative resistance to the Vichy government.

'Violette told me that he hadn't gone down too well in France, but with the situation worsening, she assured me that was changing and he was garnering more supporters. She also told me that Resistance groups were now operating throughout France.

'"The Germans didn't expect Britain to put up a fight. And with the Americans now in the war, it's only a matter of time before the tide turns," she told me.

'We ordered tea and cake – a rather tasteless one due to the rationing – and she asked what I'd been doing. I told her about the hat shop and about life in the Wallace household with the Poles.

'"And does the work in the hat shop pay well?"

'When I told her it barely covered my board and lodgings, she put her cup down and looked at me thoughtfully.

'"Hmmm, I might have something for you," she replied.

'I asked what it was.

'"Put on a pretty dress and join me for cocktails on Saturday afternoon – The London Club." She scribbled down the address.

'When I arrived, the place was packed. Violette – fashionably dressed as always in a simple, midnight-blue silk dress, over which she wore a long string of pearls – came over to greet me, a cocktail glass in each hand. "Here, *chérie*," she said, kissing me on both cheeks and offering me a glass. "There's someone I want you to meet."

'We edged our way through the crowd of people to a corner of the room divided into intimate booths by artistically etched tinted glass. A man got up to welcome us.

'"Well, if it isn't Claire," he said, shaking my hand. "I knew you'd make it, old girl." It was Hugo Manning, and quite frankly, he was last person I expected to see.

'I looked at Violette, who winked and shrugged her shoulders cheekily.

"And now, if you will excuse me, I must mingle. I'm sure you two must have lots to talk about."

'He filled me in on the situation in France, in particular the forced evacuation of the Jews and the camp at Auschwitz, which I'd often talked about with the Poles at the boarding house. I had hoped it was only a rumour but Hugo assured me it wasn't.

'"A lot has happened since you left, Claire. It's not just the Jews. No one is safe."

'"But the government...our own people!" I answered. "Surely they can't stand by and allow that."

'"You mean the puppet government – the collaborators."

'On seeing my empty glass, Hugo called over a waiter, took another cocktail from his tray and placed it in front of me. "Here you are, old girl. You look like you could do with another."

'He lit a cigarette, handed it to me, and then lit one for himself. "Violette told me you were working in a hat shop," he said, blowing the smoke out of the corner of his mouth. "Somehow I don't see you as the needle-and-thread type, and I am prepared to offer you something better."

'My face reddened at his comment, and instinctively, my hand reached up to touch the cream fascinator with a single grouse feather securely tucked into a band of pink ribbon, that Grace Wallace had kindly lent me for the occasion.

'"I told you before I wasn't cut out to be a journalist, if that's what you had in mind?"

'"You were better than you thought," he laughed, "but no, it's something different." He leaned forward and in a soft voice asked, "How would you like to go back to France? I won't beat about the bush, you have something we're looking for and I'd like you to hear me out before you answer."

'It was then that he told me he was working for the Special Operations Branch – a sort of undercover group directly under Churchill's control. Apparently, their mission was to "set Europe ablaze", which at that moment struck me as ironic as I thought it was already ablaze. He said his area of concern was France. He thought me suitable for an operation they had in mind as I was fluent in French and English and more than adequate in German.

'And I can vouch from experience that you are a capable young woman."

'"Thank you, Hugo, you flatter me," I replied sarcastically.

'But he was deadly serious. He wanted to recruit me for something the War Office called F Section. I would need about four to six months' training and then I would be dropped back into France for a mission. At that point he couldn't say for how long, but he assured me that I would be flown out again after the mission was complete. He didn't mince words: no matter how much I trained, I would be putting my life in danger and he would understand if I said no.

'I asked if he had any idea where I would be dropped, thinking that somehow or another I might end up in Paris.

'He stared directly into my eyes, and after a few minutes replied, "Brittany."

'At that point, my head started to swirl. I thought about Marcel. Those last two weeks together flashed before me and I felt a sharp pain in my chest.

'"Well?" he asked. "What's your answer?"

'"When do you want me to begin?" I replied, without even a second thought.

'He leaned back in his seat and smiled. "I knew could rely on you," he said. "You will be perfect. There is one important thing you must do first, though, before we can proceed."

'"And what might that be?"

'"You must meet with a colleague of mine, she'll have a little chat with you first. If all goes well, and I believe it will, you'll be required to sign the Official Secrets Act. You cannot discuss this with anyone, not even Violette. I know she's involved with the Free French but we keep our business separate. Do I make myself clear?"

'And Violette?' Sarah asked. 'Didn't she guess what you were up to? After all, she put you back in touch with him for a reason, didn't she?'

'I told her I'd joined the FANYs and would be either allocated to first aid or drive a truck for the army, but she just laughed and said she knew Hugo was involved in some sort of hush–hush work. "Always was one for keeping things close to his chest, but whatever it is you've got yourself mixed up in, be careful."

'I was put in touch with a woman in Baker Street. She interviewed me twice, just to satisfy herself that I was the right kind of person for their "special mission", as she referred to it. We usually spoke in French, occasionally in German. Apparently she thought that would be an added advantage. I saw Violette several times until I left London for a place in the country where I was to do field training. She never asked anything else and she didn't even know when I left. Even that was a secret. Although I think she guessed as the closer that day came, the more melancholic I became.'

Sarah had been so caught up in her mother's story that she had failed to notice the restaurant had emptied. The owner was sitting by the cash register smoking a cigarette and waiting to close up.

'Come on, Mum. We'd better let this man get some sleep. We can continue the story tomorrow.'

Back at the cottage, Sarah asked if her mother would be all right.

'I'm not an invalid, you know,' Claire replied. 'In fact I feel like a burden has been lifted from my shoulders.' She paused for a moment. 'Not sure how I'll feel tomorrow though.'

Sarah gave her a long hug. 'You'll be just fine.'

Lying in her bed that night, Sarah mulled over her mother's story. She had heard of these brave women who had fought in the Resistance, and she was well aware that many had never returned. For a while their stories had gone unheard. When their exploits became known, they had been called heroines, capable of fighting beside any man. What was it Claire had said they told their friends and relatives they were? FANYs – First Aid Nursing Yeomanry – that was it. But it was something to be proud of, not something to hide. So why had Claire kept it from them all this time? And Violette, why had she gone along with this charade? It was a conspiracy of lies, and Sarah wondered where it would end.

In the next room, Claire Bradshaw also found sleep hard to come by. She wrapped a blanket around her shoulders and sat by the open window, breathing in the heady scents of wisteria and honeysuckle in the still night air. She fixed her gaze on the outhouse. The new moon cast an eerie blue tint over it, throwing long shadows across the courtyard. The door and windows had had a new coat of paint and the creepers had claimed much of the walls but otherwise, it was just as she remembered it from all those years ago. Through her tears, she saw him, his body bent over the typewriter. After a while, he looked up and their eyes locked. Now she could sleep.

It would be another few days before Claire felt able to continue her story. Sarah waited patiently. Patience was something she was learning fast.

Chapter 7

France, Summer 1943

Claire woke up to find herself in bed in a room no bigger than a closet, and she had no idea where she was or how she got there. The smell of a wood-burning fire combined with tobacco smoke coming from the next room drifted through the air. She tried to get up but a searing pain in her right ankle caused her to let out a sharp cry. The door opened and a woman entered carrying a bowl of steaming hot coffee. After three years of ersatz coffee back in London, the taste of real coffee was more than welcome.

'Take it easy,' she said, handing Claire the drink.

'Where am I?' Claire asked.

'Amongst friends. You passed out on the rocks last night and they brought you here. You're safe, that's the main thing.'

Claire suddenly felt anxious. 'My suitcase...'

The woman put her hand up to quiet her. 'It's fine, you were lucky. Another second and the fierce waves would have washed you and your suitcase back out to sea. *Mon Dieu*, it was one of the worst storms in ages. A blessing in disguise though as it kept the Germans away.'

Claire slumped back onto the pillow. 'Where am I?' she asked again.

The woman didn't answer. Instead, she left the room to fetch Claire's clothes. They also smelt of woodsmoke.

'You were drenched to the bone when you arrived and I took the liberty of undressing you before you caught pneumonia. It didn't take long for them to dry out in front of the fire.'

Claire blushed when she realised that underneath the warm duck-feather quilt, she was completely naked.

'My leg,' she said, grimacing with the pain. 'Is it broken?'

'You twisted it badly, that's all. Nothing to worry about, the swelling will go down in a day or two. For the moment, take it easy.'

After she'd gone, Claire was aware of hushed voices – men's voices –

coming from the next room; too low for her to hear what they were saying.

The bed was pushed up against the wall and she pulled herself up to look out of the window. It was still dark outside. The building was enveloped in a thick mist but judging from the ethereal blue light beginning to filter through, it was almost daybreak. As her eyes adjusted to the darkness, she could just make out that she was in a farm dwelling. In the yard, silhouetted against the inky-blue mist, were two cars which she presumed belonged to the men in the next room. She reached for her clothes. They were still nice and warm. She must get up. Swollen ankle or not, time was passing while she lay in bed, and time was something she could not afford.

Three men were sitting around the table when Claire entered the room. Their Sten guns stood propped up against a sideboard next to a stiff yard broom. The younger, good-looking one with dark, tousled hair and piercing black eyes introduced himself as the man who had saved her from drowning. A much older, broad-faced man with a large moustache sat next to the fire poking the embers. Above him, strung across the width of the wide fireplace, was a makeshift clothes line with an assortment of men's clothing left hanging to dry. The one man she had expected to see was not among them.

The younger man stood up and offered her his seat. Gritting her teeth in pain, Claire hobbled towards them. The woman reached for the coffee warming on the grate by the fire, poured her another drink and passed her a chunk of bread, butter and goat's cheese. It seemed ages since she'd eaten and she was famished. Another man placed a glass in front of her and filled it with brandy. To ease the throbbing pain which was now spreading through her leg, she drank it in one gulp. The men smiled.

'That's what we like to see,' one of them said. He attempted to pour her another but Claire pushed his hand away. She needed to keep her wits about her.

The men told her they belonged to the Resistance and she was in the home of Monsieur and Madame Cloutier, about ten kilometres from where she'd landed.

'This coastline is heavily patrolled,' the younger man continued. 'Because of the weather you were delayed but fortunately the storm was so severe, the Germans probably thought no one would risk being out at sea in such weather. Your *agent de liaison* – Henri – was with us when you arrived. The two of you were to have travelled on to Rennes but due to the injury to your ankle, you were in no position to walk and Henri entrusted you to our care until you are able to walk again.'

At the mention of Henri, Claire breathed a sigh of relief. 'I'm sorry, I'll get going as soon as it gets light,' she told them.

Monsieur Cloutier rose from his seat by the fireside and threw her a stern look. 'On that leg you won't get very far. You'll put us all in danger.'

Claire conceded he was right.

'It's already been decided, Mademoiselle Bouchard. You will stay here until you can walk properly. My wife will take care of you. Henri has left instructions for you to continue to Rennes alone.'

A week later, and wearing a heavy old coat over her dark green tweed skirt and cream blouse, Claire covered her hair with a headscarf, donned a pair of *sabots* and said goodbye to Madame Cloutier. She climbed up next to Monsieur Cloutier at the front of a horse-drawn cart laden with hay.

'You'll be quite safe,' he said. 'The Germans are not likely to stop us. They have requisitioned hay from farms around the area. It's to be offloaded in Fougères and sent to Germany. Apparently their animals have more need of it than our own.'

The cart trundled out of the yard towards the road. When they reached the outskirts of Fougères, Monsieur Cloutier brought the cart to a standstill. After checking no one was in sight, he pulled Claire's suitcase out from under the hay and placed it on the road. Handing him back Madame Cloutier's old coat and headscarf, Claire exchanged her *sabots* for a pair of black court shoes, pulled out her matching suit jacket from under the hay, and donned a cream felt fedora edged with a dark green ribbon that matched her suit perfectly. Within minutes, she had transformed herself.

'How do I look?' she asked after dabbing a little powder on her face and applying a touch of deep red lipstick.

'As pretty as a picture,' Monsieur Cloutier replied.

Claire snapped shut her powder compact and put it back in her handbag.

'*Bien*,' she said, pulling on a pair of cream gloves and flicking away any traces of hay.

'Just one more thing,' said Monsieur Cloutier. 'A message came through last night from Henri. Someone will meet you on the train – he is also going to meet Henri.'

Claire shot him a cool glance. 'Why didn't you mention it earlier?'

Monsieur Cloutier shrugged his shoulders. 'It was Henri's idea – he didn't want to worry you.'

'What's his name?'

Again, Monsieur Cloutier shrugged. 'I'm sorry, I don't know.'

'How will I recognise him?'

Monsieur Cloutier detected a hint of nervousness in Claire's demeanour. He pulled out a cigarette packet, took out one for himself and handed her the rest. 'You won't, he will recognise you.'

With that, he snatched up a sprig of apple blossom from amongst the hay and pinned it to her lapel. In the distance, a car could be heard heading towards them.

'Hurry,' Monsieur Cloutier said, as he climbed back onto the cart. 'You have no time to waste. The Caen–Rennes train arrives in just under an hour.'

He flicked the horse's reins and waved her farewell. Tucking her handbag under her arm, she took a deep breath, picked up her suitcase and started walking towards Fougères. For the first time in weeks, she was alone, and though she hated to admit it, she felt a frisson of fear.

A thin crowd was already forming when she arrived at the station. German soldiers patrolled the area, watching over the French gendarmes who checked the travellers' documents nervously.

'Where are you going?' one of them asked.

'Rennes,' she replied confidently. 'I have work there. I'm a school-teacher.'

A German soldier standing nearby glared at her. He came over, snatched the documents from the man's hand and began to inspect them himself.

'You're from Paris,' he remarked. 'What are you doing here?'

Claire was just about to answer when two trucks carrying French prisoners arrived. Another officer called his men over and prisoners carrying suitcases and cloth-wrapped bundles were hurriedly offloaded and led away at gunpoint across the train tracks to a goods train in a siding. The German soldier stormed away, muttering obscenities at passengers as he pushed past them.

The French guard shrugged his shoulders. 'It's not a good day. Saboteurs have blown up part of the tracks. The Caen–Rennes train is delayed. You'd better make yourself comfortable. Goodness knows how long it will take to fix it.' He indicated the prisoners about to board the goods train. 'And with the filthy mood the Bosch are in, I don't like their chances.'

Claire made her way to the large waiting room. It was already full but a woman nudged along the seat to make room for her.

'That's the third lot of deportees in under an hour,' she said. 'They're not wearing the Star of David so no doubt they're going to a transit camp and on to Germany, poor bastards.'

'I heard the line has been blown up.'

'Serves them right,' the woman scoffed.

The atmosphere in the waiting room was stifling and the children began to get restless. Outside a group of soldiers stood about talking animatedly, swearing and looking at people malevolently. It was late in the afternoon when a message came over the loudspeaker that the train was about to arrive. Whilst they jostled on the platform, soldiers and guards alike continued to walk up and down asking to see documents again and using any excuse to rifle through someone's luggage.

Claire found a compartment and placed her suitcase on the overhead luggage rack and sat down to read. Within minutes the compartment was full. The last person to enter was a shabbily-dressed man of thin build with a raincoat slung over his arm. He looked around the compartment, doffed his hat towards Claire and after hoisting up his suitcase on top of hers, squeezed in between two occupants opposite her and began to read his newspaper. She noticed his shoes were muddied, and by the look of his five o'clock shadow, he hadn't shaved in days. Every now and again he looked at her from over the top of his newspaper. Claire thought him highly agitated.

The train began to gather speed. After they had passed the first village, the door to their compartment slid open and the ticket inspector, accompanied by two plain-clothed men, asked to see their papers. Claire offered hers first and gave the men a sweet smile. They did not reciprocate her friendliness. When they came to the man opposite, they looked closely at his papers.

'Would you care to come outside?' one of them said, with a coldness that made Claire's flesh crawl. 'We'd like to ask you a few questions.'

In fear, the other passengers looked away when he stood up. Claire noted the telltale thin trickle of sweat that ran down the side of his forehead. He was clearly scared. He threw her a quick glance as he exited. The door slammed shut and she heard their footsteps moving away down the corridor. A few seconds later they heard a scuffle and a gunshot. Her fellow passengers looked at each other in silence. Claire's hand instinctively reached for the crucifix around her neck. She fingered it nervously, resisting the urge to open the door and look. For a brief moment the rackety sound of the train's wheels appeared louder. Then she heard a door slam.

When the man failed to return, Claire waited for a few minutes and then got up to have a look. A guard spotted her and told her to return to her seat, but she feigned severe stomach cramps and asked where the toilets were located. The man indicated further down the corridor. When she passed him, she noticed bloodstains near the exit door. Clearly they had shot him and thrown him out of the train. Alone in the toilet, she grasped the small sink and splashed water onto her face. This was exactly the sort of danger they had spoken of in her training. No one was immune.

The train arrived in Rennes shortly before curfew. Claire reached for her suitcase and realised the man's suitcase was still on top of it. She waited until all the occupants had left the compartment before pulling it down; she would take it with her. She also noticed his overcoat was still hanging on the hook next to his seat and quickly searched the pockets. Apart from a few francs and a handkerchief, there was nothing to identify him.

Claire couldn't have arrived in Rennes at a worse time. The area in front of the railway station had taken a hit during a bombing raid and was swarming with soldiers. She made her way past the French inspectors and plain-clothed Germans scanning the platform for a sign of something amiss and stood by a kiosk next to a fire-blackened building in the square outside the station as she had been instructed, and waited. Within minutes a man approached her from the shadows of a doorway and introduced himself as Jean-Claude.

'You made it. And Gilbert, did you meet up with him? He was supposed to be with you.'

He looked towards the station expectantly. His words jolted her. The man on the train must have been Gilbert – her contact. She started to describe him and told him what had happened.

The man spat on the ground in disgust. 'Bastards!' he exclaimed. 'He had something of importance for us.'

Claire then understood that the man had recognised her by the apple sprig pinned to her lapel, as Monsieur Cloutier said he would. That was why he kept looking at her, and why he had entrusted the suitcase to her for safekeeping. Jean-Claude told her he had boarded the train when the tracks were sabotaged. He must have realised the Germans were on to him.

'You might find whatever you're looking for in there,' she replied dismally, pointing to the suitcase.

Henri was waiting for her in his tiny flat on the top floor of a half-timbered row of buildings in Rue d'Abbeville in the old area of Rennes. With him was a man wearing thick, dark-rimmed glasses, who he introduced as Didier, the agent in charge of radio operations in the field, and Stefan the forger, who wasted no time in checking Claire's documents to see if they were up to scratch. After peering at them closely under a magnifying glass and running his fingers lightly over the paper for the right texture, he handed them back, commenting that London was to be commended on such an excellent job. He also gave her a new identity card in her real name, which was to be used for anything unrelated to the Resistance.

Henri looked at Jean-Claude as if waiting for an explanation about Gilbert. Jean-Claude shook his head from side to side and momentarily looked at the ground.

'I'm afraid he won't be joining us,' he answered. 'Thankfully, he had the foresight to leave the suitcase with Marie-Elise here.'

They opened Gilbert's suitcase, moved aside a few clothes and pulled out several dark blue velvet bundles and unwrapped them.

'He didn't fail us,' Henri said. They're all here.'

Claire's heart missed a beat when she saw what they were after – crystals for Didier's radio. Didier looked relieved. He made a comment about the operators in Normandy. They had been warned that the Funk-Horchdienst might have intercepted their calls, or worse still, someone might have talked.

'The German interception service is equally as adept as we are,' he told Claire. 'They may have been able to counterfeit our operators. At the moment, London is not telling us a thing.'

The more Didier spoke, the more Claire became aware of his appalling French. She wondered how on earth the Special Operations Executive SOE could have sent him over. She had only been back in the country for just over a week, but already she knew any accent invited curiosity, let alone a bad one.

Henri saw Claire's face pale when she saw the crystals. He poured her a glass of wine and asked if she'd like to freshen up before supper. She nodded a meek yes.

'You can sleep in my bed tonight,' he said, indicating a room off the kitchen. 'I'll sleep on the couch. First thing in the morning I'll take you to Saint-Etienne. The school is already anticipating your arrival. The last teacher was a Jew, as were several of the students. One day they just failed to turn up. That's what happens here now. A knock on the door in the middle of the night and then...*puff* – gone – to who knows where.'

Claire followed him into the room. He picked up a large enamel jug from the washstand and went to fill it with hot water from a pot on the stove.

'Supper will be ready in about ten minutes,' he informed her, and closed the door behind him.

Claire slumped down on the bed and held her head in her hands for a few moments. She couldn't shake the image of Gilbert out of her mind – the way he started to sweat when the men called him outside, the look in his eyes when he walked out of the compartment. Hugo Manning had warned her that this was not a job for the faint-hearted and yet she had still wanted to do it. So far she had survived one of the worst storms at sea in ages and narrowly missed being associated with Gilbert on the train. This was only the beginning and she was well aware that her life of a courier was fraught with danger, a notch above that of a radio operator. There was no turning back.

She took a deep breath and pulled herself together. Like the kitchen, the bedroom was small and cramped but it was spotlessly clean. An empty glass and a bottle of Calvados sat on a wooden tray on the bedside table and in the corner of the room, under the eaves, was a marble-topped washstand on which Henri had placed two clean towels and a fresh bar of soap. She picked it up and smelt it. Lavender! A luxury. Clearly, Henri was a man acquainted with the finer things in life. If the attention to detail he paid to the Resistance matched that of his apartment, then she was in good hands.

She pulled out the small pistol from under her garter and placed it next to the Calvados. Then she took off her blouse and proceeded to remove the heavy bandages wrapped around her body, which concealed a large amount of cash. They were wet with sweat and she was relieved to be rid of them. One by one she laid the wads of notes on the bed and then soaped herself down with the warm water, savouring the luxury of the moment. Such a simple thing, and yet it felt so good. She slipped on a fresh, clean dress, tidied her hair in the mirror and put the slender crucifix back around her neck. It had been a parting gift from Hugo Manning.

'Don't lose it,' he'd said at their last meeting. 'It contains your cyanide pill.'

When she returned to the kitchen, Didier, Stefan and Jean-Claude had gone. The table was set with a clean red-and-white chequered tablecloth on which was placed a plant-pot of white geraniums sitting on a deep-sided saucer, and if it hadn't been for the pistol sitting next to it, it would have looked like any other domestic scene throughout France.

Henri dished out a large helping of mutton stew that had been simmering gently on the stove. Over supper he discussed the situation his group,

Chevalier, was facing. The men in the Resistance, especially those who'd fled into the countryside and joined the Maquis, were desperate for guns and money and not enough was arriving. He had told London of their plight and they'd promised to step up the drops but it took all his skills to placate the men, many of whom were increasingly risking their necks and those of the local villagers by venturing back to their homes to quell their hunger. The Germans had turned up the heat, especially after the successful raid on Saint-Nazaire and the destruction of the Normandy Dock a year earlier, and rationing stretched everyone's endurance. On top of that the Milice, who for the most part were members of the NPB – the Parti National Breton – were always looking for an excuse to rat on their enemies and earn a few more francs and extra food. He also told her that they were having difficulty with some of the groups who took sabotage into their own hands.

'It makes it difficult for them to have faith in us when we can't always give them what they want. The money you brought with you will placate them for a while. Let's hope there's plenty where that came from.'

She asked him about Didier. Why had London sent an agent whose French would put them in danger?

Henri laughed. 'He's an excellent "pianist" – extremely thorough and an expert at camouflage. He's been watching over some of the newer lads. The crystals that Gilbert left with you will be put to good use. Don't worry about him. He was an engineer in the army with a liking for the theatre and amateur dramatics.'

'Well, let's hope he can make use of his thespian skills if he's questioned,' Claire smiled.

Henri also knew Hugo Manning. They had been friends since their days at Oxford. His father was a Frenchman from Brittany who moved to England after he married. He worked for MI6 before the war broke out, and later moved over to the SOE sometime after it was established. His Breton accent and his experience in the field were welcomed by HQ Security & Planning in F Section, and he was considered to be one of their best *agents de liaison*.

'I believe you also knew Hugo before the war,' he said, mopping up his stew with a large piece of bread. 'Are you a journalist as well?'

Claire laughed. 'I can't say that I know him at all really, and I am not a journalist. I had just lost my mother and was wondering what to do with my life when he offered me an assignment during the Phoney War. I went to Northern France to check out the troop movements – which at that time was hardly anything. I was based in Reims, and while I was there I also had a look around the champagne houses. Hugo seemed to think I did a good job but I thought it a useless and extravagant exercise. He probably only offered me the job to please a close girlfriend. It might come as a surprise to you but I really am a teacher.'

'Well, he's found you the perfect foil then. You'll blend in well. But don't think for a minute that Hugo was sending you on a wild goose chase when he sent you to Reims. He may not have used your information for journalistic reasons, but he definitely would have reported on your work back to London.'

Claire had come to that conclusion herself.

Henri stressed that she was to use her real identity in Saint-Etienne. 'The only people who will know you as Marie-Elise will be the headmaster and his wife as they are a part of our network. Other than that, you will only use Marie-Elise when you do work for us. Is that clear?'

'Absolutely,' she answered.

'And Manon, that is only for us – for the SOE.' His face had a no-nonsense look, leaving Claire in no doubt that he was a man not to be crossed. 'Never give that name to anyone else.'

Chapter 8

Claire settled into her teaching job with ease. The school was located in a small village called Saint-Etienne, north-west of Rennes. The undulating patchwork landscape of fields and woods dotted with ruined castles was a welcome relief after the grimness of London. L'école Saint-Etienne had a handful of pupils of varying ages. In Paris, she had taught English and German. In Saint-Etienne she would be only be required to teach French. Before the war, English had been a part of the curriculum, but after the occupation it was cancelled by order of the Vichy officials. It was now a requirement for every school to teach the Breton language, and for that a teacher could supplement her income by another six hundred francs a year. She was also required to teach history, which was subject to scrutiny, and as she and the headmaster were the only teachers, maths and a little natural history and biology had also been added. It was also impressed upon her that all subversive discourse was to be avoided at all costs as children had a habit of repeating things to their parents and not everyone was against the Germans.

The headmaster, Antoine Chauvignon, and his wife, Mireille, lived next to the school on the Rennes road within walking distance of the town and were fervent members of the underground, especially after the sudden departure of the Jewish schoolteacher. They were most welcoming, but Claire had been advised to keep to herself as much as possible. It wasn't simply a case of dropping by whenever she felt like company, as she might have done under normal circumstances.

'You're new to the area,' Henri had warned her. 'You can't seem to be overly chummy – windows have eyes. And the Bretons are a conservative lot, it'll take a while before they adjust to a Parisian in their midst.'

'Brittany is a hotbed of political ferment,' Antoine told her. 'The PNB are in bed with the Germans and Vichy has given in to their demands and lifted bans that were in place before the war. They are a bunch of thugs –

fascists and racists, and their policies are no better than the Nazis'. I am a Breton, but I despise these people. They have turned us against each other. The problem is that that they have very powerful allies in the Germans here, so we have to be on guard.'

He gave her a list of names to watch out for; Miliciens, or ordinary people who were 'undependable', as he called them, due to their stance against the Free French and de Gaulle, whom they considered to be troublemakers. Others were Vichy supporters or belonged to the PNB. Some of them had children at the school.

'Mayor Bourgoin is on our side, however, even though he might be seen entertaining the odd German official in the Hotel de la Poste, as is the priest, Father Gambert. They have been known to turn a blind eye to many an incident that could have seen a number of people taken into custody.'

Claire thanked him for his advice and made a point of memorising the names he had given her. She asked him about the school syllabus and the Breton classes.

'In 1941 the ban on teaching Breton in the schools was lifted. I now take those classes myself. You don't have to concern yourself with that. We are required to do our bit as far as cultural and folkloric events go, but that's hardly a problem. I don't know how long you will be with us, Henri never told us and we don't ask too many questions. All I can say is that we will endeavour to look after you the best we can while you are here. I think you'll fit in very well.'

She was given the apartment once occupied by the Jewish teacher. It belonged to the school and therefore had not been requisitioned by the Germans. Not that there were any Germans in Saint-Etienne, but they did make the occasional appearance and search, though otherwise they kept a close eye on the town through the gendarmerie and their informants, the Milice. The apartment was above a garage owned by Gaspard, a widower, who lived in a one-room apartment at the back of the premises. It could be accessed from a door in the street and up a narrow flight of stairs and it overlooked the tree-lined Place de l'Église, named after the tiny Romanesque church, St. Etienne, from which the town took its name. Directly opposite was a bistro, L'Arlequin, outside of which hung a metal sign in the shape of a harlequin. Apart from the bistro there was a bar, a *tabac*, a barber's and a grocery store whose ancient, dusty shelves appeared to be filled more with old ceramic jars and glass bottles than food.

The apartment was slightly larger than Henri's and had two rooms.

The furniture was mismatched but adequate: an old, faded brown leather couch and a chintz-covered chair, a dining table and a bookcase on which Antoine had thoughtfully placed books about Brittany, including a detailed map which he was sure she would put to good use, a few literary classics, and a Bible. Thankfully, there was also a radio which Antoine had recently acquired with some difficulty because he told the authorities a teacher must be able to listen to programmes in the Breton language. A tiny sink and stove stood in an alcove, which was divided from the toilet and bath by a folding screen naively painted with rococo swirls over which an excessively thick coating of lacquer had been added, causing it to crack and flake away in sections with the dampness from the bath. At the far side of the sitting room was a bedroom just big enough to hold a bed and a nineteenth-century hand-carved wardrobe, which clearly looked out of place.

It was by no means the most luxurious place she'd ever stayed in, but it was clean and it would have to do. After all, she would probably only be there for six months at the most. She was, however, grateful for the narrow French doors that opened onto a ledge of a balcony with a view over the Place de l'Église. It meant she could monitor the comings and goings easily.

Antoine arranged with Gaspard to give Claire a bicycle, which she took to with great enthusiasm, often cycling for miles at a time after school hours, exploring the countryside. Apart from a brief meeting with the mayor, who welcomed her to the town without prying as to why she had chosen to leave Paris to teach in a place like Saint-Etienne, it was exactly as Henri had predicted: everyone was wary of this stranger in their midst, but as the children grew to like her, the parents also began to accept her. After a couple of weeks she was a familiar figure in the neighbourhood, and even one or two people she had been told to avoid tipped their hats to her when she passed.

Every now and again she ate with the Chauvignons or ventured across to Bistro L'Arlequin for something to do, having observed from her apartment that the place was often empty. L'Arlequin was a humble, unsophisticated family-run business owned by Sophie Lemoine and her daughter, Angélique. The interior was old and badly in need of a fresh coat of paint which, given the situation now, was not likely to happen. An assortment of papier mâché and wooden harlequins hung on the walls, interspersed with family photographs of women dressed in the Breton costume. Half-length lace curtains, white tablecloths and an old piano, over which hung the obligatory framed photo of Marshal Pétain, gave it a homely appearance. Due to severe rationing the food at L'Arlequin was basic, often consisting of dried pulses, a soup or a pie of some sort, and usually accompanied by vegetables acquired from the surrounding farms. Madame Lemoine was an excellent cook and always knew how to bring to life the most basic of ingredients.

Angélique was about the same age as Claire, and she took a liking to her. She was an attractive girl with long, dark hair and a fine bone structure, but she appeared to be in poor health. Her warmth and hospitality were a huge welcome for Claire on many a lonely night and after a week or so, Angélique confided to her that she had a boyfriend who lived in another village but often disappeared for days on end, and sometimes weeks at a time. She never knew when he would turn up and worried about him constantly. Claire guessed he'd joined the Maquis, as had many of the young men in the area, fearful that they also would be sent to Germany to aid the war effort.

Apart from this, most evenings were spent alone in the apartment listening to the radio, which Antoine had stressed she must always keep tuned in to a Breton station when not listening to the BBC.

It had been several weeks since she'd heard from Henri and Claire was beginning to wonder what had happened. In England she had been trained as a courier, which meant gathering and dropping off information at designated safe houses – letterboxes. She was also there to gather information about the enemy such as troop movements, all of which was to be passed on to Henri, her *agent de liaison*. She had also trained as a radio operator with her own code, even though that was not her primary role, and in the long, lonely hours she spent alone, she conscientiously practised her Morse code – just in case. Now she was here, a completely new person with a new identity, but so far she had put little of this training to use. She enjoyed her work but the days were beginning to drag and she found herself longing for action.

Several days later Antoine and Mireille asked her over for a meal after school.

'There's a message from Henri,' Antoine said. 'He wants to see you. Go to Rennes tomorrow. He'll be at the apartment. And don't worry about your lessons. I can manage until you get back.'

Claire went to Rennes by bicycle, taking the circuitous route through the winding back roads because it would attract less attention than going by bus and wouldn't take longer than a couple of hours at the most. Besides, the buses were infrequent and often never showed up at all due to fuel shortages. Halfway there, she stopped to rest at the side of the road next to an old stone bridge that crossed over a stream, unwrapped her bread and cheese that Mireille had thoughtfully packed for her and lay back in the grass to savour the beauty of her surroundings. The spring air was still and warm and she was surrounded by the soothing sounds and smells of nature – birds chirping, the humming of bees in the fields bursting with wild flowers – and one could be forgiven for forgetting there was a war on at all.

She thought of Paris and her old life, of Marcel and what would have happened if he hadn't drowned. It didn't seem real, and yet there was not a day that passed that she didn't think about him. Had she accepted the invitation to come to Brittany because of him? She had said yes to Hugo without even thinking. During the lonely evenings of the past few weeks she had even found herself poring over the map of Brittany, tracing the road towards the cottage where she had spent the happiest few days of her life.

A thundering noise approached, and a convoy of motorcycles with sidecars mounted with machine guns and armoured trucks filled with German soldiers passed her, bringing her back to earth with a jolt.

Claire arrived in Rennes in the early afternoon. Cycling through the old town, she marvelled at its charm. It appeared busy after Saint-Etienne. The shops were open but a quick look through the windows told her there was little for sale. Instead it was the cafes and bars that seemed to be doing the most business. Chairs and tables spilled out onto the narrow pavements lined with wooden planters bursting with colourful geraniums.

She checked the time. She wasn't due at Henri's until five o'clock. There was time for a drink. She propped her bicycle against the wall, sat at a table outside a bar and looked at the menu. It had taken her just under two hours to get there and her legs ached. She rubbed her calves vigorously and thought about her meeting with Henri. It dawned on her that she knew so little about these people; perhaps it was better that way. The waiter came over to take her order just as an open-topped chauffeur-driven Mercedes-Benz passed. The street was narrow and she caught a good look at the occupants – a beautiful, elegant, platinum-blonde woman wearing a small hat with a veil and feather, and a small boy about five years of age who caught her eye as they passed. Seeing the small Nazi flag fluttering on the bonnet, the waiter swore under his breath. The car turned the corner and had just disappeared from view when they heard a loud crash followed by screams.

'My God,' Claire said, jumping up from her seat. 'What was that?'

People walking nearby stopped and looked at each other nervously. A few turned and walked in the opposite direction and others disappeared inside the cafes.

Claire started in the direction of the bang, but the waiter pulled her back. 'Leave it,' he whispered. 'Didn't you notice the flag? Better not to get involved.'

Claire remembered the look on the child's face and shook herself free from his grasp. She ran to the corner and saw that the car had mounted the pavement and crashed into a wall. The impact had been so intense that the bonnet was completely buckled, and the hiss of steam combined with a bilious black smoke meant it could catch fire at any moment. The driver lay slumped across the wheel and the woman was still in the back seat, cradling her son and screaming for help.

'*Mein Sohn, mein Sohn. Bitte Hilfen sie.* My son, my son. Please help me.'

Her leg had jammed against the driver's seat on impact. Two men stood nearby, staring.

'Come on,' Claire called out angrily. 'Don't just stand there. Help them out before the thing catches fire.'

Spurred on by Claire's bravery, the men started to drag the chauffeur from the car, which was by now spitting flames from the mangled bonnet.

'Not much we can do for him,' one of them said, checking his pulse. 'Looks like he may have had a heart attack.'

The woman screamed in pain when Claire attempted to move her, and the boy had a bad cut across his brow and the blood was seeping steadily through his blond curls onto his mother's cream silk blouse. He was unconscious and she refused to let go of him.

'*Er ist ein epilectic,*' she cried, tears streaking her perfectly made-up face. '*Er konnte zu stehen.*'

'She's telling us her son's an epileptic,' Claire told the men. 'She's afraid he could die.'

Claire coaxed the struggling woman to let go of her son and they finally managed to get them away from the burning car and into the doorway of a cafe before an explosion occurred, shattering the nearby windows. The boy started to shake violently but Claire's experience as a teacher had equipped her to handle epileptics.

Addressing the woman in German, Claire reassured her all would be well. '*Ich verstehe. Ich spreche Deutsch.* I understand. I speak German. All is well, your son will be fine.'

She took off her cardigan and folded it into a makeshift pillow to cushion the boy's head. Then she turned him on his side and held him gently until the convulsions subsided.

'The authorities have been notified,' a woman from the cafe opposite called out. 'An ambulance is on the way.'

After a while the boy regained consciousness. Claire stroked his cheeks, assuring him he would be fine. Minutes later gendarmes and German armoured cars pulled up and began to close off the area.

Claire grabbed her cardigan to leave before everyone was detained and questioned. 'You'll be fine,' she told the woman.

'A thousand thanks, Fräulein. I don't know how to thank you. Where do you live?'

'I don't live in Rennes,' Claire replied. I'm just visiting a friend.'

With that she hurried back to the cafe, which was now empty, picked up her bicycle and pedalled away.

'You shouldn't have interfered,' Henri said sternly. 'The Germans will think it was some sort of attack and start questioning everybody.'

The rest of the men in the room looked at each other in despair. No one uttered a word but it was clear from the look on their faces that they agreed with Henri.

'It's not possible,' Claire replied whilst washing the blood from her cardigan. 'There was no ambush, no random attack – the woman will testify to that. It seems that the chauffeur may have suffered a heart attack.'

'All the same…'

'I'm sorry, Henri. I couldn't stand back knowing there was an innocent woman and child who could have died.'

'A *German* woman and child,' one of the men said disdainfully.

Claire was becoming frustrated. 'And if they *had* died, all hell would have broken loose. Is that what you would have preferred?'

Henri threw his hands in the air, palms upturned in a gesture of reconciliation. 'All right, let's forget it. We've more important matters to attend to.' He looked at the clock on the sideboard. 'Yves is late. We'll have to start without him.'

The group of men seated themselves around the table as Henri laid the map out and told them that there was to be a drop in three days' time.

'It's to be here, not far from the Sourisseau farm, north-west of Montauban. It's a wooded area but part of the land is flat and has been cleared for grazing. The Sourisseaus are willing to stick their necks out and allow us to use it. Their son left a while back to avoid being sent to Germany. He is with the Maquis and their two daughters belong to the Resistance.'

Claire looked closely. She had driven by the spot on her excursions and had once stopped to look at the ruins of a twelfth-century abbey in the vicinity.

Henri lit a cigarette and sat back in his chair. 'I know it's not our usual area but we can't take any chances – the Germans got wind of the last drop in Normandy. London thinks there's a mole and has advised changes. Gilbert probably could have told us more but it's too late for that now.

'When we get the all-clear, we meet up here.' He tapped his finger on an area of the map and went on to describe the exact place. 'From here it's about fifteen minutes to the drop zone. Make sure your men are ready.'

He turned to Claire. 'Wait for the BBC broadcast for confirmation and then leave. It shouldn't take you long to get there. It's a full moon and the weather is expected to be fine.'

There was a knock on the door.

'It's Yves,' a low voice called out.

Henri unlocked the door. Claire recognised him straight away. It was the man who had been at the Cloutier farm: the same one who had caught her when she slipped on the rocks.

'What happened?' Henri asked, mildly annoyed. 'It's not like you to be late.'

'Parts of the old area are blocked off. There was an accident and the Germans are snooping around, calling on witnesses and checking the area as usual.'

'Yes, I know,' Henri said, glancing towards Claire. 'Someone important, by the sounds of it.'

'You could say that.' Yves smiled. 'Apparently it was the wife and son of SS Sturmbannführer Hoffmann.'

The men looked at each other in silence.

'*Merde!*' Didier said, reaching into his tobacco pouch to refill his pipe. 'Shit!'

Yves scanned their faces. 'Why should that be of concern to us?'

One of the men looked towards Claire. Her cheeks were flushed.

'Because Marie-Elise—'

'Enough,' Henri blurted out angrily. 'Let's not go down that track again. No point crying over spilt milk. Let's get back to business.'

The meeting lasted for another half an hour and everyone except Yves and Claire dispersed.

'You will make it home before it gets dark if you leave now,' Henri said to Claire. 'Otherwise you can stay here again. It's up to you.'

'Thank you, I'll take you up on your offer. I'm too tired to cycle all the way back, and anyway, I'm hungry.'

'So am I,' Yves added. 'Let's go and get something to eat.'

They walked a short distance to a bistro in one of the back streets. The place was full but the owner recognised Henri and Yves and seats were hurriedly found for them in the yard at the back where a lively trio was playing music to a small but appreciative group of customers. They sat down at a makeshift table under a canopy of wisteria from which hung colourful paper lanterns, and ordered a bottle of wine. The evening was pleasantly warm and the convivial atmosphere meant everyone could forget their worries for a few hours. An accordionist was sitting in a corner playing melancholic music for a group of men flirting with two women. The waiter brought over their wine and a plate with a single blood sausage and a few slices of bread.

Yves poured them all a glass and proposed a toast. '*Vive le France,*' he said with a broad smile.

'*Vive la France,*' Henri and Claire repeated.

One of the men flirting with the two women overheard. He picked up his glass and raised it towards them, stood up and turned to the crowd. '*Vive la France*, comrades.'

One by one, everyone stood and raised their glasses. The owner tactfully closed the door.

'And now some dance music,' the man said. 'Something lively.'

The violinist quickly put his violin on his shoulder and started to play. He was joined by the banjo player and lastly the accordionist, who stepped out onto the floor and began to sing. The man who had stood up and proposed a toast pulled one of the girls onto the floor and started to dance, a sensual mix of waltz and tango. Others joined.

'I love bal musette,' Claire said. It reminded her of happier times in Paris with Violette.

'Want to dance?' Yves asked, pulling her up before she could answer.

He grasped her around the waist with one arm, and with the other, held her hand tightly, manoeuvring her into the centre of the floor. Every available space was filled with couples dancing cheek to cheek.

'How's that ankle of yours?' he asked. 'No lasting injury, I see.'

He pulled her closer until she rested her cheek on his. The music, the atmosphere, the cheap wine, his body pressing against her breasts suddenly made her tremble with pleasure. It was ages since she had felt the closeness of a man. Yves was rugged and he was unsophisticated, but in one move he had made her feel alive again. The music stopped and the accordionist walked around the tables with a bag. Coins were given, along with words of appreciation. Henri threw in a handful of francs while Yves went to pay the bill.

'You have an admirer.' He smiled. 'Be careful.'

Claire left Rennes early the next day. Out of curiosity, she cycled by the area where the accident had taken place. The wreckage had been cleaned up and the barriers removed. She stopped to have a look at the damage caused to the wall. Workmen were repairing it. A trail of dried blood led to the place where she'd carried the boy. They were lucky, she thought to herself. It could have been worse.

She noticed the woman from the cafe opposite peering through the window at her. Seconds later, she was in the doorway, heading towards her and calling.

'Hey you, Mademoiselle! People have been asking questions. You didn't report...'

Claire jumped back on her bicycle and pedalled away quickly. Before she turned out of the street, she turned and looked back. The woman's shouts were beginning to attract attention.

Chapter 9

In the still of the evening, Claire paced the floor anxiously awaiting the BBC's nightly roll call of coded messages. Finally, she heard it. The drop was on. The following evening she checked her pistol one more time, grabbed her jacket and crept down the stairs to the shed at the back of the garage where she kept her bicycle. Thin strips of light through the shutters told her that Gaspard was still up. Thankfully he was quite deaf, a godsend when she wanted to listen to the radio.

Quietly unlocking the door, she stood cautiously in the doorway and surveyed the square. There was not a soul to be seen. A full moon, the colour of mercury, shone brightly in the sky, casting a ghostly glow over the roof of the Romanesque church and illuminating the paper-thin wings of lime-green elm blossom. Across the square L'Arlequin had long closed its doors and was now in darkness. She wheeled her bicycle out of the square and then set off at a fast pace to the rendezvous point. At a certain point in the road, a light from the hedgerow signalled to her.

'Over here,' a voice called out.

A man appeared out of the darkness and told her to leave the bicycle behind the bushes, where he quickly threw a mound of branches over it until all that she could see was a section of the handlebar poking out.

'Follow that path.'

Claire did as she was told and a few hundred yards further on, she arrived at a woodsman's cottage. A group of young men stood outside, smoking and chatting. Some of them looked to be no more than sixteen – far too young to be putting their lives in danger.

She counted at least a dozen men and two women crammed into the small room. Henri was sitting next to Didier, who was listening to his radio. With them was Yves, who pulled up a chair for her.

'Any news?' Claire asked.

Henri shook his head. The atmosphere was tense. Occasionally someone spoke in a hushed voice. Everyone looked at Didier expectantly. Suddenly he cautioned everyone to be quiet. With one hand firmly on his earphones he scribbled something on a pad and handed it to Henri.

'A signal for you, sir.'

At 23.33 hours exactly, the drop was confirmed.

'Fine,' Henri announced. 'It's on. What's more, there will be two drops tonight.'

The men looked at each other and then everyone started to talk at once.

'Isn't that pushing our luck?' someone asked.

'It is,' Henri replied, picking up his torch and Bren gun and heading to the door. 'But we're all seasoned here. Things are hotting up.'

The men and the two young women slung their guns over their backs and followed him out of the house into the woods. Didier acknowledged the drop, quickly packed up his equipment and departed in the opposite direction towards the farm.

Claire and Yves were the last to leave. 'Come on. Time to get your feet wet,' Yves laughed.

They followed the rest of the group along the narrow footpath, which soon disappeared into the dense woods, thick with brambles and ferns. Claire had not expected the path to be so difficult. Navigating her way through the protruding tangle of mossy tree roots, she stumbled and caught her jacket sleeve on a thorny bough. The more she tried to disengage herself, the more it stuck. When Yves realised she was caught, he grabbed her arm and pulled it with such force it ripped the sleeve, leaving shreds of the fabric on the bough.

'Can't be helped,' he said. 'Now get a move on. We've only got fifteen minutes.'

The landing place secured, the men spread out and waited. Claire crouched in the trees next to Hugo and Yves. In the night sky, clouds started to gather, drifting across the moon in a filmy haze. There would be a spring shower and they all prayed it would not break until after the drop.

All of a sudden the drone of a multi-engined aircraft disturbed the silence, becoming louder by the second. To Claire it seemed as if the whole countryside would hear it. Henri moved forward and flashed a signal. In unison, the torchbearers lit up the makeshift runway signalling the drop zone. The dark shape of the aircraft lumbered overhead, leaving in its wake a series of dark canisters parachuting down to earth. Only one chute failed to open and the canister smashed into a tree, breaking off a huge branch in the process, which thankfully cushioned the impact. The men swooped from their hiding places to secure the canisters, swiftly dragging them away into the woods to hide the evidence. Claire counted the canisters – fifteen in all – and helped them round up the parachutes. With a shortage of fabric, it was vital it didn't fall into the wrong hands. Ten minutes later, the operation was repeated. This time there were eighteen canisters, which were dragged to various hiding places throughout the area.

Henri asked Claire to stay the night at the Sourisseau farm where they would be congratulating themselves on the drop, but she refused, saying it was safer to get back to Saint-Etienne as soon as possible, but she assured him she would return the next day. She collected her bicycle and headed back home just as the sky clouded over. A few droplets of rain splashed on her face. Minutes later a summer shower broke. She arrived back in Saint-Etienne in the early hours of the morning, drenched to the bone. Shedding her wet jacket, she hung it on the back of the door. The tear in the sleeve looked bad; she would mend it later when it was dry. For the moment, she was simply too tired to think of anything except sleep.

The following day Claire cycled pass the drop zone on her way to the farm. From the road there was no sign of what had taken place the previous night. When she reached the farm, Madame Sourisseau bustled around the kitchen making lunch for the men. Everyone else was scattered around the farm, hastily hiding the evidence of the drops. Sheep pens, pigsties, milking quarters and haylofts had all been utilised to hide the contents.

The two women she had seen at the cottage were the first to arrive back. They introduced themselves as Madame Sourisseau's daughters, Dominique and Catherine. Claire learnt they had joined the Resistance when their elder brother joined the Maquis; in fact the whole family now belonged to it.

Shortly after, the rest of the men arrived including Claude Sourisseau himself, a small, thickset man built like an ox, Henri, Didier and Yves. The smells of manure and hay overpowered the kitchen. Catherine and her mother carried towels and several buckets of hot water outside into the yard for the men to wash themselves. Claire caught a glimpse of them through the window, stripped naked, soaping themselves down and laughing with each other as if they hadn't care in the world. Madame Sourisseau caught her blushing and laughed.

'When there's a war on,' she said, 'what harm will a few naked men cause? At least they are alive.'

But it wasn't just the sight of just any naked man that bothered her; it was one in particular – Yves. The thought of him pressing his lean, muscular body against hers when they danced had aroused a dormant sexual desire in her.

The two drops had secured the Resistance an invaluable cache of arms: rifles, Bren guns, handheld anti-tank guns, carbines and small firearms, grenades, ammunition and plastic explosives. Along with these were six million francs and enough cigarettes, tobacco, chocolate and cans of food to lift the men's spirits for quite a while. There were also half a dozen bottles of whisky to share between the men.

'And this is for you,' Henri said to Claire, handing her a small package with the letter M discreetly handwritten on it.

The men looked on as she opened it. Inside was a French lipstick in a deep shade of coral pink.

'Very glamorous.' Yves smiled.

Later in the afternoon, Claire returned to Saint-Etienne. One of the men had a van and was heading that way, as were Didier and Yves, who were staying with the Chauvignons for the weekend before heading back home. They offered to give her a ride part of the way there. Claire gladly accepted. They had only gone about ten kilometres when they encountered a roadblock with several armoured patrol cars. The Germans asked to see their papers and searched the van. Luckily, their documents were all in order and they were waved on. All the same, it was a worrying situation as it wasn't too far away from the drop zone. At an intersection a few kilometres from Saint-Etienne, the van pulled up and Yves opened the back and took Claire's bicycle out along with a few sausages, a large mound of butter and half a dozen eggs that Madame Sourisseau had given her.

'This is where we part company,' he said.

She thanked them for the lift and put her foot on the pedal in readiness to cycle away. Yves stopped her.

'What are you doing tonight? If you're free, maybe we could meet? Have a meal perhaps?'

Claire's face flushed. What's more, the brush with the Germans meant they should be extra cautious. 'I'm not sure that's wise...'

'Nonsense, you've been here over a month now. You can't stay a hermit forever, you know. That is, unless you have something better to do?'

He took his hand off the handlebar and she started to pedal away. Then she stopped and turned back. 'Antoine and Mireille have my number,' she called out. 'Give me a call.'

With that, she rode away, her heart lighter than it had been in a long time.

'I'll pick you up at seven sharp,' Yves shouted after her.

It was a Saturday night and L'Arlequin was packed with customers. Without the weekend takings the place would have closed its doors long ago. With no sign of another spring shower Angélique placed a few tables and chairs outside where the customers could enjoy a pleasant evening soaking up the beauty of the elm trees under the lamplight. Claire had already given her notice that a friend would be joining her. Angélique was intrigued. Claire had few friends outside the school and none of them were men.

'We'll sit outside tonight, thank you, Angélique. It's such a lovely evening.'

Angélique lit a candle, placed it on the table and stood ready to take their order, and at the same time took a good look at Claire's friend. Claire suggested the gigot of lamb with white beans and Yves ordered a bottle of red wine.

'You look lovely,' he remarked, when they were alone. 'And your new lipstick, I like it – it complements your hair.'

Claire felt a little self-conscious. She had taken great care to look her best tonight, and had chosen the navy dress with its orange and pink flowers because it matched the colour of her new lipstick. She studied him carefully. His dark, tousled hair was still a little on the unkempt side – a little bohemian, she thought, like the students she recalled in the cafes on the Left Bank. He wore a freshly pressed, white cotton shirt, rolled up at the elbows; casual, but she could see that he had made an effort for her. When he smiled, his dark eyes flashed mischievously. It had been three years since she'd felt such an attraction to someone, and she felt more than a little self-conscious.

'When will you return to Rennes?' she asked.

'It depends on how long it takes to finish my work. There are a few people in the Maquis I need to meet up with.'

At the mention of the Maquis, Claire's eyes darted around the tables. Fortunately the rest of the customers were too engrossed in their own conversations to pay any attention to them.

'How are you settling in?' he asked. 'From what the Chauvignons tell me, you have adapted well. All the same, you must be lonely.'

'I just want to get this work over and done with and then...' She stopped herself from saying she would head back to Paris. 'And then return to England.'

'I know so little about you except that you are French.' He paused for a moment. 'It's okay, I don't expect you to tell me everything, it's just that why would you want to go back to England when there's too much to do here? Don't you want to see this thing through until every last German has left this country?'

'Of course, but I have my orders. One day I will return for good.'

She wanted to know about him.

'I'm an artist,' he told her, 'mostly portraits. I studied in Lyons. My family are from there. When the Germans arrived and Laval became Prime Minister, I voiced my opinion – a little too loudly, it seems. I was warned on several occasions that I was being watched. Then they started to harass my family so I decided it was better to leave for their sakes. As it is, I now know they have still suffered. After the *Service du Travail Obligatoire* was announced in February, I was informed that my brothers were told to report to the officials one day and then sent to Germany to work as labourers – like thousands of others.

'When the Vichy government took over some of the French thought it better to volunteer, thinking they would get a better deal under the new regime. But since hearing about the appalling conditions in German labour camps the volunteers soon dried up. The Nazi war machine has a voracious appetite. They even offered to release one prisoner of war for every three Frenchmen who volunteered. I have no idea where my brothers went, or even if they are still alive. My father died when I was a child and regrettably I have not been in contact with my mother since I left. It's better that way.'

Claire was curious to know why Yves himself had not been called up. He told her that he had obtained a medical certificate saying he'd contracted TB in his teens.

'The Germans have a fear of contagious illnesses,' he laughed. 'They don't bother me now.'

He picked up his glass and wished her all the best. 'In the end we will win. That's what makes it all worthwhile.'

The Place de l'Église was busier than usual and the inhabitants were taking advantage of the warm weather to take a stroll or sit on the benches under the elms, which continued to shed their leaves like confetti at a wedding, creating pools of pale leaves on the ground and nearby benches. When Angélique came to clear away their plates, Yves commented favourably on the meal.

Angélique informed them that apple *clafoutis* was the dessert of the evening, and that as Claire was a regular customer it would be on the house. While they waited, Yves unfolded a white paper serviette, took a pencil out of his pocket and started to sketch her portrait.

She studied the drawing closely. 'You're quite good.'

'One day soon, I hope you will sit for me and I can paint you properly – in oils.'

'I'd like that, very much.'

He folded it up and put it in his pocket. 'To remind me of a pleasant evening. By the way, there's something I want to tell you. You remember the woman and child that you helped the other day in Rennes – the German woman and her son?'

Claire saw that his demeanour had changed. The charming smile of the past hour had disappeared and in its place was the same serious look she'd seen that day in the kitchen at the Cloutier farm.

'You mean the woman who apparently is married to someone important? Of course I remember. What did you say his name was?'

'SS Sturmbannführer Hoffmann. Jürgen Hoffmann to be exact – Commandant of Rennes. He takes his orders from Himmler himself but is known to be a Francophile. He is also a great supporter of the PNB. Well, it seems that people have been asking about you in the area where the accident took place.'

'Look, Yves, I just tried to help, that's all. I did what any normal person would have done in the circumstances. I saved their lives and now I'm being hounded for it.'

'Apparently you spoke to the woman in German. Is that true?'

'When I heard her calling out in German, I presumed she either didn't speak French, or if she did, the trauma had caused her to revert to her own language.'

'It's just that you are not known in the area and people are wary of outsiders, especially ones who speak German. Apparently the chauffeur did suffer a heart attack. Even so, accidents like this make the authorities nervous – the first thing that enters their head is sabotage and they have to be seen to be doing something. It will all blow over. All the same, the next time you come to Rennes, avoid that area.'

Angélique came outside with their desserts. She was just about to place the dishes on the table when a car pulled up. A young man got out of the passenger side and the driver drove away. Angélique's face paled and

111

she almost dropped the dishes when she saw him. He looked towards her as he swiftly entered the restaurant, throwing a glance at Yves as he did so. Claire noticed that the two seemed to know each other. Angélique mumbled an apology and quickly followed the man inside and ushered him into the back kitchen.

'It's Sebastian – Sebastian Levade,' Yves said to Claire. He's one of us.'

She quickly put two and two together. Sebastian Levade was Angélique's boyfriend, and she clearly wasn't prepared for him to turn up when he did.

'Something's wrong, isn't it?' Claire said.

Through the window, they saw Angélique heading back towards them. She picked up the uneaten dessert dishes and in doing so, bent over and whispered something to Yves. With eyes like those of a frightened rabbit, she looked across at Claire and went back inside with the dishes. Yves quickly got up, picked up Claire's shawl and placed it over her shoulders.

'Come on, we have to leave. Sebastian thinks there's going to be a raid. They'll be here any minute. Do you mind if I spend the night in your apartment? It's too risky for me to leave right now. Of course, if you think it too improper...'

'No, no,' she blurted out, 'not at all.'

He put his arm around her and they quickened their step across the square to her apartment.

Claire fumbled in her bag for the key and unlocked the door while Yves pulled his bicycle inside and propped it in an alcove cluttered with second-hand tyres and tin drums. Claire took off her shoes and the pair quietly climbed the stairs. They had just entered the apartment when they heard the sound of armoured trucks and motorcycles rumbling into the square from the surrounding streets. In a matter of minutes, the Place de l'Église was swarming with German soldiers, gendarmes and *milice*. Over the loudspeakers people were told there was going to be a house-to-house search and everyone was to come outside. Yves stole a quick look outside the window. Spotlights illuminated the buildings and the remaining customers in L'Arlequin were being ushered into the square.

'Quickly, undress and get into bed,' Yves said, tearing off his clothes.

'What?! Are you mad?'

'Do as I say.'

Within less than a minute the two were naked and lying in bed. There was a loud banging on the door below and shouts of 'Open up.'

'All right, all right, I'm coming. No need to break the door down,' Gaspard shouted out.

Loud voices could be heard in the hallway below. 'Outside! Quickly.'

Claire and Yves could hear the sounds of heavy boots in Gaspard's garage and apartment.

'Who else lives here?' a voice bellowed.

'A young lady,' Gaspard called out. 'The teacher, Mademoiselle Bouchard. She lives in the apartment upstairs but she's usually asleep at this hour.' He let out a sharp cry as one of the soldiers hit him and bundled him into the street.

In the semi-darkness, Yves clasped his arms around Claire in a tight embrace. Seconds later her bedroom swung open and several Germans stood pointing their guns at them.

At the sight of the young couple naked in bed, the soldiers momentarily stopped to gauge the situation.

Yves let go of Claire and sat up whilst Claire looked on timidly over the covers. A Gestapo officer pushed his way into the room.

'Didn't you hear the orders? Everyone outside.'

'I'm sorry, sir. This is all rather embarrassing.'

The officer cast an eye around the poky room. His eyes fell on the floor strewn with clothes. 'Your papers,' he said quietly and indifferently. 'Get them.'

Yves pulled the covers away, grabbed his trousers and pulled them on, deftly kicking his pistol under the bed as he did so. Claire, still blushing and with her hair tousled in such a way as if they had genuinely been caught in the act of lovemaking, reached over to the bedside table and fumbled to get them out. In doing so her hand touched her own pistol, and like Yves, she pushed it towards the back of the drawer and prayed they wouldn't search it.

The officer snatched their papers and looked at them carefully before handing them back.

'Search the place,' he said to the others, 'thoroughly.'

The soldiers went back into the apartment. Claire heard cupboards and drawers being opened and things being thrown onto the floor. At one point someone mentioned the radio. Claire told them she had papers to own one; they were in the drawer next to the bookcase. The officer went to check. Someone switched the radio on, and French music blared out loudly. She heaved a sigh of relief that she'd remembered to change the station back to the Breton one after last night's BBC broadcast.

The officer returned to the bedroom, stepped over their clothes, opened the *armoire de marriage* and had a quick look inside. After a few minutes, the other men came back and reported that all was in order. The officer picked up Claire's silk knickers between his thumb and forefinger and dangled them in the air as if mocking her. The men tried hard to suppress a snigger in front of their superior. Then he threw them onto the bed and turned to leave.

In doing so, he noticed her coat hanging on the back of the door. She had left it there to dry out after the downpour on the way back from the drop. He touched it and saw that it was still damp. At that point he noticed the large tear in the sleeve. Claire's heart pounded in her chest. She had meant to repair it. The officer looked back and studied her face for a moment. He was about to say something, but then changed his mind.

The men went back downstairs where a commotion was taking place in the hallway. Gaspard was brought back inside and questioned. Yves quickly threw Claire her dressing gown, which lay draped over the end of the bed, and hurried to the door. It was still open. He could not see what was happening below but he could tell what was taking place. Claire wrapped her robe tightly around herself and came and stood next to him. She shuddered when she heard the beatings Gaspard was being subjected to.

'Where did you get all this?' asked the officer who five minutes before had stood at the end of her bed.

Gaspard was in a difficult situation. They had found containers of gasoline and diesel oil and asked to see documentation detailing where they were purchased, but as he had bought them on the black market there was nothing to show. They hit him with their rifles when he refused to give the name of his supplier, but he was not a strong man and the beatings were severe. The men dragged him outside and ordered him into a truck filled with other bewildered men and women who were also protesting their innocence.

Five minutes later the trucks left, leaving behind a few French gendarmes who ordered the stunned inhabitants of Saint-Etienne to go home. Shortly after, the surrounding buildings lay in darkness and a stunned silence fell over the now empty Place de l'Église. Yves and Claire returned to the apartment. She picked up the clutter from the floor and attempted to put it back in its rightful place whilst Yves settled down in a corner near the balcony and watched the square from behind the blackout curtain. With nothing to do, the gendarmes left behind congregated on a bench near the church, talking amongst themselves and smoking cigarettes.

Yves sat deep in thought. 'I keep asking myself how Sebastian knew there would be a raid. The incident with Gaspard seemed to be unconnected, as if they were looking for anything or anyone to bring in. I'm sure most of the others who were hauled off were innocent too.'

'I can't stop thinking about poor Gaspard,' Claire lamented. 'I thought he ran his business by the book.'

Yves burst out laughing. 'Dear Claire, you are naive. No one does anything by the book these days.'

She threw him an indignant look.

'Goodness knows what will happen if he refuses to say where the gasoline came from. He could be imprisoned and the garage closed down – or even worse, they will make an example of him.'

Claire shuddered at the thought of what might happen. She pulled her dressing gown tightly around her. With nothing on underneath it, she realised she was shivering with fright.

'After all this I could do with a nightcap,' Yves said. 'Got anything strong?'

Claire shook her head. 'Only ersatz coffee or black tea.'

He pulled her towards him. 'I can think of something better,' he whispered in a firm voice. 'Much better.'

He lifted her chin and kissed her. His kisses intensified as he slid his lips across her cheek towards her neck. Claire had no intention of pulling away. Her desire for him was as obvious as his was for her. An hour ago she had lain naked in bed with him and yet fear had erased any desire. Now things were different. They were alone and had all the time in the world. Now she could let go. His lips rested on her earlobe, sensuously nibbling it until after a few seconds he bit her playfully. Claire felt a shiver run down her spine and let out a soft cry. His touch was playfully erotic.

He undid her belt and pulled open her dressing gown, and with the eagerness of an artist's eye, stood back to admire her firm breasts and the contours of her body. The small silver crucifix glistened against her cleavage. His dark eyes smiled in approval. She reached for his trousers and undid the belt. Her sighs excited him more. She felt his hand slide over her breasts and around her waist, pulling her tightly against him. His body was athletic and strong, and with his dark, tousled hair glistening in evening light he reminded her of the classical statues she'd once admired in the Louvre – a magnificent Greek god, made of flesh and bone instead of marble, except that they had smooth bodies whereas Yves' chest was covered in dark hair; soft and inviting. He had a distinct smell; a sweet-sour smell born of the earth – rugged and primitive, but his lovemaking was warm and tender.

She trusted herself with him and let go completely. Lost in the memories of Marcel, she allowed the pent-up desires of the past few years to explode in a way that made her feel like a woman again. They made love several times that night and each time, Marcel's face faded a little.

In the morning he brought her a cup of ersatz coffee and a slice of bread slathered with Madame Sourisseau's creamy white butter.

'Good morning,' he said, waking her up with a kiss. 'Did you sleep well?'

She snuggled against his chest as he tore away a piece of bread and popped it into her mouth.

'Mmm, I haven't slept like that in a long time.' The faint light of dawn was steadily creeping through the shutters. 'What time is it?' she asked.

'Almost time for the curfew to end.'

The doorbell rang. Claire looked at Yves anxiously.

'Stay out of sight while I see who it is.' She slid the bolt back on the door and opened it a few inches. 'Angélique!'

'Can I come in? I have to talk to you. I heard they took Gaspard away.'

Claire quickly ushered her up the stairs to the apartment and locked the door behind them.

'Where's Sebastian?' she asked.

'That's why I'm here. He asked me to find Yves and get a message out.' Angélique looked around the sitting room. 'Is he here?'

There was an awkward silence.

'Claire, your secret is safe with me, you know that.'

At that moment, Yves stepped out from behind the folding screen, still buttoning up his shirt. Angélique ran to him and grabbed his arm. She was almost in tears until Yves urged her to stay calm.

'What is it you want to tell us?'

'Sebastian said that at about seven in the evening, he and his friend stopped to have a drink at a bar in a village just off the Montauban-Rennes road. They overheard a conversation between some of the locals, who said that they had it on good authority that the Germans had got wind of a drop in the area and were conducting searches. They left as soon as they could without attracting attention and soon came across

116

a roadblock. Cars and trucks were detained and searched. People were being herded into a field and questioned. Word passed down the line that they were looking for weapons. Everyone was questioned and all cars were being searched.'

Recalling their own encounter with the patrols, Claire threw Yves an anxious glance. His face showed no emotion as Angélique continued her story.

'A commotion started in the field and the Germans standing near the vehicles went over to see what was going on. When several shots rang out, Sebastian realised they had to get away as soon as possible. They jumped back in the car and turned back. He wanted to warn everyone.'

Angélique fiddled with her cardigan nervously. 'Apart from a few hamlets, Saint-Etienne just happens to be the nearest village to where this happened. It was inevitable they would search here. Sebastian wanted me to tell you this because he says you'll know what to do.'

Yves sat down and lit a cigarette. '*Merde!* Why did they run? That would only have attracted their attention.' He closed his eyes for a moment, deep in thought. 'We have to think clearly. First thing is to get a message to Henri. Is there a telephone box in the village?'

'There's one outside the Hotel de la Poste. I could phone him myself,' Claire replied.

'There's no time to waste. I'll make a call, everyone knows me here. You would only draw attention to yourself. Go back to the Chauvignons', see if they can't do something for poor Gaspard. And you go home and tell Sebastian it's all in hand,' she added, turning to Angélique. 'And don't worry.'

He waited until she had gone, pulled his bicycle out of the alcove and wheeled it towards the door.

'You will get Antoine to do something for Gaspard, won't you?' Claire said.

He gave her his assurance. She slipped the latch back off the door for him, half expecting that he would say something about last night. But if she had expected another tender moment, a quick kiss with his goodbye, then she was wrong. He left without a word and she stood in the half-open doorway and watched him cycle away.

As soon as he left, Claire made her way to the telephone box outside the Hotel de la Poste. A few people were already queuing up to use it. She tried to look calm while she waited but inside she was a bag of nerves. Plastered on the nearby walls were several notices stating that any acts of sabotage would be dealt with swiftly and without mercy. Someone tapped her on the shoulder and she jumped in fright.

'Sorry, Mademoiselle Bouchard, I didn't mean to frighten you.' It was the father of one of her pupils, and a man thought to be an informer. 'I know I'm next in line but you can go before me if you like.'

Claire thanked him and stepped inside the box. The man stood outside watching her as she placed the coins in the slot. She smiled at him and turned away to speak.

Henri answered the phone. 'Hello!'

'*C'est* Manon. There's been a change of plan. Notify our friends. The woods are out of bounds. We must find somewhere else to have our picnic.'

The phone went dead. Claire put the receiver back and saw that the man was still watching her. She opened the door to let him pass.

'Wrong number, I'm afraid,' she said, smiling sweetly.

Sometime in the afternoon Claire heard a car pull up outside the apartment. Gaspard had arrived back, accompanied by a couple of men in trench coats and slouch hats. He could barely walk, and so the men stood either side of him and dragged him to the door. Gaspard fumbled to unlock the door but his hands shook, and one of the men snatched the key and opened it himself. At that moment the telephone rang. It was Antoine. He wanted to know if Gaspard had returned.

'He arrived a few minutes ago. He's downstairs and there are officials with him. Gestapo, I think. By the look of him, I think he's had a rough time.'

'They want to see documentation regarding where and whom he got the gasoline from,' Antoine told her. 'I want you to go to the mayor's office straight away. He's prepared letters of authorisation and should have dropped them over earlier. Something must have held him up so I want you to get them yourself. Hurry!'

Claire wasted no time. She picked up her bag and rushed down the stairs. Gaspard was in the garage rifling through a mound of papers on a workbench that doubled as his desk, whilst the men sat opposite him looking through greasy auto magazines. He gave her a downcast look as she hurried by the door into the street.

It took her less than three minutes to reach the mayor's office. Several cars stood outside, all bearing the Reich flag. Inside his office, Mayor

Bourgoin was entertaining a high-ranking German official and his officers. His secretary was about to carry in a bottle of fine cognac and a platter of canapés, but stopped outside the door when she saw Claire. The smell of cigars wafted through the reception area and laughter could be heard inside the office. For a brief moment Claire wondered if she had done the right thing by coming.

'He can't see you now. Can't you see he has important visitors?' the secretary snapped.

'It's a matter of urgency,' Claire replied, gathering her breath after her brisk walk. 'I believe he has something for me.'

The secretary, a buxom, middle-aged woman with dyed blonde hair pulled back into a severe bun, looked her up and down. 'Wait here,' she snapped again.

Claire watched through the partially open door as the secretary put the tray on the mayor's desk and then whispered something to him. He looked past the men and saw Claire standing near the doorway.

'Excuse me, gentlemen,' he said. 'I'll be with you in a moment.'

Mayor Bourgoin left the room, leaving his secretary to pour the men a drink. He closed the door to make sure they were not overheard and pulled an envelope out of his jacket pocket.

'As you see, I have been detained, but these are the papers I believe you're waiting for. They're all in order so there should be no problems.'

With that, he turned around and went back to entertain the Germans.

On the way back, Claire took a quick look in the envelope. They were papers of authorisation requiring Gaspard to keep twelve containers of gasoline aside as an emergency precaution to be used for the sole purpose of supplying gasoline to the mayor and officials of Saint-Etienne should something unforeseen occur. The signatures were official, including one from the Commissioner of the Reich in Nantes.

Claire returned to the garage and overheard the men berating Gaspard for wasting their precious time.

'You have another ten minutes,' one of them said. 'If you haven't found them by then, you will return with us and it's most unlikely you will set foot in here again.'

Instead of going into the garage, Claire went straight to Gaspard's flat, took the documents out of the envelope and placed them in an old folder between a few bills and correspondence. Taking a deep breath, she returned to the garage.

'Good morning, gentlemen,' she said, throwing them all one of her sweetest smiles. 'You've been here a while now and no one has offered you anything to eat or drink.'

Her sudden appearance took the men by surprise. They looked at her harshly without saying a word.

'Gaspard,' she continued with false bravado, and at the same time trying hard to ignore his swollen face, which had started to blossom into black bruises, 'you left some of your paperwork with me to file away. I completely forgot about it until now.'

She placed the folder in front of the bewildered Gaspard and asked the men if she could prepare them any breakfast. 'We don't have much, but there are eggs and I could make you an omelette.'

The younger of the two looked pleased with her suggestion and was about to agree, until the older one demanded to know who she was.

'I'm the teacher at l'école Saint-Etienne,' she replied. 'I occasionally help Gaspard with his paperwork when he's busy – and last week was a busy week.'

The older man made a note of her name in his notebook. While she chatted idly to divert their attention, Gaspard opened the folder and saw the documents from the mayor.

'Ah, gentlemen,' he said, finding a renewed confidence. 'They were here all along. How silly of me to forget where I put them. Thank you, Claire, I don't know what I'd do without you.'

He handed them to the older man, who looked through them and then showed them to his colleague.

Claire and Gaspard exchanged looks and waited.

The man threw them down on the desk. 'You've had a lucky escape, my friend,' he snarled.

After they'd gone, Gaspard collapsed into the chair, a trembling mess.

An emergency meeting was called in Rennes for the following weekend. In the meantime, Claire continued her teaching as normal and in the evenings, scoured the map looking for new drop sites. Hamlets and villages between Saint-Etienne and the Sourisseau farm continued to be searched, although the search stopped short of the farm. As nothing was discovered the authorities turned their attention to an area south of Saint-Etienne.

Sebastian left Saint-Etienne sometime after Gaspard arrived back. He had had quite a scare, and much to Angélique's delight, resolved to stay out of sight for a while until things blew over. The authorities might not have found anything but they were stepping up their search for men to conscript for the *Service du Travail Obligatoire*.

Throughout all this, Claire hoped she might hear from Yves; a short phone call – anything to say that he had enjoyed her company. But nothing came, and if the truth were known, she didn't expect it to. The occasional romance was something to be grabbed whenever possible in a war. All the same, she was disappointed.

Chapter 10

Leaving Gaspard to recover from his wounds in the care of Angélique and her mother, Claire cycled into Rennes. Having been warned about going through the same area as the accident, she approached Henri's apartment from the south, which added another fifteen minutes to her trip. When she knocked on the door there was no answer. She was on time, so where was everyone? An elderly woman opened her door slightly and peered through the crack at her.

'If you're after the Monsieur, he's gone out, about half an hour ago.'

'You wouldn't happen to know where I can find him, would you?' Claire asked.

The woman said she had no idea and closed the door, leaving Claire to ponder her next move in the silent, darkened hallway. She took a piece of paper out of her bag, scribbled the letter M on it and pushed it under the door. There was little else she could do but find a cafe and idle the time away for an hour or so until Henri returned.

She headed towards the cathedral, bought a copy of *L'Heure Brettone* and found a cafe opposite the Hotel du Ville in the Place de la Marie. Most of the buildings here were draped with the swastika – a far cry from Saint-Etienne where she had only ever seen two flags; one draped from the balcony over the entrance to the office where she had met Mayor Bourgoin a week ago, and the other at the Hotel de la Poste where he entertained any German and Vichy visitors.

She didn't fail to notice the number of Germans in the square, or that every other car flew the swastika. In Rennes it was hard to escape the fact that France was an occupied country; in Saint-Etienne the only things that offered a constant visual reminder of this were the photographs of Marshal Pétain prominently displayed in bars and shops, and plastered on walls and tree trunks in the Place de l'Église, notices denouncing acts of sabotage or the traitor de Gaulle.

On such a beautiful afternoon, the cafes were packed. Fashionably dressed French women laughed and chatted with German soldiers as if they didn't have a care in the world. It was a surreal picture and she was thankful she didn't have to face that sort of thing in Saint-Etienne. When the couple at a nearby table flirted openly over a bottle of champagne, murmuring expressions of love for all to see, Claire buried her head in her magazine, trying to hide her disgust.

A group of officers sat at the next table, and with her excellent knowledge of German she listened to their conversations. One of them had just returned from Berlin and laughed when he told the others that the Jews had finally got what was coming to them.

It was at that moment that Claire looked up and saw a woman pass by with her son – the same two she had saved in the accident. She quickly looked down at her magazine, flicking the pages nervously. Several of the men recognised the woman and stood up as a mark of respect, including the officers whose conversation she had been listening to. The woman stopped and started to chat with one of them. Claire prayed she would not look in her direction, but it was too late.

The boy saw her and tugged at his mother's hand. 'Mama, look who it is: the kind lady who saved us,' he said in German.

All eyes turned to Claire. The woman came towards her. There was no escaping this time. They had spotted her and there was nothing she could do about it.

'My dear Fräulein,' the woman said, offering Claire her hand. 'I have looked everywhere for you. I want to thank you for what you did. My son and I are indebted to you. If it hadn't have been for you, we would have perished.'

Claire felt her cheeks redden. 'I did what I could and I'm glad you are fine. How's the cut on your son's head?'

The young boy took off his cap and lowered his head so that Claire could see his scar.

'My, my, it's healed well,' she said with a smile. 'In another few weeks you won't see a thing.'

'Do you mind if I join you?' the woman asked.

With such an important guest in his cafe, the waiter hovered around, ready to take her order. The men who had stood up to greet her now sat back down again and the one who had been talking about the Jews looked embarrassed when he realised Claire may have understood their conversation.

'A glass of champagne, please,' the woman said to the waiter in German, 'and a glass of orange juice for my son. 'You are my guest, Fräulein. What will you have?'

'I'm fine, thank you. I still have my tea.'

The waiter returned and also brought a large helping of ice cream for the boy, courtesy of the establishment. Neither he nor his mother bothered to thank him for his generosity. Clearly they were used to being spoilt.

The boy took one of his toys out of his pocket to show Claire; a Prussian soldier made of metal. She admired it, telling him that he was a lucky boy to have such a toy.

'I have a whole army at home,' he told her. 'You must come and see them.' He turned to his mother as if to get her approval. She leaned over and planted a kiss on the top of his head. The ice cream melted in the heat. Claire winced at the sheer waste, especially when ice cream was a luxury and unavailable in most places.

'Allow me to introduce myself,' the woman said, offering her hand. 'My name is Eva Hoffmann and this is *kleiner* Oskar.'

'Claire,' she replied. 'Claire Bouchard.'

The boy also shook Claire's hand. He couldn't have been much older than four or five and yet he had a confidence beyond his years. She thought of the children at l'école Saint-Etienne. Even at such a tender age, they had the timidness of a defeated population; such a contrast with Oskar, a child brought up to believe the world lay at his feet.

Claire was in a dilemma. Clearly Eva Hoffmann was going to converse in German. She thought about Yves chastising her for speaking German and was now forced to admit to herself that she had made a grave mistake. Eva started to ask questions.

'I am afraid my French is very bad,' she laughed. 'I am having French lessons, as is Oskar, but I'm not very good.'

She asked Oskar to say a few sentences in French, which he did proudly. Claire congratulated him.

'Where did you learn such excellent German?' Eva asked.

'I studied languages at university.'

'And are you from the area? I recall that you told me you were visiting friends here.'

Claire was thinking on her feet. Even after the shock of an accident, Eva had a good memory. She couldn't afford to put a foot wrong.

I'm originally from Paris but I came here to take up a teaching post – a small school in the country.'

At the mention of Paris, Eva's eyes lit up. 'I adore Paris,' she replied, 'such a beautiful city.'

'Do you know it well?' Claire asked.

Eva was only too delighted to talk about Paris. 'I lived there for a short while. My husband was working in Paris before the war. I left Austria to be with him. My family is from Vienna. Do you know it?'

'I'm afraid not. I've never been to Austria – or Germany for that matter.'

'What a pity. It's such a beautiful city. In many way it's like Paris, so much to offer – music, the theatre… How I miss it.' She looked wistful at the thought of her home. 'I am thinking of taking a trip back but this war, you know, it's so very inconvenient.'

Claire thought how much more inconvenient it was for millions of other unfortunate souls.

'My husband has given me his word that we will go together the next time he visits Berlin, so at least I have that to look forward to,' Eva continued.

She wanted to chat about French fashion and reeled off the names of top couturiers with ease, commenting on their various styles and which women in the Reich wore their clothes. One look at Eva told Claire she was a woman of discerning taste. With her platinum-blonde hair styled into a pale silk snood, she was the epitome of elegance. Tall and slim with a healthy complexion, she reminded Claire of the archetypal Aryan woman so admired by the Nazis – blonde, strong and fertile. After a while, Claire felt less intimidated by her and decided to ask about her husband.

'Do you live near here?' she asked casually.

Eva looked at her in surprise. 'Yes, in the Villa Rosières on the outskirts of town. Surely you know of it?'

'I'm sorry, Frau Hoffmann, but as I told you, I am not from here.'

Eva burst into a giggle. 'Please forgive me, Claire – you don't mind me calling you that, do you? Fräulein Bouchard is…well, so formal, and I don't feel at all formal in your company. Besides, I would like you to call me Eva.' She moved a little closer. 'I presumed you might have known who I was because of my husband.'

Claire feigned complete surprise.

'My husband is Jürgen Hoffmann, Sturmbannführer Jürgen Hoffmann,' Eva continued, conveniently leaving out the 'SS'. 'Everyone in Rennes knows him.'

Claire didn't answer. The loud peals from the cathedral bells told her it was four o'clock. She must return to the apartment.

'I enjoyed your company this afternoon, Claire. I have no friends to speak of here. They are all friends of my husband and sometimes I get quite lonely.' Eva stood up and looked towards the chauffeur, who had been waiting nearby – another chauffeur and a brand spanking new Mercedes. Frau Hoffmann might be lonely, but as far as material things went, she wanted for little. 'Can I offer you a lift to wherever it is you're going?'

Claire politely refused. The last thing she wanted to do was to attract attention to 27 Rue d'Abbeville.

'I would love it if we could meet up again – perhaps we might have afternoon tea together,' Eva said. 'The next time you're in Rennes.' She turned to Oskar. 'And my son would like that also, wouldn't you, darling?'

Oskar agreed. 'Do come and see us, Fräulein Bouchard.'

'I would like that, Oskar, but I'm afraid it's rather difficult as I don't come here often, and with a shortage of teachers, my work takes up all my time.'

Eva looked disappointed. 'I understand. Anyway, you know where we are now and the offer still stands.'

They shook hands and walked to the waiting car. The men sitting at the nearby tables jumped to attention as Eva left. Aware that these same men were also watching her, Claire walked away in the opposite direction with a confident air that belied the dull, sickening feeling in the pit of her stomach.

Henri was alone when Claire arrived back at his apartment. He apologised for not being there when she called earlier and said that at the last minute the meeting had been changed to another place and as she had already left Saint-Etienne there was no way of letting her know. He was normally a calm, composed person and she was perturbed to find him unusually anxious; chain-smoking and with a half-empty bottle of Calvados that was rapidly emptying.

'Sorry to hear about old Gaspard,' he said. 'It appears that another garage owner – someone from the next village – thought he'd make trouble when the raids were on. By all accounts he isn't as competent as Gaspard and was losing customers to him. A few of our men wanted to rough him up a bit when they found out, but fortunately, we stopped them. It would only attract attention. He'll get what's coming to him in due course.'

He went quiet again. Claire offered to make him something to eat, which he gladly accepted. His cupboards were almost empty but she found a few eggs and made them into an omelette with a scattering of dried herbs. The bread was stale and in better times would have been thrown away, but instead she fried it in a little oil with garlic, onion and a tomato. The pleasant aroma wafted through the cramped kitchen and made him smile.

'It's a long time since a woman cooked food for me,' he said, when she placed the food before him.

'The Sourisseau women cooked for you at the farm. Surely you haven't forgotten?'

'I mean like this – alone. It's good to have a woman's touch, you know. I miss that in a job like this.'

His face looked less anxious after he'd finished eating, and he wanted to know where she went when she found no one at the apartment. It crossed her mind to say nothing about the afternoon with Eva, but Henri was an astute man and it wasn't wise to deceive him.

'Well, where did you go? You didn't get yourself in trouble again, did you?' he asked with a smile.

She cleared the dishes and then turned to face him, wiping her hands on the tea towel apprehensively.

'I bought a magazine and went to the Place de la Marie for a drink, and by chance I saw the same woman that I rescued from the accident.'

He raised his eyebrows. 'And?'

'And unfortunately she also saw me and asked if she could buy me a drink – a small thank you for saving her life. She was with her son, Oskar.'

Henri laughed loudly. 'My dear Marie-Elise, what are we going to do with you?'

Claire sat back down, relieved that he'd taken it so well. 'She introduced herself as Eva. She wanted to chat about Paris.'

'You told her you were from Paris?!'

'I had to. I also gave her my real name, so don't worry. She said she lived there for a while. She wanted to talk about fashion – nothing deep. I also told her I taught at a school, but not here in Rennes. She asked – it couldn't be avoided, and I thought it better not to lie.'

'What else did she talk about? Did she mention her husband?'

'Yes, but only at the last moment, just before she left. She seemed surprised when I appeared not to know who he was, especially after she told me where she lived.'

'Villa Rosières,' Henri replied, matter-of-factly.

'Yes, that's right. She wanted me to call on her the next time I visit

Rennes. To enjoy afternoon tea together, that's all. She gave me the impression of being very lonely.'

Henri studied her. 'Very chummy, but I think we'd better keep this to ourselves – might be wise not to let the others know. It would only cause unnecessary worry and we've got enough on our plate as it is.'

'Tell me what happened this afternoon?' Claire asked, changing the subject. 'Why was the meeting called, and why the sudden change of place?'

'As far as the meeting goes, I decided it would be better not to attract too much attention here. You see how the neighbour was. She knew I'd gone out. Buildings have eyes. The thing is, Marie-Elise, something is wrong. Someone has infiltrated various circuits and no one is above suspicion. First Gilbert – and we still don't know what happened to the others who landed with him – and then there's this latest raid. I have a sneaking feeling that the raid in Saint-Etienne and the nearby area was not related to any real information, otherwise why would they have stopped before the Sourisseau farm?

'Nevertheless, the Gestapo are closing in on several circuits. At the moment Chevalier remains alive, but for how long? Several agents have already been reported missing, but as yet none are from Chevalier. All the same, we can't become complacent. It's also common knowledge that there's something wrong with the Dutch traffic and this has made London extremely nervous about France. Some of the fists are not up to scratch.'

Claire recalled her weeks studying radio transmissions before she left England – Morse code, passwords and security checks, etc. – and she was well aware that every transmitter was recognised by his own special 'fist' – that particular touch on the keyboard which they equated to the individual touch of a piano player.

What Henri said next shocked her.

'There's something else. I'm returning to England in three days' time. London has something of importance they want to discuss with me. A plane will pick me up from where the last drop was.'

Claire was lost for words.

'I can't wait any longer,' Henri said. 'The moon is already on the wane, but I expect to be back soon so don't worry. In the meantime I'm putting you in charge.'

'Me?' she blurted out.

'Yes, you, Manon! Baker Street has great faith in you – especially Hugo. You will work with Didier. He's a good man and you can trust him.

I've arranged a meeting for tomorrow so the two of you can talk. And there's always Jean-Claude if you need more help.'

'This is all rather sudden,' Claire replied.

'It's the way we have to operate.'

'And what about the others, do they know?'

'Only Jean-Claude and Didier. A few others will be told tomorrow. You will take over communicating with all these groups.'

'Can I ask why Yves isn't aware of this? I thought you two were close?'

Henri lit another cigarette. 'Marie-Elise,' he said, looking directly into her eyes, 'don't let a little fling cloud your judgement.'

Claire's face reddened. 'What do you mean by that?'

Henri took another sip of Calvados. 'I don't care who you sleep with, my dear. That's your business. You're an attractive woman. All I ask is that you be discreet or you'll put us all at risk.'

When Claire awoke the next day, she heard voices in the kitchen. Didier had arrived. She looked at herself in the mirror and noticed the dark shadows under her eyes. Henri's words had given her a hard jolt and she had hardly slept a wink all night thinking about the situation. Clearly this was not going to be a smooth ride, and she prayed she could live up to the task required of her.

'Morning, Marie-Elise,' said Didier, lighting his pipe. 'Seems like we'll be working together for a while.'

They spent the morning making notes: every safe house, letterbox and contact in the network was discussed, and a list of all the supplies and the locations where they had been hidden was drawn up. Finally they went over Henri's departure plans. They would meet in the same place as the last landing, only this time the group would consist of a trusted few – Claire, Didier, Jean-Claude and four of his men.

'No one from the farm?' Claire asked.

'No. The plane will land and I will leave – that's it. It's not a drop. We only need torchbearers for the runway. I informed Claude Sourisseau – just in case he thinks there are trespassers on his land. The less that know the better.'

Around midday, Henri suggested they make their way to a restaurant in a village where a table had been booked for a few of the men. He wanted Claire to meet with a few men whose networks covered areas further afield: Nantes, Angers and Le Mans. They travelled by car and the route took them past a villa set in acres of parkland surrounded by stone walls and two high rows of barbed wire. When they passed the heavily guarded main gates, Claire caught a glimpse of the stately residence beyond. Its Breton slated roof with a central turret, white facade, and the formal steps leading up to the entrance gave it a quiet, restrained elegance.

'Villa Rosières,' said Henri, his eyes still on the road ahead, 'the home of Sturmbannführer Hoffmann and his family.'

They drove to Redon, a beautiful town forty kilometres south of Rennes. The restaurant was located in an old building situated on the Quai Saint-Jacques. It was owned by a member of the Resistance and used as a safe house for pilots whose planes had been shot down. The uneven design of the architecture was a foil for hidden closets in the walls, one of which hid a set of steps that led to a cellar directly under the quayside and which opened out onto the River Vilaine. A cache of arms from earlier drops had been stored there. Directly above the cellar, several outdoor tables straddled the cobblestoned pavement overlooking the river, one of which had been reserved for them.

The owner greeted them, and as if on cue, several men came out of the building and joined them. With them was another *agent de liaison* – a British agent known by his nom de guerre of Michel. A heated discussion quickly ensued as a second *agent de liasion*, known as Pascal, had sent a message to say that he had been delayed due to German road checks. Henri's face bloomed red with anger when he heard this. He had been adamant that both of them should attend the meeting, and it took him a while to calm down. In the meantime, the owner of the restaurant pointed out to Claire that he got a kick out of serving his German customers sitting on top of an arms dump. She could not help thinking that should anyone have lit one of the explosives, they all would have been blown to smithereens.

The conversation touched on those who had gone missing, the names of collaborators and the usual topic – when they would be getting more money. Food obtained via the black market took all their money and many had resorted to stealing livestock and raiding henhouses. Henri promised to do what he could. In the meantime any grievances were to be directed to Claire as she was now in charge. The men looked her up and down, and if there were any adverse thoughts, no one showed it. They were a model of French civility.

By the end of the week, Henri wired to say he'd arrived back in England. In the meantime Claire returned to her job at the school, occasionally dining alone at L'Arlequin. As promised, Didier kept in touch with her but she never asked about Yves, and Didier never mentioned anyone unless there was a message that needed passing on. As for Angélique, ever since the raid there was a silent understanding between them, but now more than ever, Claire suspected she knew she had come to Saint-Etienne for other reasons besides teaching.

Chapter 11

Over the next few days, Claire made various drop-offs at letterboxes and at the same time scoured the area for a new drop zone. It worried her that the Sourisseau farm had been close to the last German searches in the area but good drop zones were hard to find. The problem lay in the fact that any drop nearer the coast would mean the planes would encounter a barrage of anti-aircraft guns along the whole of the heavily fortified coastline.

On several occasions she returned to Rennes. Henri had made his apartment available for her. Didier also made use of it even though he lived not far away. During one of her visits Claire met the neighbour again in the lobby. The woman was pleasant but did comment on how quiet it had been lately.

'I haven't seen much of the Monsieur,' she said. 'I do hope he's all right.'

Claire took a dislike to her. Just how much was she monitoring the comings and goings at 27 Rue d'Abbeville? When she met up with Didier she voiced her anxiety but he told her not to worry, and that Henri said the woman was like that with everyone.

'Have you seen Yves lately?' she asked Didier casually one day.

'I saw him a few weeks ago. Just before Henri left for England. We called by for a drink.'

'Did he tell him I was looking after things until he returned?'

'He did. Why do you ask?'

'No particular reason. It's just that he was with us a few times and then after the raid, I never saw him again. I thought he was one of the trusted members of the group, along with yourself and Jean-Claude, that's all.'

Didier was surprised by her remark. 'As far as I know, he still is. Henri often met up with him, usually at his home or at the bistro where I believe you all went one evening. He doesn't come here unless he's asked.'

'He lives near here then?' Claire asked, looking out of the window into the street below.

'About ten minutes away on foot.'

Claire turned. 'Good. How about we pay him a call before dinner?'

Didier didn't reply.

'I would like to keep in touch with most of the men, just in case they need anything. You never know.'

Claire could see that Didier couldn't really see the point as they all knew how to contact each other, but he didn't argue. He grabbed his jacket from the back of the chair and opened the door. 'After you, Mademoiselle,' he said with a smile.

Yves lived in a less-than-salubrious part of Rennes, in an area known for its bars, nightclubs and brothels. Thankfully, at that time of the day, it appeared less seedy. His apartment was an attic in a dilapidated building occupied by artisans – cobblers and ironmongers. The outside door was already open and they entered into a long, dark passageway and headed up a narrow staircase to the third floor. The place smelt of decay – dampness, tobacco and urine. How could an attractive man like Yves live in a place like this, she asked herself? As if reading her mind, Didier said he paid no rent as he had some sort of agreement with the landlord to do odd jobs around the place – plumbing repairs and the odd painting.

When they reached the top floor, they heard a gramophone playing bal musette. Claire's heart pounded in her chest as they knocked on the door. It swung open and Yves stood in the doorway. He wore no shirt and his body glistened with sweat underneath the braces that held up his trousers. As usual, his curly hair was unkempt and he looked as if he had not shaved for several days.

'Marie-Elise! What a lovely surprise.' If he was shocked to see her, he certainly didn't show it. 'Come in, come in,' he said, standing aside to let them pass.

Didier was right about the apartment being an attic, yet despite the off-putting building, inside it was the epitome of bohemian charm. Old carpets, almost threadbare with use, lay scattered around the highly polished, dark wooden floor, adding a certain warmth to the place. A row of small windows opened out onto the rooftop and the street below, allowing the afternoon sunshine to fill the place with light. Next to one of the windows stood an easel and table covered with paint tubes and brushes, although she wasn't able to see what he'd been painting.

'I'm afraid you've caught me in the middle of painting,' he said, throwing on a shirt and turning away whilst he tucked it into his trousers. 'Now, what can I get you both to drink? What about a whisky?'

Claire heard a soft shuffling noise behind a screen near his bed. A few minutes later, a young woman stepped out, straightening her skirt and buttoning up her blouse that exposed her ample breasts. She slipped on her shoes, tidied her tousled mane of fiery red hair and acknowledged them with a polite nod. She picked up her bag from the coffee table next to Claire and walked to the door, leaving a lingering smell of perfume in her wake.

Yves gave her a peck on the cheek. 'We'll continue another time,' he told her.

Claire's face reddened with embarrassment. 'I'm sorry if we interrupted you,' she said, a little too frostily for her own liking.

'Nothing that can't wait,' Yves replied. 'You caught me in the middle of a painting session, that's all. Now, what has brought you here?'

'I wanted your thoughts on where you think the next drop zone should be. You know that area well.'

Didier shifted uncomfortably in his chair.

Yves pondered the question whilst stroking his short, dark stubble of a beard. His eyes flashed, his smile faded and his face became serious – that same look she remembered him giving her the day after the raid.

'What's wrong with the last place?' he asked.

'I just wanted to hear your thoughts,' she replied. 'Did you hear anything afterwards as to why the search stopped just before the farm?

'If I had, don't you think I would have told Henri?' he said sharply.

Claire held his gaze, hardly believing that this was the same sweet and tender man she had made love to over a week ago. He was like a chameleon; so changeable.

'How's everything in Saint-Etienne?' he asked, switching the charm back on. 'I heard Gaspard was accused of wrongdoing by another garage owner working for the Milice.'

He wanted to know how long she was staying in Rennes, and suggested they all go out for a meal later.

'There's bal musette at the bistro again. I know how you like it.'

Didier thought it a good idea; it might lower the tension between them, but Claire refused, saying she had things to do.

She got up to leave. 'Can I see what you're painting?' she asked.

Yves indicated for her to take a look. 'It's not finished yet,' he said, following her.

The painting was a nude – the voluptuous red-haired woman. She lay on his bed in a provocative pose, legs slightly apart. It was highly erotic and there was little left to the imagination. Claire could see that the paint was still wet. She also noticed the sketch he'd made of her pinned to the easel. Was this what he had in mind when he said he wanted to paint her?

'Satisfied?' he whispered in her ear.

Their eyes met briefly. How silly she had been to make love to someone she knew nothing about.

In the early hours of the morning, Claire was asleep in Henri's apartment when she was woken by the sound of someone unlocking the door. She jumped out of bed and grabbed her pistol just as a voice called out softly.

'It's me, Didier.'

Claire heaved a sigh of relief. 'You gave me a fright. What is it?'

'I've got bad news. There's been another raid. Jean-Claude and one of our agents – Michel – have been rounded up in a raid and are at the Gestapo headquarters. It happened just before curfew.'

'How did you find out?'

'Jean-Claude's wife called to tell me. They were just leaving a bar when it was surrounded. She's hysterical. What are we going to do?'

'Does anyone have any idea why there was a raid? Did they know Michel and Jean-Claude were there?'

'I don't know. We'll know more in the morning. The point is, what are we going to do about it? If they talk we're all done for.'

'Go back home, Didier,' Claire said calmly. 'There's nothing to be done now. In the meanwhile I'll think of something.'

After he left, Claire sat in the darkness, mulling over their options. In the end, everything led back to the same one thought. It was a gamble, and she was fully aware of the danger she was facing.

The next morning, Didier returned with information that some of the prisoners had been released. Six others – including Jean-Claude and Michel – were being interrogated and it was likely they could be shot or at the very least sent away. Claire asked him about the other four.

'Communists – and you know how much the Nazis hate them.'

Claire told him she had a plan but she didn't want to tell him anything else. Didier was alarmed. He pointed out that Henri wouldn't like it if she acted alone. They were all responsible for each other.

'You have to trust me,' was all Claire would say.

After lunch, she dressed herself up as best she could in the few clothes she had brought with her and made her way to a hotel near the Place de la

Marie where she booked and paid for a room in the name of Mademoiselle Bouchard. She asked the doorman to get her a taxi.

'And where would Mademoiselle like to go to?' he asked.

'Villa Rosières,' Claire replied with an air of confidence.

The doorman shot her a quick look. Clearly he was also familiar with the villa.

It took less than ten minutes to get there. Claire checked her hair and make-up in her compact mirror and then approached the imposing, ornate wrought-iron gate.

'I'm here to see Frau Hoffmann,' she said in German.

Two Alsatian dogs snarled at her until the guard quietened them. 'Are you expected?' he asked.

'No, but if you would tell her the schoolteacher has called to see her, she will know who I am.'

The guard walked over to a nearby hut and after some minutes came back with another guard, who wanted to see her papers. Seeing that they were in order, the man returned to the hut and made a telephone call to the house. Minutes later, the electronic gates opened and she was allowed through. The guard indicated for her to head to the house; Frau Hoffmann would be expecting her. All the while the dogs strained on their leashes.

Surrounded by a variety of conifers and deciduous trees, Villa Rosières was a charming house with an elegant facade that looked out onto manicured lawns interspersed with decorative marble and stone planters spilling with colourful flowers. Henri had told her it had been requisitioned from an aristocratic family who had left for America when the war started. As she neared the house Oskar appeared from the main entrance accompanied by a middle-aged, conservatively dressed woman with a stiffly coiffed hairdo. He waved happily when he saw Claire and ran to greet her.

'You came to see us after all, Fräulein,' he said, his face beaming with happiness.

'Mummy will be so happy to see you.'

He took her hand and led her into the house. The woman standing by the door, hands clasped formally in front of her, introduced herself as Oskar's nanny, Frau Heller. She bowed slightly as they passed. A maid led them through the house and onto a large veranda where Eva sat at a white wicker table, reading a magazine. When she saw Claire, she stood up and greeted her warmly.

'*Fräulein Bouchard, Was fur eine wunderbar uberrascung,*' she said, with a smile. 'What a wonderful surprise. And you couldn't have arrived at

136

a better time. You can help me choose a dress.' She indicated the pile of fashion magazines scattered on the table, and a sketch pad. 'But first, do join me in afternoon tea. You must be quite thirsty.'

Oskar reminded Claire that she had said she would look at his toy soldiers. Eva patted his head affectionately, telling him not to bother their guest. In an effort to please, Claire said she would be only too delighted to see them before she left.

Giselle, Eva's personal maid, brought out a tea trolley laden with cakes, including a small Sachertorte, which Eva proudly proclaimed was from Vienna. The maid sliced them both a small piece of the rich, dark cake and placed them on delicate porcelain plates along with a scoop of fresh cream and then left the room. Eva reached for the silver coffee pot and poured them both a cup of real coffee. After ersatz coffee, Claire was more than delighted to savour the aroma and taste the real thing.

'What brings you to Rennes again?' she asked.

'I wanted to buy a few books for the children. And I thought I'd do a little sightseeing, although I'm afraid I haven't done too much of that as yet.'

'Rennes is a handsome city,' Eva replied. 'The Romans developed it as their hub, you know. My husband told me its position makes it strategically important as it stands at the confluence of two rivers. You must visit the Grande'Chambre du Parlement. Apparently Madame de Sévigné was among those who used to observe the beau monde from one of its fine loggias decorated with gilded cornices.'

Claire glanced at the German fashion magazines on the table: *Modenschau*, *Praktische Damen und Kindermode*, *Claudine*, and lastly, a popular magazine called *Frauen Warte*, which translated as 'Women Wait' and was widely known for its Nazi propaganda as well as its fashion advice. She picked up one with a cover featuring a German peasant woman pushing an old-fashioned plough against a shadowy backdrop of a soldier's helmet in the background, and flicked through it. Among its many features on home economics and photographs of celebrities was a smiling Hermann Goering pictured cuddling his daughter, Edda.

'That's an excellent magazine for home economics,' Eva said. 'It's a pity you can't get it here. Some of our servants could do with learning a few of its tips. But it's not the best for fashion – at least, the sort of things I like. This one is better for that sort of thing.' She showed Claire the latest edition of *Modenschau*, and then her sketches. 'I'm going to Paris next week and I want to have a new gown made. What do you think of this?'

She pushed the sketch pad towards Claire.

'You are talented, Eva. It looks lovely. Is this for a special occasion?'

Eva smiled. 'Jürgen has an important meeting in Berlin soon. The Führer will be there so I must look my very best.'

Claire showed a marked interest, but not for the same reason as Eva. 'And who will be making the gown for you?' she asked. 'They look like the sort of dresses Mademoiselle Chanel is famous for.'

Eva laughed. 'They do rather, but I'm afraid the Führer doesn't approve of her creations. He abhors skinny women and thinks her designs encourage an unnatural slender silhouette – it's not good for childbearing. In fact he hates Paris fashion altogether, but he does want to see Berlin women be the best dressed in all Europe. What's more, he even disapproves of make-up and perfume. I am fond of the Führer but I am afraid he does not understand women, even if he has been known to say on more than one occasion that what he likes best of all is to dine with a pretty woman.'

Claire was amazed at how much Eva knew about the German male hierarchy's attitude to fashion.

'That's why I have sketched a combination of styles,' Eva continued. 'This is from Mainbocher, who dressed the Duchess of Windsor. Unfortunately he has now left for America, which is a great pity. And this is from Cristóbal Balenciaga, who designed for Franco's wife.' She closed the magazines and took a bite of her Sachertorte. 'I think I will go to Monsieur Lucian Lelong for this fitting. He has a very good designer by the name of Christian Dior working for him.'

'If the Führer doesn't like Parisian fashion, wouldn't it be much better for you to have a dress made by a German designer – or someone in Vienna?' Claire asked.

Again Eva laughed. 'Dear Claire, I am fearful that I would end up wearing *Tracht* – those terrible *Völkisch* creations promoted by the Deutsche Modeamt.'

Claire had no idea what she was talking about, and Eva enlightened her.

'When the Führer came to power ten years ago, he helped set up the German Fashion Institute. He wants to promote German design and German materials. There is even an Association of Aryan Clothing Manufacturers, and their labels are sewn into the garments. Of course, we all know that the Jews are very good with clothing but as a consequence of the new policies, many of the good designers have left.

Eva leaned a little closer as if to disclose a secret. 'I have heard that certain ladies married to high-ranking officers even keep Jewish seamstresses on the quiet. Of course this is only heresay, you understand. The institute likes to promote German tradition. I myself have a Tyrolean dress and I am in agreement with their cause, but it is hardly couture. I know for a fact that many of our leaders' wives still adore Parisian couture. Take Annelies von Ribbentrop for example. Even Magda Goebbels in her role as honorary president of the institute wears the very best French clothes, and several of her favourite designers are Jewish. Her hats are by the best Parisian milliners and her shoes by Ferragamo. If Magda chooses to forgo the "Gretchen" look for haute couture, then so will I.

'And then there was the incident with the hair dye. Do you know that the Führer tried to ban hair dye? Magda told me that Eva was so outraged she chastised him and the ban has been rescinded. No,' she continued with a sigh. 'I am afraid Herr Hitler does not understand women.'

Inwardly Claire was amused at the conversation and couldn't help thinking how much Violette would have loved to hear all this. After a while, she felt Eva was relaxed enough to open up a little more. It was then that she noticed a framed certificate on the wall near to where they were sitting. Eva saw her look at it. She took it down and proudly handed it to Claire for a closer look. It was her Certificate of the Cross of Honour of the German Woman. Claire had heard of these but it was the first time she had seen one.

'You must be very lonely in Rennes,' Claire said. 'I mean, after Paris where there's so much to do. But you do have little Oskar and your husband. That must be a great joy for you.'

The smile faded from Eva's face. 'I rarely see Jürgen. His work has become so demanding, especially lately.'

'I am sorry to hear that,' Claire replied.

'I don't usually bother him with talk about work but just lately I have seen the strain he is under. When I asked him what was wrong he told me that there have been several British agents dropped into France who are helping the Resistance. It seems that Berlin is putting pressure on him to find them.'

Claire pricked up her ears. 'Who exactly is putting pressure on him?' She knew she was tempting fate but she couldn't stop now.

'Heinrich Himmler. My husband answers directly to him.'

'Does he know who these people are?' Claire asked.

'I believe he's closing in on them. There was a raid yesterday. A few suspects were rounded up including one they are convinced is an

Englishman. They are being held at HQ in Avenue Jules Ferry. Jürgen was there all night. Apparently they are being interrogated. He came home early this morning in a foul mood and told me they were transporting the six still in custody to Nantes. A couple died and were transferred across the road to the hospital.'

Claire knew the Gestapo headquarters well. She also knew that the military hospital across the road – often known as Frontstalag 221 – was where the Gestapo disposed of those who died in their custody.

'The arrangements are already underway,' Eva continued. 'I believe they will leave during the early hours of the morning in order not to attract too much attention. There's a transport of prisoners already waiting in Nantes to be sent to Germany. He said at least two of them will be going to Paris. What terrible distress all this causes him. If only the French would accept us, things would be so much easier.'

At the mention of Paris, Claire felt her heart pound. She knew this meant the Gestapo headquarters at Avenue Foch. Hardly anyone survived their torture methods, and those who did were quickly bundled away to the extermination camps under the label *Nacht und Nebel* – Night and Fog – never to be seen again. She was at a loss for words, but at least she knew what was happening now.

'Let's hope it will all be sorted out soon, Eva, and you will have him back again.'

Eva said she was relieved to be able to talk to someone so understanding. Jürgen had told her never to discuss anything about his work with anyone, but her loneliness was beginning to cast a dark shadow over their relationship. She might have the luxuries that being the wife of such an important man could bring, but she was extremely miserable and Claire couldn't help feeling sorry for her. But having found out what was likely to happen to Jean-Claude and Michel, she realised she had to get back as soon as possible.

She thanked Eva for the lovely afternoon and said she really must leave as she had lessons to prepare for the forthcoming week. Before leaving she asked if she could see Oskar's toy soldiers as she had promised. Eva led her back into the house and upstairs to Oskar's room, where a private tutor was sitting in a chair by the window, supervising Oskar doing his homework.

'Are you going to show me your army, Oskar?' Claire asked in French.

Oskar was delighted. They were laid out on a large table. Most were from the Napoleonic War – Prussians, English, Belgians and French. None dated from the war that consumed them now. He took great delight in explaining all the manoeuvres taking place. Eva looked at him proudly, telling him that one day he would become a great General.

When they had finished, Eva escorted her outside and asked someone to call her chauffeur.

'No, please don't go to any trouble. It's only a short walk back and the air will do me good.'

Eva wouldn't take no for an answer. The chauffeur arrived and Claire said goodbye, promising to come again the next time she was in Rennes.

After she was dropped off at the hotel she went straight to the telephone booth in the lobby and made a call to Didier.

'Call a meeting for this evening – 6pm sharp. There's no time to waste.'

Didier was the first to arrive, along with Stefan the forger and Armand, a man in his late fifties known as 'the major' because he was ex-military, Foreign Legion to be precise, and an expert on explosives. Others followed, including Yves. Claire was forced to put her emotions regarding him to the back of her mind for the moment. Since calling the meeting, she'd realised that she would be forced to come clean about her visit to Eva and why she did it. It wasn't going to be easy as she was bound to be seen as a threat to their safety. All the same, it had produced an outcome and for that they had to be grateful.

As predicted, none of them were happy about the new friendship, but Didier came to her rescue, saying that if Henri put her in charge, he knew what he was doing and they had to trust her. The issue of the prisoners' removal to Nantes was now uppermost in their minds and they must pool their resources to rescue them.

'All I know is that the transfer of these prisoners is likely to be in the early hours of the morning,' Claire said. 'Eva Hoffmann thinks that could mean any time between midnight and dawn so as not to attract too much attention.'

'The question is, which route will they take?' asked Yves.

They all looked at Henri's map spread out on the kitchen table. Several options were discussed but quickly narrowed down to one.

'They will most likely take this secondary road as there was an ambush on the main road about a year ago and quite a few were killed,' the major said. 'There is a sharp bend just before the road crosses the river. The bridge is an ancient one and was not built to take heavy traffic. Any trucks will be forced to slow down here.'

The others agreed.

'And there is a steep embankment, ideal for concealment. The thing is,' added Yves, 'the roads must be watched from the Gestapo headquarters until this point. It's about a ten-minute drive.'

'Five minutes,' one of the men observed. 'When no one's about.'

When it came to the getaway vehicle a problem arose. If there had been more time, they could have purchased a car somewhere with forged documents. Now the options were limited. Someone suggested stealing a car from a known Milicien. The men chuckled.

'Good idea,' someone said. 'We all know a few of those. Kill two birds with one stone. I'd love to see them wriggle their way out of that.'

'No,' Claire replied. 'A car is out of the question because of the curfew. We will have to get there the usual way – on foot or bicycle.'

The men considered their options. Yves suggested they use a boat to get the men away. The embankment was an ideal cover for it. Everyone liked the idea. Didier then surprised them all by saying Henri had stored a few Wehrmacht uniforms for times like this.

Claire asked how many.

'About half a dozen.'

The major suggested that the team stopping the truck with the prisoners could use them.

'I don't know the sizes,' Didier replied.

'*Merde!*' the major exclaimed. 'This isn't a bloody fashion parade. If it gets us near the driver without alerting those in the back, I don't give a damn!'

'Just so long as we don't shoot each other,' someone laughed.

After much discussion, the elaborate plan was hatched. At least six people would be in the main group where the kidnapping was to take place. Lookouts would be installed everywhere else from their informants in the military hospital overlooking the Gestapo headquarters to the bend at the river. Two of the best marksmen would be positioned to fire shots at the tyres of any vehicles either leading or following the one with the prisoners. This should leave the prison truck isolated. The major would lead the ambush itself. Jean-Claude and Michel would be hurried away to a waiting boat near the bridge. Claire was emphatic that all this must be over with in less than five minutes.

'And we use silencers,' she added. 'Less noise but it means we have to act at close range.'

The men agreed. The discussion then centred on the prisoners themselves. After they had been freed, what were they going to do with them? It was dangerous for them to be in Rennes. They all agreed that the best place to take Jean-Claude and Michel would be Redon. In Redon they would have to lie low for a while until false identity papers were supplied. Michel could assume a disguise and a false identity and would be assigned to another group, but Jean-Claude was different. He would want to see his wife and that would be impossible; his family would be watched day and night. He could not return to Rennes at all until the Allies landed, and at that moment that date was anyone's guess. Claire said they would look after his wife financially but at no point should she be told anything other than that Jean-Claude was safe. As for the other four, it would be impossible to leave them behind. They would have to be released and left to their own devices.

'That's about it,' Claire said finally. 'Yves, you take care of boat and get Jean-Claude and Michel to Redon. I will meet up with the major.'

'Is that wise?' Yves asked.

'Do you think because I am a woman I can't play my part?' Claire snapped. 'I am in charge of this operation and I want to see it go according to plan. Now, if there are no more questions we'd all better get a move on?' She looked around the room, studying each face for a few seconds. 'Right, off you go, boys. We will meet up in a few hours.'

'Are there any contingency plans?' someone asked.

'No,' Claire replied sharply. 'This is it. We need luck on our side and must think quickly if plans change. And by the way, you will all get a little extra something for your troubles.'

They all departed except for Didier. Claire didn't want him near the area, mainly because of his appalling French and also because she wanted him to radio London should something go wrong.

'Where are the uniforms?' she asked. I'd better try one out myself.'

Didier moved the kitchen table and pulled back the threadbare rug, revealing a section of the floorboards that hid a cache of guns and the uniforms.

'*Mon Dieu!*' exclaimed Claire.

Didier laughed. 'You were sitting on them all the time.'

It was just before curfew when Claire arrived at the meeting place near the river. The major and his men were already there. She gave them their German uniforms, which they hurriedly changed into. The major whistled when he saw her.

'The best-looking German I've seen for a long time, but it's hard to hide a beautiful face.'

Claire ignored him. She pulled her hair back into a tight roll and smudged dirt over her face in the hope that in the confusion, no one would recognise her as a woman.

'Have you seen Yves?' she asked. 'Did he manage to get the boat?'

'He's already waiting,' the major replied.

They attached the silencers to the barrels of the sub-machine guns, took up their positions and waited. After curfew everything went quiet. Claire positioned herself in the recess of a doorway to an old warehouse. On the wall was a freshly pasted poster with a man's face. Underneath the photograph were the unfortunate man's name and the words *Shot for sabotage*. It was a stark reminder of what would happen should things go wrong.

The major was a few metres away, out of sight, yet within earshot. The rest of the group hid in the area and around the embankment.

After the first hour of waiting, Claire began to doubt whether she had done the right thing. Would the prisoners really be transferred? She only had Eva's comments to go on – tenuous at best, and by her own admission, she rarely saw her husband these days. What if Eva had failed to grasp the real circumstances? After all, she was not privy to the everyday running of the Gestapo – or was she? Self-doubt churned in her stomach to the point of making her feel ill, and a relentless thirst clawed at her throat. After another two hours, still nothing had happened. The major came out of the shadows to see if she was all right.

'What if I made a mistake, Armand?' she said.

'As you said yourself, it's the only thing we've got to go on at the moment. Let's just be patient and see.'

At around four in the morning signals started to be passed down that two vehicles had left the prison gates and were heading their way. The first was a black Citroën. Behind it was the army truck carrying the prisoners.

Everyone took up their positions. When the Citroën neared the bend, the major signalled to let it pass. Less than a minute later, they heard the sound of gunfire. The driver was shot in the head and the car spun out of control, careering into the bridge wall where it hung precariously over the water. The major's men rushed out, and after making sure there were no survivors, pushed the car into the river. From their vantage point on the boat by the embankment, Yves and his men watched the partly submerged car slip past them with the fast current until it eventually slid under the water.

Meanwhile, the major and Claire rushed out of hiding and quickly assembled a makeshift roadblock. When the truck turned into the road, confronted by what they assumed to be three Germans, they came to a halt. Before the driver and passenger had a chance to realise it was a trap, the men fired on them at close range. Using the silencers meant that the men in the back of the truck did not suspect an ambush, but they did know something had happened. Two of the soldiers poked their heads out from under the tarpaulin and were immediately shot dead. The rest of the guards, realising they were under attack, attempted to defend themselves. In the ensuing melee, one of the soldiers tried to surrender and it was Claire herself who shot him. No one could remain alive.

The major's men hastily pulled the prisoners out of the truck and into a doorway. They had been handcuffed, two together. Luckily, the men had had the foresight to bring bolt cutters with them.

Free at last, Jean-Claude and Michel were whisked away to the embankment. The remaining four prisoners, confused by the appearance of Frenchmen in German uniforms, were too astonished to move.

'You're free. Get out of here – now,' Claire said in a low voice. 'Before the Germans suspect what has taken place.'

The reality of their freedom didn't take long to sink in and they made a run for it.

Claire quickly grabbed the sack with the men's clothes, ran to the embankment and after throwing it down towards the boat, scrambled down. It was steeper than she expected and in her haste, she slipped and started to roll, almost falling into the water until Yves put his leg out to stop her.

'That's the second time I've stopped you from falling into the water,' he said with a grin.

When Didier arrived back at Henri's apartment the next morning, Claire had already left Rennes. The apartment was spick and span with nothing to suggest what had taken place hours beforehand. He moved the table and rug and pulled up the floorboards. The German uniforms lay carefully folded and hidden away again. On top was a scribbled note in red lipstick.

A fine night's work.

M

'Well I never,' he said with a chuckle. 'What a woman.'

Chapter 12

It was Mireille who told Claire about Yves. The day after she arrived back in Saint-Etienne, she had dinner with them after school. They wanted to know all about the episode in Rennes. After they'd eaten, Antoine left the room to give a private lesson to one of his pupils. Mireille cleared the table and started to wash the dishes. Claire picked up a cloth to dry them.

'Do you think I did the right thing in befriending Eva Hoffmann?' she asked.

'My dear, I cannot answer that for you. You must be careful though. These people will be watching you.'

'But I haven't exactly lied to her. She thinks I'm a schoolteacher from Paris and moved here for another post – somewhere away from the troubles – and part of it is true, of course.'

Mireille sighed. 'Surely *you*, of all people, someone who could implement a scheme as you did this weekend, could not possibly think the Germans – not to mention the Vichy officials – are incapable of putting two and two together?' She dried her hands and began to slice two apples. 'Sooner or later, they will want to know who Eva's new friend is, if they don't already. Does she know where you live?

'I checked into a hotel just in case anyone followed me.'

'You had it all worked out, didn't you?'

Claire thought she recognised a hint of sarcasm in her voice.

'I *had* decided that I would not pursue the invitation to call on her, you know. In fact I really did want to avoid seeing her again. But that was before I heard what happened to Jean-Claude and Michel.'

'Yes, but it could have backfired. What if her husband had been there?'

'It was a calculation on my part that he wouldn't be. We all know he's a busy man.' Claire wanted to change the subject. 'What do you know about Yves?' she asked.

'You mean, do I trust him?'

Claire blushed. Was she that obvious?

Mireille smiled. 'I see that you like him and it's hardly surprising, he has a way with women. That's probably why Henri gave him a certain job to do.'

Claire looked confused. 'I'm not sure I follow you. What sort of job?'

'He works the street girls and the brothels, gets information on which girls have been keeping the Germans company.'

Claire's throat dried at this news, and she coughed to get a little air. 'Why on earth didn't anyone tell me?'

'Perhaps they would have, especially Henri, but after Yves spent the night with you, Henri thought it better to let sleeping dogs lie. He uses his work as an artist to get to know them – the bohemian lifestyle, it suits him, don't you think? Not everyone is cut out for that sort of work, but Yves is a natural and the women trust him.'

So that was what the woman was doing in his apartment, Claire thought to herself. A part of her even felt relieved at the news, although why he couldn't have told her himself, she wasn't sure.

It was late when Claire left the Chauvignons and the road was in almost total darkness. In the distance, the lights of Saint-Etienne twinkled under the canopy of the vast Milky Way. She would just manage to make it home before the curfew blacked everything out. Throwing her heavy satchel with her students' notebooks over her shoulder, she walked on for another few minutes, listening to the sounds of the night – a cow moving behind a hedge; a small animal scurrying through the grass. All of a sudden she felt uneasy. Her sixth sense, always on high alert, was telling her something was wrong. She heard the sound of a vehicle approaching from behind and turned to see who it could be, but the glaring headlights made it impossible. Her heart racing, she picked up her pace.

As the car approached it began to gather speed. Blinded by the lights, she stepped to the side to let it pass. For a moment it seemed as though the car would continue towards the town. When it drew level with her it screeched to a halt and two men jumped out, pointing their guns at her. They indicated for her to get in the car but she refused and tried to walk on, saying there must be some mistake. In a matter of seconds, she was knocked unconscious and bundled into the back of the car.

When she woke she found herself blindfolded and bound to a chair with her hands tied behind her back. She had no idea where she was or how long she had been there but she was aware of a throbbing pain at the back of her head.

She tried to wriggle free of the ropes but it was impossible.

A door opened and she heard footsteps coming towards her. She begged to be let free, saying again that there must be a mistake. No one answered. Whoever it was checked her head wound and she felt what seemed to be a wet sponge wiping the wound. It stung. After a few minutes the same person clamped his hand on her arm, pulled up her sleeve and gave her an injection before leaving the room. She struggled desperately to wrench herself free but her strength soon ebbed away until she felt as weak as a rag doll. Her head felt heavy and her thoughts swirled into the vortex of a tunnel. She heard voices – men's voices – but in her drug-induced state of mind they were incomprehensible and she had no idea where they were coming from. At that moment everything went black and she slumped forward.

When she came to, she found herself lying on a bed in a spacious bedroom decorated with period furniture. No longer bound and with the blindfold gone, she tried hard to focus on her surroundings. She struggled to sit up but her body was still weak. Thankfully she was still dressed and appeared to be fine apart from feeling light-headed and the dull throbbing at the back of her head. She reached down and pulled up her skirt to check her pistol. It was then she realised she had left it behind in her apartment. She looked around for the satchel containing the schoolbooks and her identity papers but it was nowhere to be seen.

She heard the sound of someone unlocking the door and an elderly woman entered carrying a silver tray laden with food and drink.

'Your breakfast, Mademoiselle,' she said.

Claire was rendered speechless by this sudden turn in events and watched in disbelief as the woman placed the tray on a table by the bed and left, leaving the door unlocked. The aromas of freshly baked bread and real coffee sharpened her senses. Slowly she eased herself up and sat for a while on the edge of the bed, staring at the contents of the tray: fresh orange juice, croissants, rolls, jam and fresh butter. Her throat was parched and she reached over to pick up the glass of orange juice but her hands shook and it slipped, splashing most of it on the tray.

What was all this, she asked herself? What were they going to do to her? She had played these little games during her training in England – tests to see how well she coped. But this was no game. It was real and she was scared.

All of a sudden she heard the door open and jumped up nervously. A man wearing the Gestapo uniform of an SS Sturmbannführer entered the room, closed the door behind him and stood looking at her. When he lifted his cap, emblazoned with the matte silver Waffen-SS eagle and *Totenkopf* ('Death's Head') emblem, Claire's jaw dropped. For a split second, she thought she was dreaming. She bit her lip to stop herself crying out. It couldn't be possible. Had the bump and the injection affected her mind? Was she going mad? They stood for a few moments, staring at each other. And then he spoke.

'Hello, Claire,' he said, addressing her in French.

How could she forget that voice? It was the same voice she had heard over and over in her head for the past three years. She stood mesmerised; memories flooded her brain. A pain in her chest made it hard to breathe and her legs started to give way. One hand reached for the side of the bed but she miscalculated and slid to the floor in a crumpled heap and wept freely in great spasms.

'No!' she cried out, covering her grief-stricken face with her hands. 'No! Noooo!'

The man came towards her and she felt his hands grip her shoulders and gently pull her up. He wrapped his arms around her, pressing her close to him and holding her head against his chest. In these few precious moments of suspended reality, they clung together as if nothing else mattered.

'I hoped it wouldn't be you,' he said, 'but in my heart of hearts, I knew it would be.'

He sat her on the bed and sat next to her, his arm around her shoulder. The tears continued to stream silently down her cheeks and she stared at him, not comprehending. She had remembered every detail of his face: each freckle, the curve of his eyebrows, his mesmerising eyes – and the scar, that thin red streak that swept towards his ear and which was so much a part of him. In three years he had hardly changed. Finally, she uttered his name.

'Marcel, please tell me this isn't true – that I'm imagining all this.'

He wiped away her tears with the tip of his finger and she closed her eyes to breathe in his scent; a scent she had never forgotten. He turned her face towards his and kissed her, that long, lingering kiss – so sweet, so tender, so arousing – that she had savoured years before. It was still the same. Nothing had changed, yet everything had changed. He had not drowned after all…and the world was at war.

'Why?' was all she could think to say. A pathetic little 'why', yet in that one word she wanted to know everything.

'I knew this would be a shock, that's why I asked them to drug you.

Don't worry, they didn't give you anything too strong.'

The initial shock was now suddenly replaced with anger. She pulled herself free from him and slapped him hard across his face. 'You bastard!' she screamed. 'Bastard! Bastard! Bastard!' she continued, hitting out at his chest. 'Why did you leave in that manner? If you had wanted to leave me, couldn't you simply have told me it was over rather than fake your own death?'

Marcel grabbed her wrists. 'Calm down.'

She stopped fighting. Sitting beside the only man she had ever loved, she wanted him as badly as she had always done. Only now this desire was superseded by something else; something even stronger – survival.

She stared at his uniform. 'Why are you wearing *this*?' She touched the twin silver SS bolts, the runic badges on the corners of his collar. 'Are you a Nazi as well as a liar?' she asked with utter disdain.

Claire scrambled to gather her thoughts. 'Don't you think we should start at the beginning,' she said angrily, 'and that you should tell me who you really are and why you faked your death? You owe me that at least.'

He stood up and walked towards the window. The pride that he always took in his dress now encapsulated itself in his uniform and she couldn't help noticing how handsome he looked in it.

'You are right. I do owe you that,' he replied, looking out of the window. 'Do you remember the day we met, on the train from Reims?'

Claire wanted to say how could she forget, but instead listened.

He turned to face her. 'I saw you in the hotel. I believe I told you so.' He smiled, more to himself than Claire. 'It was then that I was attracted to you. I couldn't get you out of my mind. What you did during the day, I never knew, but I noticed a man always dropped you off in the evenings and that you were alone. I did think about asking if you would like to join me for a drink, but thought better of it. Then I overheard you say you were leaving for Paris and I decided to try and catch the same train.'

'Why didn't you tell me all this when I met you, when we became lovers? Why did you lead me to believe it was a coincidence that we met on that train?'

Marcel sat down on the window seat, supporting his back with a huge silk cushion. The sunlight streaming through the windowpanes highlighted the scar on his tanned skin. His manner seemed so relaxed. Even now, after learning all this, she still felt a powerful electric current in his presence.

'I was there on business – my clients took precedence at the time so I didn't see the point. It wasn't relevant.'

Claire recalled their conversations with the utmost clarity. 'What I don't understand is why you waited so long to see me again if you were so attracted to me. Besides, it *was* by accident that we met that day in the bookshop, wasn't it?'

'That's certainly true. In fact I thought I'd never see you again but it didn't stop me thinking about you.' He paused for a moment, deliberating over his words.

'You are simply not making any sense,' said Claire.

He walked over to her and sat by her side again. 'I didn't see you again because the truth is, I was married.'

Claire felt as though someone had stuck a knife in her heart and twisted it. That such a love as they had held for each other had been built on a lie – it was incomprehensible. She doubled up, fighting the urge to vomit. He put his hand on her back and pulled her back up, forcing her to look at him.

'I couldn't stop myself from falling in love with you, Claire. You must believe that. I knew it was wrong but I couldn't let you go. What we had was real, but how could I tell you I was married?'

'And so you faked your death to spare me the truth?'

'I had no choice... There were other reasons for that also.'

She looked at the German uniform again. 'Who are you, Marcel? Tell me who you really are. You can't be French if you're wearing this.'

'You're right. That was another reason I couldn't tell you the truth.'

'I want to know everything. *Everything!* Do you hear?'

'I am, as you see, very much a German.' Pride swelled in his voice. 'The Germans were hated in Europe when we met. You would never have seen me again if you knew who I really was.'

Claire narrowed her eyes. 'But your name,' she queried. 'Marcel – it's French.'

'Marcel is French for Marc. I used my middle name. I'm sorry.'

'And that was also a lie about coming from Alsace?'

'I'm afraid so. Years ago there *were* members of the family from Alsace, but after everyone moved to Germany our names changed.'

He continued his story. 'I was here in France on behalf of the German government, recruiting sympathisers for our cause. In particular, I liaised with certain Bretons who wanted an independent state. They were deemed helpful to the cause.'

'The PNB,' Claire said, more as a statement of fact than a question.

'Two of their leaders came to Berlin after the French government cracked down on them. They hoped Hitler would support their ambitions to declare separation from France, but it meant an alliance with Germany. When the French government found out, they were tried in absentia on the grounds of treason. That was on 7th May 1940. And then France was invaded three days later, those same leaders offered us their services and of course we were only too delighted to accommodate them. They have been invaluable in finding willing turncoats amongst the Breton POWs who for the most part, were happy to support the armistice.'

Claire thought about the trouble the Breton Nationalist Party had caused. In the eyes of most Frenchmen they were traitors, fascists and racists whose manifesto was on a par with the Nazis'. She read their newspapers, especially L'Heure Bretton, which was established in July 1940. In particular, she read the long columns filled with lists of ordinary people who were fined or jailed for publicly insulting members of the occupying force; a student was sentenced to a week, a laundress to three months and a railway worker to six months. The lists grew by the month. The PNB despised the Vichy government but Vichy was now forced to keep them sweet because of their Nazi allies. Furthermore, Antoine and Mireille had often talked about the man who was now the Prefect of all Brittany – Jean Quenette. He was responsible for the promotion of cultural linguistic and folkloric traditions, which l'école Saint-Etienne had been forced to implement, and his spies were everywhere, including the parents of some of her pupils.

Marcel went on to say how he had been on friendly terms with Lieutenant Colonel Hotz, the Commandant of Nantes, since the '30s. Hotz was considered a Francophile, yet that didn't stop him from being assassinated in October 1941 by an agent of the Communist FTP Resistance. Reprisals were swift. Over a hundred hostages were shot. Many Bretons were appalled at the scale of the revenge. Claire was in England at that time and only heard about it after she met up again with Violette and Hugo Manning.

But one thing Marcel didn't talk about was that since the introduction of the Service du Travail Obligatoire in February, the ranks of the Resistance in Brittany had swelled. He had no need; it was common knowledge. She had come to an area rife with factions and dissent.

'And this association with the PNB, was it the reason why you wanted us to spend time at the cottage?' asked Claire.

'I had business there. I could have gone alone, but I wanted you with me.'

Claire studied his face for a few moments. The scar across his cheek had not faded, and neither had it marred his looks. Sorrow veiled her eyes.

'As a foil for your dirty business?'

'No! I had fallen in love with you and I saw it as a chance for us to be together. I knew that this was impossible in Paris.'

'But we were together for two whole weeks. How did you conduct your so-called business?'

'Do you remember those walks I used to take alone in the mornings, when I was gone for about two hours?'

Claire remembered vividly. Blinded by love, it had never occurred to her to ask him where he went or if he met anyone. How foolish she felt now.

'I met with our agents. It wasn't for long but it was enough for us to carry out our business.'

'And the day the Germans broke through the Ardennes... Did you know that was going to happen?' She recalled the last time they made love. It had been different – more passionate, more violent. Now she understood why.

He shook his head. 'I knew an invasion would take place but I had no idea when, or even where, but I had hoped it would have been when we returned to Paris. That way I could simply have disappeared from your life.'

Claire arched her shoulders, straightened her back and drew in a breath. 'And so you faked your death to spare me the pain of separation? Wouldn't it have been easier to have come clean and ended it? At least I would have had time to get over the lie.'

Marcel watched her struggle with it all. His answers were inadequate and he knew he had broken her heart. Now, more than ever, he had to convince her or he would lose her trust. He pulled her to him. She struggled but was no match for his strength.

'Damn it,' he said, shaking her angrily. 'I never asked for this war. Like it or not, we're in it, but what happened between us was real and neither of us can change that.'

His compelling eyes looked deeply into hers, melting her resolve. She was choking with passion for him. In that instant they both recognised they wanted each other as much as they had ever done. He pushed her back onto the bed. This time she didn't struggle. He frightened her, but currents of desire and excitement flooded through her body. With one hand he held her down and with the other he deliberately and methodically unbuttoned her blouse. Claire wanted to cry out, yet her voice remained trapped. For a moment he stopped, staring into her eyes with a wildness he could not control.

He pushed her bra aside, exposing her firm breasts, and saw her nipples were hard with desire. Her chest, with the silver crucifix draped across her left breast, rose and fell gently with each breath, arousing his senses and inviting him to caress her breasts whilst at the same time, his other hand reached under her skirt. Claire closed her eyes; memories of that perfect spring came flooding back and she started to shake and tremble. Inching his way downwards, he smothered her body with kisses, occasionally biting her flesh, causing her to let out cries of ecstasy, whilst at the same time tugging at her silk knickers to pull them down. When he had removed them completely, he parted her legs, allowing him the freedom to explore that part of her body he already knew so well.

When he finally entered her, Claire cried out with a mixture of pain and pleasure. It was just like the last time they made love – wild, hungry and violent. Their bodies shuddered in unison and in that moment, both of them knew that what they shared, they would never share with anyone else.

Afterwards he drew her to him and whispered softly in her ear. 'My darling, you will always belong to me.'

Claire's lower lip trembled. 'The truth is, I belong to someone called Marcel – someone who doesn't exist.'

He held her tightly, cradling her head. What had she done? This was wrong but she could not help herself. Even now, knowing this conspiracy of lies, he had made her feel alive again.

They made love several times during the next few hours, neither wanting to ask anything more of the other, but it couldn't last. When he thought he had won her over again, he sat up, pulled on his trousers and handed her the glass of the orange juice from the tray.

'And now, Claire, I want to know why you are here.'

The question brought her down to earth with a sudden jolt and she realised that the last few hours of precious intimacy had almost clouded her judgement. Their bodies may have belonged together but their ideals could not have been further apart. Her lover was not the man she thought he was; he was not French, but German. Worse still, he belonged to the hated Gestapo – there was no escaping that fact. The warm glint in his eyes had become an icy stare. She sat up, naked and vulnerable, and sipped from the glass, playing for time. Careful questions demanded careful answers. If she could convince a man like Marcel, she was saved. If not, she knew nothing would save her. Whatever the outcome, it was crucial he did not suspect her involvement with the Resistance or the SOE and the British. Too many lives were at stake.

'When the Germans took Paris, I didn't want to live there any longer,' she began. 'It wasn't the Paris I knew in happier times. I had also lost my job. As a teacher of English and German, the school no longer had a place for me. For a while I toyed with the idea of becoming a secretary or a translator, but the only people hiring German translators were the Germans and the Vichy government.' Claire lay back on the pillows and pulled the sheet up to partially cover her breasts. 'And to be honest, I didn't find that appealing. I had a little money put aside but due to rationing and the added expense of buying basics on the black market, the money soon ran out and I had to find a job. I thought I might have better luck finding a teaching job in the country. I answered a few ads and that's when I saw there was a vacancy at Saint-Etienne.'

She eyed him carefully to see how he reacted. It was hard to tell, and so she continued. 'When I arrived, I was told I had taken a Jewish teacher's position. It seems that she was deported to Poland along with several other Jews.'

At the mention of the Jewish teacher, Claire was convinced she saw a flicker of distaste in his eyes and wondered if he had been responsible for their fate.

'I am not allowed to teach English and no one knows I speak German as I don't want to arouse anti-German sentiments.'

Marcel smiled and gave a slight nod of approval at her discretion.

'That's it, I'm afraid. There's not much else to say. As you see, I have not been living the same exciting life that I used to lead.'

For once, Claire was thankful she had forgotten her gun. Trying to explain that away would have been quite a different matter.

He sat back down on the end of the bed and gathered the sheet in one of his hands and slowly started to pull it away. His eyes savoured her body as it fell away. Claire relaxed a little, thinking she had convinced him that she was innocent of any wrongdoing. She arched her back coquettishly in readiness for him to make love to her again, but instead, he grabbed her ankle and squeezed it tightly until she cried out in pain.

'But you left Paris just before we occupied the city,' he replied.

Claire sat up quickly, her arms reaching out to him to stop. 'You're hurting me!' she screamed.

'What did you do between then and coming here? Where were you during those two years?'

Claire struggled to shake him off and when he let go, she slumped back on the bed. She had been silly to underestimate him, yet she was also angry. He had toyed with her emotions like a cat plays with a mouse, just to get her to talk. How could he do this to her if he truly loved her as he said? Even more alarming was the fact that he knew she had not been in Paris.

This time his voice softened. 'Answer me, Claire, or do you have something to hide?'

Once more, Claire gathered her thoughts. 'When I lost my job, I went to stay with friends in Provence. I met a man there, we became close and decided to marry but he was sent to work in Germany. When I didn't hear from him, I decided to try and look for another teaching job. That's when I came here.'

She held her breath. A huge smile crossed his face. He pulled her up off the bed and wrapped her in his arms.

'This man, did he mean a lot to you?'

'Not as much as you did,' she replied. 'I was trying to fill the void you left in my life.'

He lifted her fingers to his lips and kissed them, softly and one at a time. 'To me you are still my Claire.'

'And to me you are still my Marcel.'

The plan had worked. When the SOE wanted to give her a new identity, it was Hugo who had insisted on keeping her real name – for a moment like this. To all intents and purposes, she was still the French woman from Paris. Most important of all was the fact that Marcel still had no idea of her connections with England, or her SOE codename of Manon. For that, Claire fingered her crucifix, deeply relieved.

After making love one more time, he lifted the receiver of the telephone on the bedside table and called for someone to bring in her things. Almost immediately a young adjutant entered the room with her identity papers and satchel. Seeing Marcel in his trousers, his braces hanging down loosely either side his naked torso, and Claire lying naked in the bed, he averted his eyes. She felt cheap.

'Get the car. Fräulein Bouchard is going home.'

The young officer clicked his heels, held out his arm and called out, '*Heil* Hitler' before leaving. Marcel handed her the papers and her bag.

'Get dressed. It's time you went home. Your pupils will be missing you.'

She looked at her watch. It was four o'clock in the afternoon. Antoine would be wondering why she hadn't turned up for school. Somewhere nearby, church bells chimed four times. As she dressed she peered out of the window to see where she was. The architecture of the house suggested that she was in a nineteenth-century manor house set in acres of parkland, and beyond was a thick forest that hid the house completely from the outside world. A sweeping driveway snaked its way from the main gates to the front of the house. At one point the forest dipped and she caught a glimpse of water, glistening in the afternoon sun. The sea, she thought to herself. We must be near the English Channel.

'And us?' she asked. 'Will you disappear from my life again as you did before?'

He shook his head, and his eyes avoided hers. 'Claire, this is not going to be easy.'

'No,' she answered curtly. 'You are German and I am French. We belong to different sides.'

'I don't mean that.'

'Then what do you mean?'

'Have you forgotten that I told you I was married?'

'How could I? But tell me one thing: Are you still married and, if so, where is your wife?'

He fell silent for a moment before continuing. 'I'm afraid I have to tell you that I'm still married. Very much so... In fact, you know her.'

Claire stared at him blankly. His words rang in her ears and a suffocating pain tightened in her chest like a rubber band. Slowly she backed away as it dawned on her what he was trying to tell her.

'Mother of God,' she groaned. 'It can't be...please tell me it's not so.' Her voice started to tremble. 'So *that* is how you found out about me?'

'I'm afraid so, Claire. Eva Hoffmann is my wife and Oskar is my son. Everyone knows me as Jürgen Hoffmann – very few know me as Marc.'

Claire though she would faint, but he reached out and held her in his arms. Her mind went blank. Several minutes passed before either could speak, and when they did it was Marcel who spoke first.

'When she told me you had saved them after the accident, I tried to find you. I had no idea then that it was you – even after you met again in the square. But after you came to the house to visit her, things started to add up – a teacher from Paris. When she described you and told me your name, I knew it had to be you.'

The reality of the situation hit home. Whilst training in England Claire thought she had prepared herself for every possible situation and a part of her was hardened to the work she was doing, yet nothing had prepared her for this. She should have heeded her colleagues' advice and left well enough

157

alone. Now she was trapped. This latest revelation had shaken her to the core, but it also made her realise even more that she had others to think of. At all costs, she had to protect their identities.

The young adjutant knocked on the door. Marcel grabbed Claire by the arm.

'You must forget Marcel ever existed – for both our sakes.'

She tried to pull away from his tight grip. 'That's impossible. You are asking me to forget my past – something that was precious to me.'

His grip tightened further. 'This is not a game, Claire. Things have changed and we could both end up dead. Do you understand? No more Marcel. Now trust me.'

The adjutant entered, accompanied by two plain-clothed Gestapo officers. Marcel told them to tie her hands behind her back and blindfold her. When she started to struggle, the look in his eyes rendered her mute. With that, he turned on his heels and left the room.

Minutes later, she was led down a flight of stairs and into a waiting car. The church bells chimed again. Five peals. They had a distinct sound, and Claire tried hard to memorise it. That small piece of information combined with the fact that the house was near the sea were the only things she had to go on to remember where she had been held captive.

Sometime later the car drew to a standstill. The men pulled her out, took off her blindfold and untied her and drove away without uttering a word. In the distance was Saint-Etienne. She had never been so happy to see this small village in her life as she was now. She picked up her satchel and headed home – a changed person. The same thoughts kept spinning around in her head. Her lover was not dead; he was not even French, and worst of all, his name was not Marcel; it was Sturmbannführer Jürgen Marc Hoffmann, Gestapo leader and husband of the woman she had befriended. Overcome with a combination of elation and fear, she stood by the side of the road, clasping her stomach, and vomited. In the space of almost twenty-four hours the woman known as Claire Bouchard – alias Marie-Elise, codename Manon – had seen her world turned upside down. She hardly recognised herself.

Chapter 13

The moment Claire's head hit the pillow she fell into a deep sleep. When she woke several hours later, it was almost nine in the evening and she was aware of someone moving about in the apartment. She threw on her robe, grabbed her pistol from the drawer of the bedside table and quietly opened the door to see who it was. Someone moved in the small kitchen and she carefully took aim. A man stepped out carrying two mugs of steaming hot ersatz coffee.

'*Mon Dieu!* Careful with that thing. It could do a lot of damage.'

'Yves!' Claire exclaimed, lowering the gun. 'What on earth are you doing here?'

Yves walked straight past her and put the mugs on the table.

'How did you get in?' she asked, shocked and annoyed to find him there.

'Gaspard let me in. We were worried about you.'

Claire belted the robe tightly around her and sat down at the table.

'Antoine alerted us when you didn't turn up for school. Both he and Mireille were worried and when no one answered the phone and Gaston said he'd not seen you at all, they called us.'

'Us?' Claire queried.

'Didier to be exact, and he called me. I came over straight away. Mireille said you left their house later than usual and as it was dark, she watched you from her bedroom window until you disappeared from view. She also said that a car passed by soon after. She didn't think anything more about it until you failed to show up today.'

Claire put her elbows on the table and propped her head on her folded hands, staring out at the elm tree shimmering in the lamplight. 'Who else knows?' she asked after a while.

'No one.'

She looked him squarely in the face. 'Are you sure?'

Yves didn't take too kindly to being interrogated like this. 'What happened?' he asked. 'Did the Gestapo take you in for questioning? If that is so – and I suspect, judging by your reaction, that it is – we have a right to know, wouldn't you agree?'

Once more, Claire felt trapped. She couldn't lie and she couldn't tell the truth, but she did owe them an explanation as they had obviously been extremely worried about her. In the end, she decided a half-truth would be the safer option.

'You are right. It was the Gestapo who pulled me up. I was blindfolded and driven to some place...I have no idea where, but it wasn't Gestapo headquarters in Rennes. This was a château or a mansion, judging by the little I saw.'

She deliberately omitted to tell him it was near the sea. For the moment, she would keep that to herself.

His face showed concern. 'What did they want from you?'

When she didn't answer, he tried to help her along. 'Did it have anything to do with your friendship with Frau Hoffmann?'

Claire corrected him. 'Acquaintance...she is not exactly a friend.'

He shrugged his shoulders, took out his cigarettes and offered her one. 'Call it what you will,' he said, leaning across the table to light her cigarette.

Claire took a deep drag and slowly exhaled the smoke.

'They wanted to know who I was. When they saw my identity card they could see I was from Paris. I told them it was Frau Hoffmann who invited me to the house and that was that. Nothing else really.'

Yves looked surprised. 'And they believed you?'

'Well, they must have done because they let me go. I was blindfolded and dropped off just outside Saint-Etienne a few hours ago.'

'Then why did they wait all day to bring you back? You were gone for almost twenty-four hours. A lot can happen in that time.'

'I have absolutely no idea. I was left alone in a small room for most of the time.'

'And they didn't attempt a little roughing-up?' he asked. 'I mean, they're not exactly the politest of people...'

Claire cut him short. 'Why wouldn't they believe me?' she said, rather too confidently for Yves' liking. 'My papers were all in order and I am who I said I was – a teacher from Paris.'

'Did you recognise your interrogators?'

'I had never seen them before.'

'And would you recognise them again if you saw them?'

Claire wasn't sure where Yves was heading with this line of questioning, and she wanted the conversation to end.

'I'm back, aren't I?' she snapped. 'Yes, it was traumatic but they didn't harm me so let's forget it. I'm quite exhausted by all this.'

Yves looked at the clock. 'Fine. If we hurry, we can still get a bite to eat at L'Arlequin before they close. You look as if you could do with a good meal – you're as pale as a sheet.'

Claire desperately wanted to be alone but she felt she had to accommodate his request. After all, they had been worried for her safety and she owed them some gratitude. The thought of L'Arlequin's meagre menu of hock, pulses or turnips and beets was the last thing she wanted to face, but to appease him, she agreed.

'Okay,' she replied. 'But please allow me to take a shower first.'

She disappeared behind the screen and ran the water. He saw her throw her robe over the screen and heard her pull the shower curtain back and step inside the bathtub. The fresh fragrance of soap and soft clouds of steam filled the room. Yves became worried when she appeared to be taking too long and went to see what she was doing. A trickle of water was starting to flow across the floor towards the screen.

'Claire, are you all right?' he called out anxiously.

When she didn't reply, he pulled back the curtain and was shocked to see her sitting in the bath in a foetal position in tears. He quickly turned off the water and grabbed a towel. Too distraught to resist, Claire let him wrap the towel around her. He pulled her to him, rocking her like a baby. This was not the woman he had come to know and he feared the worst. Regardless of what she told him, the Gestapo must have made her suffer, but if she did not want to talk about it, he would not press her; he respected her far too much for that.

When Claire arrived at the school the next day, Yves had already left for Rennes and Antoine was anxiously waiting for her.

'We were worried sick about you. Yves told us what happened but thank God you're safe.'

Antoine was like a father to her. He fussed about throughout the day, popping his head around the classroom door to see if she was all right. But as much as Antoine showed concern, Mireille was quite a different story. She appeared distant and tried her best to avoid her. When Antoine offered to see Claire back home after school, Mireille suddenly remembered she had something urgent she wanted him to attend to. Clearly she still believed Claire's visit to Eva was a threat to them all.

As usual, Claire dined alone at L'Arlequin that evening. Angélique tried to engage her in conversation but she had too much to think about to pass the evening with idle chatter. A full day had passed since she had seen Marcel – twenty-four hours which felt like a lifetime. In that time, she had thought of little else except him. In those twenty-four hours her life had changed, and for better or worse she had to find a way to deal with the situation. Just how she was going to do this was another matter. She also thought about Yves; he *had* cared after all, but now it was too late. When she thought about their lovemaking, it no longer set her on fire. Marcel had seen to that.

She wondered if she should stop thinking of him as Marcel; after all, 'Marcel' never really existed, except as a lie. Yet she couldn't bring herself to think of him as Sturmbannführer Jürgen Hoffmann, husband of Eva, father of *kleiner* Oskar, either. At first she decided that the only way she could deal with this was to think of him as Marcel – the man who had really loved her. To think of him as anything else would have meant what they had shared was a lie, and that thought was unbearable. But after the initial shock, the reality of the situation finally sank in and she recalled his last words and the look in his eyes which told her they could both be killed if she remembered him as Marcel.

It occurred to her that in this bizarre turn of events, she also wasn't the same person. The tables had turned and now she was the one living a lie. She decided to do as he asked. Henceforth she would think of him as Jürgen Hoffmann like everyone else. All these thoughts led to one conclusion. She had to protect her friends whatever the cost, and if that meant returning to England, then so be it. Her mind had never been in such turmoil. How she wished she had Henri to talk to. But would he understand?

She had been so distracted by her thoughts that she failed to notice she was the last customer left in L'Arlequin.

'Are you all right?' Angélique asked. 'You're not your usual self. You seem far away.'

'Nothing that a good night's sleep won't cure,' Claire replied.

Angélique watched her walk across the square – a lonely, sad figure. It was obvious something was wrong but if her friend did not care to confide then there was little she could do to help her.

A couple of days later, Yves left a message with the Chauvignons. Henri was returning in the next few days. Claire greeted the news with mixed feelings. They asked her if she wanted to be in the welcoming party when he arrived. She gladly accepted.

'Fine,' Yves said. 'Listen for the broadcast and then make your way to the usual place. We will meet you there.'

Claire sat huddled in a ditch next to Yves, waiting for the Lysander to appear over the treetops. At exactly 01.00 hours on a late summer morning, the plane rumbled overhead, dropping its human cargo with astonishing accuracy. Henri parachuted right into the middle of the paddock along with several containers of arms and ammunition for the Resistance. To his astonishment Claire threw her arms around him and planted a kiss firmly on his cheek. The men gathered around him, slapping him on the back in a warm gesture of welcome.

'Good to have you back, my friend,' Didier exclaimed. 'How was old Blighty?'

The containers safely hidden and the contents stored away, the group made their way to the Sourisseau farm, where Madame Sourisseau and the girls had prepared a hearty rabbit stew especially for Henri.

'Good to be back,' Henri said, relaxing over a strong glass of Calvados. 'You don't find this in England.'

The wild chatter in the Sourisseau kitchen was more akin to a party atmosphere than a clandestine drop. They were all eager to know Henri's news. As evasive as ever, he told them little except what they wanted to hear – that the war would be soon be over, but that they were to expect the Germans wouldn't give up without a fight.

'Rommel has been defeated in North Africa and the Italians have surrendered even though Mussolini has escaped and set up a Fascist government. With the tide turning in favour of the Russians in the east, it can't be long now before there's a final victory.'

'What about the reported attempt on Hitler's life in March? Did you hear any more about that?' one of the men asked.

Henri shook his head. 'Unfortunately these failed attempts only serve to strengthen his resolve to crush any opposition, but the Allies have started bombing Germany around the clock and the bombing of Hamburg in particular has dealt a blow to their morale. Devastation to the ports and infrastructure is bound to have an effect.'

'Well let's pray it's sooner rather than later,' remarked Madame Sourisseau. 'So many of our men have been sent there.'

Henri tucked into his meal lustily and Madame Sourisseau fussed around him like a mother hen, scooping more of their precious rabbit stewed in wine onto his plate as soon as it was empty.

'Rationing in England is like here – demoralising,' Henri told them. 'How I've missed this home-cooked food.'

When he'd finished, the Sourisseau sisters wanted to know all about London. He told them about Noel Coward's play *Present Laughter,* which had premiered two months earlier in London and which he was fortunate enough to see, despite the air raids doing their best to ruin the show. They spoke about how London was coping with the bombing, and about the latest music, which served to uplift the people's spirits. The girls often listened to Glenn Miller and Tommy Dorsey, whilst Madame Sourisseau favoured Bing Crosby. An argument ensued about whose recording of *Stardust* was the best and for a while, the mood at the farm lifted, each one wanting to contribute to this light-hearted debate.

By three in the morning, everyone had left except Didier, Yves and Claire. Henri wanted to know all about Jean-Claude and Michel and the kidnapping. He listened carefully and said very little. Claire cautiously defended her position in planning it all, adding that the men were now in safe hands. Didier and Yves looked at Henri's face, waiting for his reaction.

'You did the right thing, Marie-Elise. And I agree, if you had not acted then they would not have survived.'

Claire was relieved to hear him say that, but the late night and the events of the last few days were catching up with her and she excused herself, saying that she must return to Saint-Etienne and get some sleep before school started. Henri offered to see her out. Claire picked up her bicycle, which had been propped up against an outhouse, and together they walked in silence to the farm gate. She turned to thank him, saying that she was relieved he'd had a safe trip back and that she was glad to have him back directing Chevalier again.

'I know you placed great faith in me, Henri, but I'm afraid not everyone agreed with my unorthodox way of doing things.'

Henri took a packet of cigarettes out of his pocket and offered her one. 'Let's get one thing straight,' he said, lighting a cigarette and handing it to her. 'You have not failed me at all – or London. You did what we would have expected you to do. These things are to be expected and I applaud your actions. It's the other situation that came as a surprise.'

'I haven't got a clue what you're talking about. What "other situation"?'

Henri studied her face as he inhaled, carefully looking for the right words. 'The man you know by the name of Marcel.'

Claire's heart missed a beat. 'Henri, for God's sake, what are you talking about?'

Henri smiled. 'I know more than you think, Marie-Elise. London has filled me in.'

Claire was lost for words.

'We need to talk, but not here – not now. Go back home and get some sleep. I will be at the Chauvignons' tomorrow. We'll discuss this further after school finishes.' He pulled her bicycle away from the stone wall, indicating she should get on it. 'Get some sleep. I'll explain tomorrow.'

When the school bell rang at the end of the following day, Claire collected her books and hurried over to the Chauvignons'. The couple had conveniently gone into Saint-Etienne, leaving her alone with Henri.

'Sit down,' he said to her. 'There's a lot to discuss.'

Claire braced herself for what was to come next.

'The time has come for me to tell you why you were chosen for this mission. Some of what I am about to tell you will not sit comfortably with you, but hear me out.' He cleared his throat. 'When Hugo recruited you, he was aware of your affair in Paris with a man called Marcel.'

Henri's words chilled Claire to the bone. She had seen and heard so much over the past week that it seemed nothing could get any worse, and yet here she was again, being bombarded with yet more lies and deceit – and this time from someone she had believed she could trust.

'It seems that you met him on an assignment in Reims,' he continued.

It occurred to Claire that many people seemed to know more about her life than she did. 'Go on,' she said.

'When Hugo sent you to Reims, he knew that the Germans had their eyes on the champagne houses should they attack, as did the houses themselves. You even reported back that they were blocking up some of their cellars in readiness. The French Deuxième Bureau and British Secret Service had their eyes on several suspects working for the Nazis – Marcel was just one of many. These men worked for the Abwehr Foreign Espionage Section in Berlin and they had offices throughout France, generally masquerading as a legitimate business. Marcel was conveniently employed by one of these agencies – a law firm situated near the Champs-Élysées. The company had dealings with Germany and were known to be Nazi sympathisers. This was his cover, and his primary role in France was to recruit sympathisers to the German cause for the purpose of espionage.

'He made several trips throughout France and especially to Reims, as the Nazi elite, with their taste for luxury, had their eyes firmly set on plundering one of France's greatest luxury exports – fine champagne. And in this they have been successful. Between 1939 and 1942 alone, the wine production fell by almost half and the Weinführers managed to take away not only the best, but massive amounts of a lesser vintage for the army. The great wine and champagne houses were a barometer of things to come, and the best restaurants were also aware of this. That's one reason John Dufour said he was working for Le Saint-Pierre.

'Various groups were keeping each other in the loop. Hugo had his own people at Le Saint-Pierre and they notified him of all suspect clients and their customers – Marcel was high on this list. Hugo was also notified when you were seen with him. Photographs proved to him it was you. You were both watched during that time. Someone even reported back to Hugo the exact time he left your apartment the night you entertained him.'

When Henri stressed the word 'entertained', Claire felt a cold shiver run down her spine. They knew everything about her.

'There seems little doubt that he would have tried to recruit you also, had it not been for the fact that you displayed a distinct anti-Nazi stance.'

Claire thought back to that evening at Le Saint-Pierre. The beautiful memory was suddenly tarnished. She recalled being upset when Marcel said that France and Germany would make a good alliance and that the British should not waste their time siding with the Poles. And then there was the fact that he mentioned Maurice Chevalier's Russian wife was Jewish. Why, she asked herself, hadn't his comments rung alarm bells? Why had she chosen to ignore those remarks just because she was falling in love with him? Hearing Henri's words, the missing parts of the jigsaw that Marcel himself had omitted began to fit together, and it all started to make sense – why he never told her where he worked or went.

'When did you find all this out?' she asked despondently.

'I was told as soon as I arrived in London.'

She held her head in her hands and sighed deeply. 'He did love me though, Henri. I am sure of that.'

Henri put a comforting hand on her shoulder. 'You were the innocent victim in all this.' He paused for a moment. 'Then of course, he mysteriously disappeared, you came back to Paris and Hugo helped arrange your papers so that you could leave France.' He lit another cigarette while he gave her time to let his words sink in. 'Although things might have worked out differently if you and Violette hadn't met up again in London,' he added.

Claire looked him squarely in the face. What was he trying to say?

'When Violette told Hugo you were in London, he realised how valuable you could be for us. London had already discovered that Marcel had not mysteriously drowned as originally thought, and Berlin had rewarded him with a plum job for services rendered. But then you know that, don't you, Marie-Elise?'

Claire could find no words with which to answer him. She now understood that she had been thrown into the lion's den and her life was now at stake. She had to play the game their way or not at all.

'Meeting up with you again gave Hugo the idea to use your relationship with him to gain access to his inner circle. Some might call it callous – others the right thing, given the circumstances: that anything that would rid Europe of the Nazi regime was a sacrifice we had to make. That's what the SOE is all about, as you well know. Hugo knew that when you realised he had not drowned – that he was still very much alive – you would try to see him again. That's when he decided to send you to Brittany. The thing is, I don't think anyone expected it would work out this way.'

'What do you mean?'

'They didn't expect you to make friends with his wife. They thought you would realise who he was in time – when you saw a photograph of him, or in person – and then try and make contact with him, but when they heard you had gone to Villa Rosières, well, that changed things. It all happened sooner than expected.'

'I never saw him when I went to see Eva. It was a calculation on my part that he wouldn't be there,' she replied.

'But you must have known he would want to know who his wife's visitor was?' His words echoed Mireille's.

'Not particularly. At the time, I just knew I had to use our friendship to try and get information from her.' She shook her head in disbelief. 'I really don't believe what I'm hearing.'

She felt trapped, and began to pace the room. 'My God, what you will all do to get a result – it staggers me. You have *all* used me just to get to him. Political prostitution – isn't that what you call it?'

Henri chose to ignore her comment. 'Now let's come to the crux of the matter, Marie-Elise. You found out who he really was when the Gestapo took you away, didn't you?'

His eyes scrutinised her face. She was unable to hold his gaze.

'I know what a shock it must have been when you discovered that the man you thought of as Marcel had not drowned after all, and even worse, that he did not exist in the first place – that he is an officer of the German

Reich, none other than SS Sturmbannführer Jürgen Hoffmann. It cannot have been easy. If it's any consolation, it came as quite a shock to me also.'

Claire slumped back in the chair. He watched her reaction like a hawk. Her nerves were on edge and she struggled to keep her cool.

'You *did* meet up with him again, didn't you? When you were taken by the Gestapo.'

She wondered how he knew, or was it simply a bluff? Whatever had happened, it was vital she show the strength he expected of her. This was a matter of life and death and she could not forget it. Most importantly, they were at war, fighting for the same cause. The war had changed everything and there was no turning back.

Claire was exhausted; she could not fight this any longer. She turned away, desperately fighting back the tears. Fearing he might have pushed her too far, Henri walked over and put a brotherly arm around her shoulder.

'This has not been easy for any of us, Marie-Elise,' he said softly, 'least of all me, who has come to know you very well. But we have a job to do and we must do it by whatever means necessary.'

She looked up at him, her eyes full of sadness. 'I know,' she answered. 'I just need a little time to get over the shock.'

Over the next few days, the reality of the situation began to sink in. Claire had indeed been used as a pawn in a game that held little choice for her, and Henri had left her in no doubt as to the situation she faced: she either went along with all this, doing it the SOE's way, or she would be airlifted out of France within the week. If she tried to communicate with Hoffmann in any way, she would face the consequences, and she knew what that meant. Henri gave her time to think it over. One way or another she was to let him know by the weekend.

In the meantime, she busied herself with her teaching or went for long bicycle rides in the country to clear her head. After four days, she called him.

'Okay,' she said, 'I'm with you. Tell me what you want me to do.'

There was a pause at the other end of the line for a few moments.

'Good girl,' he replied. 'I will be in touch.'

With that, there was a click and the line went dead.

The following day, Antoine interrupted her class to say Henri wanted to meet with her at a bar in a village halfway between Saint-Etienne and Rennes.

'If you leave now, you will be back before nightfall,' he told her.

The village was little more than a hamlet. Claire knew it well as she had ridden through it several times before.

Henri was sitting at one of the small wooden tables near the window. Apart from the bartender, there was no one else around.

He ordered her a glass of wine and pushed his plate of blood sausage and cheese into the middle of the table for her to share with him. Claire picked up a few slices with her fingers and ate them greedily. The ride had made her hungry. Between them, they finished off the food before Henri started to talk.

'I know this is not easy for you but we are all indebted to you for making this decision. Hugo told me you were a woman of principle and I agree. And for what it's worth I do hope Marcel, as you call him, does love you – it will make your job much easier.'

'Do you know how it feels to double-cross someone you love, Henri?'

'No time for sentimentality. The war does not allow it.'

His abruptness no longer shocked her. In fact, she wondered if she could ever be shocked by anything again.

'Okay, before we go on any further, let's get something straight,' she said, letting out a deep sigh. 'Marcel no longer exists. We will refer to him as the man everyone knows him as – Jürgen Hoffmann. That way I can separate my life into the past and the present.'

He nodded in agreement.

'So where do we go from here and what do you want me to do? I can't simply go to Villa Rosières as I did before.'

'If I am a good judge of character I would say he will find a way to make contact with you. We just sit and wait. You are the temptress he cannot do without, and in his position, what the Sturmbannführer wants, he gets.'

Claire winced. She felt like a prostitute.

'As I told you the other evening, this war will not go on for much longer. The Allies are preparing for a final onslaught and the Germans know it. The intelligence we have gained so fair is invaluable and the Resistance remains ready to act. We need all the information we can get on what the Germans are doing. Anything you uncover will be helpful – you proved that in Reims.

'Most importantly, we will be aware of Hoffmann's movements. Our worry at the moment is that some of the circuits have been compromised. Agents have simply vanished without a trace and it's likely this will continue if we don't get to the bottom of it all. There have been far too many coincidences to ignore. You've more than proved yourself in the short time you've been here. I applauded your initiative when Michel and Jean-Claude were taken into custody – it's just the sort of quick thinking and daring action we like. If you were on the inside, you would be able to put this to good use – a trusted friend who no one would suspect.'

Henri continued. Claire listened.

'I want you to carry on as before. When he contacts you, let me know. Until then, lie low – and avoid Rennes.'

'Just one thing,' she asked. 'Who else is aware of this?'

'Didier, of course, and Antoine, but we have agreed to keep this from Mireille. She's rather nervous at the moment, what with the raid in Saint-Etienne, and hearing about your friendship with Frau Hoffmann has only made her more anxious. So for the time being, she will continue to think of you as a courier, nothing more.'

'And Yves, does he know?'

'Yes.'

Claire frowned.

All Henri would say was that Yves had a wide network of informers and could be trusted. Claire remembered the red-headed model in his flat. They spoke for a while longer, leaving Claire in no doubt that all this had been worked out in London.

'Just follow your instincts, Marie-Elise – like you always do. We will take it from there.'

When the meeting was over, he kissed her on the cheek and they parted ways. After everything that had happened, it surprised her that her feelings for Hoffmann, as she now knew him, were as strong as ever. She considered herself to be an intelligent woman, and an honourable one at that, so what was it that drew her to a man who had deceived her, other than that he was a good lover? Surely she should have been repulsed by him, yet she didn't feel that way. On the contrary, knowing what she did now excited her even more. After their affair, a part of her had died and she wanted to bring back to life what she had lost. The fleeting fling with Yves had awoken a desire in her again, but it was not for him. It was for what she had lost as a woman – a living, breathing creature who was made to be loved as Hoffmann had told her that first night. No one could possibly understand. Indeed, she couldn't even understand it all herself.

One thing she did know was that this was not going to end well. For now she would grab what little happiness she could.

Chapter 14

Henri was right: Claire did not have to wait long for something to happen. At the end of July, she was in the classroom at l'école Saint-Etienne when she heard several cars drive into the playground. Moments later, the classroom door opened and Antoine entered. She knew from the look on his face what it was all about. He wanted her to accompany him back to his office. Instinctively, the children knew something serious was happening and did as they were told when she asked them to carry on alone for the moment, telling them she would return shortly.

'The Gestapo,' Antoine whispered to her as they approached his office. 'They asked me to fetch you.'

Inside she was met by half a dozen men dressed in plain suits. Her heart missed a beat when she saw Hoffmann was with them.

He shook her hand. 'Mademoiselle Bouchard, it's an honour to meet you,' he said with a warm smile.

Claire felt a lump rise in her throat. All eyes were on her as she struggled to retain an air of self-confidence and dignity.

'To what do we owe this honour, sir?' she asked.

'I believe that just recently you became acquainted with my wife and son. I wanted to thank you personally for coming to their rescue at the scene of the accident. Without your quick thinking they would have died when the car exploded and I am indeed indebted to you.'

'I was only doing my job as an honourable citizen, sir.'

'We tried to find you to thank you but you left no name and address. Luckily for us, you met them again and we were then able to locate you.'

'Have I done something wrong, sir?' Claire asked.

'Not at all – I am here to offer you a proposition. I would like you to tutor my son, Oskar.'

Claire held his gaze for a few seconds. Mixed feelings churned her stomach. Like Henri, she had been sure Hoffmann would try to see her again, but she hadn't expected it to be under these terms. And the idea of involving Eva and little Oskar in this was something she had wanted to avoid at all cost.

'I am flattered by your proposal and you have a dear son who I took an immediate like to, but I already have my work here.' She looked across at Antoine. 'Besides, I am happy here and it will not be easy for Monsieur Chauvignon to replace me. Teachers are in short supply these days.'

Hoffmann smiled. 'You are indeed an honourable lady, Mademoiselle Bouchard, and I applaud your loyalty. Let's see what the good headmaster has to say.'

All eyes moved to Antoine, who seemed at a loss for words. He didn't want to push her into the Sturmbannführer's company, yet he could hardly disagree. After a moment of silence which seemed like an eternity, Antoine suggested that the school would manage; Mireille would be able to take Claire's classes until they found someone else.

'May I ask what this would entail?' she asked.

Their eyes locked. 'You will receive an excellent salary and have your own room at the Hôtel d'Armorique in Rennes, and you will be free to come and go as you see fit.'

'Can I ask if Frau Hoffmann is amenable to this? I would hate to be an imposition on her after she has been so kind to me.'

Hoffmann laughed. 'We have discussed it at length and she would be delighted. She already thinks of you as a friend and I know that Oskar has also taken a liking to you.'

He had it all worked out, and yet Claire could not help but feel bad about Eva and Oskar becoming caught up in this web of lies and deceit. After what had taken place, the thought of facing them filled her with dread. She forced these feelings to the back of her mind.

'If Monsieur Chauvignon is agreeable, then I have no objections. When would you like me to start?'

'At your earliest convenience: the sooner the better.'

This time Antoine came to her aid. 'Please do not worry about us, Claire. We will manage. The good gentleman is offering you an excellent position and I know you will do a fine job of tutoring his son. We will be very proud of you.'

Claire agreed to move to Rennes over the weekend with the intention of starting her new job the following Monday. Hoffmann shook hands and thanked Antoine for his time. He informed him that the school would receive extra privileges for his cooperation. What he meant by that was not specified.

*

The following Sunday Claire moved into the elegant nineteenth-century Hôtel d'Armorique where a suite on the fourth floor was already waiting for her. Since the occupation this elegant hotel had become the home of several top Nazi officials, and enveloped in a world of Reich propaganda, life here afforded every comfort possible. The bar and cocktail lounge, with their ceiling-high mirrors and tapestry-backed chairs, were filled with officers and their mistresses drinking the finest of champagnes and French wines, and one look at the menu, with its *sole meunière*, game dishes and an array of patisserie to suit the sweetest tooth, was a far cry from the virtual starvation the French people were forced to endure. It was like stepping into another world.

She also noticed how well dressed the women were here – and how beautiful. Henri had warned her that most of them were the French mistresses of Nazi officers. Wearing the same dark green suit and matching cream fedora that she had worn when she left the Cloutier farm for Rennes, she felt rather dowdy.

Claire cast her eyes around her new accommodation. She knew when she accepted the position that a room at the Hôtel d'Armorique would be more than a notch above the cramped apartment she had become accustomed to in Saint-Etienne, but she hadn't expected this. Her suite consisted of two tastefully decorated rooms bordering on the luxurious – a bedroom and a sitting room. Leading off the bedroom was a large bathroom, the centrepiece of which was a claw-footed bath over which were draped sumptuous white towels. The rooms were light and airy and overlooked a garden courtyard in which meals could be served under the shade of the trees. Flower arrangements and a gramophone player, next to which were a pile of French and German records, added the personal touch. A bottle of *premier cru classé* – Pauillac Château Latour 1929 – stood on a silver tray on the coffee table in the sitting room. With it was a crystal bowl of fine chocolates – a luxury she had not eaten in a long time. Propped up against the bowl was an envelope with her name neatly handwritten on it.

Mademoiselle Bouchard,

Welcome to your new home. I trust everything is to your liking.
    My wife and I are having a garden party at Villa Rosières this afternoon. You are most welcome to join us. My secretary has been notified and a car is at your disposal.

The note was written on official Reich paper. It was formal but she wouldn't have expected anything else. She put her suitcase on the bed and pulled out her clothes. Inside was a secret compartment, which she carefully prised open with the aid of her nail file. She pulled the pistol out of her suspender, placed it inside and smoothed back the lining. A soft click locked it back into position again.

Then she changed into her only good dress – the same one she had worn the night she dined with Yves. It reminded her of just how ill prepared she was for socialising. The only piece of jewellery she had was the crucifix, which she wore constantly but which now looked out of place. She zipped the dress up at the back and stood in front of the oval cheval mirror, looking at herself as if she were a stranger. This was the first time since she had arrived back in France that she had seen herself in a full-length mirror; her old apartment did not possess such a luxury. She studied herself for a while. Who was she, she asked herself? How had it come to this?

The car pulled up in the driveway alongside a fleet of black cars, all of which bore the Reich flag. As she neared the house she could hear music coming from the grounds on the other side of the house; the garden party was in full swing. No matter how hard she tried, Claire felt completely unprepared for this moment. Over and over again, she told herself she must act perfectly normal when she faced Eva. But what would happen when she saw Hoffmann? Would she give herself away? She hoped not. She reminded herself that under no circumstances was she to let slip the name she had come to know him as.

It was Eva, dressed in a bottle-green traditional Austrian dirndl, who came to greet her. Hoffmann was not with her.

'*Fräulein Bouchard, es ist so schön Sie weider zu sehen.* It's so good to see you again, and I am thrilled that you have accepted our offer to teach *den kleinen* Oskar.'

Claire felt as if her legs would give way until Oskar, accompanied by the dour Frau Heller, ran into the room and greeted her by shaking her hand.

'Welcome, Fräulein Bouchard. Papa made me very happy when he told me you were going to be my teacher.'

Eva laughed. 'He has done nothing but talk about it since he found out.'

Oskar was a child who appeared older than his five years, due, Claire surmised, to his formal upbringing. Clearly, he was being groomed to take his place in the world – Hitler's Reich, where duty and tradition spoke volumes. Like his mother, he was attired in traditional dress – short brown lederhosen with stiff leather braces.

'You're looking very smart in your lederhosen, Oskar,' Claire said to him.

Eva informed her that today was a special day. They had important visitors from Berlin. Claire started at the news.

'That's why I am dressed in this,' she laughed, sweeping her hands downwards with a flourish. '*Tracht!* No couture this afternoon, I'm afraid. They like to see German women in this ridiculous dress.'

Claire commented that even so, she did look beautiful in it. The dress itself might be *völkisch mode* but it was made of expensive fabric – dark green silk which contrasted with Eva's platinum hair, which she had elegantly styled into a roll – and the design of the bodice curved underneath the bustline emphasising Eva's small breasts and giving her an almost girlish innocence. Underneath the dress she wore a crisp, short-sleeved white cotton blouse. Eva might frown at her outfit but to Claire, she looked as if she had just stepped out of the pages of *Deutsche Modeamt.*

'I'm glad you were able to join us this afternoon. Let's go outside and you can meet some of our guests.'

A large marquee had been set up in the centre of the lawn and a band was playing a lively tune and several couples were dancing. Claire scanned the guests for a glimpse of Hoffmann but saw no sign of him. They approached a slim and sultry dark-haired woman and a middle-aged man wearing thin-rimmed glasses.

'Claire, let me introduce you to two old friends, Herr Doktor Franz Zeidler and his wife, Julie. They are from Berlin.'

Claire was introduced as Oskar's new teacher from Paris.

Franz Zeidler clicked his heels, took Claire's hand and bowed. 'It's an honour to meet you, Fräulein Bouchard. Frau Hoffmann has been telling us how fortunate she is to have found you. Oskar is very lucky to have you as his teacher.'

Julie Zeidler was rather more reserved. She held Claire's gaze for a while before transferring the champagne glass in her right hand to her left, which held a long, black cigarette holder, and shaking her hand.

'Eva tells us you are the one who saved her after the accident. We applaud your quickness of mind. It's a pity that more of your countrymen do not show the same kindness.'

'Perhaps you have not met the right people, Frau Zeidler. We French are most hospitable.'

Julie gave her a half-smile. 'So, you are from Paris. Which arrondissement, may I ask?'

'The 20th, not far from the Cimetière du Père-Lachaise. Do you know Paris?'

'My husband and I stay at the Georges Cinq or the Ritz when we are in Paris. I'm afraid we don't go into the suburbs. I don't think we would be welcome. What do you think, Fräulein Bouchard?'

At that moment Claire was aware of someone approaching from behind.

'Jürgen!' exclaimed Eva.

Claire spun around. This was the moment she had dreaded.

'Welcome to Villa Rosières, Fräulein Bouchard. We are honoured to have you with us. I trust you have settled in well. If there is anything you need, please don't hesitate to ask.'

'Thank you. Frau Hoffmann has made me most welcome,' Claire replied.

It was a difficult moment, but one that both of them handled well. In fact, Claire surprised herself at how easily she adapted to the situation. The joy of being in his presence again, and the dangerous game she had exposed herself to, gave an added frisson of fear and excitement. It was Eva that marred this joy. Seeing the way she looked at him left Claire in no doubt of her love for him.

'Jürgen, *liebling...*'

Her words were lost as the band struck up a German song and several of the guests came out of the marquee to dance.

Eva wanted Hoffmann to dance, but he refused. Her smile faded and to save her from the embarrassment of rejection, Franz Zeidler stepped forward to accommodate her wish.

'Allow me, my dear,' he said.

When the pair walked away, Julie stepped closer to Hoffmann. 'You always liked to dance,' she purred, looping her arm through his. 'What has happened to you?'

'Not today, Julie. I have too much on my mind.'

He gave a quick glance towards Claire, who discreetly looked away.

Julie playfully chastised him. 'You spend far too much time with your work. Surely you can allow yourself a little time to relax?' She turned to Claire. 'Do you like to dance, my dear?'

'Very much,' she replied. 'Although I can't remember the last time I went to a dance.'

'Jürgen is a very good dancer, aren't you?' Julie added, in a teasing, coquettish manner. 'Do you know,' she continued, turning back to Claire again, 'there was a time when we couldn't tear him away from the dance floor. Do you remember those times, Jürgen, before the war?'

Claire couldn't help wondering why Julie was embarrassing him with this conversation. He removed her arm from his and took a step towards Claire.

'Yes, you are quite right, Julie. I should allow myself more time to relax. Perhaps Fräulein Bouchard would care to dance?'

With that, he ushered Claire towards the band. She couldn't help but notice the look of utter disdain on Julie's face. For whatever, reason, Julie had taken an instant dislike to her and she could only hope that she didn't try to poison Eva against her.

Throughout the dance, neither uttered a word, yet she noticed how he occasionally squeezed her hand and pressed her breasts into his uniformed chest. A few guests stopped to watch them and applauded when it was over. Hoffmann bowed and escorted her back to the guests.

'You are so beautiful,' he whispered in her ear. 'I don't know how I will look at you without giving myself away.'

'You dance well, Fräulein,' Julie said, the half-smile crossing her face again.

Hoffmann excused himself, saying that he had things of great importance to discuss with several of his guests. Before leaving, he turned to Claire.

'Fräulein Bouchard, I do hope you will honour us by dining with us this evening.'

'Thank you, sir. I would like that very much.'

After he left, Julie murmured something to Eva about how inappropriate it was to have a teacher dining with such notable guests. Eva ignored the comment, but after their dance Claire sensed Eva wasn't too happy with the idea either. Was the real Eva starting to show her true colours? Claire had hoped they might be friends, yet in an instant she had been made to feel that she was just another of the Hoffmann household staff. She was racked with mixed feelings. Despite Hoffmann wanting her there, this was not going to be easy. If her mission was to be successful, she could not lose Eva's confidence.

Claire asked to be excused in order that she might prepare for Oskar's lesson the following day. She sensed Eva was somewhat relieved at this suggestion as she called for someone to show her the way to Oskar's classroom.

'We dine at seven sharp,' Eva called out as she was leaving. 'Don't be late. Jürgen despises lateness.'

*

At a quarter to seven, Claire made her way to the dining room. Herr Zeidler was the first to spot her.

'I am afraid you have me for company this evening.' He smiled. 'We are seated together.'

An antique clock chimed seven times and the guests were ushered to their places. Thankfully Claire was not seated near the frosty Julie, who had been placed next to Eva and Hoffmann. The table looked a picture of refined elegance. Eva had certainly spared no expense this evening. A row of silver candelabras lined the centre of the long table, and between each one was a bowl of variegated, freshly cut pink roses. The dinnerware was Sèvres porcelain decorated in shades of pink, and on the rim, amidst a decoration of foliage arabesques and animals, was the cipher of Louis XVI. Herr Zeidler picked up a carafe of burgundy and poured Claire a glass. Hoffmann gave a speech to welcome his guests and they all raised their glasses for a toast to the Fatherland.

'*Prosit*,' they replied in unison. 'To Deutschland.'

The servants brought out the food – silver trays filled with everything from roast goose to venison with a rich red-wine sauce accompanied by an assortment of seasonal vegetables. This was a far cry from the meagre food served up at Bistro L'Arlequin. In the short time she had been in Brittany, meat, with the exception of pork knuckle or rabbit, was rarely on the menu. It was years since Claire had eaten this well. The last time was at Le Saint-Pierre.

She soon discovered that the guests, including Dr Zeidler, were from the Ministry of the Interior run by Heinrich Himmler himself. One of them was a small, wiry man with a narrow face and cold grey eyes known as Karl Wenk. He reminded her of a staid bank manager rather than a man of power. Claire knew him to have been a close friend of Reinhard Heydrich, who had been assassinated in Prague the year before and since his death Wenk stepped up his ruthless campaign of reprisals and torture. Yet here in the midst of a pleasant garden party on a warm afternoon, these men who had been especially recruited by probably the most feared man in the Reich could not have been more cordial. They complimented Eva and Hoffmann on a wonderful meal and the fine wines, and flattered the ladies on their dress. Eva in particular looked stunning. She had shed her *Tracht*

178

for a sleek, silver lamé dress with a plunging neckline. To complement it, she wore a necklace and matching bracelet of diamonds and emeralds that sparkled in the flickering candlelight. Claire could not help wondering why Hoffmann had fallen for her when he had Eva, the model Reich wife with the film-star looks.

Apart from the occasional glance, Hoffmann ignored her. It was Julie who seemed intent on gaining his attention. She had a flirtatious manner which didn't seem to bother her husband in the slightest. The conversation turned to Eva's forthcoming trip to Paris. She told them she had made appointments with couturiers before going on to Vienna and Berlin. Julie informed her that Chanel had closed down her couture house, although she was still promoting her perfume.

'She's become a close friend of ours since she took up with Baron von Dincklage,' Julie said with a knowing smile. 'They spend most of their time together at the Ritz.'

The guests laughed. Chanel's love affair with Dincklage was an open secret and Claire had been appalled when she heard about it.

Then out of the blue, Hoffmann suggested that Eva might like to order a few clothes for Claire. The room fell silent.

'As Fräulein Bouchard has generously agreed to teach Oskar, I think it only fitting that she has a wardrobe befitting her new role.'

Everyone looked at her in stunned silence.

'That's most kind, sir, but I have clothes in Paris. Perhaps I can get them sent here.'

'Nonsense, I won't hear of it.' He turned to Eva and put his hand on hers. 'I think that's the least we can do, don't you, *liebling*?'

'*Ja, ja…*' Eva stammered in a soft voice. 'Of course.'

Julie was so appalled by this suggestion that she reminded him Eva already had a fine seamstress in the house.

'Julie, my dear, Claire risked her life to save Eva and Oskar. Have you forgotten that already?'

His terse reply put Julie back in her place. She sighed indignantly.

'Of course not. It's most generous of you to offer to do this for her.'

Not only had the offer of being outfitted by Paris' top couturiers shocked them, but also the fact that he had dropped the formality and was now calling her Claire. It had even shocked Claire herself.

After dinner, the guests assembled in the reception room where a pianist had been hired to play Chopin. Claire sat as far away from Julie as possible. The pure notes of a prelude sent shivers down her spine. She closed her eyes, savouring the sheer delight of the music. Memories of the last years spent nursing her mother flooded her thoughts. How Gerty had loved Chopin. A feeling of shame brought a flush to her cheeks.

'Are you all right, Fräulein?' asked Karl Wenk, who was sitting next to her. 'Perhaps you would like a little air?'

Claire thanked him for his concern. 'I'm afraid the music brings back memories of my mother. I used to play Chopin for her before she died. He was her favourite composer. And what about you, Herr Wenk, do you like him?'

'*Ja, ja, natürlich.*' He leaned over and added in a soft whisper, 'For a Pole, he is excellent.'

Chapter 15

The following day, Claire began her new role as Oskar's teacher. He was a charming and engaging child, polite and eager to please, and Claire felt a great affection for him. She watched him as he pored over his textbook, calling out the basic French verbs with ease, and complimented him by telling him he was a natural learner and a fine student.

'In no time at all, you will be speaking like a true Frenchman,' she said with a smile.

His face beamed with pride.

At lunchtime Giselle entered the room to say that Eva wished to see her.

Claire found her in the drawing room going over the menu with the housekeeper. As usual, Eva was immaculately dressed, this time wearing a simple, black crepe dress accentuated by the addition of a fine, red silk scarf tied around her neck in such a way that her initials, E.H., hand-embroidered into a goldwork monogram in one of the corners, shimmered in the light. It was so simple and so beautiful. Claire couldn't stop looking at it.

'Sit down, Claire,' Eva said when they were alone.

At first she wanted to find out how the day had gone with Oskar. Then she came to the reason why she had asked to see her.

'I will be leaving for Paris tomorrow. Jürgen and I have been having discussions and he suggested that I go with Julie and the Herr Doktor. I will arrange for my couturiers to have something made for you.'

'Look, Eva,' Claire interrupted. 'I've told you, I already have clothes in Paris. I will send for them immediately.'

'*Ja, ja,* but Jürgen has insisted.' Eva slipped one long leg under the other and sat back in the chair. 'The thing is, we had planned to go away together – the family, that is – and then on to Vienna and Berlin. Now it seems that's not possible and so I shall stay with Julie and Franz in Paris for a

181

short holiday. There is the matter of Oskar's education, you see. We cannot interrupt that. The previous teacher was German and so would have come with us. Jürgen has pointed out that as you are French, it would not be wise. A French lady accompanying us could be viewed unfavourably. I am sure you will understand this. When I mentioned it would be fine for the two of us to go alone and leave Oskar in your capable hands, he wouldn't hear of it.'

The news that Hoffmann would no longer go to Vienna and Berlin as planned filled Claire with a mixture of happiness and apprehension, and she couldn't help feeling that Eva now regretted agreeing to her becoming Oskar's tutor.

'Herr Hoffmann doesn't have to cancel his trip on my behalf. I know how much you were looking forward to going away with him and if I can have a word with him, persuade him perhaps that Oskar will be fine with me.'

Eva shrugged her shoulders. 'My dear, do not flatter yourself that you have the power to change my husband's mind. It's his important work that keeps him here. Besides, I could not possibly go to Vienna without my son. With the situation as it is, one never knows what could happen.'

Eva's remark was cutting, yet Claire also saw sadness born out of frustration on her face.

'I'm sorry. Please excuse my tongue. I shouldn't have said that. This is not your fault. I know my son is a good student and he will blossom under your tutelage, but Jürgen is right when he says we cannot interrupt that. It's just that – well, I had hoped we would be together for a while. I see so little of my husband as it is. I hate this war.'

She walked over to her writing desk and scooped up a pile of fashion magazines. 'Here, take these. In the morning before I leave, you can tell me which dresses you like.'

The following day, Eva left for Paris, and that night Hoffmann came to Claire's room at the Hôtel d'Armorique. Neither spoke a word: words were not necessary. When she woke in the morning, he was gone. She rubbed her face in the pillow where he had lain, breathing in the lingering scent of their night of sexual abandon.

Claire settled into her new role with absolute perfection: a teacher to Oskar during the day, and Hoffmann's lover by night. She soon discovered that the whole of the fourth floor of the Hôtel d'Armorique had been allocated to him. He had his own suite and offices overlooking the square and several rooms were reserved for important guests, in particular those from Paris or Berlin. Claire's own suite was located at the end of the corridor adjacent to Hoffmann's personal secretary, Erich Schneider, who spent much of his time working there rather than at Gestapo headquarters.

With Eva still away and Hoffmann at the Gestapo headquarters during the day, Claire set about exploring Villa Rosières. She had observed that an area near Oskar's room was always roped off and soon discovered that Eva and Hoffmann's private rooms were in that part of the house. Returning there after lunch one afternoon, she noticed the rope had not been put back. With no one around, she decided to take a look. Halfway along the corridor was a recess with a set of heavily carved doors flanked by a pair of art nouveau lamps.

As she reached to turn one of the handles she heard voices coming up the stairs and quickly flattened herself in the shadows of the recess. She soon recognised the voices as belonging to two of the maids who were bringing fresh linen to put in one of the bedrooms, and breathed a sigh of relief when they headed in the opposite direction. She turned the door handle, entered the room and quietly closed the door behind her.

A quick glance and the lingering scent of floral perfume told her this was Eva's bedroom. Her toiletries covered the dressing table and an array of framed photographs took pride of place on the dressers and bedside tables – Eva alone in a sultry pose, Eva and Jürgen in front of a building decked with Nazi flags, Eva and Oskar when he was a baby. Claire's eyes fell on one photograph in particular – Eva with three other women. It was taken at the Berghof in Berchtesgaden. The women were all wearing *Tracht*. Standing next to her were Eva Braun, Annelies Ribbentrop and Margarete Speer, wife of Hitler's favourite architect, Albert Speer, and a close friend of Eva Braun.

To the right of the room was an adjoining door. It led to the other master bedroom – Hoffmann's. His uniform hung on a rail next to the wardrobe, under which had been placed a pair of highly polished boots. Like Eva's room, exquisite pieces of antique furniture filled the room, and on one side, facing the main door, was a gilt-embellished mahogany writing bureau. On it was a photograph of Oskar – the only photograph in the room – and several piles of paperwork including half a dozen manila folders stamped *GEHEIM* – secret. Claire quickly flicked through them. One of them caught her attention. Her heart pounding, she made a mental note of their contents – permits; reports from Vichy officials with a few scribbled notes in the margins; maps of Brittany's submarine bases, naval defences, rail and road networks; and another with a list of names divided into categories – *Subversive, Juden, Kommunisten*, etc. Most had been crossed with the words *Abgeschoben* and *Ausgeführt* – deported and executed.

Before she had the chance to look at the last two, she heard the maids' voices in the corridor. They entered Eva's room. One of them made a comment about the adjoining door being open. Claire quickly placed the folders back into position and ran to the main door, praying they wouldn't enter the room. The door was locked, but the key was still in the lock. She turned it and it gave a loud click. Thankfully the maids were still talking and didn't hear it. The door opened into the corridor next to Eva's room and she saw that the maids had left the door wide open. She could hear them talking as they cleaned the room. She waited a few seconds until the coast was clear and headed back to her room. At that moment, Frau Heller appeared at the top of the stairs. She looked surprised to see Claire.

'Fräulein Bouchard, *Kann ich Ihnen helfen? Can* I help you?' she asked. 'This area is out of bounds. *Verboten!*' She stressed the word.

'I was looking for Oskar. It's almost time for his afternoon lesson. I can't find him anywhere. Have you seen him, by any chance?'

Her eyes narrowed. '*Nein*, Fräulein. Perhaps you will find him playing in the garden.'

Claire thanked her and gave her one of warmest smiles. 'Thank you so much.'

Frau Heller's eyes followed her down the staircase and then she turned and put the rope back into place.

Before going to Rennes Henri had given Claire strict instructions that she was to report to him within the first few days to put their minds at rest that all was going to plan. It had been decided that she would not meet him near the hotel as she was sure to be under close surveillance, at least for the first few weeks. It was not only by the Gestapo, who would be keeping a close eye on her, but the French also, and for any Frenchman unaware of her mission she would be viewed as a collaborator, and probably the worst kind of all: a *collaboratrice horizontale*. In the end they decided it was better if she could find an excuse to leave the house, and that was easier said than done as she was convinced everyone there also had her under surveillance. Henri rarely let his feelings show; he had that stiff way about him that Claire had come to associate with the English. But she knew that if she left it much longer he would be worried and might try to contact her and that could put them both in danger. She decided to meet him the following day after

Oskar's morning lessons were over.

During lunchtime she made her way to the gate when one of the guards called out, 'Halt', and asked her where she was going.

'I'm going for a short walk.'

The guard told her it was *verboten*.

Claire was outraged. 'What do you mean, *verboten*? You have made a mistake. I am not a prisoner here. I am the teacher and free to come and go as I like.'

The guard stood his ground and was soon joined by another, who wanted to see what the fuss was about.

'We are only obeying orders,' he told her.

'Get Herr Hoffmann on the phone, please,' she ordered angrily. 'He will confirm this.'

When the guards told her that was not possible, she marched back into the house. The first person she saw was the butler.

'I need to speak with Herr Hoffmann immediately. Can you give me his number?'

The butler solemnly told her that under no circumstances were the household staff to call him. 'It's *verboten*,' he added.

Claire was in a dilemma. Then she remembered Frau Heller. As Oskar's nanny, she was bound to be able to contact him. She rushed up the staircase to her room, which was across the hallway from Oskar's, and knocked on the door.

Frau Heller did not look too pleased see her.

'Please, Frau Heller, can you help me? I need to speak to Herr Hoffmann. Do you have his number?'

Frau Heller's back stiffened. The look on her face told Claire she relished the thought of being privy to something Claire wasn't.

'I am afraid that Herr Hoffmann does not like to be interrupted at work unless it is an emergency – which is not the case.'

'Fine!' Claire exclaimed. 'Then you leave me with no other option.'

She rushed over to Oskar's room in the hope that he would have his father's number in case of an emergency. Frau Heller came after her, angrily telling her that she must not interrupt his afternoon sleep. The commotion woke him up. Claire ran over and sat on the side of his bed.

'Oskar, tell me, do you have Papa's telephone number at work? I need to talk to him.'

Frau Heller protested but Claire took no notice. Oskar rubbed his eyes and then gave her a piece of paper with the number written on it.

'Thank you, Oskar. You are a good boy.' She gave him a peck on his forehead and tucked him back under the sheets. 'Go back to sleep. We'll continue our lessons in a few hours.'

Claire walked past the indignant Frau Heller, almost knocking her out of the way. Downstairs she found the butler and Giselle talking in low voices. She asked to use the telephone and Giselle directed her to the reception room. When she was alone, she dialled the number. It went straight to Hoffmann's desk at Gestapo headquarters. When he heard her voice there was a few seconds of silence.

'Fräulein Bouchard, is everything all right? Oskar…is he…?'

Claire noted his formality. 'Herr Hoffmann, Oskar is fine. It is not about him. May I remind you that when I took this position I was told that I was free to come and go as I please? Today I tried to go for a walk and was told that I am forbidden to leave the grounds. Now I feel like a prisoner. This is unacceptable.'

He apologised, telling her that he would speak to the guards immediately. A click on the other end of the phone told her that the conversation was finished. She picked up her bag and went back into the hallway. The butler and Giselle looked at her without saying a word. She walked out of the house and back down to the gatehouse. When she got there one of the guards was talking on the telephone. After he put down the receiver, he stepped outside and opened the side gate.

'*Enschuldigen*, Fräulein Bouchard,' he said apologetically. 'I had my orders.'

It took Claire a full fifteen minutes to make her way through the park to a small square on the outskirts of Rennes, where several cafes were still doing a brisk business. She had been particularly cautious to meander through the gardens at a leisurely pace just in case someone was following her.

Cafe Martine, with its red awning and small marble-topped tables that reminded her of Paris, stood in the centre. She sat inside and took a seat near the window. A young woman came over to serve her. Claire asked for a particular wine; a code she had been told to use. The woman scribbled something on her pad and went out to the back. Moments later, Henri appeared and sat down with her.

'I was beginning to wonder what had happened to you,' he said with a smile. 'You had me worried. Is everything all right?'

The waitress brought them glasses of Calvados, which Claire drank in one gulp. Without waiting to be asked, the woman poured her another and left the bottle on the table.

'Nothing that I can't handle,' she replied, a little too confident for Henri's liking.

'Do you have anything for me?' he asked.

She told him about the visitors from Germany – Wenk, Julie and Franz Zeidler – and about Julie taking an instant dislike to her, and about Eva leaving for Paris for a while.

'Well, at least you will have him to yourself.' Henri smiled.

'Eva's very disappointed. She puts on a brave face. I feel sorry for her.'

'Don't,' Henri snapped. 'She's German and will defend her husband to the last. Don't let her apparent naiveté deceive you.' He lit two cigarettes and offered her one. She took a long drag and another sip of Calvados and told him about the folders on Hoffmann's desk, but that she had been interrupted before she could see them all. She gave him as much information as she could, but without writing it down there was simply too much to remember it all.

'Can you get me a small camera?' she asked.

'Leave it to me.'

'How soon can you get it?'

'Go to Mass at the cathedral. You'll get it there, but it won't be me who will meet you. Then meet me here on Tuesday at the same time. It doesn't give you long but we have to act as soon as possible.'

'And what if something goes wrong?'

Henri raised his eyebrows. 'For all our sakes, especially your own, you'd better pray it doesn't.'

He stood up, paid the waitress and left. She watched him until he disappeared around a corner and then returned to Villa Rosières.

That night, Hoffmann came to her room again, but instead of coming to her bed, he sat in the chair opposite her in the shadows, staring at her, reminding her of that night in Paris when he had asked her to take off her clothes. Except that this time the look on his face told her all was not well.

She sat up, naked, a cold chill running down her spine. 'What's wrong?'

After a few minutes he called her over. 'Come here,' he ordered.

His mood frightened her, and her thoughts turned to her gun. It was back in the suitcase. Earlier in the day, she had reminded herself that she must keep it nearby at all times, especially after the suspicious look Frau Heller had given her. Yet there were other innocuous-looking weapons secreted around the place which she could use, should the occasion occur:

the blade in the sole of her heel and the pen that doubled as a dagger, to name just two items. Now they were on the opposite side of the room.

Nervously she did as she was told. He indicated for her to kneel in front of him. Her knees sank into the carpet. He leaned forward to run his hand through her hair. His breath smelt of alcohol. She closed her eyes in readiness for him to kiss her, but instead he grabbed her hair and pulled it back, forcing her body to arch in a painful curve. She screamed in pain, trying to tear his hand away. Then with one almighty push, he shoved her to the ground. She tried to make her way back to the bed but he yanked her body around to face him.

'Let me go,' she cried out, tears stinging her eyes.

'You would never deceive me would you, Claire?' he asked in a soft voice.

'Why do you ask such a question? Can't you see I love you?' she cried, hammering at his chest wildly. 'Remember it was *you* who deceived me. Do you think I would willingly come back to someone who had deceived me in the first place – or make love to another woman's husband, hidden away like a kept woman, if I didn't love you? Answer me that. Do you?'

Shaking with fear and anger, she tried to get up and walk away, but he stopped her, pushed her onto the floor and began to undress. His face mellowed and she could see he was hard with desire. She reached up and deftly unbuttoned his trousers whilst at the same time covering him in kisses. Her sharp words had the desired effect and his foul mood changed back to the caring lover once more. Within minutes he was naked beside her, rolling her over the carpet and releasing all of his anguish and pain into her body as if possessed. Afterwards they lay together, wrapped in each other's arms.

'I'm sorry,' he said. 'I've had a very bad day and you are the last person I should take it out on.'

Claire looked at his face for a long time, stroking it gently with her fingertips as if he were a child, and at the same time trying bravely to fight back the tears. Deep down she knew this affair could not go on for much longer, but she also knew that whatever happened in this dangerous game she was playing, she would love him no matter what. She reached over, pulled the sheet from her bed and covered them both.

Throughout the next morning, Claire could not get Hoffmann's mood out of her mind. In the clear light of day, she wondered if he really did have suspicions about her. And if he did, then she knew what he was capable of.

Henri had warned her. 'A man like Hoffmann doesn't get to be where he is without being ruthless,' he had said. 'Don't let your guard down.'

At the weekend Hoffmann left Rennes for a few days. Claire had no idea where he was going and she didn't ask. Neither mentioned his angry mood again — it was if it hadn't happened. But he did warn her about venturing too far without an escort. Whether innocent or not, Claire was all too aware of what was happening to French women who were suspected of fraternising with the enemy. In order to appease him, she said she would go to Mass on Sunday by car.

Chapter 16

On Sunday Claire donned her green suit and cream fedora and left for the evening Mass at Rennes Cathedral. The chauffeur dropped her off at Place des Lices and parked the car nearby. Soldiers carrying machine guns were everywhere, patrolling the street and conducting random searches on the local parishioners.

As instructed, she sat on the far side of a row of chairs next to the pulpit. After a few minutes, a woman emerged from behind one of the stone pillars and sat down next to her. She knelt on the stool in front of her to pray. Claire had no idea who she was but after she had finished her prayers, she got up and left, leaving a black embossed prayer book, small enough to fit into her handbag, on the floor. Claire quickly picked it up, opened it and silently mouthed a prayer as if reading from it. The inside had been hollowed out and in the cavity was a small camera and a roll of microfilm.

She had less than forty-eight hours to accomplish her mission and get back into Hoffmann's room and photograph the documents, but the task was not going to be easy as the unpleasant Frau Heller watched her like a hawk, waiting for any opportunity to report her to Hoffmann.

Fortunately the following day was Frau Heller's day off and she was in Rennes. When the coast was clear Claire made her way back to Hoffmann's bedroom the same way as she had before – through Eva's room. She headed straight for the writing bureau only to find nothing there. The paperwork had gone. Frantically she searched the room but to no avail: the folders had completely disappeared. She wondered if he might have taken them away with him, or whether he had taken them to Gestapo headquarters. If it was the latter, then she had lost her chance of ever seeing them again. She was in a dilemma, and time was running out. Then it occurred to her that there was another place he could have left them – his suite at the Hôtel d'Armorique.

The Hôtel d'Armorique had become an extension of Gestapo headquarters and those rooms not reserved as guest bedrooms were now being used as offices. Claire noted that Hoffmann's secretary Erich Schneider divided his time between both buildings. He was an affable person, young, blond and good-looking, and like most of the young men in the hotel, athletically built, the result of years devoted to sport in the name of the Fatherland – the heroic Aryan male just as Eva was the perfect Aryan wife. Schneider was always on hand to see if she needed anything but she had purposely avoided having anything to do with anyone at the hotel in case anyone suspected her affiliation with Hoffmann was more than a business arrangement. Perhaps that had been a mistake. She needed him now to gain access to Hoffmann's suite.

When she returned to her room, she saw his door ajar. He was engrossed in his work and failed to notice her. She knocked on his door and he looked up, surprised to see her standing there.

'Fräulein Bouchard, is everything all right?'

'Fine. I've had a busy day and I thought I'd have a nightcap before I retire for the night. Would you like to join me?' she asked.

'That's very kind of you but I must finish my work before Herr Hoffmann returns tomorrow.'

Claire apologised for interrupting him and turned to go to her room. Schneider put down his pen and called her back.

'All right,' he answered. 'I could do with a break anyway.'

Claire arranged for a chilled bottle of schnapps, two glasses and a platter of sandwiches to be brought up to her room. When they arrived she emptied a sleeping draught, which she'd kept hidden in the lining of her suitcase, into one of the glasses and filled it with schnapps.

Schneider looked pleased when she handed it to him.

'Ham sandwiches,' she said, pushing the plate towards him, 'and a few gherkins to go with it. It will remind you of home.'

Schneider lifted his glass and toasted her health. '*Prosit!* To the Fatherland,' he said, drinking it in one gulp.

'*Prosit!*' she replied.

Claire passed a full ten minutes with him in idle conversation until she was sure the sleeping draught was beginning to have an effect, then she bid him goodnight and retired to her room, leaving the door ajar, and lay on her bed and waited.

After a while she checked on him. He was snoring loudly and his head lay slumped on the table, barely visible over the typewriter. She quickly cast her eyes over the piles of paperwork on the desk for the key, but it was not there. Then she noticed a bulge in his right-hand trouser pocket and carefully pulled out a large bunch of keys. Schneider suddenly groaned and shifted his head in an effort to make himself more comfortable. She jumped back in fright, but he was still asleep.

Cautiously, she made her way down the corridor to Hoffmann's suite. It seemed to take forever to find the right key but eventually her patience was rewarded. She pulled out her torch, thankfully a necessity now placed in each guest room due to the frequent black-outs, and shone it around the room. Vast amounts of paperwork lay strewn everywhere. She had always wondered why he never invited her here, why he came to her instead. Now she understood. This was not a place for entertaining guests of any persuasion. This was his private office, away from prying eyes – an extension of Gestapo headquarters without the distractions – and if she was caught here she was in no doubt about what would happen to her.

She began to search, thankful for the soft carpets underfoot that cushioned her steps. It didn't take long to locate the files; they were on a coffee table next to a half-empty bottle of cognac. She picked them up and took them over to the desk, switched on the desk-lamp and one by one, placed the papers in the shaft of light and started to film, making sure everything was placed back in the original order.

The minutes ticked away and she realised she'd been there at least ten minutes – far longer than expected. She must get a move on before someone noticed the secretary asleep at his desk. When she pulled out the last folder her heart skipped a beat. It was marked *Chevalier*. Inside were notes mentioning a man known as Agent 12658. Her eyes scanned the document and at the bottom of the first page she noticed a reference to a man called Pascal, who she quickly ascertained was the agent who had failed to show up in Redon. Reading further, it became clear that Pascal had been caught up in a raid and under torture, had 'turned'. The notes went on to say that several agents had been caught or shot upon landing on French soil. Those captured had been sent to Fresnes or Avenue Foch in Paris. At least ten had already been executed.

On the very last page, she felt a lump rise in her throat. Henri's name was there, along with that of Michel – the agent she had met in Redon. Thankfully there were no photographs with which to identify them. Her hands trembled as she photographed these last pages, but it was the last one that really shocked her. *Agent de liaison – Manon*. The name seared itself like a burnt image on her brain. Again, there was no photograph. She stuffed the camera back into her blouse, placed the files back on the coffee table and hurried out of the room.

The secretary was still asleep, his head leaning on his SS armband. She placed the keys on the floor next to his chair and returned to her room, mulling over the events of the past few months: every agent, every safe house, each drop and who had been there. Now she knew why Henri had been so angry when Pascal failed to show up at the meeting at Redon. Most of all, she wondered how long it would take for Hoffmann to put two and two together.

At about three in the morning she heard the low drone of aircraft. She knew that sound by heart – a bombing raid. She jumped out of bed and peeked through the blackout curtains. The air-raid sirens sounded as wave after wave of bombers heading inland and the lights of tracer bullets streaked the sky. The drone became louder and closer, turning into a deafening roar. Voices called out in the corridor and someone banged her door. Suddenly there was an almighty crash and the hotel shook.

'Raus! Outside, Fräulein, quickly!' The noise had woken the secretary from his deep sleep.

Claire quickly removed the film from the camera, stuffed it in her skirt pocket and put the camera back in the prayer book under a magazine.

The corridor was swarming with SS officials making their way to the stairway rather than taking the lift, which was no longer operating. Some carried boxes of important documents whilst others, clearly caught in the act of lovemaking, rushed out of their rooms with their girlfriends still buttoning up their clothes. The secretary pushed Claire down the stairs towards the garden where the makeshift air-raid shelter was already filling to capacity. Claire's thoughts were for Oskar – he was terrified of air raids and they brought on his epileptic seizures.

After the raid passed over they headed back into the hotel. Claire tried to call Villa Rosières but the lines were down. She pleaded with Schneider to take her there in case anything had happened to Oskar. Knowing the boy was his superior's son, he acted quickly.

Outside, the damage was clear. The heavily-sandbagged Hôtel d'Armorique had hardly suffered – just a few loose tiles and broken windows – but at the far end of the square another hotel and ministerial building had taken a direct hit. Smoke billowed from the ruins and the dead and wounded were being transported to waiting trucks and ambulances.

Because of extensive damage, the drive to Villa Rosières took longer than usual. The fire brigade was busy putting out fires and pulling people from the ruins. The debris of shattered lives lay everywhere – mangled furniture, glass, torn fabric, scattered paper and charred bodies in the throes of death. More than once they were forced to double back and find an alternative route and they were stopped several times before they finally arrived.

When they did, Claire got the shock of her life. A bomb had landed close to the perimeter wall, destroying a large section of it, and where the road had been there was now a massive crater. Centuries-old trees lay sprawled and broken across the road in the tangled mess of barbed wire that had topped the stone wall and spotlights flashed up and down the road, illuminating the soldiers, guards and dogs as they hurried to clear up the mess.

With the electricity down Villa Rosières was in almost total darkness and the servants were busily placing oil lamps and candles in the rooms. For once Frau Heller was pleased to see her.

'Fräulein, come quickly. It's *kleiner* Oskar. He's having another fit. *Gott im Himmel*, help us.'

Claire rushed upstairs to Oskar's room and was shocked to find him pinned down on the floor by Giselle and another maid to stop his little body jerking uncontrollably. One side of his face was cut and bleeding and foam bubbled out of his mouth.

Claire pushed the women aside, grabbed his pillow and crouched down beside him. 'Get me a towel and warm water,' she ordered, laying him on his side and undoing the top buttons of his pyjamas.

Within minutes, Giselle returned with a basin of water. Claire dipped the towel into it, wrung it out and gently placed it on Oskar's head. Her soothing touch and soft voice calmed him down. She held him in her arms, pressing the warm towel on his forehead, his cheeks and his chest. His eyes stared listlessly into space.

'How long did the fit last?' she asked.

Frau Heller couldn't be sure; the bomb dropping nearby had distracted them.

'Well, it was severe this time,' Claire replied. 'He could have died.' She chastised them all for holding him down. 'Never do that again. You will make it worse.'

She lifted his little body onto his bed and lay beside him, saying she would stay with him all night, just to be on the safe side.

When she woke up sometime just after dawn, Hoffmann was standing at the foot of the bed.

'*Mon Dieu!* You gave me a fright. How long have you been here?' Claire said.

'I just got back. Schneider told me what happened. Is Oskar all right?'

'I'm afraid it was bad this time. He hit his face on something when he fell.'

'Thank God you were here,' Hoffmann replied, squeezing her hand affectionately.

He'd just leaned over to kiss her when the door opened. Claire quickly pulled her hand away.

'I'll take over now, Fräulein Bouchard,' Frau Heller said, her eyes noting the fleeting movement of their hands.

Claire stood up. 'It might be best if we cancelled Oskar's lessons for today. He needs to rest.' She turned to Hoffmann. 'I'll get Schneider to take me back to the hotel.'

'Fine, but please join me for breakfast before you depart. I'll see to it that Giselle has the table set for two.'

He departed, leaving the two women alone. Claire bent over Oskar, kissed his forehead and walked out of the room. She had only gone a few steps when she remembered the roll of film. Instinctively, her hand reached into her skirt pocket to check on it. It wasn't there. Panic struck when it dawned on her that it must have slipped out when she was lying on the bed. She ran back into the bedroom. Frau Heller was on the other side of the room tying back the curtains.

'I think I may have dropped something,' Claire said, running her hand underneath the blanket.

'Is this what you were after?' said Frau Heller, her arm outstretched to reveal the roll of film in the palm of her hand.

Claire spun around. 'Ah, thank you,' she replied, walking towards her.

Frau Heller closed her hand tightly around it before Claire could take it. 'I wonder what Herr Hoffmann would have to say about this?' Her words were menacing.

'If you make trouble I will make sure you are sacked,' Claire threatened, lowering her voice. 'And you will never work again. Do you hear me?'

'I don't know what your game is, little French woman, but it will end badly for you. Mark my words.'

Claire snatched the film from her hand and left the room. Outside she took a deep breath to calm her frayed nerves. The woman was trouble. She had to go.

*

In the breakfast room she found Hoffmann opening a bottle of champagne.

'Isn't it a bit early for that?' Claire said.

He showed her the label: a vintage Dom Pérignon. 'It's never too early for the finer things in life.' He handed her a glass. 'And that includes you.'

The breakfast table had already been laid for two with an array of cold cuts of meat, eggs, cheese and bread, a veritable feast in a time of famine. He pulled out a chair for her.

'Is there any damage to the house?' Claire asked, opening a linen napkin and spreading it over her lap.

'Besides a few broken windows and damaged crockery, no. We were lucky.' He handed her the platter of meat. 'Thank you for what you did for Oskar, my darling. You saved him – again.'

'I know this is not what you want to hear,' she replied after a while. 'But you must consider sending him away, back to Germany – or Vienna. These bombings are only going to get worse. It's too risky for him here. He puts on a brave face but the fits get more frequent and worse each time.'

Hoffmann looked thoughtful, but said nothing.

'When is Eva returning?' Claire asked.

'At the weekend.'

'Then they must go away together. It's just a precaution, Jürgen.'

Hoffmann put down his knife and fork, wiped the corner of his mouth and reached for the champagne.

Claire continued. 'Italy has almost fallen, the Russians are forcing the Germans to retreat and Germany is being bombed around the clock. You *have* to consider it.'

He turned and looked her squarely in the face. 'How do you know all this?'

Clare realised she had said too much.

'I overheard conversations at the Hôtel d'Armorique. It's hardly a secret.'

'Defeat is something I cannot contemplate.'

She changed the subject. 'I missed you, you know. I was worried you might not return – from wherever it was you went to.' She leaned closer to him. 'I missed our lovemaking,' she whispered in his ear, 'and the smell of sex that lingers in my bed and on my body afterwards.'

'I will come to you this evening.' He smiled. 'Be ready.'

196

She acknowledged her agreement by brushing his cheek with her mouth.

*

Claire slid the magazine with the film inside it across the marble-topped table. Henri deftly pocketed it.

'What's wrong? You look as though you've seen a ghost.'

Her voice was barely audible. 'They know, Henri,' she said. 'About Chevalier – you, Michel…and me.'

He took a sip of ersatz coffee and stared out of the window, mulling over her words. When she told him what took place, how she'd had to get into Hoffmann's suite and what she'd uncovered, Henri wasn't at all surprised.

'It was only a matter of time, Marie-Elise. Leave it to me, we'll change all the safe houses and letterboxes immediately. At least my suspicions about Pascal were correct. Why couldn't he have simply taken his cyanide pill?' he said, disgusted at the thought that someone could betray their colleagues.

'This is serious, isn't it?' she said dolefully. 'Hoffmann's clever. It won't be long before he suspects me as well. Thank God he doesn't have any photographs. I'm also worried about Frau Heller. She found the film on the bed.'

Henri let out a long sigh. 'It's things like that that will get you killed – get us all killed. What is your true assessment of the situation with her? Do you really think she will talk?'

'Unfortunately, yes. Fortunately, Hoffmann is rarely there these days but she may well say something to Giselle or the butler. At the moment it's only her word against mine but as I am French it won't take much for them to doubt me.'

'If you want to walk away now, you have my backing. Say the word and we'll get you out of here immediately.'

'No. It's too late now. We have to see this through. It won't be long before the Allies make a move on France. They need us. The other information contained in the film is enough on its own to cause immense disruptions when we are eventually called upon to act, not to mention strategic positions for use in bombing raids.'

'When did you say Eva was coming home?'

'In a few days' time, and Frau Heller has Eva's ear. That's my main worry.'

Henri looked her squarely in the face. 'We have to get rid of her, you do understand this, don't you?'

Claire nodded. 'I can't do anything in the house. It's far too risky.'

'Does she ever leave Villa Rosières?'

'Yes. Sunday is her day off but she also goes to Rennes to have her hair done, usually on a Friday afternoon during Oskar's lessons. Then she meets a friend for afternoon tea.'

'What does she look like?'

Henri made a mental note of Claire's vivid description. He particularly wanted to know what type of handbag she carried.

'It's one of Eva's cast-offs: smoky-grey and made out of crocodile, I believe.'

'Good. I want you to find out where and when the next trip will be and leave a message with the man who runs the kiosk in the square near the Hôtel d'Armorique. Leave the rest to me.'

The cafe was beginning to fill. Two Germans sat at a table nearby with a couple of French girls. Until now Claire had always despised these women – horizontal collaborators. But was she really that much different to them? The thought sickened her.

'How's Yves?' she asked. 'Do you see much of him these days?'

Henri looked away. 'He's with the Chauvignons. The Germans have started their searches in the area again. Now I'll have to give him the disturbing news about Chevalier and Michel to add to his list of worries.'

'And Didier?'

'He moves about a lot these days. This week he's somewhere near the Sourisseaus', training some of the Maquisards.'

More Germans entered the cafe and Henri decided it was time to leave.

'We'll meet somewhere else next time. In the meantime, see what you can learn about Pascal. Perhaps they're keeping him somewhere out of Rennes. It may be where Hoffmann disappears to. I'll leave it to you to find this out.'

'I only hope we're not too late,' said Claire.

He didn't answer, but his look conveyed a deep sense of unease.

Hoffmann didn't come to her that night, nor the next, and neither did she see him at Villa Rosières. It troubled her greatly and she sought out Schneider in the bar later in the evening to see if he could shed light on his whereabouts. Music played in the background; the unforgettable, deep voice of Zarah Leander – Hitler and Goering's favourite singer. Night after night they played her songs. They reminded the men of Germany. Schneider looked grey and tired and was drinking heavily, and he was in no mood to talk except to say that a group of *miliciens* had ambushed some of their men, causing heavy casualties. Claire asked where this took place and he mumbled something about it being near a village outside Rennes. When he started to curse the French, Claire decided not to pry further and left. She would just have to have patience.

In the meantime she did manage to find out that Frau Heller was going into Rennes on the following Friday to pick up a few things for Eva's return, and to get her hair done as usual. That same evening she followed Henri's instructions and headed for the kiosk under the pretence of buying a magazine and left a coded message with the man there. It was then that she noticed the poster.

WANTED FOR ESPIONAGE
A reward of 1,000,000 francs for information leading to the arrest of the woman known as 'Manon'

Claire felt sick to her stomach. Instead of going straight back to the hotel, she walked the streets of Rennes until it was almost curfew, checking the hundred of posters plastered on the walls. Their names were all there. It was official; she was now a hunted woman.

Back in her room, she tried to take her mind off the posters by running a long bath but even the sheer luxury of the warm, scented water could not ease her stress. The rest of Chevalier would also have seen them by now. None of them were safe. Autumn was drawing to a close and with it the prospect of a harsh, cold winter with little or no heating meant further misery and hardship for most of the French population. A million francs would lure someone to talk sooner or later.

Thankfully, there had been no mention of Marie-Elise – the name by which most members of the Resistance knew her. That alone told her it was another agent who had betrayed them and no other suspect than Pascal had been named in the file, but that didn't mean the Gestapo didn't have other files with other names. The number of airmen and agents either captured or missing had grown enormously over the summer months, as had the reprisals, and with each reprisal the Gestapo were more desperate, more bloody, and netting more innocent civilians than ever. The ranks of the Maquis swelled, meaning more places had to be found to hide them and more food, clothing and weapons were needed. The Resistance was chasing its tail.

Soaping her body with the soft sponge, she thought about Schneider's comments about the ambush outside of Rennes and wondered if it was anywhere near Saint-Etienne. Living at the Hôtel d'Armorique amongst the privileged few, of which she was one, had done nothing to dampen the affection she still held for the village and the friends she'd made there. Not a day went past when she didn't think of them and the hardships they must be enduring. In the hotel life went on as normal. If there were power cuts the hotel had its own generator; if there were food shortages elsewhere, here there was an overabundance; and while everyone else drank inferior wine, the hotel made sure its cellar was stocked with the finest. In the bar and lounge, where music played until the early hours of the morning, affairs of the heart continued to flourish. She wondered if any of these *liaisons d'amour* would outlast the war.

She thought of her own *liaison d'amour*. It could not last, but how it would end was not something she was ready to contemplate.

Her thoughts were interrupted by the sound of someone in the bedroom. She sat up and listened, her eyes fixed on the pistol hidden under a white hand towel. After a minute or so she heard music: Rosita Serrano, the Chilean nightingale. Along with Zarah Leander and Marika Rökk, she had been another German favourite until she was accused of giving money to Jews sometime during the year. Since then, people had stopped playing her records for fear of being hauled before the authorities. The fact that this music was playing could mean only one thing: Hoffmann had arrived. Only he would dare flaunt the ban on her music.

He opened the door and a faint smile crossed his face when he saw her lying there. He took off his jacket and started to undress, carefully folding his uniform over a chair. Claire watched his every move: the curves of his buttocks as he bent over, every sinew, every muscle, bronzed, taut and athletic. He was perfection itself – even with the fine scar across his cheek, which only enhanced his features.

'I've been worried about you,' Claire said, lying back in the water.

He didn't answer. Instead he sat on the edge of the bath, leaned over and took the sponge from her hands and began to soap her chest and breasts. She loved the absence of shame between them in their nakedness. It had been like that from the start. She closed her eyes, recalling the two weeks they had spent at the cottage by the sea in 1940. Every evening they had bathed together in the rustic tin bath in front of a log fire, pampering each other, washing each other's hair, and making love. After all that time his touch still remained the same.

He swivelled his body around to join her, pushing her legs apart to make room for him. The water lapped around her neck, occasionally splashing onto the tiled floor. She took the sponge back and began to soap him as he done her. When she reached his groin she felt him hard with desire. He pulled her towards him until her breasts swung against his chest, and at the same time he slid further into the water, forcing her to open her legs wider to accommodate him, pushing her onto him while they made love. In the heat of the moment, the tumultuous events of the past few days faded and for the moment she was his. Nothing else mattered.

Afterwards they sat in her room, listening to music and drinking a bottle of Château Lafite Rothschild. She sat on the carpet, leaning back against his knees and drying her hair.

'I've neglected you,' he said, running his finger in a circle at the nape of her neck. 'And I'm sorry. You know I can't talk about my work, suffice to say that we have intelligence on groups in the area who are working to undermine us: the FFI, the Maquis and London. We have intercepted messages and broken codes and at last have them firmly in our sights and intend to crush them – every man, woman and child. Foolishly, they underestimate us.'

'Is that what's taken you away?' she asked casually.

'Our raids are bearing fruit but we need to keep the insurgents out of reach until we've finished with them. The High Command in Berlin will not rest until every last traitor is dead. On top of this I am aware of competing interests in Berlin.'

This was the first time he had spoken about his work and she hung on every word.

'Take Wenk for instance – even Schellenberg. They've become so paranoid just lately that when you understand the depths of envy and malicious intrigue men like them are capable of descending into, you must watch your back. All of them want to ingratiate themselves with Himmler, and of course the Führer himself.'

He told her that when he went away it was to a place in the country where they could conduct their interrogations away from prying eyes.

Immediately Claire thought of the place she had been taken to the night she was kidnapped; yet from the little she had seen it bore no resemblance to a prison. She felt a deep urge to ask more but decided to tread slowly. The less she asked, the more he would tell her. It was the way he was. Instead she changed the subject.

'I was thinking I might take a trip back to Saint-Etienne at the weekend to visit Monsieur and Madame Chauvignon and see if there's anything they need for the school. Besides, I think you might be busy with Eva.'

He smiled and drew her to him, pulling the towel away from around her body. 'Fine, I'll have someone take you there.'

Chapter 17

At 2.30pm on Friday afternoon Claire was teaching Oskar in his room when she saw the car with Frau Heller in the back seat head towards the gate. She knew this would be the last time she would see her.

Half an hour later Frau Heller arrived at the hairdresser's in 2 Rue du Bassin and took her seat alongside other customers as usual. She was told her usual hairdresser was ill that day and another would see to her. The new hairdresser was a woman in her mid thirties, a seemingly chatty person with a warm smile who spoke a little German. Whilst she washed her hair, taking care to massage her scalp for several minutes, Frau Heller failed to notice another woman pick up her grey crocodile bag from the floor beside her chair and walk behind the counter with it. In less than a minute it was returned to the same place.

When she was ready to leave, Frau Heller picked up her bag and was about to open it until the hairdresser put her hand out to stop her.

'Not today, *gnädige Frau*. You are a loyal customer and this is on us.'

Outside, Frau Heller checked her watch and then started to walk down the street towards the cafe where she was to have afternoon tea with her friend. It was a short distance, but she would never make it.

It was Erich Schneider who told Claire what had happened later that evening at the Hôtel d'Armorique.

'I have some bad news for you, Fräulein Bouchard. Frau Heller was found dead in an alleyway not far from the Place des Lices.'

Although Claire knew something dreadful was going to happen to Frau Heller, she was not prepared for her reaction and instinctively covered her mouth with her hands. It had been one thing to kill the Germans when they rescued Jean-Claude and Michel but somehow this was different. She was complicit in the death of a woman she had come to know and whether she liked her or not, the family would be devastated.

'What happened?'

'Apparently she always took afternoon tea with her friend when she went into town. As you well know, Frau Heller was a stickler for punctuality and when she failed to show up, the friend made a few enquiries. It was then that someone reported finding a woman's body sprawled against a wall when he took a short cut through the alley. She had been shot through the head.'

'Was it a robbery gone wrong?' Claire asked. 'Did someone panic when they found out she was German?'

Schneider shrugged his shoulders. 'That doesn't appear to be the case. Her bag was still at the scene of the crime. The gendarmes alerted us straight away but it's what we found in the bag that has us puzzled.'

'What do you mean?'

We found propaganda leaflets in her bag, and a wad of notes – about fifty thousand francs to be exact.'

This time, Claire genuinely was shocked. 'Why would she carry propaganda? She doesn't speak French.'

'They were in German and obviously intended for us. Yet Frau Heller was not the sort of woman who would do anything against the Fatherland. It's quite out of character.'

'What does Herr Hoffmann have to say about this?'

'Naturally he is most upset, as will be Frau Hoffmann when she returns – they were quite close. He thinks it's a message of some sort and has vowed retribution. The problem is, this is not something he wants to get out. The contents of her bag make this a messy affair and Herr Hoffmann has more than enough on his plate at the moment without worrying about this. The High Command in Berlin is already putting pressure on him.'

Claire thanked him for letting her know.

'I believe you are going to Saint-Etienne tomorrow. Herr Hoffmann has asked me to take you. Is there anything you need?'

Claire asked him to wait while she wrote down a list of things; mostly foodstuffs which she knew the Chauvignons would welcome. Schneider clicked his heels together and raised his arm sharply in the Hitler salute.

'Gute Nacht, Fräulein. Schlafen Sie gut.'

Claire closed the bedroom door and stood for a few minutes with her back leaning against it, thinking about Frau Heller's death. It was the first time she had seen Henri eliminate someone, and she was impressed.

It had been almost two months since Claire had seen Antoine and Mireille and she got the shock of her life. In such a short time they looked much older. Antoine's grey hair had thinned to the point where he was now going bald and he had difficulty in walking due to severe arthritis. But it was Mireille who shocked her the most. Her skin was blotched and scabby, and like Antoine's, her hair had also thinned. She also complained of severe pains in the chest. Clearly the occupation was taking its toll. Even so, they were happy to see her.

Schneider put the basket of food on the table and told them he would be back the next day.

'This calls for a celebration,' Antoine said when they were alone. He reached in the cupboard for his last bottle of Calvados and three glasses while Mireille emptied the basket. Tears streaked her blotched complexion when she saw what Claire had brought. A large ham, sausages, cheese, a packet of real coffee, which she sniffed with utter delight, and a variety of tinned food. There was also a large apple strudel laced with walnuts and chocolate. It was a favourite at the Hôtel d'Armorique and Schneider had made sure they saved one for her.

'And something special for you both,' Claire added, handing them each a gift-wrapped package.

Mireille's hands shook as she untied the string, taking care not to tear the lovely wrapping paper. When her eyes fell on the three metres of apricot polyester, she crossed herself and gave thanks to God for Claire's goodness. For Antoine, Claire had secured ten packets of cigarettes and a pouch of tobacco.

'God bless you, Claire,' Antoine said, wiping away his tears with the back of his hand. 'I know what you're doing is not easy...'

He was so overcome with emotion he couldn't find the words.

Claire reached out and put a hand on his. 'I'm fine. You don't have to worry about me. Tell me, what's been happening here? How's the school? How are Gaspard and Angélique?'

'Didn't Henri tell you?'

'Tell me what?'

Antoine and Mireille looked at each other. 'There's been a lot of raids just lately. The Germans are on to something. A few nights ago, the village of Saint-Vincent was raided. They found two British airmen hiding. A skirmish occurred and they were shot trying to escape. The family who hid them were all shot. And Sebastian Levade, Angélique's boyfriend, is in hiding again. This time there's a price on his head.'

Claire felt sick to her stomach. Henri had purposely avoided telling her all this.

'This is terrible news,' she declared mournfully. 'Is she all right?'

'The Germans took her in for questioning but she said she hadn't seen him for a few months and had no idea where he was.'

'And does she?'

'We have hidden him in one of the farmsteads. She knows he's safe, that's all, but he's a headstrong fellow and has been warned to stay put or risk being killed by his own people if he attempts anything silly.

'There's something else. A couple of days ago Mayor Bourgoin and Father Gambert were taken away for questioning. The mayor was accused of giving favours to those who are thought to have spoken out about the government and Father Gambert is accused of subversive activities – trumped-up charges by the *milice* again. We have no idea where they are. Henri's sources say they are not at Gestapo headquarters in Rennes. We are wondering if it's the same place they took you, somewhere in the country.'

Claire thought of Hoffmann's remark about interrogations away from prying eyes but she thought better of saying something for fear of alarming them, especially Mireille. Mireille cut a slice of strudel and handed it to her. Her hands shook badly. She said she wanted to apologise for being cool with her before she left for Rennes.

'I'm sorry, Claire, I had no idea what was going on. When Antoine told me the move put your life in danger, I felt ashamed. Please forgive me.'

'It's alright. We thought it best at the time not to worry you. Anyway, tell me, did you manage to find another teacher?' Claire asked.

'We didn't look,' Antoine replied. 'We've managed alone so far. The room above Gaspard's is still yours.'

Claire asked if Hoffmann made good on his promise to look after the school as compensation for her leaving, and was pleased to hear that he had indeed been true to his word. Antoine told her that a man he had never met before called at the school and handed him an envelope with several thousand francs in it.

'We've put some aside for heating at least one classroom over the winter and the rest we've used helping those less fortunate.'

Their unselfishness touched her. They were both ill and some of that money should have gone on vitamins and medicines, but they were impossible to come by. She asked about Yves.

'He's here at the moment,' Mireille said. 'He's been at the Sourisseau farm for a few days. I think he'll be back tonight.'

Later in the evening Claire returned to Saint-Etienne. The trees had shed most of their leaves, which lay in thick, decomposing pools around their bases, filling the air with a faint odour of dampness, and the last rays

206

of sun cast a glorious warmth across the landscape, bathing the fields in a soft, wine-tinted glow. Breathing in the fresh country air, she realised how much she'd missed this little Breton village with its quaint charm and easy manner. It was a simple life and one she thought she'd never get used to after Paris, but the war had thrown them together and now here they were, all relying on each other for survival.

Walking through the quiet streets towards the square, Claire was confronted by the same posters she had seen in Rennes. Antoine had warned her about them but it still unnerved her to see them here, where she had thought she was safe. Henri's poster was also there, and this time a new one had been added too – for Sebastian Levade. Worse still, his photograph was on it. She knew Angélique would be beside herself with worry.

Gaspard was still in his garage when Claire arrived. He welcomed her like a long-lost daughter, telling her how dull life had become without seeing her cheery face at the end of the day.

'It's not the same here any more,' he lamented. 'People are afraid of their own shadows. I pray that I will live to see all this end soon because I don't know how much more we can take. I presume you've heard about the mayor and Father Gambert? They are suspected of helping the Resistance. If they slapped me around for a few cans of gasoline, I can only imagine what they must be doing to them.'

Like Antoine and Mireille, Gaspard had also lost weight, and had developed a nasty cough. He reached for his tobacco pouch to roll another cigarette.

'You should get that seen to,' Claire said. 'It sounds bad.'

He shrugged. 'One of the few pleasures left to me now.'

One look around the garage told Claire business was not going well.

'I've taken to repairing bicycles now,' he laughed. 'Those who still have a car can't get gasoline.'

He wanted to know about Rennes; how the people fared? Were they worse off than the villagers? Claire told him that everyone was suffering; perhaps more so in the towns where they had no access to farm produce.

'People queue from sunrise to midday but having a ration card doesn't mean you'll get something. People are at their wits' end.'

The one thing she desperately wanted to tell him, she couldn't: that the Allies were preparing to land.

Claire spent the rest of the evening in her old apartment, curled up in the old chair by the window reading a book and clutching a hot water bottle to her stomach. Over the past week, she had felt nauseous and no amount of rest or medicine had been able to quell it. Tonight was just one of those times. She thought about Eva, and was no longer sure of their friendship. Behind closed doors she and Hoffmann had managed to shut out the outside world. Cocooned in their desperate need for one another, they were living a lie that threatened to implode. The sensible Claire told her she should walk away; the honourable Claire told her she must serve her country and support her fellow countrymen to the very end; the romantic Claire told her she just wanted to be with him one more time.

Just before midnight she heard a noise at the window. Someone was throwing small stones. When she peered out from behind the blackout curtains she saw a figure huddled under the elm tree. It was Yves, and he gestured to her to let him in.

'You gave me a fright,' Claire said, holding open the door while he wheeled his bicycle into the darkened hallway. 'And you certainly are developing a habit of turning up unannounced.'

'I'm sorry. I only just heard you were here and I needed to speak with you. I thought it best not to telephone in case the line is bugged.'

He followed her upstairs to the apartment, took off his beret and laid it on the table along with his woollen scarf while she lit the stove to boil water for tea. He had grown a beard, which framed his dark complexion. It suited him, and she told him so.

When she placed the steaming hot drink on the table he grabbed her wrist.

'I've been worried about you.'

Claire pulled her arm away. 'I would have thought you'd be too preoccupied,' she replied curtly.

Her comment amused him. 'By that I presume you mean Kristina – the model?'

'Is that her name?'

'So you're still angry with me for not seeing you again?'

'Of course not,' she lied.

'I'd like to think that what we shared here that night was special, at least from my point of view,' he said.

'You have a funny way of showing it. You virtually ignored me.'

'We are at war. It's not good to get too attached. Life can be snuffed out in an instant.' He snapped his fingers as if to emphasise the point.

Claire pulled the chair out and sat at the table opposite him. 'Yes, that's what everyone keeps reminding me.'

She hated herself for being so hostile towards him when in reality she was pleased to see him. In some strange way his presence was reassuring. There was something intangible between them – perhaps not love, but a sense of closeness born out of admiration for each other.

He took a sip of his drink. 'I know you have an attachment to Hoffmann. Henri told me everything.'

'Everything?!'

'That you were lovers before the war began, and that he lied to you.'

His words stung. 'It wasn't quite that simple,' she answered uncomfortably. 'He was afraid to tell me he was German, and anyway, he was married. He could hardly tell me that, could he? It came to an abrupt end when the Germans marched in. It really doesn't matter how or why, the point is I'm here because London knew he was still alive and they are using me to get to him.'

'No one's forcing you. Henri gave you the chance to walk away. They could have given you another assignment.'

She looked at him. 'I'm not like you. I can't just ignore my feelings, turn them on and off like a tap.'

'Perhaps that's what attracts me to you: your single-minded attitude to the job in hand, persistently turning a blind eye to any risks.'

She folded her arms on the table and looked into his eyes. They understood more than she had given him credit for. 'I love him, Yves.'

He put his hand on hers. This time she didn't take it away. 'I know. And if the circumstances were different, I'd say he was a lucky man. I presume his wife doesn't know?'

'I don't think so. She's been away. The truth is, I don't know how much longer this will last. When the Allies land, what will happen then? A victory for us means he will face execution if caught.'

'You're a brave woman,' he said.

'Not really. It's the hand I was dealt, so I must get on with it. There will be enough time to reflect when it's all over.' She pushed her hair back and took a deep breath. 'Now, what was it that you wanted to talk to me about?'

'The place they took you to when you were kidnapped – you said you had no idea where it was.'

'That's right.'

He leaned forward as if about to disclose a great secret. 'I think I know where it is.'

Claire sat up straight. 'Where?'

'A manor house on the coast, about thirty kilometres past the Sourisseau farm.'

'How did you find this out?'

'Some of the Maquis noticed an unusual amount of activity in the area – trucks carrying what looked like prisoners, and Reich cars – important ones like Hoffmann's. The house is set on a large estate surrounded by farmland and woods. It belongs to a Viscount de Lefebvre. His wife Martha's family are Hungarian – old school and pro-Nazi. The viscount now lives in Paris and hasn't been there for a while. Over the past few months the property was rumoured to have been taken over by the Gestapo. The gamekeeper keeps the Maquis supplied with the odd rabbit, and it was he who alerted them.'

Claire had never told anyone what she saw from the window, but it did sound remarkably like the same place. She reached over to the bookcase and pulled out the map.

'Can you point it out?' she asked, smoothing out the map.

When Yves put his finger on a particular spot, Claire's heart raced.

'You've gone pale,' he said. 'Do you recognise the place?'

Claire nodded. It was all starting to fall in place. 'It's near the cottage where we spent two weeks in 1940 and where Marcel – I mean Hoffmann – disappeared, presumed drowned. And now that you mention it, I do recall there being a manor somewhere in the area but I never saw it.'

Claire stared at the map for a while, the enormity of his words still sinking in.

'The cottage is somewhere here,' she said, pointing to a turn-off along the coastal road. 'So the manor must be here.' She slid her finger along the paper. 'He used to go for long walks in the morning. At the time I never bothered to ask where he went, but I've since learnt that he visited other agents. If what you say about the family is true, then they must have been complicit in his disappearance. And I do know that the Gestapo is carrying out their dirty business away from prying eyes. Both Hoffmann and Schneider told me.'

Yves folded the map up and put it back on the bookshelf. 'There's something else. When Father Gambert and Mayor Bourgoin were taken away they were last seen heading in the direction of the coast, not Rennes as we would have expected. I don't know of any other place they could have gone to except the manor.'

'Does Henri know about all this?' she asked.

'Yes. He's with Didier at the Sourisseau farm. He's teaching one of my men how to play the piano.'

She laughed. Didier was an expert pianist and none of the men he had taught had been caught so far. In over a year, that was an impressive achievement.

'What happens now? How can we find out for sure what's going on there?'

'I've issued a few photographs to the Maquis. Most already know of Hoffmann even if they've never actually seen what he looks like, but there might be another man with him who I believe you've met. Karl Wenk.'

Claire looked shocked. 'Wenk?! I thought he'd gone back to Berlin?'

'It appears not. He may be the mastermind behind what's going on there. Berlin wants to stamp out the Resistance at all costs. He's their man here, sent directly by Himmler.'

Claire shook her head in disbelief.

'Where is Hoffmann now?' Yves asked.

'At Villa Rosières, I would think. Eva returns this weekend. And then there's the messy business of Frau Heller. Everyone is bound to be deeply affected. I don't believe he would leave them all until after the funeral.'

His eyes focused intently on her. 'I've proposed to Henri that we try and get you out of there. Villa Rosières has become far too dangerous now.'

He waited for her reaction but she seemed to take it in her stride. She had expected this. Yet as he placed his beret on and picked up his scarf in readiness to leave he was well aware that she had her breaking point, and that it would be reached sooner rather than later.

Chapter 18

The moment Claire arrived back at the Hôtel d'Armorique, the manager called her over to say she had a visitor. When she enquired who it was he looked embarrassed.

'Frau Hoffmann,' he replied, rather sheepishly. 'I'm afraid she insisted on waiting for you in your room.'

He shrugged his shoulders as if to say there was nothing he could do to stop her.

Eva was sitting on the couch in the sitting room looking through some of the gramophone records when Claire entered her room. She didn't get up and neither did she apologise for being there.

'You have excellent taste in music,' she remarked, setting the records down on the coffee table next to a newly opened bottle of Bordeaux and a half-empty glass. 'You didn't tell me you like German songs.'

Claire ignored the remark. 'How are you, Eva? You look wonderful. Paris agrees with you.'

'I had a wonderful time. I only wish Jürgen could have been transferred there instead of here.' She gestured towards the bedroom. 'I have taken the liberty of laying out your new wardrobe. I hope you approve.'

Claire pushed the door ajar and saw an array of clothes neatly arranged on the bed. 'Oh, Eva, I don't know what to say. They are beautiful.' She picked up an emerald-green, rayon crêpe, calf-length cocktail dress and held it up against her body. 'It's simply wonderful. I've never had anything so beautiful.'

She noticed another peeking out from a mound of tissue paper – an evening ensemble consisting of a jacket and skirt. The straight, full-length skirt was made of heavy crêpe, but it was the short, cap-sleeved jacket that took her breath away. It was made of black velvet and encrusted with gold braid ribbon in a lattice pattern over the entire surface, with added buttons, cabochons, beads, etc.

'I hope they fit. Monsieur Lelong assured me that they would,' Eva said, watching Claire's reaction. 'And I took the liberty of getting you another suit.' She pointed to a light brown tweed outfit with a claret velvet collar and cuffs laid out over the chair. 'I think the one you wear when you come to teach Oskar is rather too severe for you. Anyway, the sleeve has a tear in it. My seamstress will fix it for you.'

At the mention of the tear, Claire's heart missed a beat. She had tried to fix the sleeve herself after it had torn on the night of the first drop. She had thought she'd done a good job considering that part of the fabric was missing, but to Eva's eagle eye, that was obviously not the case.

They returned to the sitting room. Eva had another surprise for her. She opened her bag and took out a small package. Inside was a copy of Eva's favourite red silk scarf.

'I noticed how you admired mine and found a similar one. I had one of Monsieur Lelong's embroiderers monogram your initials on it in goldwork as is my own.'

Claire picked it up and held it to her cheek. It was soft and delicate and the embroidery was exquisite.

'I am touched by your generosity. How can I ever repay your kindness?'

'Red suits you,' Eva replied with a half-smile that seemed slightly mocking. 'And it matches your lipstick perfectly.'

She sat back on the couch, her long legs crossed to the side. With her platinum-blonde hair swept back into her favourite snood, she looked incredibly beautiful. She was stylish, and under normal circumstances, self-assured, yet something about her had changed.

'So you've heard about what happened to Frau Heller,' she said.

Claire took a seat opposite and poured herself a glass of wine. 'I still can't believe it. Have they found out who did it yet?'

Eva tried to fight back the tears. 'I don't think they will. Do you?'

Claire nodded. 'Herr Hoffmann will try, I am sure.'

'I feel responsible. It was me who persuaded her to come here with us. Her family was against it.' She paused for a moment. 'But that's not the reason I came here tonight.'

Claire held her breath, wondering what she was about to hear.

'I was wondering if you knew where my husband was?'

Claire looked stunned. 'I thought he was at Villa Rosières. He was looking forward to welcoming you home.'

'He was not there when I arrived and I haven't seen him all weekend. I've asked everyone else but no one will tell me anything. That's why I came here. I know Jürgen sees you as…a close confidante.'

Eva paused before using the words 'close confidante'. It made Claire feel uneasy.

'I'm sorry, I have no idea. I've been in Saint-Etienne.'

'I see,' Eva replied coolly. 'Then I must simply wait for him to return.'

Claire felt extremely uncomfortable. The air was thick and Eva changed the conversation to Oskar's French lessons and his recent epileptic fit.

'We are indebted to you. That's twice you have saved his life.'

'Should it happen again, the household is better equipped to deal with the situation,' Claire replied.

'Tell me, as a friend – do you believe Germany is losing the war?'

Claire was careful with her words. 'You have seen how the air raids are intensifying. The British and Americans are relentless, the German Army has lost the fight with Russia, North Africa is lost and so is Italy. In adversity we have become friends but the fact remains that I am still French and you are German. For the moment the most important thing is to survive.'

'Julie has gone back to Germany,' Eva said. 'She wanted me to go with her but I refused. I thought my place was here with my family but now I'm not so sure. Frau Heller's murder has made me rethink. I believe the French will not be happy until we are all dead. I am not afraid for myself. I will die for the Fatherland by my husband's side, but my son…I cannot allow that.'

'That is a matter for your good selves. I cannot comment on that, but I can say that the constant bombings are not good for Oskar's health.'

Eva departed shortly after, leaving Claire to wonder what had happened to Hoffmann. He did not come to her that night, and it would be another few days before he was back in Rennes. In the meantime, Claire's nausea intensified, causing her to take to her bed and miss her weekly rendezvous with Henri.

Claire was just about to leave Villa Rosières when Hoffmann returned home. Wenk was with him.

'Ahhh, the charming Fräulein Bouchard. How are you? Herr Hoffmann tells me you are an excellent teacher.'

'I have a fine student.' She smiled.

Eva came out of the drawing room to greet them. It had been a few weeks since she and Hoffmann had seen each other and she threw her arms around his neck and kissed his cheek. He did not reciprocate her warmth, and Eva looked hurt.

Filled with embarrassment for Eva, Claire bid them all goodbye and made her way to the door, but no sooner had she stepped outside than another bout of nausea and a sharp pain in her abdomen caused her to double over. Before anyone could reach her she collapsed on the steps in a crumpled heap.

When she came to she found herself lying on the couch in the drawing room, disoriented and her vision out of focus. The jumbled voices and images of people standing nearby swirled in and out of her mind as though in a dream. After a while the fog cleared. Eva saw her try to sit up and came over.

'You gave us a nasty fright. You could have hurt yourself. Take it easy for a while, Jürgen has called the doctor.'

She fussed over her, tucked a rug back over her that had slipped onto the floor, and handed her a glass of water.

Claire took a sip and apologised for being such a nuisance. 'I really don't know what came over me. I must have eaten something that disagreed with me.'

Hoffmann entered the room with the doctor. After giving the Hitler salute to Wenk, the doctor pulled up a chair and sat down next to Claire.

'Now, young lady,' he said, opening his black bag, 'let's see if we can't get to the bottom of this.'

Judging by his accent, the doctor was a Czech German, a man in his late fifties who sported a greying goatee and a thin moustache. After taking Claire's pulse and temperature he shone a small torch in her eyes.

'Has this happened before?' he asked matter-of-factly.

'No. This is the first time,' she lied. 'I'm sure it's nothing to worry about.'

He helped her sit up and leaned her forward, tapping his fingers on her back. After putting his instruments away, he handed her his card.

'You will be fine to go home now but I would like to see you tomorrow in my surgery. I will give you a thorough examination, just to be on the safe side. Let's say around midday.'

The following day, Claire did as she was told and visited his rooms a short walk away from the Hôtel d'Armorique. His nurse ushered her straight through.

'Go behind the screen, Fräulein, take off your clothes,' he ordered, 'and lie on the bed.'

She heard the flicking sound of his rubber gloves and felt a deep sense of unease.

When he appeared he laid a hand gently on her abdomen and looked her squarely in the face. 'I think you know why we're doing this, don't you, Fräulein Bouchard? When did you last menstruate?'

Claire could not find the words to answer him, and the doctor proceeded with his examination. After what seemed like an intense invasion of her body, he tore off his rubber gloves and stepped back behind the screen.

Claire's hands trembled as she put her clothes back on. The moment had come that she had dreaded for several weeks.

The doctor took off his wire-rimmed glasses, placed them on the table and swivelled his chair towards her, his hands folded together in his lap. Like others, he had heard rumours of an affair between Hoffmann and his son's French teacher but decided it was better not to mention anything. 'You are with child, my dear,' he said. 'By my reckoning you must be at least a month – possibly more.'

Ever since the first bout of sickness, Claire had thought she might be pregnant and had watched for signs, checking her breasts for the slightest swelling or soreness. There had been blood but not the usual amount, giving her cause to think it may have something to do with the enormous stress she was under. But it was the last time she and Hoffmann had made love that she really knew the truth. It was as if her nipples were on fire, and she had cried out when Hoffmann caressed them, albeit gently.

'I thought you might have been when I saw you last night but as I see you are not wearing a wedding ring I thought it best to be discreet,' the doctor continued.

'I appreciate that, and would be most grateful if we kept this to ourselves. It might put my teaching post with the Hoffmanns in jeopardy. I'm sure you understand.'

The doctor assured her that her secret was safe but advised her to discuss her predicament with her 'fiancé' before it showed. Was he also telling her he would be willing to give her an abortion? She couldn't be sure.

Claire left the surgery in a daze. Eva had given her the day off but she certainly didn't want to go back to the Hôtel d'Armorique. She couldn't get the doctor's words out of her mind – 'a month – possibly more'. She walked the streets for a while to clear her head and found herself in the seedier area of Rennes – in Yves' street. The place was buzzing with daily activity: women hanging out their washing on lines strewn up across stairways and out of windows, children playing noisily in the streets and dogs curling up in darkened doorways. Here and there the smell of fried food wafted from a window, and someone could be heard screaming abuse at someone else who didn't bother to answer. She wondered why on earth Yves chose to live in this neighbourhood, but then she remembered that the Germans avoided squalor for fear of catching a disease.

She climbed the staircase, which had been freshly scrubbed, and knocked on his door. Claire was the last person he expected to see. He pulled her inside quickly and peered down the corridor.

'It's okay,' she said. 'I'm not being followed.'

The apartment smelt of turpentine and paint. He had been working on a painting and Claire took a quick look. It was not the same red-haired model. This one had dark curly hair, but was just as attractive.

'*Mon Dieu*, Marie-Elise! What's happened? You look terrible.' He hastily threw a paint-splattered shirt on and sat down next to her. 'Shall I call Henri?'

Claire shook her head from side to side. 'I'm afraid Henri can't help me with this one,' she said with a thin smile. 'I've just learnt I'm pregnant.'

Yves let out a long whistle. For once he was speechless.

'I need a strong drink?' Claire said. 'Something to steady my nerves?'

He pulled out a bottle of Calvados and poured her a tumbler full, which she savoured with relish. Both sat in silence for a while, neither knowing what to say. In the end, Yves asked her how far gone she was. When she said perhaps just over a month, it was difficult to say, his mind raced back to the night she had been kidnapped. He thought it might have been a result of being tortured and raped until Claire told him it was definitely Hoffmann's. He asked if she planned to keep it.

'I can't decide.'

Yves looked sorry for her. 'If you keep it, the family will know. Is that wise?'

'No. I'm not even sure how Hoffmann will react, let alone anyone else.'

'Does Eva suspect there is something between you?' he asked.

'I believe so. At first I wasn't sure. We had been so careful to restrict our intimate moments to the Hôtel d'Armorique but just lately he has stayed away far too much, including the weekend she arrived back from Paris. She even came to the hotel asking me if I knew where he was.' Claire shook her head again. 'If she gets wind of the pregnancy, I can't even say there is a man in my life. She once asked me that and I told her I had a fiancé who was now in Germany – you know the cover story. If I make out there is someone now she would pressure the Gestapo to find out who it is. I don't think Hoffmann would allow that, but there's Wenk to consider. He answers to Berlin, not Hoffmann.'

'Then you have to get rid of it, Marie-Elise, as soon as possible. Otherwise your life is in danger. You must tell Henri. Get out before it's too late.'

'And what about my work? I can't leave now.'

'*Merde!*' he exclaimed. 'You're a stubborn woman. You've already done enough. All the information you've passed on has saved lives and prepared us for the Allied invasion. It won't be long now.' He lit another cigarette and blew out a long breath of smoke. 'Look, I know you love this man – although for the life of me I can't understand why – but—'

Claire raised her hand and slapped him hard across the face, and Yves put out his hand in a gesture of conciliation.

'All right, I apologise. I overstepped the mark.'

'That's right, you did,' she replied angrily. 'Don't ever judge me, okay?'

Yves refused to be silenced. He tried another tack. 'What will happen when we win the war? Have you thought about that? A Frenchwoman cohabiting with a German is bad enough, but getting pregnant by an SS officer will see you killed. That's a certainty. The SOE will stand by you, as will the Resistance, but I can't vouch for the people who don't know what's been happening. A child makes it hard to explain. Surely this must have crossed your mind?'

Claire agreed to give it some thought and asked that he keep it between the two of them for the moment. He gave her his word. She got up to leave.

'Whatever I decide to do, I won't endanger anyone in the group. You have my word on that.'

She held out her hand. He shook it forcefully.

'And I am here for you, my little fighter,' he replied. 'You have my word on that also.'

At around midnight, Hoffmann entered Claire's room. Sleep was impossible and she had lain awake listening to records. He undressed, pulled back the sheets and wrapped his arms around her waist. What resolve she had had to tell him now dissipated.

'How are you feeling? You had me worried.'

'It was as I thought,' she replied. 'I had eaten something that didn't agree with me. The doctor gave me medicine and I am to return if it persists.'

She placed her lips over his so that he couldn't say anything. He responded to her kisses like a fire kindled by a gust of wind and they made love with their usual intensity, as if the world and all its troubles didn't exist. Afterwards, she lay in his arms and he fondled her plump breasts. The bedside lamp was turned down low and he couldn't see her flinch as he caressed her nipples. No, she decided. She couldn't tell him now. She would wait until it showed.

'I've missed you,' she whispered in his ear. 'And it worries me when I don't know where you are. You must take care.'

He laughed. 'My darling, I wish I could tell you − take you with me, even.'

She caught his mood. 'Where *do* you go?' she asked, snuggling into his chest. 'At least tell me so that my mind will be at rest. When you keep secrets from me, I feel you don't trust me.'

Again he laughed. She had not seen him like this for a while. It was as if the heavy weight he had been bearing had lifted somewhat.

'Okay. Have it your way,' she teased.

He was in the mood to talk. 'It may not be for much longer. We have the traitors firmly in our sights.'

'Who are these traitors?' Claire asked, trying to hide the tremor in her voice.

'We have been monitoring radio traffic about a group called Chevalier and have located several drop zones, one of which is near to a farm long suspected of dispersing weapons to the Resistance. Our patience has finally paid off. Someone has come forward to claim his reward and provided us with the information we've been looking for. It's only a matter of days before we round them up.'

Claire drew her legs up and placed her chin on her knees whilst Hoffmann ran his finger up and down her spine. He could not see the fear in her eyes.

'My darling, do not worry. These people will not defeat us.'

'Where is this farm?' she asked, not expecting him to answer. He surprised her.

'Not far from where you used to teach. They have two daughters, both as lovely as you. Who would put their daughters' lives in jeopardy, I ask myself? It's a big mistake.'

Claire knew he was talking about the Sourisseau farm and Dominique and Catherine. Had someone seen her there, although it had been a while since she was there? Who was it that betrayed them? Who could sell their soul to the devil for a few million francs? The bastard, she thought to herself. I would kill the person with my own hands. Her mind raced over the inevitable scenario should anyone be tortured. Her name would crop up and the Gestapo would leave no stone unturned until they found out her real identity. She felt nauseous again, and for the first time in their relationship, found she could not reciprocate her lover's affection.

'I'm tired,' she said softly when he tried to make love to her again. 'I think the medicine has made me drowsy.'

The kiosk owner in the square was laying out his newspapers when Claire approached. After verifying their code, he handed her a magazine and asked what he could do for her.

'I have to see Henri this afternoon – the usual place.' She counted out the exact money into his hand. 'Tell him not to be late. It's a matter of life and death.'

She slipped the magazine into her bag and returned to the waiting car. It had crossed her mind to have another day off; tell Eva she was still recuperating, but the thought that she might call by the hotel to check on her was something Claire wanted to avoid at all costs.

There had been another bombing raid and it took longer than usual to reach Villa Rosières. Oskar was already at his desk with Eva by his side. Her normally clear blue eyes looked dull and her complexion looked sallow. She had been crying.

'Have you recovered?' she asked, as if nothing was amiss. 'We were worried about you.'

Claire assured her she was fine and the illness had passed, but Eva seemed in the mood to talk.

'The new outfit suits you,' she continued. 'It fits perfectly.'

Claire wondered for how much longer: perhaps another month – two at the very most.

Eva brushed back Oskar's hair, a habit she had acquired when she was nervous. '*Kleiner* Oskar has been reading to me in French. Papa is extremely happy with his progress and has promised to buy him more soldiers.' She brought up the subject of Frau Heller. 'I keep thinking about the fact that she wanted to speak to me. Giselle said she seemed anxious about it. Do you have any idea what it could have been?'

Claire replied that Frau Heller had mentioned to her that she would like to return to Vienna for Christmas. Perhaps it was that. After several minutes of small talk, Eva got up and left. Claire was relieved. It was going to be a long and torturous day and being around Eva only made her more nervous. When she left at the end of the afternoon, she noticed Eva watching her from an upstairs window. There was little doubt that she knew something was wrong.

Henri was late, which was unusual for him. She would give him fifteen minutes, a time agreed upon by all the contacts. After that, if the contact failed to appear, they were to get away as soon as possible. Claire was the only customer in the bar until a group of four young men and a woman entered and sat on the other side of the room. Their voices were too low for her to hear what they were saying but by the looks on their faces, it wasn't good.

The fifteen minutes had almost passed when she saw Henri through the window, but instead of coming to the cafe he was walking along a pathway in the park with a newspaper tucked under his arm, a sign that she was to leave and follow him.

As she paid the waiter two cars pulled up outside and several men entered the premises wearing official Milice uniforms, followed by two plain-clothed officials – the Gestapo.

'*Documents d'identité, s'il vous plaît,*' one of them called out.

Claire handed her papers to one of the Gestapo, who examined them and then handed them back to her. His face seemed familiar although she couldn't recall where she had seen him. Was it at the Hôtel d'Armorique? She couldn't be sure.

'You may go, Fräulein,' he said, indicating the door with a flick of his head.

As she opened the door a shot rang out. One of the young men had tried to leave by the back entrance and was shot. He lay on the floor writhing in agony. The second Gestapo agent aimed a pistol at his head and fired. The girl screamed and was pulled aside along with the other three men and forced to face the wall, hands above their heads. Claire watched in horror as the man who had examined her papers kicked the woman's legs apart and ran his hand over her body, searching her pockets roughly whilst holding the gun at the back of her head. She protested her innocence but her cries fell on deaf ears. Seconds later the man fired and the woman slumped to the ground, her brains splattered over the faded blue-striped wallpaper. He turned around and saw Claire still standing in the doorway.

'Go! Leave now.'

Claire hurried across the road as another two cars arrived, the occupants swiftly entering the adjoining buildings. Without looking back she walked briskly in pursuit of Henri, but he was nowhere in sight. She couldn't hang about, and followed the path to the other side of the park.

She heard a whistle. Henri was waiting for her behind a tree. He approached her, looped his arm through hers, and they quickly continued on their way through the wrought-iron gate into the busy street. In a state of nervousness, she fired questions at him in rapid succession.

'Who were those people? How did you know there was going to be raid?'

'The street was too quiet. I smelt a rat. Call it gut instinct if you will. And no, I didn't know the people. This sort of thing is going on all the time now.'

She poured out the reason she wanted to see him and she felt his arm clasp hers a little more tightly. He swore under his breath. Minutes later they slipped into a side alley to a safe house. A peephole in the centre of the door slid open and a pair of grey eyes framed by dark-rimmed glasses stared out at them. Didier. He slipped the chain from the lock to let them in, checking the street behind them. Henri slung his cap on the table where Didier was in the process of setting up his transmitter.

'No time to waste,' he told Didier. 'You have to let London know straight away. There's a drop on tonight.'

The master pianist immediately began tapping out the information Claire had given them. He was halfway through the message when a high-pitched noise startled him. The line was jammed.

'Damn,' Didier said, 'Something's wrong. I have a nasty feeling about this. We have to get out of here straight away.' He quickly packed the transmitter into its case. 'Notify everyone immediately. From what you've told me, they already have the Sourisseau farm in their sights. It's probably surrounded as we speak.'

'The Chauvignons!' Claire blurted out. 'We must warn them.'

Henri picked up Didier's telephone and dialled the school, but the line was dead.

'Not sure how this is going to pan out, Manon,' Henri said, straightening his cap. 'It could be a while before we meet up again but whatever happens from here on, I want you both to know you've done a sterling job and London is proud of you.'

His demeanour frightened her. Henri's calmness was something that had given them all strength. And he rarely used her codename. Why now of all times?

'In the meantime, lay low. You know the safe houses. And should you want to walk away now, you have my blessing.'

Claire shook her head. 'Never,' she answered defiantly. 'I came here to do a job and will see it through until the Allies land. And you still need me.'

She followed him outside. Didier bid them farewell, locked the door behind them, picked up the suitcase and left by the back door.

'*Bonne chance*, my friend,' Henri said to her, giving her a peck on the cheek. 'You're one of the bravest women I know.'

He turned on his heel and started to walk away.

'Wait,' Claire shouted after him. 'Where are you going?'

He looked back without stopping. 'Where do you think?' he replied.

Claire had a sinking feeling that she might not see him again, and it scared her. In an instant, she ran after him.

'You're not getting rid of me that easily,' she told him. 'I'm coming with you.'

The light was fading when the black Citroën pulled up outside the Chauvignons'. The place was in darkness. Claire banged on the door, and when there was no answer she tried the handle. It was locked. They took out their guns and went around the back and found that door also locked.

Claire glanced at Henri. He cocked his pistol, ready to shoot.

'*C'est moi* – Claire,' she shouted, banging on the window. '*Ouvrez la porte.*'

She heard a soft scraping sound like someone moving a chair. A light flickered inside the kitchen.

'*C'est moi,*' she called again.

The latch clicked and the door opened. Claire and Henri aimed their pistols. He pushed her aside and threw back the door. Standing next to the sink holding a tiny candle stood Mireille, shaking like a leaf. Claire ran towards her.

'What on earth's happened?' she asked. 'Are you all right? Where's Antoine?'

Mireille could hardly speak. 'They came for him,' she said. 'In the afternoon. A car came to the school. They bundled him into the back and drove away.'

'Who's they?' Henri asked, checking through the windows.

'The Gestapo.'

Claire sat her down and threw a shawl over Mireille's shoulders. She looked even frailer than the last time she saw her. 'Do you have any idea why, or where they might have taken him?'

Mireille shook her head. 'They drove towards the village. That's all I know.'

The clock on the mantelpiece chimed eight o'clock. Henri pulled Claire aside.

'Look, I can't hang around here. I have to get going to the drop zone.' He lowered his voice to a whisper. 'You're going to have to stay here and handle this alone.'

Claire felt a stab of irritation, but she knew he was right. Mireille couldn't be left alone.

'Move the car behind the shed over there,' she said. 'No one will think to look there. Unfortunately Gaspard took my bicycle back so you'll have to go on foot. I hope you make it in time.'

She returned to the house.

'What shall I say if they come for me?' Mireille asked. 'I don't think I am strong enough to stand up to their questioning.'

Claire opened the glass door of the dresser and took down two glasses and an almost empty bottle of Calvados. 'We might as well finish this off,' she said. 'It will do you good.'

She picked up the last few pieces of kindling wood from a basket next to the fireplace and lit a small fire. Over the next hour, she discussed with Mireille exactly what she should say if the Gestapo should reappear.

'You don't know anything,' she concluded. 'And neither does Antoine. You are both too busy with the school. Have you got it?'

Claire felt as though she was talking to a child but Mireille was beside herself and she had no other choice. One wrong word and the Gestapo would pick it up.

Chapter 19

Jürgen Hoffmann stood in the shadows of the farmhouse doorway, peering through his field glasses towards the stone tower silhouetted on the hilltop not far away. Except for the tower, little remained of what was once the thriving twelfth-century abbey apart from a few stones and a dry well. The rest of the buildings had long been pilfered to help build the farmsteads that dotted the area. The tower provided an excellent vantage point from which to survey the countryside, and Hoffmann and his men had taken advantage of this to post a lookout.

At around 9.30 at night a winter frost was beginning to settle and a thin mist veiled the moon, casting a ghostly light over the undulating landscape. According to their intelligence, the drops would take place at 11.25pm exactly. At long last, after months of planning, his patience was about to pay off; the British would be dealt a mortal blow. He was about to net the big fish – Henri, head of the Chevalier network – and if he was lucky, there would be others with him, including the elusive Agent Manon, the woman no one seemed to be able to identify. He smiled to himself. The reprisals and rewards had paid off. People had squealed. You never could trust the French.

He stepped back inside and joined his men, who waited by the field telephone on the table. In the corner of what had been the kitchen and living quarters of the small cottage were the occupants themselves, an old couple who despite their years, sat bound and gagged against the wall. Next to them stood a young officer, his sub-machine gun aimed in their direction. The fear in the couple's eyes was palpable. They were not the only ones to find themselves in this situation; all the other farms and houses within a radius of several kilometres had been commandeered as well, their occupants suffering a similar fate. All except the Sourisseaus.

Hoffmann took out his cigarette case and pulled out a cigarette. A subordinate quickly offered him a light. He sat in an old, upholstered armchair chair, one leather-booted leg cocked out on the unlit grate, and waited.

His mind flashed back to his private life; to how complicated it had become. Heaven knows, it was the last thing he needed when Berlin was putting pressure on him. He thought of Claire, naked in his arms. He smelt her flesh, warm and inviting. Even now, when so much was at stake, all he could think about was her. She was the only woman he could trust. Not even Eva could compare with her. Eva, the beautiful and loyal wife, picked out by Hitler and Goering themselves. She loved him, he knew that, but it was not the same. Eva deserved better; she was a good woman.

And then there was Oskar. He loved the boy dearly but his epilepsy was a curse. How was it that two people such as he and Eva could produce a boy with such a defect – both of them perfect specimens of the Aryan ideal? Goodness knows how much longer they could keep his disability a secret. What would the future hold for him?

An hour later, the lookout flashed a signal from the tower and the telephone rang. He jumped up to answer it.

'They've started to move into the woods,' he told his men. 'It's time to go.'

He picked up his pistol and put it in his holster. His men had deliberately been told to stay hidden until the Maquis had moved in to give them a false sense of security. Now there was no way out. A battalion of battle-hardened men, backed up by armoured vehicles hidden at strategic points along the roads, started to make their way towards the woods.

Inside the woodsman's cottage, everyone was accounted for. Having been forewarned by Henri that he might be late due to meeting Claire, Yves had taken charge. Everyone was questioned. Had they spotted anything out of the ordinary? Earlier there had been reports of armoured divisions in the area but they appeared to be heading for the coast – nothing to do with them. A few mentioned that the hamlets close by were unusually quiet and not even a dog bark had been heard, but this was dismissed as the inhabitants going to bed early due to the onset of winter and lack of heating.

Didier had not arrived either and Yves used another pianist – a member of the local Maquis whom Didier had trained himself. There were to be two drops. In the second they were to expect two jeeps – 'gifts' for the approaching D-Day. Jacques tapped nervously, constantly wiping away the beads of sweat on his forehead, and Yves chastised him for making them all nervous.

After a while the men left the hut for the drop zone. Before long a soft droning noise could be heard, and in less than a minute the Halifax burst out over the treetops and dropped its cargo into the landing strip with expert precision. The men darted around, cleaning up the evidence, and a few minutes later a second plane appeared, its precious cargo of jeeps floating to the ground like a surreal dream. The men darted out of hiding again.

All of a sudden spotlights illuminated the area, catching them off guard. A voice boomed over a loudspeaker. Everyone who did not give themselves up would be shot on sight. In the mayhem that followed most of the men tried to escape back into the woods, only to be blocked by groups of German soldiers with sub-machine guns. Bursts of gunfire echoed from all directions and bullets sprayed the drop zone, kicking up mounds of dust in their wake. Within minutes at least fifteen men lay dead or dying. The drop zone had become a killing field.

Yves managed to flee. He made his way from the main thrust of the action back to the woodsman's hut, hoping to call for help. As he scrambled through the thickets of brambles, instinct made him stop. He inched closer until the hut was in sight.

What he saw shocked him. Outside stood half a dozen Germans and nearby, sitting on a log near the door, was Hoffmann himself. With him, smoking a cigarette, was Jacques the pianist. Yves wiped his brow with the back of his sleeve. So he was the traitor – a trusted member of the Maquis.

Yves knew he was putting his life in danger but he had no other option. He aimed the Bren gun towards the hut and began firing. The pianist flew back off the log, riddled with bullets, and the rest of the men started to fire indiscriminately into the thicket but were soon mown down in a hail of bullets. Someone darted forward to protect Hoffmann and was caught in the crossfire, falling into a crumpled heap over his body.

Miraculously, Hoffmann was unharmed. He lay under the man's body until the firing stopped, blood spurting from the dead man's neck soaking his uniform and sticking to his skin. When he stood up and surveyed the scene, all his men were dead. He took out his revolver, and in a rage, fired into the thicket. By then it was too late: Yves had slipped away into the night.

Claude Sourisseau was near the farm sheds checking on a hiding place for the guns when he heard the planes fly over and the sound of gunfire. He turned and ran back to the house to warn the women. They were in the kitchen preparing a meal for the men. When the door burst open, Madame Sourisseau dropped a plate in fright.

'Get out now,' Claude shouted. 'The Germans have ambushed the drop zone. They'll be here any minute.'

Dominique ran to the window. Vehicles appeared over the brow of the hill, heading towards the farm.

'Too late, Father,' she said. 'They're already here.'

The girls threw on their jackets, grabbed their guns and left by the back door. Madame Sourisseau, still wearing her food-smeared apron, protested. She didn't want to go without her husband but he thrust her old jacket into her arms and pushed her out of the door, saying he would see her soon. Catherine tugged her mother's arm and they hurried behind the milking shed towards the woods. Claude Sourisseau hid his gun in the chimney, cleared the table of the telltale food that awaited the Resistance and threw it outside as if it were pigswill. Then he calmly sat down at the table and waited.

A few miles away in a clearing on the other side of the drop zone, Henri had heard it all. He knew things had gone wrong long before the shooting began. When he neared the tower that was a lookout for the Maquisards he heard voices. Two Germans were talking to each other at the top of the lookout. At the bottom, sprawled on the rocks, lay the body of a Maquisard.

Realising the area was under surveillance, he took a circuitous route to the woods. When he reached the last field at the edge of the woods leading to the drop zone he heard vehicles approaching along the narrow lane and jumped into the ditch, narrowly missing being spotted by a convoy of armoured trucks. He crawled on his belly to an opening in a stone wall and watched helplessly as further down the road the trucks stopped and groups of armed Germans jumped down and disappeared into the woods. It flashed through his mind that he should fire a warning shot but he quickly dismissed the thought as he would never escape, and as the leader of the group, it was vital he didn't get caught. He retraced his steps until he was a fair distance away. Then he heard the planes fly over, followed almost immediately by machine-gun fire. For once in his life he found himself praying.

The Germans burst through the farmhouse door. Others dispersed towards the farm buildings. Claude Sourisseau feigned surprise when he saw them. An officer demanded that his men search the house for the rest of the family.

When they reported there was no one else there, the officer pistol-whipped Claude across the face, splitting his cheek open and sending him sprawling onto the floor. He ordered his men to stand him up and tie his hands behind his back. The officer forced him under one of the long, dark beams across the kitchen ceiling and threw a rope over it. He pulled up a chair, sat in front of him and began to question him.

'You can save yourself, Monsieur, if you just tell us what we want to know. Let's begin with your son. Where is he?'

'I haven't seen him for a while. They told me he'd gone to work in Germany. Why don't you look there?' Claude answered defiantly.

Someone punched him in the solar plexus with such force he jerked forward, choking in pain.

'Come now. You and I both know that he didn't report for duty in Germany, therefore we have reason to believe he joined the Maquis.'

Claude Sourisseau refused to budge. He maintained he had no idea where his son was, and that he had never heard of an organisation called Chevalier. As for a man who went by the codename of Henri, he asked which one was the officer referring to – he knew many.

The officer jumped up in a rage and pistol-whipped him again whilst the men stood either side of him to stop him from falling. This time the gash opened further, exposing his cheekbone.

The door opened and a man called the officer outside. Claude struggled to stop himself from passing out in pain. It wasn't long before the officer returned.

'So you don't know anything?' He smirked. 'Then what do you say to the cache of arms under the floor of the pigsty?'

When he mentioned another two hiding places filled with ammunition, Claude Sourisseau knew his luck had run out. The Germans had left no stone unturned. Through a combination of pain and hopelessness, his mind began to wander. He no longer comprehended the officer's words; they had become a distant blur.

When one of the men tied the noose around his neck, he barely knew what was happening. It was useless to struggle; he was going to die anyway. The last thing he recalled was his wife before the war, standing at the table where the Germans now stood. She was churning the butter and was pregnant with their firstborn. She kissed him on the lips. The noose pulled tight and his feet lifted off the ground, a trickle of urine running down his trousers.

The Sourisseau sisters and their mother had almost reached the riverbank when they heard the dogs barking. The Germans were closing in on them.

No matter how hard she tried, Madame Sourisseau could not keep up with her daughters. She was overweight and unfit and the escape route was proving to be too much for her. It was one thing to look at the route on a map in the comfort of her kitchen and another to implement it. Twice she had caught her foot in a rabbit hole and her legs were a mess of cuts and bruises. Each time she fell, her daughters picked her up. She had become a liability. After they heard explosions and saw flames shooting towards the sky and realised the farm had been torched, Madame Sourisseau lost heart. With the farm gone, hopes that her husband would be alive dimmed. The girls tried to coax her to move on.

'I can't,' she wailed. 'Go without me. I'm holding you back. You'll never make it with me.'

The sisters looked at each other. It was impossible to leave their mother here. Just one mile away were the river and the boat which would take them to freedom, but in their mother's state one mile might as well have been ten. Dominique grabbed her sister's arm.

'In the name of God, Mother, we have to go.'

The girls pulled her up one more time. She took a few more steps but it was useless. They would never make it. An argument ensued. They refused to leave their mother. In the end it was agreed that Catherine should go ahead alone as she was by far the fittest. Dominique would take her chances with their mother. She prepared her Sten gun and pistol and they hid themselves behind a rock, hoping that by some slim chance the Germans would miss them.

'Here,' Catherine said, giving them her own gun. 'You'll need this more than me.'

She kissed them both goodbye and ran towards the river. The small boat was lodged firmly in the mud under the bushes. She pushed and shoved until it finally loosened and slipped into the water. Then she jumped in and started to paddle away quickly downstream.

In the meantime the dogs had picked up the women's scent and they were discovered. Dominique was not going out without a fight. She emptied the first round in their direction, but the Germans had the upper hand. The first bullet struck her in the shoulder, causing her to fall back against her mother. In agony she reached for the second gun, but before she could sit up another bullet penetrated her left breast. She slumped forward, exposing her mother to a barrage of machine-gun fire. It was all over within a matter of minutes.

*

From his hiding place, Henri watched with dismay as the night sky lit up in a warm orange glow streaked with crimson. He knew what this meant. The Sourisseau farm was on fire. He arrived back at Saint-Etienne in the early hours of the morning, tired and distressed. After persuading Mireille to get some sleep, Claire was alone in the kitchen, curled up in Antoine's favourite chair. One look at him told her things had not gone well. Henri winced as he peeled off his boots. His feet were swollen and blistered. She rushed to get some warm water to bathe them. When she returned, she found him sobbing. She lit a cigarette and passed it to him. His hands were shaking.

'We were too late, weren't we?' she said.

'If I had only got there earlier, none of this would have happened.'

She had no words to comfort him. As the leader of the network, he took full responsibility. That was Henri.

'We always knew we were living on borrowed time but the Germans must have had this planned for a while. They wanted to catch as many of us as they could, and they did a good job. I have no idea how many were killed but it must have been a lot.'

'And Yves?' she asked, finding it hard to say his name.

Henri shook his head. 'We will have to wait and see.'

When he told her about the Sourisseau farm, she gasped in disbelief.

'We have to leave straight away,' he told her. 'Get back to Rennes before daylight. I need to warn the others.'

'And Mireille? What will we do about her? If they come looking...'

'Wake her up. We'll take her with us. There's a safe house near Rennes. She can stay there.'

231

Chapter 20

The fallout from the raid had far-reaching consequences. The Sourisseau farm lay in ruins, and Monsieur and Madame Sourisseau and Dominique were dead, along with at least fifty others from the Resistance and the Maquis, several of whom were strung up from the lamp posts of the surrounding villages as a reminder of what would happen if you provoked the Reich. More than another fifty were now in the hands of the Gestapo. Despite the Milice trying to pin something on Antoine, he was released after twenty-four hours and reunited with Mireille in Saint-Etienne a few days later.

Throughout the following days, posters announcing summary executions were plastered on the buildings in Rennes and throughout the countryside. Claire searched through the list of names with a sense of sheer hopelessness. Several of the names she recognised. With each posting her eyes scanned for those she was closest to, in particular Yves. And then there was Catherine. What had happened to her?

Throughout all this Claire did as Henri asked and kept a low profile. Fortunately, her sickness seemed to have passed and she went to Villa Rosières as usual. She saw nothing of Hoffmann and very little of Eva, who now appeared to have accepted the fact that Hoffmann was hardly ever at home and thankfully for Claire, had stopped asking if she'd seen him.

With Hoffmann away and Eva more and more withdrawn, Claire felt an acute sense of isolation. She had no friends, and missed the companionship of those in Chevalier. The long, dark, cold nights of winter were drawing in and Christmas was just around the corner. This would be her first Christmas in France since 1940. It was the time of year she and Gerty had always looked forward to. What this Christmas held for her, she had no idea. It was less than a month away, yet she couldn't make plans. Her main thought had now become one of survival.

It was dark when she arrived back at the hotel. At this time in the evening the place was usually filled with guests but tonight it was almost deserted. She went into the bar where the barman was busy cleaning the glasses for something to do.

'Where is everyone?' she asked.

'I don't know. It's been like this all day.' He looked towards the street. 'Earlier there were enough armoured trucks around to fight the Russians.'

He offered her a drink, which she accepted gladly. The barman was French and a man who kept himself to himself – the wisest thing to do, given his customers – but Claire had detected the occasional hint of animosity towards the Germans, especially when he saw them flirting with a pretty French girl.

With hardly anyone around she decided to dress for dinner and dine in the restaurant rather than spend time alone in her room. An elderly couple and a middle-aged man were the only other guests. The pianist was playing a melancholic German tune, which under the circumstances Claire thought a good reflection of the mood in the place. He gave her a nod as she walked to her table. She felt sorry for him. Night after night he played a repertoire of German songs until the early hours of the morning. Tonight he was accompanied by a violinist, who moved around the almost empty room with a dramatic air.

The waiter took her order – a meat dish prepared in a rich goulash sauce with a side dish of sauerkraut. It was accompanied by a fine Bordeaux. Another man entered with his girlfriend and sat in a corner at a table marked reserved. The violinist made his way over to them and began to play a love tune with a haunting Hungarian melody. The woman was clearly charmed. Claire finished her meal with a fine cognac, reflecting on the drop that had gone wrong. She couldn't stop thinking about Yves – his wild, curly hair and bon vivant ways. You never knew what to expect with him. The thought that he might have been killed filled her with dread and she found herself fingering the silver crucifix around her neck and saying a little prayer for him.

When she left the restaurant she bumped into Erich Schneider coming out of the lift. He was carrying a large pile of manila folders and accidently dropped some on the floor, scattering their contents around their feet. He apologised and bent down to pick them up.

'No, no,' Claire replied. 'It was my fault. I should have looked where I was going. Here, let me help you.'

As she picked them up, her eyes quickly scanned the contents. One of the folders was stamped *Manoir de Sevigny*, and amongst the pages that had slipped out was a list of names under the heading *Interrogation for Clandestine Activities by Order of the Reich*. To her horror she saw the names of Mayor Bourgoin, Father Gambert and most chilling of all, Catherine Sourisseau and Angélique Lemoine's fiancé, Sebastian Levade.

A man approached them and she noticed Schneider stiffen. He snatched the papers from her.

'Do not bother yourself, Fräulein. I can manage myself.'

Clearly, he was worried that she might have seen something she shouldn't.

His arms full, he was unable to salute the man standing behind them. 'Herr Koenig, *Guten Abend.*'

Claire turned around. Looking her squarely in the face was the man who had checked her papers in the cafe – the same one who had shot the young girl in cold blood. Her face paled.

'We meet again, Fräulein,' he said, bowing graciously.

Claire acknowledged him with her sweetest smile. 'Yes, indeed we do – Herr Koenig.'

Schneider moved aside and Claire stepped into the lift. When the door closed, she leaned against the rail to steady herself. A terrifying feeling that everything was closing in on her brought on her nausea once again, and for the second time that night, she reached for her crucifix.

In the safety of her room Claire pulled down the suitcase from the top of the wardrobe, took out the pistol from the hidden compartment and slipped it under her pillow. Then she lay down on the bed and waited, only this time it was not Hoffmann she expected to call on her in the early hours of the morning, but the Gestapo.

She was wrong. Shortly after, the sirens started up, piercing the stillness of the night. Anti-aircraft guns fired tracer bullets into the dark sky as wave after wave of Allied bombers flew over, heading inland towards the Loire Valley. Claire quickly dressed, slipped the pistol into her bag and rushed into the corridor. The first bomb dropped just as she reached Hoffmann's room, and an explosion could be heard coming from the direction of the railway station. The lights flickered and then went off.

At that moment, Koenig appeared from the room with Schneider carrying a briefcase of what Claire surmised to be top-secret documents. Together the three of them scrambled down the fire escape by torchlight. Within minutes of entering the shelter another huge explosion rocked the ground, cracking the roof and showering them with debris. Claire was thrown from the bench onto the ground but was unharmed. Koenig had been sitting nearby and helped her up.

'Thank you, Herr Kommandant,' she said, brushing a film of pale grey plaster from her clothes and hair.

He leaned closer, his grip tightening on her arm. 'I know your little game, Fräulein. You might have deceived Herr Sturmbannführer Hoffmann, but not me.'

'Fräulein Bouchard, are you all right?' Schneider called out through a cloud of dust.

Claire shook herself free and scrambled towards him, clutching her bag tightly in her arms. 'I'm fine, but I'm worried about Herr Hoffmann.'

He assured her the commandant would be fine. He wasn't in Rennes.

'Oh, I see,' she remarked.

Whether it was the rush of adrenaline that came from the air raids or the fact that she was still in shock due to recent events and the unknown fate of her friends, she didn't know, but she suddenly threw caution to the wind.

'Yes, I suppose there's no reason to drop bombs around the Manoir de Sevigny is there? After all, what good would that do?'

She had said it in a low voice so that only Schneider heard her. His look was one of shock.

'I wasn't aware that the Herr Kommandant had told you about that place,' he replied.

She leaned closer. 'I have known for a while. He trusts me implicitly.'

Schneider smiled. 'Fräulein, even Frau Eva doesn't know this. You understand, it's top secret, if anything was to leak out…'

Claire squeezed his arm. 'I understand,' she said in a low whisper. 'You don't have to worry, but perhaps it's better if we don't mention it again.'

Schneider agreed.

The raid lasted several hours and throughout it all the sounds of bombing and explosions seeped through the thick walls. It was cold and the air smelt dank and earthy. After a while Claire's nostrils became used to the odour, but the nausea returned and someone passed her a bucket so that she could be sick. Schneider took off his jacket and wrapped it around her shoulders. Throughout all this Koenig sat across from her on the bench, his hands resting on the briefcase on his knee. His eyes never left her. He had the same cold look he had given the young woman in the cafe before he ruthlessly shot her. If only she could remember where she'd seen him before.

Finally the siren stopped sounding and they filed outside. The building next door had taken a hit and part of the wall had fallen into the hotel garden. Shards of glass glistened in the rubble. The Hôtel d'Armorique was heavily protected by walls of sandbagging, but it wasn't enough to stop the windows from shattering or a section of the roof from caving in. Fires lit up the night sky and every now and again an explosion sent bilious clouds of smoke into the air. Much to her dismay, Claire noticed that the kiosk where she bought her magazines and passed her messages also lay in ruins.

Koenig's words continued to play on Claire's mind. Frau Heller had been dangerous, but Koenig – well, that was something entirely different. He was in the Gestapo and as such could call on Hoffmann at any time. She needed to warn Henri, but with the kiosk in ruins, she was no longer able to leave a message. To add to her anxiety, a week had now passed since the raid and still there was no sign of Hoffmann. The only good thing was that Koenig was no longer around.

The weather had taken a turn for the worse. The winter frosts were setting in and every now and again there was a light sprinkling of snow. At Villa Rosières, Eva occupied herself by decorating a huge Christmas tree in the drawing room with Giselle, much to the delight of Oskar, who anticipated more soldiers in his Christmas stocking. When they'd finished, she called Claire in and asked what she thought of it. It looked beautiful. The happy memories of Christmas spent with Gerty in their apartment in Paris now seemed to belong to another era – a distant, bittersweet memory.

Sweeping bands of coloured ribbon and silver and gold baubles hung from the green branches, interspersed with small candles. At the top was a star, which Eva had made herself out of cardboard and painted silver. With the roaring log fire in the background, it looked a picture of yuletide warmth. In Eva's world, Villa Villa Rosières was an island free from the reality of war.

She asked if Claire had any plans for Christmas. Perhaps she was going back to Paris? Claire told her she had been thinking of spending Christmas with the headmaster and his wife in Saint-Etienne.

The telephone rang and Giselle answered it. The call lasted only a few seconds.

'Who was it?' asked Eva.

'Someone from Avenue Jules Ferry. I didn't catch his name. He said Herr Hoffmann wants you to go there straight away.'

Eva looked perplexed. She had always been told to avoid going to

Gestapo headquarters. Giselle fetched her coat, a full-length sable with matching Cossack hat. Not for the first time did Claire wonder why Hoffmann had fallen in love with her when he had such a glamorous wife as Eva.

'I wonder what he wants,' she said to Claire as she pulled on her long black gloves.

Oskar looked downcast. 'Is Papa coming home tonight?' he asked.

Eva ruffled his hair. 'I hope so, my brave soldier, but Papa is a very busy man. He has important work to do. We must have patience.'

As soon as she left, Claire and Oskar returned to his room to continue his studies. She gave him a written exercise and went to sit in the window seat with a book. The phone call had made her uneasy. Something was wrong, very wrong. Hoffmann would never send a message like that. And then it dawned on her. It was a trap.

She jumped up, and grabbed her coat and bag. 'Oskar, carry on for a while without me. There's something I have to do.'

She ran downstairs, and under the pretext of suddenly remembering that she had an important appointment with the doctor, asked Giselle to ask one of the chauffeurs to take her into Rennes straight away.

'Hurry,' she said to the driver. 'I'm late.'

The weather had worsened. The sky was a darkened grey mist and a steady rain had turned the earlier sprinkling of snow into slush, making driving hazardous. To add to that, several roads were blocked due to the heavy bombing. Claire knew that Eva must have taken a different route through the park into the old area with its winding, narrow streets. They had gone barely two kilometres when she realised there was not a soul in sight. Even in such weather there was usually someone about, hoping to get lucky with their ration coupons or searching for a stick of firewood to throw on a fire that would barely warm a kettle.

Minutes later her fears were realised. Eva's car stood in the middle of the road, the windows laced with bullet holes. The driver slammed on the brakes, skidding to a halt only a few feet from the car.

'*Mon Dieu*,' Claire screamed. 'My God! No, no! Not this!'

They ran to the car but it was no use. The driver's body lay slumped against the shredded leather seat and when they opened the back door, Eva's body slid out onto the wet road, the soft sable soaking up her blood. She had been shot in the head from the back and the side. Her beautiful face was unrecognisable − a mass of splintered bone and platinum hair streaked with dark red. Claire reeled against the car to steady herself. She looked around; the perpetrators had melted back into the landscape. They had thought this out well. She walked back to the car in a daze. When would this damned war end?

It didn't take long for news of Eva's death to circulate. Condolences came from as far away as Berlin and Himmler himself ordered that no stone be left unturned until the culprits were caught and executed. Eva's death impacted on Claire in ways she had not imagined. She had always known she would come face-to-face with death when she took the job – Hugo Manning had made sure of that.

'This is war, old girl,' he had said when he gave her the crucifix containing the cyanide pill. 'Kill or be killed. It's as simple as that.' As a consequence she had trained herself to believe that a German death didn't matter. It couldn't, or she would not have been up to the job. Even when she had killed the soldiers to rescue Jean-Claude and Michel she had still remained detached. Only the intimate moments with Hoffmann were real. But with the deaths of her companions and now Eva, something inside her changed.

It wasn't that Eva was the enemy, or her lover's wife, but something else. *Kleiner* Oskar, the child she had unwittingly grown to love. He didn't deserve this. How could the wounds of the next generation heal after all this, regardless of which side they were on? She had to snap out of this melancholy before it made her vulnerable.

Hoffmann returned to Villa Rosières the evening of Eva's death. Neither he nor Claire could find it in them to look at each other – both bore the burden of guilt. Through Giselle, he asked if she could move into the house to be with Oskar for a while.

Christmas Day was one of the most miserable and darkest days Claire had spent in a long time. It snowed all day, shrouding the house in melancholia. Hoffmann invited a few of his Gestapo friends around for lunch and Claire spent the day with Oskar, making sure that he got his wish of more soldiers to add to his collection for his Christmas present. In the afternoon, she took him outside to throw snowballs and make a snowman but nothing could put the light back into his sad blue eyes.

By early evening, the visitors had all left. Claire had just settled Oskar into bed when the door opened. It was Hoffmann, and he wanted to know if she would join him for a Christmas drink in the drawing room.

When she entered the room, he stood in front of the fire with his back to her. He walked over to the dresser filled with an array of wine and spirits, and poured them both a fine cognac. Once again she recalled Hugo Manning's words: 'Mark my words, the best wines will be the first to go. The top brass of Nazi Germany have a taste for the finer things in life.'

He handed her a cognac, together with a small present wrapped in embossed red-and-silver paper.

'Your Christmas present. I had hoped to give you this under more pleasant circumstances.'

'I'm afraid that I don't have anything for you,' she replied.

He watched her open it. Inside was a small leather box on which was written the name *Cartier*. It was an exquisite diamond necklace studded with rubies.

'I hope you like it,' he said with a smile. 'I took great care in making sure it matched your hair and eyes.' He took it from her. 'Allow me to put it on.'

She took off the crucifix and placed it in her pocket while he draped the Cartier around her neck.

'Perfect,' he said, turning her around. 'Much better than the crucifix.'

'That was a present from my mother,' she replied. 'That's why I wear it.'

She looked at herself in the large mirror over the fireplace. He was right. It did match her eyes and hair.

'I don't know what to say, Jürgen.'

He kissed the nape of her neck. 'Then say nothing.'

She turned to face him. The warm atmosphere of the room, dominated by Eva's tree adorned with candles and the crackling sound of logs on the fire, belied the reality of the moment. His eyes penetrated hers. She wanted him to take her in his arms, to tell her it was all a dream, but it was never going to be. Eva's memory had come between them. She lifted a finger and traced the fine scar on his cheek.

'My darling,' was all she could say. 'How I wish it could all be different.'

He took her hand. 'I have been thinking about what you said – about getting Eva and Oskar away from here. You were right, and I should have done something earlier but I've been so tied up in my work. It's too late for Eva now, but not for Oskar. I have decided to send him back to Vienna to live with his grandparents.'

She nodded. 'You have made the right decision. When?'

'In the next few days. The Zeidlers are in Paris and I've made arrangements with them to take him.'

'I see,' Claire replied. She pulled away from him and sat down on the couch. 'I know it's for the best but I have grown rather fond of him and will miss him dreadfully. And what will become of us? I have no reason to come here after he has gone.'

He sat down next to her, staring into the fire. 'I cannot live without you, Claire, and I don't want to lose you a second time.'

'Nor I you, but my life is already in danger. Without a job, I cannot stay at the Hôtel d'Armorique either. You are hardly there these days. If I stay, people will become suspicious and tongues will wag. You know perfectly well what happens to French women who fraternise with the Germans. Even here, I am not entirely safe. Frau Heller despised me and the servants barely tolerate me. Eva protected me from all that. I will return to Paris.'

He turned to look at her. 'No. I will not let you go. You will come with me.'

Claire looked exasperated. 'Where? Tell me.'

She knew she had pushed him into a corner. It was another risk she was willing to take, and once again it paid off. Someday soon she was afraid her luck would run out. Hoffmann referred to a place he called top secret because it was used for intelligence-gathering, but he still didn't divulge the name or anything else about it. She didn't tell him she was already aware of it.

Oskar left Rennes for Paris in January 1944. Claire was sad to see him go.

'Will we meet again, Fräulein Bouchard?' he asked.

'We will, when the war has ended. In the meantime I want you to continue your French lessons. Will you promise me that?'

She gave him a French edition of a book as a keepsake, with a dedication written in French: *To Oskar, a student who shows great promise. Your friend and teacher, Fräulein Bouchard.*

'One day when you grow up to be a successful young man, you will be able to read this, and when you do, I would like to think you will remember me. It's by a very famous American writer,' she told him.

He read out the title, trying to formulate the words. '*The Great Gatsby* by F. Scott Fitzgerald. What's it about?'

'It's about a man who loves someone so much he reinvents himself to win her back.'

Oskar looked puzzled. He wasn't sure what she meant.

'Oskar, one day you will understand that all good books teach us something. This one is very special. It teaches us that we can be anything we want, but we can't always have *who* we want.'

'And I have something for you.' He reached into his pocket and pulled out one of his toy soldiers. 'It's Frederick the Great. Papa said that even your Napoleon Bonaparte admired him.'

Claire was deeply touched. 'That's certainly true. I shall treasure it.'

She gave him one last hug and stood in the driveway waving him goodbye until the car turned out of the gate. Choking back her tears, she headed back into Villa Rosières to pack her things.

Claire was told that she would be departing Rennes in a few days' time. In the meantime she had to let Henri know what was happening. No one had tried to make contact with her since the raid and she was worried. Every day she scanned the newspapers and took walks around the city centre to check out the latest posters. The list of executions and deportations grew by the day. Thankfully, Yves' name was still not among them. With the kiosk in the square no longer there, she had no one to turn to.

In the end she decided to forgo her instructions and go to his apartment. She went during the busiest time of the day – mid-morning, when the streets were filled with people queuing for food. She wore her old coat and a headscarf in an attempt not to stand out. In Yves' neighbourhood the people were out and about, trying to get on with their daily work as best they could, dodging the beggars and street urchins who had multiplied since she was last here. Some had set up temporary shelters made out of rubble and broken furniture from bombed-out homes in the alleyways and abandoned yards. She held a handkerchief to her face to block out the stench of the insanitary conditions. It reminded her of a scene from *Les Misérables*.

When she turned the corner into Yves' street, she heard a whistle clearly directed at her. She looked around and saw a man wearing a faded brown coat and a Breton cap standing in the shadow of a doorway. He waved her over and then disappeared inside the house, leaving the door slightly ajar. With one hand on the gun in her pocket she cautiously pushed the door open. It led to a darkened stairwell. A voice called out from the top of the stairs.

'Psst! Over here.'

She recognised the voice. It was Didier.

'You gave me a scare,' she told him. 'I was ready to shoot you.'

'And I you,' he laughed. 'What are you doing here?'

'I could ask you the same thing. I gather you've heard about Eva's death?'

He nodded. 'It wasn't one of us, if that's what you're thinking.'

He led her into a dimly-lit room decked with several couches upholstered in rich red velvet and a bar at one end. The walls were filled with mirrors and the occasional painting of women – mostly nudes, one of which she recognised as the red-haired woman Yves had been painting. Two heavily made-up women in low-cut dresses sat by the window smoking and playing cards.

'Can you give us a moment alone?' Didier said to one of them.

They stubbed their cigarettes out and left through a door covered with a heavy curtain, leaving behind the odour of cheap perfume. Claire didn't need to ask what sort of place they were in.

'The dark-haired one is called Maya,' Didier said. 'She owns the establishment.'

'What's going on, Didier?'

'You are lucky I was on watch. See that black car parked outside the bakery?' He moved the lace curtain aside so that she could get a better look. 'It's the Gestapo. They're watching Yves' place. They raided it the day after the fiasco near the Sourisseau farm. Everyone who goes to his apartment is pulled in for questioning. It gets worse. My place was also raided, as was Henri's. They found the uniforms we wore when we rescued Jean–Claude and Michel. Somebody squealed, and they squealed loudly.'

Claire shook her head in disbelief. 'Are they okay?' she asked, afraid of what she might hear.

'Henri has gone to ground, moved out of the city for a while till things cool down.'

'And Yves?'

'No one has seen him since that night.'

'What do you think happened?' she asked him.

'Only Yves can tell us that. I have my suspicions, though. I think I trained the traitor myself. It's a hard thing to live with.'

She put a hand on his knee. 'It's not your fault. We've always known something like this could happen.'

'True, but it doesn't make me feel any better,' he said. He lit his pipe and took a long look at her. Her face seemed a little rounder. Something about her had changed but he couldn't put his finger on what it was. 'And you?' he asked. 'How have you been?'

'Hoffmann has sent Oskar back to Germany. I have no job and I can't stay on here, so he wants to take me away.'

'Where to?

'He wouldn't tell me where, only that they use it for intelligence purposes.'

'I am aware of the place,' Didier replied. 'I was in the discussions when Henri and Yves suggested finding a way to get you there. He said you think it's near the place where you spent some time with him in 1940.'

'Is there anything you don't know about me?' she answered sarcastically.

Didier grinned. 'Not much, Marie-Elise. That's why we're survivors. We make it our business to know these things.' He sucked on his pipe, deep in thought. 'Where did you stay?' he asked. 'Tell me everything.'

'Is this really necessary? It was over four years ago.'

'It's all necessary.'

'There's not much to tell. We didn't go far – to the beach, dinner in the local restaurants…that's about all really.'

She spent the next ten minutes telling him about the cottage, the landscape of the area, how large the nearest village was, etc.

'If this is the place, do you think you could find that cottage again?'

'I'm sure of it. That is, if I am allowed the freedom to move about.'

'It all fits in with what the Maquis have told us,' he said. 'I will make contact with them – tell them to keep an eye out for you. Use the code to communicate with them. I assure you we will keep you in our sights.'

'Do you think Yves and Henri have gone there?' she asked nervously.

'I don't know. If they are alive, they will resurface when the time is right.'

He sat back in the chair and studied her again. She was definitely not her normal self and unaware of her pregnancy, he put it down to the strain they were all under.

'You can still walk away, you know, right this very minute. You don't have to go back to him if you don't want to. I can get you out of Rennes today.'

'You sound like Henri,' she laughed. 'He kept telling me the same thing. No, Didier, I will see this through.'

Chapter 21

It was one of the worst winters in living memory and the ground was covered in a thick blanket of white snow. As they neared the coast they became enveloped in a thick fog and Schneider took a wrong turn on several occasions. She had no idea where they were, but when they turned into the rutted, narrow lane Claire recognised the place immediately. The cottage where she had spent that fateful summer in 1940 was less than a kilometre away. Though the hedgerows were now laden with snow and the ditches with their rabbit holes were filled with glistening white snowdrifts, she knew every step of this lane by heart. A lump rose in her throat. It was here that she'd spent the happiest two weeks of her life, and in her bones she knew it was here that it would all end.

When they reached the fork in the road, instead of veering left to the cottage, the car turned right – towards the Manoir de Sevigny. Another several more kilometres they pulled up outside a large wrought-iron gate emblazoned with a coat of arms. To one side was a configuration of what appeared to be farm buildings.

Two guards appeared carrying sub-machine guns. They recognised Schneider and waved him through. Claire scanned her eyes past them towards the farm buildings. Outside one of them a man was hanging up half a dozen ducks under the eaves. They locked eyes momentarily. Was he the gamekeeper Yves had told her about?

The car drove up the hill towards the house. Tyre marks from heavy trucks had left furrows in the snow and mud, making this last part of the journey a bumpy ascent. Towards the top of the hill the mist cleared, and when the house came into view Claire recognised it immediately as the place she had been held captive. From the outside it looked impressive, an elegant nineteenth-century stone building with a gabled roof. So this was the infamous Manoir de Sevigny, she thought to herself. Schneider turned the car into a gravel car park situated in front of the house and parked next to several Reich cars. At this point the truck tyres veered left towards the other side of the house.

Claire had no idea what to expect but when they entered the building she got the shock of her life. The place was teeming with people. On the first floor men and women sat at desks tapping away on their typewriters, whilst others appeared and disappeared with mounds of paperwork from one of the many doorways in the adjoining corridors. It was clear that she had entered one of the most important intelligence headquarters in Brittany. It reminded her of a place in England Henri had once mentioned – Bletchley Park, known only to insiders as Station X. That was also supposed to be top secret.

Schneider approached a conservatively-dressed young woman of slim build with dark, shoulder-length hair. After a short conversation she came over and introduced herself as Fräulein Brigitte Kopkow. Claire wondered if she was related to the infamous Horst Kopkow, the SS counter-intelligence chief in Berlin in charge of *Sonderbehandlung* or 'special treatment'.

'I believe that you will be staying with us for a while,' she said, affecting a warm smile. 'We have prepared your room, so if you wouldn't mind following me.'

Claire did as she was told while Schneider went out to the car to fetch her belongings. After her accommodation at the Hôtel d'Armorique, she wasn't entirely sure what to expect, but this time she had been given the adjoining room to Hoffmann's – the very same room she had been in when they were reunited. Except for vases of fresh flowers – red and white carnations – nothing had changed. Even the bedcover with its madder toile de Jouy pastoral scenes was still the same. There was one thing that stood out, however – the radio on one of the tables. Had they forgotten she was French?

These new arrangements signified a new phase in their relationship: Hoffmann was no longer hiding the fact that she was his mistress. How Claire despised that word – 'mistress'. It conjured up something sordid; something she had never believed their love to be.

'If there is anything else you need, Fräulein Bouchard, please don't hesitate to ask,' Brigitte Kopkow said, after checking all was in order.

She put her hand on the door handle to leave. 'And there's one other thing,' she added, as if was an afterthought. 'We observe a strict code of conduct here, that is to say that certain areas are out of bounds and you must not fraternise with any of the people working on the first floor. They are under orders not to talk with anyone other than their immediate colleagues.

A breach of these orders could result in serious consequences for them. There's also the matter of the east wing. It's completely out of bounds to anyone without a pass. Other than that, you are free to go anywhere. We have a dining room and a recreation room with a library.'

As soon as she was alone Claire looked out of the windows to gauge the layout of the estate. The fog was beginning to clear, and from one of the windows she could see the east wing. The truck tyres headed in that direction and turned the corner. At the bottom of the estate near the gate were the farm buildings she had passed. The church bells chimed on the hour – 5pm. Now she recalled their distinct sound, and the memories came flooding back. They were from the church on the other side of the cottage in the tiny village of Plouville. She took a deep breath. Coming to grips with the workings and layout of the Manoir de Sevigny was not going to be easy.

In the evening many of the workers left the manor house and returned to their accommodation in Saint-Brieuc and were replaced by others for the next shift. Intelligence work continued around the clock.

Brigitte sent a message that dinner was to be served in the dining room at 8pm sharp. Apparently dinner at the manor was an elegant affair and she should be dressed appropriately. She sorted out her clothes. Only Eva's new outfits would be suitable here; her old ones were far too dowdy. The crucifix was the only thing she was rarely parted from, and even then it was for a short time. She took it off and placed it on her bedside table. Tonight would be one of those times. She would wear Hoffmann's present. It would go well with Eva's black crêpe outfit with the gold braid ribbon.

She was putting the finishing touches to her attire when Hoffmann entered. He took off his jacket, undid the top buttons of his shirt, and turned the radio on. It was tuned to a German station playing music.

'How do I look?' Claire asked.

He smiled. 'Perfect.' He took her in his arms and pulled her to him. 'Now I finally have you to myself. Your presence will bring a little light back into my life.'

They were the last to enter the dining room. Everyone else was already seated at the banquet table. Claire took her place next to Hoffmann, who was seated at the top of the table. To her right was a man who introduced himself as Herr Maximilian Gassner, a colleague of Sturmbannführer Hans Kieffer of Gestapo HQ at the Avenue Foch in Paris.

Claire got the shock of her life when she noticed his companion for the evening: the red-haired woman with long curls like the Medusa's head whom she had met in Yves' studio – Kristina. Gassner introduced her as Lili. When they acknowledged each other, the look in Kristina's eyes told Claire that they were here for the same reason.

She cast her eyes around the table at the other guests, twenty in all. One face in particular stood out: Karl Wenk, and he gazed at her with a mixture of interest and disdain. Two other officers also had female companions. She wondered how they viewed her.

Dinner that evening was a sumptuous affair. A glistening roast pig on an enormous platter took centre stage and was meticulously carved and placed onto exquisite Meissen plates alongside vegetables and roast potatoes. This was accompanied by precious fine red wines served in crystal glasses. It surpassed anything she had experienced at Villa Rosières.

After complimenting Hoffmann on the meal and the excellent choice of wines, Gassner tried to engage Claire in conversation.

'If you will allow me to say, Fräulein Bouchard, the dress suits you to perfection. Was it made in Paris?'

Claire's face reddened. She thought of Eva and the last time she had laid eyes on her in the snow.

'Thank you,' she replied. 'It's from the atelier of Monsieur Lelong.'

'Jürgen tells me you are from Paris. Whereabouts, may I ask?'

'The 20th arrondissement,' she told him.

Gassner was interested to know more. Where exactly did she live? Why did she leave? Remembering that he was associated with the Gestapo at Avenue Foch, Claire tried to be as evasive as she could, afraid they would look into her background and the missing years in France – not even Hoffmann could prevent them doing that.

Thankfully Gassner's attention turned away from her when Wenk stood up and proposed a toast to Hoffmann. The meal had been in honour of his latest achievement – the surprise attack on the Resistance and the capture of most of the Chevalier network. The men stood up and congratulated him.

'Soon all the perpetrators will be brought to justice,' Hoffmann replied. 'It's only a matter of days.'

Someone started to sing, and everyone except the women joined in.

'*Deutschland, Deutschland, über alles*
Über alles in der Welt...'

The combination of rich food, her pregnancy and the fact that they were toasting the demise of her friends caused Claire to experience another bout of nausea. She whispered something to Hoffmann and excused herself to go to the ladies' room. Seeing her distress, Kristina quickly placed her napkin on the table and told Gassner she was going to see if Fräulein Bouchard was all right.

In the ladies' room, Claire ran cold water over a hand towel and patted her brow. At that moment Kristina burst into the room.

'Are you all right?' she asked. 'You looked as if you were about to faint.'

'What on earth are you doing here?' asked Claire. 'And do you have any idea who that man is you're with?' After firing questions at her in quick succession, she apologised.

'No need,' replied Kristina, opening her bag and taking out a small perfume spray. 'Madame Maya sent us.'

'Us?' Claire queried.

'Myself and the other two women. She heard from a colleague that certain members of the Gestapo wanted a few women to keep them warm during the cold nights. It seems that they were reluctant to use girls from the area, most likely because they didn't want anyone to know where this place was. Madame Maya belongs to the Rennes Resistance. We all do. She works closely with Henri, Didier and Yves.'

At the mention of Yves, Claire's heart missed a beat.

'Have you heard from him?'

'Nothing, none of us have. But if I know Yves, he will be doing everything in his power to get back at the Germans.'

'Then you don't believe he's dead?'

Kristina threw her head back, the red tresses falling down her back. 'Certainly not,' she said, spraying perfume on her wrists. 'He's far too clever for that.'

'Are you staying here tonight?' Claire asked.

'Of course. They have a little party planned,' she said with a wink. 'Let's hope it's not going to be too eccentric. Some of them like to let their hair down.' She returned the perfume to her bag and then applied a rich coral lipstick. 'I have a message for you from Didier. He says it's urgent. The gamekeeper will make contact with you tomorrow.'

Kristina raked her hands through her hair. It was the first time Claire had really studied her, and she found her quite beautiful in an exotic way.

'I'm sorry I was rude to you the first time we met,' Claire said.

Kristina laughed. 'It's quite all right. And if it helps, Yves feels the same about you.'

'I'm not sure what you're getting at.'

'It's as plain as the nose on my face, *mon amie*. You were quite jealous that day but you had no need to be. Yves is in love with you but he is too proud to say it.'

Her words took Claire by surprise. Had her feelings that day been so transparent? But Yves...in love with her! That was something she hadn't contemplated.

They heard footsteps approaching and Fräulein Kopkow entered the room.

'We have been worried about you, Fräulein,' she said. 'Is everything all right?'

Claire picked up her handbag. 'Absolutely fine, thank you, but please tell Herr Hoffmann I wish to be excused. I think I will have an early night.'

Claire had been asleep for several hours when she was woken by voices coming from the adjoining room – Hoffmann's room. A thin stream of yellow lamplight streaked the carpet from the partially open door. She checked her watch. It was 5.30 in the morning. She got out of bed and moved to the door to listen. She recognised the two other voices with him – Wenk and Gassner. The conversation appeared to be about the capture of someone important in the early hours of the morning. The telephone rang and Hoffmann answered it.

'Bring him here,' he said, and slammed the receiver down.

'What else do you have?' Wenk asked. 'What about the woman?'

'Koenig thinks he has uncovered something of importance,' he replied. 'We will know more tomorrow.'

The men departed and she heard Hoffmann put on the radio. Music played for a while and then he switched it off and entered her room.

'How are you, my darling?' he asked. 'You have me worried. This illness of yours seems to persist. I think I should call the doctor again.'

'No, no. It won't be necessary. It must have been the rich food.' She pulled him to her. 'Come and lie with me. Let's not waste our time together.'

The nakedness and warmth of her body excited him. Claire gave herself to him as she had always done, only this time it was different. For the first time the love that had been so deep, so perfect, now had a crack in it.

When she went downstairs for breakfast, Kristina and the girls had already left and the communications experts were changing shifts. Claire ate alone in the dining room, which had long been cleared from the previous night's banquet. Someone brought her scrambled eggs and a thick slice of rye bread accompanied by real coffee, added a few more logs to the fire and departed.

She thought about Hoffmann's conversation with Wenk and Gassner. Who had they captured? She found herself praying it wouldn't be Yves. But there was one thought that she kept going over and over in her mind: what was it that Koenig had uncovered? In Rennes, Claire had been more confident of keeping control of her relationship with Hoffmann, but here it was different. Here she had to contend with his superiors, who held sway over both their lives.

She finished her breakfast and returned to her room. The fog had cleared and the snow was beginning to thaw. She looked out of the window and saw a man walking towards the house carrying a brace of ducks – the same man she had seen outside the farm buildings. She decided to go for a walk. Everyone else on the ground floor appeared far too busy to notice her leave.

Outside, the biting cold air hit her cheeks like a jagged knife and she pulled up the collar of her overcoat to cover them. She had no idea where she was going except that she was heading towards the one man she prayed was her connection with the outside world. As they neared each other she saw him drop a small piece of paper, but when she passed he did not acknowledge her, and neither did he look at her.

She bent down and picked up the paper. On it was written: *The orchard at the changeover of shifts.* She tore the paper into shreds and bit by bit, scattered them throughout her walk.

When she returned to the house, Fräulein Kopkow was at her desk. She asked if Claire felt better. On the surface she seemed pleasant, but Claire knew she would be on the lookout for her putting a foot wrong.

It didn't take long for her to discover that the orchard was behind the house just past the walled vegetable garden, and could be reached through the kitchen. Hoffmann was out with Wenk and wouldn't be back until late. At around 7pm when the changeover of shifts occurred, Claire slipped out of the kitchen and made her way to the vegetable garden. She pushed open the wooden door and walked through a maze of empty vegetable beds towards another door, which opened into the orchard. The trees, now devoid of their leaves, ran all the way down a slope which bordered onto a wood.

Within minutes of being there, she heard a whistle. She cocked her pistol and slowly walked over to a gnarled cherry tree where two figures emerged to greet her. The first was the gamekeeper, who introduced himself as Bernard, the other, Yves. She was so overjoyed to see he was still alive she threw her arms around his neck, smothering him in kisses.

'Steady on! What did I do to deserve that?' he said, giving her that cheeky grin of his.

'You're alive, thank God, that's what.'

They moved back into the shadow of the tree.

'We have been so worried about you. Not even a word!'

Yves put his finger to his mouth. 'Ssh! The estate is heavily patrolled.'

'You were right about this place,' Claire said. 'It's one of the most important intelligence centres in Brittany.'

'What else have you found – anything about the men being held captive, for instance?'

She shook her head. 'At the moment all I know is that the east wing is out of bounds. Give me a day or two.'

'No time, Marie-Elise. Come with us – I want to show you something.'

They silently inched their way back towards the house and hid next to a small hothouse, which opened up onto a lawn.

'Over there.' He gestured. 'That's the east wing.'

They could see two sentries sitting on a stone wall guarding the doors of the back entrance of the manor. A series of darkened low-barred windows spanned almost a third of the building, and above them was the ground floor of the manor. Bernard pointed out that the brightly lit rooms were where the prisoners were interrogated.

'They keep the codebreakers and intelligence units separate – on the first floor, well out of earshot of the screams. Most of them wouldn't have a clue what was taking place.' He pointed to a section of the wall a few metres past where the guards sat. 'And that's where the executions take place – within earshot of the poor sods in the cells.'

Claire scanned the outside of the building. 'Where on earth do the trucks go?'

'Through those doors,' Yves replied. 'There's a ramp that leads to the cells in the basement. It's a death sentence for those who enter. We have to get these men out as soon as possible.

'There's something else. You're not going to want to hear this, but Henri has been captured. They're holding him in Rennes but I have it on good authority they're bringing him here.'

'So that's who it is,' she replied. 'I overheard them say they thought they'd caught someone important.'

'At the moment they're not sure who he is and they're bringing him here to identify him.' He gave her a small photograph. It was impossible to see the face clearly in the dark.

'Who is it?' Claire asked.

'The man who can identify him – Agent 12658, better known to us as Pascal. It's a duplicate of his ID card. He's a double agent and he's in there. Your job is to find him and eliminate him before Henri gets here. Fortunately he has no idea who you are so you'll be safe.'

'So Henri was right after all.'

Yves sighed. 'I'm afraid Pascal wasn't the only traitor. There was someone else, a Maquisard who Didier trained – Jacques the pianist. I saw him with Hoffmann at the woodsman's cottage the night of the raid on the drop zone. I have no idea if they were connected, though.'

'This Jacques, where is he now?'

'I took good care of him. Hoffmann was luckier. I thought I'd shot him but it appears not.'

They heard a noise and two trucks appeared around the corner. The guards opened the doors and the trucks disappeared down the ramp into the building. Yves checked the time.

'Watch carefully,' he said to her.

After a while the doors opened and the trucks reappeared and drove away. A few minutes later, the guards resumed their post.

'Sixteen minutes, twenty-five seconds exactly,' Yves said, checking his watch again. 'The longest they've been in there was an hour.'

'What are you saying?' Claire asked.

'There's a pattern here. This is the moment the area is unguarded: when they are at their most vulnerable.'

He pulled her back into the relative safety of the orchard and handed her a folded piece of paper. 'Take this and study it. It's a map of the building – an old one, but it will still give you an idea of the layout. You will see that the basement of the east wing was used as a wine cellar and storage area. They were converted into cells when the Gestapo took the place over. There isn't time to talk now. Tomorrow we'll map out a plan of action. I want you to go to the cottage. No one has been there since the war except for the Plouville Maquis.'

'How will I get there?' Claire asked. 'I can't simply walk out of the main gate.'

Bernard pointed to an area where the orchard petered out into the wood. 'Make your way down there. There's a narrow footpath. I'll meet you at the end where it crosses the road.'

Claire looked to where he pointed. From where they stood, there was no sign of a footpath and she prayed she wouldn't get lost.

'There's one very important thing I have to ask you,' she told Yves. 'Hoffmann – is there any way we can…?'

'Spare him?' Yves said, finishing her sentence for her. He shook his head. 'With his record, I doubt it.'

'What if we could get him to hand us information – something that could help the Allies – or give us Wenk?'

Yves looked at her. He understood her silent plea. 'And do you really believe he would do that?'

Claire didn't answer.

When she returned to the house, she realised that amidst her happiness at seeing Yves alive, and the devastating news of Henri's capture, she had completely forgotten to tell him that Koenig had uncovered something of importance. She quickly returned to her room, locked the door, pulled out her suitcase, took her pistol out of the secret compartment, checked it and put it her bag. Now more than ever, she needed it on hand.

Hoffmann wasn't expected to be back for at least another hour, giving her enough time to study the map and the photograph of Pascal. He had dark hair, a broad face and a thin moustache, which Claire surmised he had probably shaved off by now. After committing his face to memory she tore it into tiny pieces and flushed the image down the toilet. Next she spread the map out on her bed and memorised every inch: every room, corridor, staircase and entrance, every closet and toilet. Her training and the events of the past few months had sharpened her mind for this sort of thing.

But the news of Henri's capture had come as a bitter blow. He was invincible, or so she had thought. And how was she going to find Pascal? With so many people around it was like looking for a needle in a haystack.

She heard someone turn the key in the door to Hoffmann's room and hurriedly slid the map under the heavy Aubusson carpet by the side of her bed. Footsteps walked across the room and switched on the radio. The same German radio station played *Lili Marleen* and other nostalgic songs she had come to recognise.

When no one came through their adjoining door she took a look for herself and found Schneider sitting at Hoffmann's desk, looking through a folder of papers. When he saw her enter, he snapped them shut.

'Fräulein Bouchard, you startled me. I thought you were downstairs having dinner. How are you feeling? Much better, I hope.'

'I came up to have a lie-down, but now that you mention it, I am rather hungry. Do you have any idea when Herr Hoffmann will be back?'

Schneider shook his head. 'Something important came up. I am afraid he won't be back until tomorrow afternoon. He's gone to Rennes.'

'I see,' Claire replied. 'In that case I shall dine alone – unless of course you would care to join me?'

Schneider's face reddened at her suggestion. 'I'm afraid not. The dining room is for officers and their guests only. Besides, I have work here.'

She returned to her room to make sure everything was as it should be before dressing for dinner. Tonight she would wear the red silk scarf Eva had given her. It occurred to her that she should lock the adjoining door before leaving, but she thought better of the idea as it might look suspicious. She wondered what Schneider thought of her. When had he found out that she and Hoffmann were lovers? It was hard to tell with him. He was the loyal German who kept his emotions to himself.

Except for a few officers whose faces she recognised from the previous evening, there was no one in the dining room that she knew. They stood up when she entered to acknowledge her, just as the men had done for Eva in the square in Rennes several months back. The irony didn't escape her. She felt like the cuckoo in the nest. The meal was delicious – rabbit stew in red wine – but after a few mouthfuls she pushed her plate aside. The thought of Pascal identifying Henri made her feel ill.

One of the men got up to leave, and as he did, he dropped something – his pass. As soon as he left the room she picked it up and put it her bag. She had to act now.

Schneider had gone when Claire returned to her room. In the quiet of the evening she took off her crucifix and carefully slid aside a section of the back. The cyanide pill popped out and she put it in her pocket along with her pistol. Then she went into Hoffmann's room and checked the desk where Schneider had been working. As expected, the file he had been working on was not there, but she did manage to find an empty folder. Grabbing a pen, she wrote the words *TOP SECRET* on it, and below, *Agent 12658*. On top of the desk was an official Reich stamp and inkpad. She picked up the stamp and brought it down with a thud at the bottom of the folder.

It was 10pm and the night shift would be well and truly settled in by now. A group of men and women worked at their desks on the first floor. She walked straight past them and down a long corridor towards the east wing. A man at a desk outside a large set of double doors asked to see her pass.

'Where are you going?' he asked.

Claire's heart was pounding. 'I have an urgent message from Herr Sturmbannführer Hoffmann. I am to contact this man for an identity check tomorrow. Where can I find him?'

She reeled off Pascal's identity number and gave the man a quick glimpse of the folder. The fact that it had the official Reich stamp was enough to set his mind at rest.

The man pulled out a pad from the drawer and checked through a list of names until he came to one on the second page. He told her she was in the wrong area.

'The ground floor,' he said. 'Room 26.'

She thanked him and walked away. The ground floor was where Bernard had told her the interrogations took place. Room 26 was at the far end of the corridor. Next to that was the entrance to the basement. She knocked on the door.

A voice called out in German, '*Herein.*'

Claire loosened her scarf, draping it elegantly around her neck and shoulders, and checked her pistol and the cyanide pill in her pocket. When she entered the room, a man was looking out of the window towards the orchard with his back turned to her. It was obvious he was expecting someone else.

'Have they brought him?' he asked.

'Who, sir?' Claire asked, closing the door behind her.

On hearing her voice he spun around and glared at her. She recognised him immediately. He was a little thinner perhaps, and his face looked grey and haggard. Whilst on the surface he might have appeared a free man, his face bore the telltale marks of a recent Gestapo beating.

'Who are you?' he asked.

'Herr Hoffmann's secretary,' she said with a smile. 'I'm afraid he has been delayed and asked if you could take a look at this before he gets back.' She put the folder on the desk.

'What is it?'

'I have no idea, sir.'

He pulled out a chair and sat down to read it. When he opened it there was nothing inside.

'What the...?!' he said, swearing angrily.

He looked up and saw Claire pointing the gun at him. 'Hello, Pascal,' she said. 'You don't know who I am, do you?' She walked around to his side of the desk, and with her free hand, whipped away her scarf. 'No, I didn't think so. Let me jog your memory.

'Manon,' she said, pointing the barrel of the gun at his head. 'The elusive Manon. I believe you've been looking for me. Well, here I am.'

He backed his chair away a little as she neared him, but with the gun aimed at him, he had nowhere to go. She stepped behind him.

'You see that picture over there?' she said, indicating a large framed photograph of Hitler on the wall with the gun. 'Look at it. It will be the last image you will see.'

Before he understood what was happening, Claire slipped the scarf around his neck and made as if to strangle him. When he raised his hands to try and free himself she quickly pressed the cyanide pill into his mouth and clamped it shut. In less than a minute he was dead. After positioning him upright in his chair, she retrieved the folder and left the room.

Chapter 22

The following morning Claire dressed in the most casual clothes she could find. Knowing the route would be muddy due to the recent snow and rain, she found a pair of navy slacks and a dark ribbed pullover, over which she intended to wear her old tweed jacket that she had worn during the nightly drops, but she couldn't find it. She must have left it at Villa Rosières or the Hôtel d'Armorique. The next best thing was her overcoat, not the most appropriate for a walk through the woods but it would have to do.

When she reached the wood at the end of the orchard, Bernard was already waiting for her. He asked her to take off her shoes, which he put in his rucksack, and he gave her a pair of wellington boots.

'It's muddy and slippery,' he said. 'Better to walk in these.'

As she put them on he looked at her light-coloured overcoat and threw her a look of disapproval.

'I had nothing else to wear,' she told him.

She followed him into the woods until the track crossed the narrow road at a point past the main entrance to the manor. When the coast was clear they crossed over into the woods again. A sign read *Forêt de la Sevigny: Propriété privée*. The track meandered through ferns and bracken, their wet, feathery fronds glistening in the shafts of light that penetrated the canopy, and a symphony of birdsong filled the air. At a certain point the track led down a steep slope towards a stream. The recent snow had melted and the ground was wet and slippery. Bernard took off his overcoat and gave it to her.

'Here, put this on in case you fall. We don't want you dirtying your nice clean coat, do we?' he said with a smile.

He had been right to make her wear it. She stumbled twice and at one point slithered down the slope in an ungainly manner, only coming to a standstill when she caught a low branch.

After they'd crossed the stream, the track opened up into a field, which Claire recognised in an instant as the field at the back of the cottage. A Maquisard was waiting for them and escorted them through to the courtyard and into the cottage kitchen, where a welcoming committee including Yves and Didier awaited her.

'Good to see you again, Marie-Elise,' Didier said.

The news that she had eliminated Agent 12658 was met with thunderous applause.

'I'm proud of you,' Yves said. 'We all are.'

'Any news of Henri?' she asked.

'Our sources said they will be bringing him here, probably within the next twelve hours, but at least we don't have to worry about Pascal now.'

'There's something else,' she continued. 'The SS officer – Koenig. He's uncovered something of importance.'

'Do you have any idea what?' Yves asked.

Claire shook her head. 'I'm afraid not, but I've seen him somewhere before and for the life of me, I can't remember where. He's taken a great dislike to me, that's for sure.'

'Okay,' Yves said to everyone. 'Time is slipping by. Let's get down to business. If we want to save Henri and the others we must act tonight. At a specific time during the evening the coastal road to Saint-Brieuc is to be blown up. Lookouts will be posted along the turn-off to the manor and throughout the woods. By then the manor will be totally surrounded. The thing we have to do is to get those trucks going to the manor first and replace the Germans in the truck with our own men. As soon as the trucks go through the doors in the east wing. Bernard's men will be in the orchard, which gives us added strength. It's imperative that we get everyone out of those cells and away as soon as possible. No one must be left behind.

'There's another thing. I also have it on good authority that the officers will be entertaining again tonight – probably to celebrate their recent successes with the Resistance. The girls have been notified to keep them busy.' He turned to Claire. 'They will be at your disposal, should you need them.'

The importance of what they were about to do was etched on the faces of everyone in the room. Failure was not something they could contemplate.

'There's a man in Plouville, a gendarme by the name of Hubert Perrot who flirts as a double agent,' Yves said. 'He has been known to act as a liaison officer for the Gestapo. He is known to most in the manor, especially the guards. We are going to get him on our side. When he sees he has no other option, he will comply. Another thing: everyone who enters the premises will be wearing Wehrmacht uniform to fool the guards.'

The meeting concluded. Yves asked Claire to go to Plouville with him before she returned to the house. Bernard accompanied them, showing them a back way across the fields.

Plouville was about half the size of Saint-Etienne; little more than a hamlet but it did have a small church – the one whose distinctive bells she had heard from the cottage and the manor. The gendarmerie was an old brick building on the main street that had once been used as an infirmary for the sick during World War I. It was lunchtime and the streets were empty. The three sauntered into the gendarmerie, catching Hubert Perrot asleep with his feet on his desk in front of the wood heater and snoring loudly. When Yves pressed his semi-automatic against his temple a startled Hubert instinctively reached for his gun until he realised his hopeless situation. Bernard closed the door and kept a lookout whilst Claire took his pistol and placed a piece of paper in front of him.

'What do you want?' he asked, his eyes wide with terror.

'We have had you in our sights for a while now,' Yves said. 'Your little game with the Germans has not gone unnoticed.'

Hubert protested that he had no idea what they were talking about.

Bernard pointed out his comings and goings at the manor. 'Every single trip noted,' he said. 'You're a wanted man. We could have had you killed before but we are giving you one last chance to redeem yourself.'

Claire pushed the paper towards him. 'Read it,' she hissed.

Hubert's hands were shaking like a leaf.

'I, Hubert Perrot, gendarme of Plouville, willingly acknowledge that I helped the Germans against my fellow countrymen for monetary gains.'

'Now sign it,' she added.

Hubert protested until Yves pushed the gun further into his temple. Claire handed him the pen.

'Someone's coming,' Bernard called out. 'It's his wife.'

He stood behind the door as Madame Perrot, a willing beneficiary of Hubert's gains, appeared with a basket of food. On seeing what was taking place in the room, she dropped the basket and turned to run. Bernard hit her on the back of the head, knocking her unconscious. Her bulky frame fell on the doorstep and he pulled her inside. Hubert cried out until he was pistol-whipped by Yves.

'Sign,' Claire said again. 'Or we kill you both.'

When Bernard pointed his gun at Madame Perrot's head a terrified Hubert signed the paper.

Claire picked it up and put it in her jacket pocket. 'As we said, there is another way out for you.'

She went on to tell him that they had it on absolute authority that the Allies would be landing in the next few weeks, and that the Germans would be forced to surrender or be killed.

'The Allies already have you down as a traitor,' she told him. 'But I doubt you'll live that long. Your countrymen will get you before then.' She glanced across the room at the crumpled body of his wife. 'And her too.'

'What do you want me to do?'

'We are offering you one million francs to work with us. If all goes according to plan, this paper you just signed will be destroyed and we will make sure you receive a pardon and are released after the war.'

Hubert thought quickly. One million francs was far more than the meagre pickings the Germans had given him. It was enough for him to buy them a decent house.

'Okay. I'm with you. I give you my word.'

Claire extended her hand, and they shook hands.

'Get your coat,' Yves said. 'You're coming with us. Remember, one wrong move and you're dead.'

They took his keys, along with several crates of alcohol commandeered from the Resistance, whilst Yves walked him to his car around the corner. With the barrel of the gun in his sights, Hubert reversed the car outside the gendarmerie. They bundled Madame Perrot's limp body into it and drove away. A few kilometres along the coastal road, Bernard directed them down a bumpy back road towards the cottage, where Madame Perrot was immediately bound and gagged and taken to one of the outhouses.

It was almost two in the afternoon and Bernard said they had better be getting back before someone noticed Claire was missing. Yves walked part of the way back with them, going over their plans. At the brow of the hill, they parted ways.

'Bernard will keep an eye on you,' he said, and turned to go back to the cottage.

'Wait!' she called after him.

He turned back to face her.

'Thank you,' she stammered, 'for everything.'

He gave her a wave. Within a matter of seconds he had disappeared into the woods.

Back in the orchard, Claire changed back into her shoes and returned to the house. As usual, the place was a hive of activity and she was pleasantly surprised to find that no one had missed her at all.

Claire was reading in the library when Schneider came in and said Hoffmann had returned and wished to see her straight away. She was also told that the meeting was to be in his official office on the ground floor, not in his private room as she had expected. When Schneider avoided her eyes she knew it was serious. She picked up her bag with the gun inside and clutched it under her arm. She could run, but where would she go? She wouldn't last a minute.

Hoffmann was not alone. Gassner and Wenk were with him. One look at his face told her it was all over. Hoffmann indicated to Schneider to take her handbag. It was useless to protest. He gave the bag to Hoffmann and left. Wenk was seated in a leather chair next to Hoffmann's desk, one leg crossed casually over the other, smoking a cigarette. Gassner stood by the window, staring at the light sprinkling of fresh snow accumulating on the windowsill.

'Sit down, Fräulein Bouchard,' said Wenk menacingly. 'I think you know why you are here.'

Claire looked at Hoffmann. He was visibly agitated.

'I have no idea,' she replied.

Wenk leaned over to pick up a thick file from Hoffmann's desk. He smiled at her as he flicked through the papers; a cruel smile that told her he was not one to play games.

'From the moment I laid eyes on you at Villa Rosières, I knew you were up to something. I tried to warn Herr Hoffmann but I am afraid he was besotted with you and would not listen to reason.' He looked across at Hoffmann, and back to Claire. 'I must admit that you do have a certain seductive charm, and we are only men after all. Monogamy does not come easy for some men but we turn a blind eye – except when the woman in question happens to be French.'

Claire felt trapped, but she was surprised at how remarkably cool she was under pressure.

He looked at her file. 'Herr Gassner has dug a little deeper into your past. It seems that you told Herr Hoffmann that when the Germans took Paris, you lost your job and didn't want to live there any longer. You also said that you toyed with the idea of becoming a secretary or a translator, but then decided to stay with friends in Provence until finally finding a teaching job in Saint-Etienne.'

'Yes, that's correct,' Claire replied.

'But is it, Fräulein Bouchard? When we sent someone to your apartment to check, we were told that you left before our army reached Paris. You never returned. Isn't that correct?'

'No, I'm afraid that is not true.'

'Our records indicate that a German officer was billeted in your apartment during the first month of the occupation. The concierge said you never returned.' He paused for a moment. 'Who is lying?'

'I did go to Provence to visit friends for a while.'

'Again, we have no record of you ever being in Provence. And the teaching job you applied for – it was never advertised.'

Claire thought quickly. 'It was word of mouth. Someone told me they had lost a teacher and were in need of a replacement.'

Wenk looked at the file again and showed her a photograph. 'Was it this man who told you about the job?'

When Claire saw the photograph of Henri, she felt a lump rise in her throat. 'No,' she replied after a quick glance. 'Who is he?'

Wenk laughed. 'Have it your own way, Fräulein.' He picked up the phone on Hoffmann's desk and asked for Dieter Koenig to come in.

Koenig entered the room carrying a box and her old jacket. Her heart pounded in her chest. Now it suddenly hit her where she had seen him before. He was the officer who had caught her in bed with Yves during the raid in Saint-Etienne. They had been ruthlessly efficient and there was no way out. She glanced at Hoffmann for support but his eyes avoided her.

Wenk got up and picked up the jacket. He brought it close to her. 'The sleeve was ripped, I believe.'

'Yes, that's correct. I must have caught it on something. I repaired it a few days later.'

'Correction: Frau Hoffmann's seamstress repaired it for you.'

'Frau Hoffmann thought her seamstress would make a better job of it than I had done. And as you see by the workmanship, that is so. You can hardly see the tear.'

Wenk turned to Koenig. 'Herr Koenig, what can you tell us about the evening you noticed the coat?'

Koenig's eyes blazed with the steady fire of fanaticism. He was a ruthless sadist who took pleasure in the demise of others. Now Claire was his prey.

'We were conducting a raid in the village of Saint-Etienne. Fräulein

Bouchard did not obey orders to go outside, and when we searched the building we found her in her room – in bed with a man.'

Wenk glanced at Hoffmann. He had listened patiently but now his eyes flashed with anger. To Claire it seemed that the fact that she had been caught in bed with another man was far worse than the crimes Wenk was determined to associate her with.

'Go on,' Wenk said.

'When I was about to leave I saw the jacket hanging on the back of the door. It was quite damp. I knew that there had been a thunderstorm the night before during the hours of curfew. It was then that I noticed the large tear. I thought it unusual as it was almost the length of my hand. The Fräulein looked embarrassed when she saw me looking at it.'

'And what happened next?'

Koenig was not sure how to approach his next statement, and waited until Hoffmann himself told him to continue.

'After that I saw her in Rennes at the Hôtel d'Armorique and was told she was...' He considered his words. 'Herr Hoffmann's son's teacher. At about the same time, we had been conducting searches in the woods, and that was when we came across this.' He opened the box. In it was a section of the branch with the torn threads still attached. 'On closer inspection we saw that the threads matched, and knew it was from the same jacket.'

He turned to Hoffmann. 'I'm sorry, sir. I couldn't tell you before. We needed the jacket to put two and two together, and I asked Herr Schneider to get me the jacket.'

Claire then understood that Schneider had taken the jacket when she had dined alone. That was why he was in Hoffmann's room. On the outside she appeared calm, but on the inside she knew there was no way out. After so much care, it was something like this – a tear in an old jacket – that had really given her away and placed her at the scene of the crime: the landing zone.

Wenk put the jacket down. 'Agent Manon,' he said. His voice chilled her to the bone. 'We were informed by one of our agents – a man who unfortunately took his own life last night – that one of the women in the group Chevalier was a woman sent by F Section in London. We have interrogated every other woman in our hands, one of whom I believe you know as Catherine Sourisseau, the sister of the woman who died along with her mother. You, my dear, are the only other woman left in the group.'

He drew his face close to hers. She peered into his ice-cold eyes with as much hatred as he gave her.

'You, Fräulein, are the woman we have been looking for – Manon.'

Claire stared at him. Her defiance angered Wenk and he began to pace the room like a wild animal. He turned to Koenig.

'Bring him in.'

When Koenig returned he was accompanied by two burly guards dragging a man through the door – Henri. At the sight of him Claire felt a sharp pain in her chest. She momentarily clutched her stomach, trying hard to stop the bile that rose in her throat. She had never seen a man so badly beaten. He was barely alive. His body was like a limp rag doll, his legs broken and his face a swollen mass of cuts and black bruises. He had also lost an eye. The stench of urine and blood overpowered the room, forcing Gassner to open the window. His fate seemed clear and she wondered why he had not taken his cyanide pill.

Koenig grabbed Henri's matted hair and yanked his face towards her, whilst Wenk showed her Henri's photograph again.

'My patience is running out. I am asking you one more time. Do you know this man?'

Claire prayed that Henri would forgive her. 'I have never seen him before,' she replied.

Wenk nodded and the men dragged Henri out of the room, leaving a trail of bodily fluids on the polished wooden floorboards.

'It is lamentable that such a fine man as Herr Hoffmann should have seen fit to have become mixed up with you. Berlin does not look favourably on such matters, but because of his excellent record in the service of the Reich, we are willing to put this behind us. You, however, Fräulein, leave us with no other choice. You will be executed tonight at 10.30pm with the rest of the traitors.'

On hearing those words, Claire's legs started to buckle and she reached for the back of the chair. She now wondered if using the cyanide tablet on Pascal had been a wise thing.

Wenk turned to Hoffmann. 'In the meantime, she is yours to do with as you wish.' He raised his hand. '*Heil* Hitler!'

The men left the room, leaving her alone with Hoffmann. Claire sank into the chair. Hoffmann picked up her bag and emptied the contents onto the table. Along with her lipstick was her gun. Never before had she seen such sadness in his eyes.

'Would you have used it on me, Claire?'

She shook her head. 'No,' she lied. 'It was for my own safety. I was receiving death threats because of fraternising with the enemy.'

'This gun alone was enough to have you shot.' He put the gun in his drawer and the rest of the contents back in the bag and handed it back to her.

'Do you believe them?' she asked, her voice barely a whisper. 'That I am guilty of espionage?'

He got up and sat beside her. No matter how hard she tried she couldn't stop the steady flow of tears that ran down her cheeks.

'It's too late for that now. I should not have pursued you as I did,' he said, handing her his handkerchief. 'I should have left well alone.'

He would never know that F Section had always intended that she should find him, and that their chance meeting had only brought this little game forward.

'I do love you, you know – with all my heart,' she said.

Both knew they had a mere five hours together before it would all be over, but neither could bring themselves to acknowledge that fact. He pulled her up onto her feet.

'Come on. Let's go back to our rooms.'

She followed him outside into the corridor. Guards had been posted on every floor, yet no one moved or uttered a word as they made their way towards their rooms. Inside his room, Hoffmann held her in a tight embrace, just as he always did when they were alone. His hand reached out to switch on the radio. A melancholic song played.

'The radio was a test,' he told her. 'Wenk's idea to see if you would try to listen to the BBC. He thought he would catch you out. Happily you did not fall into his trap and I thought it would satisfy him.'

It had crossed her mind to try it, but her sixth sense had told her not to touch the radio. Still, what good was all that now?

Their eyes locked. There was no need for words; both knew what the other wanted. She went to her room, opened the wardrobe and pulled out a silk dress the colour of fresh butter and laid it on her bed. In the next room the music continued to play – Hildegarde, Rosita Serrano, and music that had outlived the Weimar Republic. She undressed and showered, sprayed her body with a fine perfume and slipped the dress on.

Hoffmann was sitting in his chair by the bed. A bedside table lamp cast a warm yellow glow over his face, accentuating his fine scar.

She turned the music up a little louder and stood in the centre of the room. As she had done that first night in Paris, she slowly began to strip for him. Now as before, her actions thrilled them both. In her nakedness she caught a glimpse of herself in the mirror. Her body had changed; her breasts were fuller and her belly rounder. He commented on this but it was not the comment she had expected. He put it down to their lovemaking.

'You have gained a little weight, my darling. Making love has changed you. The curves in your body are comparable to the finest Greek sculpture. From the very moment I saw you naked, you excited me, and now, even after everything we have been through, you still exert the same feeling over me.'

Claire desperately wanted to tell him she was carrying his child; that she must be at least four months gone. But what did it matter now anyway? In a few hours she would be dead and he would know nothing of the child inside her. It was better this way.

Chapter 23

It was just after 7.30pm when the car carrying the three girls from Saint-Brieuc turned off the coastal road into the narrow lane. The night sky with its waxing moon lay shrouded behind gathering rain clouds, casting an eerie blue-black glow over the darkened landscape, silhouetting the passing trees and hedgerows into abstract shapes reminiscent of a theatrical backdrop. When they neared the fork in the road the driver spotted a man in the headlights, waving his hands at him to stop. It was Hubert Perrot, and the driver recognised him. When he stopped Hubert came towards the car.

The driver wound down the window. 'Is everything all right? I have orders to take the women to the Manoir de Sevigny.'

A group of Maquisards suddenly appeared and surrounded the car. The driver was forced out at gunpoint and ordered to take off his chauffeur's uniform. When he protested, he was strangled. The girls sat patiently while the men hid the body in the bushes.

After a few minutes the new chauffeur got into the car – Didier. With him was Hubert. They continued towards the gate. Two guards came towards them to inspect their passes and take a look inside the car. Hubert and Kristina wound down the windows, and as Hubert showed his pass, Didier lifted his gun with the silencer attached, and narrowly missing Hubert's head, fired two bullets with such accuracy that they struck both guards cleanly between the eyes. Another guard rushed out of the building but was shot dead by Bernard, who had been waiting nearby. Hubert jumped out of the car and together, he and Bernard dragged the bodies back inside the building. The incident was over in less than two minutes.

'Well done,' Kristina said with a smile to Didier as they drove away. 'Two perfect shots.'

The car drove on towards the manor and pulled up outside the entrance. Didier stepped out and held the door open for the girls. One by one the three women, decked out in their finest party dresses, got out of the car and after showing their passes to the guards, went inside, leaving him to park the car alongside several others and wait. He sat in the car and lit a cigarette, surveying every angle of the manor and the grounds. He had less than four hours to wait.

The party was well underway when the girls arrived. A buffet of fine food lined one side of the room and a small orchestra was playing in the corner. Kristina cast a quick eye around the room. There were probably about forty people, mostly men, although she spotted several women whom she quickly ascertained were probably codebreakers who had formed a relationship with the officers.

An SS officer stepped forward to welcome them and offered them a drink. One of the girls quickly looped her arm through his and pressed her breasts against him provocatively. When Gassner spotted Kristina his eyes lit up, and the events of the past few hours were momentarily forgotten.

She sidled up to him, brushing her lips against his ear. 'Are we in a playful mood *heute Nacht, mein Herr?*' she whispered coquettishly.

He had no need to answer. Kristina was one of Madame Maya's best girls, effective both at getting what she wanted from the men, and giving them a good time in the process. He gave her a glass of champagne, which she pretended to sip. Whilst others refilled their glasses the three girls secretly discarded theirs. If you wanted to stay alive, you needed your wits about you. Sex with the enemy was a dangerous game, as they well knew.

After a couple of drinks, Gassner wanted to take Kristina back to his room. She asked for one of the other girls to accompany them, promising an experience he wouldn't forget. He willingly agreed. In the privacy of his room, they undressed him and made love to him. As each girl took her turn, the other laced his drink with a sleeping draught.

By 9pm Gassner was fast asleep and the girls returned to the party. Throughout the next hour, little by little, they laced the drinks of several other officers. After a while, the combination of good food, music and drink left the men in a state of blissful intoxication. Only Wenk was immune to their seductive powers. He didn't drink or socialise with the other officers and left the room quite early in the evening after gorging himself on an abundance of seafood.

To Kristina and the girls, all appeared to be going well except for one thing – she had not laid eyes on Claire all evening. They were all supposed to be at the party, and with only a few hours before the raid, it was unthinkable that Claire would not have made contact with them. Something was drastically wrong. Kristina pulled one of the girls aside and told her she was going outside to inform Didier. When she made her way to the entrance, she noticed guards everywhere and knew something was amiss. The guard outside asked her where she was going and she told him she had accidently dropped her lipstick in the car.

Didier was sitting in the car rubbing his hands together, desperately trying to keep warm, when he saw Kristina hurrying towards him.

'She's not here,' she said, trying to catch her breath.

'What do you mean? Of course she's in there.'

'We were supposed to meet at the party. She hasn't shown up. Something's wrong.'

The guard watched them, and together they pretended to look for her lipstick.

'Carry on regardless, with or without her. Now get back inside,' Didier said, 'before they come looking for you. And try to keep that guard distracted for at least a minute. I don't want him looking this way.'

Kristina hurried back to the house. When she neared the guard, she held her lipstick up to show him.

'Found it,' she said with a smile.

She opened her bag to put it away but 'accidently' dropped it, letting it roll down the steps. The guard bent down to pick it up for her, oblivious to Didier, who was directing two flashes of light towards the entrance to the manor to signal that something was wrong. A single light flashed back from the wood, acknowledging him.

By 9.30 pm there was still no sign of the trucks, and Yves started to worry. What if there were no trucks arriving that night? Time was running out, and if all else failed they would go through the woods with Bernard's men and take their chances by storming the east wing on foot. But that would surely result in a bad outcome for all concerned. Added to his worries was the fact that he had just received news from a member of the Maquis that Didier had flashed that something was wrong. All was not going to plan, and he had no idea what it was.

Yves was not a religious man, but he began to pray. Knowing it was luck rather than a miracle, at 10pm they saw headlights turn into the lane. Two trucks rumbled slowly down the rutted lane. When they reached the fork in the road half a dozen of the Maquis forced the trucks to stop.

In the back of the trucks the prisoners, shackled together and with their hands tied behind their backs, heard a voice speaking in German ordering the drivers to get out and line up against the hedgerow. On Yves' orders the Germans were shot in the back of the head and quickly stripped of their uniforms. Thinking that they were also about to be shot and their bodies dumped in the middle of nowhere, the prisoners held their breath as the tarpaulins were flung open. A group of young men in German uniforms greeted them in French.

The prisoners had been so badly beaten they had to be helped out of the trucks but despite their ordeal, they cried with pure joy at tasting the freedom they never thought they would see again. One of the Maquis gave a shrill whistle and more of the men came to their aid, spiriting the prisoners away into the safety of the woods. The rest of the Maquis jumped into the back of the truck and drove away.

It was almost 10.30pm. When the trucks reached the gate, Bernard and his men had already left and they were waved through by members of the Maquis.

At 10pm Wenk, accompanied by half a dozen of his most efficient Waffen-SS soldiers, knocked on Hoffmann's door and entered. Claire was sitting on the end of Hoffmann's bed in her butter-coloured dress. Her hair was carefully brushed and her make-up perfectly applied.

'It's time,' Wenk said matter-of-factly.

Hoffmann walked towards her and offered her his hand. She took it willingly and stood up. With her free hand, she smoothed down the creases of her dress and checked her hair in the mirror. Wenk ordered his men to tie Claire's hands behind her back. When Hoffmann protested, Wenk took his gun out of his holster and pointed it at him.

The procession made their way downstairs towards the ground floor and the east wing, where they were joined by Koenig. Fräulein Kopkow stood in the reception hall next to Schneider, whose face bore a deep sadness at the events taking place. In the background the strains of a tango could be heard coming from the party; a little gaiety that broke up the solemnity of the occasion. Someone unlocked the door to the basement and Claire stepped into a darkened stairwell that led to the cells. The foetid stench of urine and blood was so overpowering that she stumbled against the wall and vomited.

In the basement the guards stood around preparing for the next batch of prisoners. Wenk ordered all the cells to be opened. Every prisoner without exception was to be taken outside to face the firing squad. One by one the guards began to drag the men outside: Father Gambert, Mayor Bourgoin, Sebastian Levade, who cried like a baby when he realised what was about to happen, and finally Henri, who by this time seemed to have no idea what was taking place. There was only one woman with them – Catherine Sourisseau, her dress torn and her face black and swollen. When she saw Claire tears streamed down her face. It took them fifteen minutes to drag the badly beaten bodies outside and line them up against the wall. Claire was the last to leave.

In the dining room, Kristina checked her watch. The band played on. By now a few couples had retired to their rooms, taking advantage of the moment to engage in sexual pleasures, whilst others continued to drink the evening away. The girls had long finished lacing the drinks with sleeping draughts and were monitoring the results closely. Now all they could do was wait. Someone dressed as one of the household staff would inform them when they were to make their getaway. They had no idea who it would be and were at the mercy of someone they had never met.

Meanwhile, outside in the car park, Didier watched the two trucks turn the corner to the east wing. Despite the freezing cold, he wound the window down, his ear acutely tuned to what was about to take place.

When the trucks rounded the corner towards the entrance to the cells, Yves realised they were too late. The area was floodlit and the prisoners were being led towards the execution area. He had to think quickly. If they opened fire now, no one would stand a chance and it would all be in vain. He knew Bernard and his men would have the area staked out, and so with the entrance door already open, he signalled to his men for the trucks to enter the basement as they had originally intended. The trucks rumbled down the ramp into the building just as Wenk and his men were about to lead Claire outside.

Seeing Claire like this momentarily threw him off guard. It was the last thing he had expected. He reached for his gun and was about to fire, until one of his men stopped him.

'Not now, *mon ami*,' the man cautioned, 'or we're all done for.'

Claire was aware that Yves' men would be in the trucks but she did not look his way in case she aroused suspicion. In her mind, it was all over anyway and she would face her death with dignity.

The prisoners were already lined up against the bullet-riddled wall when Claire joined them. Wenk asked her if she preferred to be blindfolded, to which she replied no. She looked at Hoffmann standing between two of

Wenk's henchmen. Never before had she seen him so powerless.

In the orchard Bernard and his men took aim and waited. They had prepared for the event to the best of their abilities, including infiltrating men into the building to set off a series of explosives. But nothing had prepared him for this new turn of events. When he realised Claire was also to be executed he urged the utmost caution.

Inside the basement the cells were empty and the SS guards stood near the doorway watching the scenario unfold. Yves and his men casually got out of the trucks as if they were about to unload the new prisoners and stood behind them as if to watch the spectacle themselves. Swiftly and silently, the guards were disposed of and their bodies deposited inside the cells. Yves returned to the doorway and aimed his gun at Wenk.

Wenk told the men to take aim at the prisoners, but at the last minute pulled Claire aside. Bernard and Yves watched carefully, ready to fire.

'Herr Hoffmann,' Wenk said, 'in the name of the Fatherland I will give you the honour of eliminating this enemy of the Reich.'

He offered Hoffmann his gun. Hoffmann stepped forward and took it. Claire's heart beat violently but she refused to show her fear. Their eyes met and she smiled. She had loved him to the point of delirium, but equally she had loved her country and had served it to the best of her ability. She had no regrets.

Wenk waited. Hoffmann raised the gun, pointing it at Claire, and in a split second turned it on Wenk, shooting him in the head. With that one shot the place erupted in a hail of gunfire. Hoffmann was hit and spun around, knocking Claire to the ground. With her hands tied behind her back she was powerless to move under the weight of his body. All she could feel was warm blood soaking her body. In the heat of the moment and filled with the rush of adrenaline, she had no idea whether it was Hoffmann's blood or her own.

Under the protection of the Maquis' sub-machine fire, the trucks drove up the ramp, stopping next to the prisoners, who were dragged into the back. At the sound of gunfire other SS guards started to pour into the basement from the ground floor but the Maquis were ready for them, mowing them down with their machine guns. Two grenades were hurled at the doorway, causing a part of the vaulted ceiling and doorway to cave in. Their job done, Bernard's men melted back into the woods whilst the trucks did a quick circular turn, picking up Yves and the rest of his men, and hurtled back towards the gates.

In the dining room, the girls had no idea what was taking place, but at 10.30pm a waiter carrying a champagne tray told them it was time to leave. He hastily put the tray down and left with them, locking the door from the outside. Their actions were noticed immediately and someone started banging on the door. The waiter made a quick dash to a nearby pot-plant standing next to a large sculpture and lit a fuse.

'Hurry,' he shouted to the girls. 'Through the kitchen – that way.'

The girls made a quick dash towards a stairway, but when Kristina looked back the man seemed to be having difficulty with the fuse. She turned to go back and help him. The music had now stopped and the banging on the door echoed loudly in the corridor. At the last minute the fuse took hold and the fire snaked its way towards the doors. The man ran towards Kristina and pushed her down the stairs. When they reached the kitchen they heard a loud explosion. The explosives had done their job. The kitchen staff looked on in fear as the strangers fled past them.

At the first sound of gunfire the guard left his post to see what was happening. Didier quickly turned the car round and drove towards the far end of the car park, not far from the kitchens. When he saw the girls running towards him he revved the car. The girls jumped into the back seat and the car took off. The waiter was nowhere to be seen. One of the girls grabbed a Sten gun lying under a blanket on the floor behind the passenger seat and fired shots at the tyres of all the cars in the car park, ensuring no one would be able to follow them.

As they neared the entrance, Kristina and Didier wound their windows down to throw a grenade. At that moment the guard reappeared, accompanied by others, and they opened fire, forcing Didier to swerve out across the lawn. He had managed to throw his grenade successfully in their direction but in the melee, Kristina was hit before she could throw hers. When she fell back into the car one of the other girls tried to prise the grenade from her hand. It was too late. It exploded, engulfing the car in a blazing inferno. There were no survivors.

The trucks managed to get away. There had been casualties but they had successfully managed to save all the prisoners from execution, including Claire. In the process they had infiltrated the manor and blown up the codebreaking and intelligence rooms.

When the trucks arrived back at the cottage, Yves gathered everyone together. Claire was still in shock that she was alive and unharmed but the

Maquis had lost several men. Every death was one too many and the news that Didier and the girls had not made it left them all reeling. Not only was Didier's death a personal tragedy for Yves and Claire, but the fact that they were now without his radio skills made it difficult for them. Claire was the only one left who had been trained as a radio operator and she had not put those skills into practice since leaving England. Yves told her to take the radio and leave for a safe house in Fougères, where she was to make contact with London. They were to take Hubert's car, and Bernard would go with her.

Henri's injuries were so bad he was delirious, and one of his legs had turned gangrenous and needed to be amputated straight away. It was impossible to risk doing an amputation at the cottage and it was suggested that they get him to a village about an hour's drive away where there was a doctor who belonged to the Resistance. Yves would take one of the trucks and drive him there. The other prisoners deemed to be in urgent need of treatment would also go with them, including Catherine Sourisseau and Sebastian Levade. Mayor Bourgoin and Father Gambert were to go in the second truck with the Maquis. The rest would make their getaway on foot.

Wenk and Koenig were now dead. Yves had wanted them alive, but that was not to be. Only Hoffmann had been taken captive. He had been shot several times and lay unconscious in the back of the truck along with several dead Maquisards. When Claire realised he was still alive she wanted to see him, but Yves refused.

'He won't live,' he told her. 'It's only a matter of hours. By the time we reach the doctor, he will be dead.'

Claire protested; she wanted to take one last look at him.

'Don't be a bloody fool,' he shouted angrily. 'This is no time for sentiment. If you persist I will shoot you myself.'

He stormed outside, slamming the door behind him. In the thoughtful silence that followed he lit a cigarette, mulling over what to do with the man who had caused them so much grief. In the distance the night sky was tinged with orange and red streaks. The explosions had set off a series of fires and the manor appeared to be burning out of control. They had to move quickly before the Germans sent out reinforcements from Saint-Brieuc and other towns.

Bernard joined him. 'It's time to leave, my friend. It's too dangerous here.'

Yves agreed. 'Make sure she gets to Fougères,' he said to him. 'She's headstrong and I don't want her doing anything that will put us all at risk.

We are lucky to be alive.'

'What are we going to do with Hubert and his wife?' Bernard asked. 'A signed piece of paper is no guarantee they won't turn on us, and we can't take them with us.'

In the end it was decided to kill them. They drew lots as to who would be the executioner. Bernard drew the short straw. After everyone left the cottage, he marched Hubert into the outhouse where his wife was tied up, and shot them both. As Yves had said to Claire, this was not the time for sentiment.

The car and two trucks drove away down the narrow, rutted lane to the coastal road. When they came to the first crossroads, Yves brought his truck to a standstill to wish everyone good luck before they parted ways. When he approached the passenger side of Hubert's car, he tapped on the window. Claire ignored him. Instead she stared ahead at the headlights. The enormity of what had just taken place was hitting home. He tapped again, loudly this time until she wound down the window.

Yves put out his hand. Claire looked at him and shook it.

'Take care, Marie-Elise,' he said. 'God willing we will meet again soon.'

Tears streaked her dirty face. She looked at him but could find no words to answer him. She watched him get back in the truck and drive away. None of it seemed real.

The fallout from the raid was to have even worse consequences than the raid on the drop zone. The Germans left no stone unturned in their determination to find the perpetrators. Being so close to the coast it was thought that the raid might have been a prelude to the impending Allied invasion. It was to be a night of terror. By 2am the roads were teeming with armoured vehicles and roadblocks intensified. Anyone not able to identify himself was shot instantly. Throughout the next few days the Germans torched whole villages. Hostages were taken and men and women executed, many out of sheer revenge, but the fact remained that the Resistance and the Maquis had delivered a huge blow to the German morale.

Even villages as far away as Saint-Etienne were not immune. Fortunately Yves had got word to Antoine and Mireille to go into hiding as soon as possible. In the early hours of the morning, they drove into the village where Gaspard, Angélique and her mother had already been notified to wait for the special knock. They must be ready to leave before the Germans arrived. Their association with Claire, Mayor Bourgoin,

Father Gambert and Sebastian Levade made them targets and they would not escape this time. Madame Lemoine was frightened and puzzled and couldn't understand why she was being forced to flee her home.

'I don't understand,' she kept repeating. 'I haven't done anything wrong.'

Angélique put her arm around her. It was useless trying to persuade her it was for her own good. For now she had to trust them.

Yves managed to get Henri to a doctor just in time to save him, but unfortunately they couldn't save his leg. Catherine Sourisseau left Brittany for a safe house in the Alps near the Swiss border, along with Father Gambert and Mayor Bourgoin. She remained in a bad way for a long time, having endured being repeatedly raped and beaten, and although she survived, was never able to have children. Sebastian Levade never lost his hot-blooded ways and his hatred for the Germans and soon rejoined the Maquis. His knowledge of the area proved invaluable in aiding the American troops after the landing at Normandy. He married Angélique in 1946 and together they continued to run Bistro L'Arlequin until her death years later.

Under the next full moon, Henri boarded the Lysander and was evacuated back to England. Yves would not see his old friend again. He was killed in one of the last bombings over London. The amount of information Chevalier, and Agent Manon in particular, had passed on to F Section was invaluable and much of it would be used in the weeks leading up to D-Day.

In Fougères, Claire was able to enjoy a few weeks of peace and freely transmit to London, who praised the group's courage.

'You've done an excellent job,' came the response from London. 'Now come home.'

She was given strict instructions when and where the next landing was to take place. She never turned up.

Chapter 24

Côte d'Émeraude, Brittany, September 2001

Claire Bradshaw lay fast asleep on her bed. Sarah closed the shutters, covered her with a blanket and picked up the empty teacup and half-eaten slice of Mrs P's fruit cake and returned to the kitchen. After gathering up the remains of a late lunch she made herself a drink and sat down to collect her thoughts. She had had a happy childhood, and whilst she had been loved by Claire, she had always felt closer to her father. It was always Peter who was the apple of their mother's eye. This holiday had changed all that and she had never felt so close to her mother as she did at that moment.

The war had changed so many lives and it was understandable that few wanted to talk about their experiences. The fact that her mother had joined the Resistance and never told them had shocked her to the core. Sarah couldn't even begin to understand the courage Claire had shown. It was unimaginable – equal to anything she'd read about in books or seen in films. But she did recall that whenever there had been a programme on the television about the bravery and heroism of the Resistance and the awards they were to receive, belated in many cases, her mother had turned the television off. Now she knew why. Her love for the man who had turned out to be a prominent and ruthless German Gestapo leader had haunted her ever since. How could she have told her story? No one would have believed it. Certainly she – Sarah Carrington with a failed marriage behind her – was in no position to judge. She had never experienced a love like that and probably never would.

The weather was perfect and she decided to get into the car and drive to the beach. A walk would do her good. She parked the car on the clifftop next to a cluster of windswept bushes. A soft breeze warmed her cheeks as she made her way down the steep, winding steps, clutching the safety rope for good measure. It was a sweeping, dramatic landscape and the cliffs were nothing less than majestic. Pleasure boats and yachts bobbed on the water that glistened like a mirror in the afternoon sun. She walked to the beach where her mother had lain with her lover. Several bathing boxes had now been erected and families played with their children, searching for crabs in the rock pools and building sandcastles. It was a world away from worn-torn France.

When she returned to the car, she saw a figure sitting on a bench under the shade of a tree. The man waved.

'Ça va?' he called out.

It was Monsieur Leroux. 'Everything's fine,' Sarah replied.

She thanked him for the fresh eggs and bread he'd placed on the doorstep that morning. He asked after her mother.

'She's taking an afternoon nap. It's a habit she's got into since she became ill.'

He seemed quite saddened at that revelation. 'I'm sorry to hear that. She looks so well.'

'I'm afraid she's more fragile than she looks. She's just getting over a second heart attack. That's why we came here. She needed a holiday.'

He suggested taking her to a certain restaurant in Tréguier. 'It does a very good *cotriade*,' he said. 'Fish stew with sorrel and leek. It will do her good.'

Claire Bradshaw looked the best she'd looked in ages. She wore her favourite dress of cornflower-blue cotton with a print of tiny clusters of flowers, and she added a string of pearls that John had given her as an anniversary present. The relief at telling her daughter her story had lifted a heavy load off her chest and she was thankful that Sarah had not been judgemental. She thought Monsieur Leroux's suggestion of *cotriade,* a fine one, and she had never visited Tréguier.

The restaurant was in a side street not far from the river. A row of window boxes filled with pink and red geraniums added a burst of colour to the medieval wood and stone. Inside it was quiet, cosy and casual and the walls were filled with old photographs of Bretons in national costume. Claire remarked that it reminded her of L'Arlequin.

Sarah ordered the meal while her mother studied the wine list. In the end she took the waiter's advice and ordered one of their limited editions from the Loire Valley.

'Why did you decide to stay in France?' Sarah asked. 'After all, you had achieved so much and you were ordered to return.'

'Think about it, Sarah. How could I?' Claire replied.

'You mean the pregnancy?'

'Of course. I didn't want the SOE in London to know I was pregnant. It's as simple as that. I had left it too late to have an abortion and the only man who could have performed one safely was Hoffmann's doctor. I couldn't have risked going to a local French doctor. I should have acted earlier.'

'Why didn't you?'

Claire smiled. 'I suppose somewhere in the whirlwind of events, and especially after Eva's death, I hoped the war might be over sooner rather than later and we might have had a life together.'

Sarah looked perplexed. 'But even love could not have blinded you to the fact that you must have known Hoffmann would have been tried for war crimes and most likely been executed?'

'In those last few weeks I was living from day to day. I did things I can't even bear to think about. I sold my soul to the devil and it has haunted me ever since. My main objective was to aid my fellow Resistance comrades and the SOE. There was no time to act in a rational way as one normally does. I don't expect you to understand.'

'Tell me one thing, Mum. When you think of him now, and especially after you met Dad, can you say you truly loved this man?'

Sarah waited for her mother's response.

'I will love him to the day I die, my darling,' was the answer.

After what she had heard, if the truth be known, Sarah hadn't really expected any other response.

'Then what did you do? How did you live?'

For a while, Claire skirted around the question. Instead she commented on the wine. It was excellent, and they ordered another bottle.

'We were all in hiding for weeks. I couldn't risk going back to Saint-Etienne and I certainly couldn't go back to the apartment in Paris. I was a wanted woman and the Gestapo would have been looking for me. The woman who ran the safe house in Fougères had no idea what I had been doing. We just didn't ask questions. She took in too many lodgers to risk becoming involved with their lives. But by then I couldn't hide the fact that I was pregnant and I told her I had a fiancé – a member of the Resistance who had been killed. It was she who suggested I go into a convent.'

Sarah looked shocked. It was hard to comprehend. Her mother – the reliable Claire Bradshaw; the woman who played bridge, followed the local hunt, was a member of the Women's Institute, had for years held garden parties to raise money for various charities and who won prizes at the local horticultural show for her carnations; a woman who was in many ways more British than the British themselves – in a convent in Brittany because she was pregnant by a Gestapo officer. After this, Sarah thought nothing would ever shock her again. She had to pull herself together for her mother's sake.

'Where was this convent?' she asked.

'Near Rennes. It was run by the Sisters of Nazareth. There were so many girls there in the same situation as me – it broke my heart. Most had been raped by the Germans and others had fiancés who had disappeared so my story didn't seem out of place. We all did work to earn our keep. I made baby clothes, helped prepare food, etc. The nuns ensured our days were kept busy to take our minds off things.

'But there was one thing that kept my mind occupied. The Mother Superior had allowed me to smuggle in Didier's radio. She took a big risk and we could have all been killed. During those last few months she became my link with the outside world. Twice weekly, one of Madame Maya's girls called at the convent. She was never allowed inside but would pass coded messages, which I would send to London. Chevalier was never broken. Yves had taken over Henri's role.'

'Yves! So you saw him again?' Claire asked.

'No. I just received the messages. I had no idea where he was but I did know they were from him.'

Claire stopped for a moment to gather her thoughts. Tears welled up in her eyes and she took another drink to steady her nerves. 'And then at the end of June I gave birth to a son. He was so beautiful, so perfect, I cried with joy. Of course I knew I couldn't keep him and I put him up for adoption immediately. I just wanted him to have a good home.'

Sarah reached across the table and squeezed her mother's hand tightly. 'Oh, Mum. I don't know what to say.'

Claire wiped away a tear. 'By then we were only weeks away from D-Day. The bombings were relentless but the Resistance were well prepared. When the Americans liberated Avranches on 1st August we knew it was only a matter of days before we'd be liberated as well, but the Germans put up a fierce resistance. With the fall of Rennes imminent we suddenly found ourselves with extra food looted from Gestapo headquarters. Eventually members of the Resistance slipped through the lines and were able to tell the Americans where the Gestapo headquarters were. On the 2nd the Germans started to flee, and on the 4th Rennes was finally liberated. Many of the remaining Germans had slipped away during the night towards Saint-Nazaire. Those who remained had to be protected from the French. Settling old scores had become a daily occurrence and the innocent were killed as well.'

'Did you see any of your old friends?' Sarah asked. 'After the liberation, I mean.'

Claire shook her head. 'I did try to find Yves but was told he had gone to fight in Saint-Malo and then Brest. The garrison there had some of the best German fighters including a crack parachute division. The city fought on for another six weeks and Brest was left a smoking ruin and casualties ran into the thousands. By then I'd left Brittany.'

'Is that when you went to Normandy?' Sarah asked. 'Where you met Dad?'

Claire nodded. 'After the Mother Superior took my child, I was in a state of depression. I didn't want to stay in Rennes a day longer and asked the American commander if I could go to Normandy to take care of the wounded, but he persuaded me to help the Red Cross in Rennes treating the Allied prisoners of war. They were in a terrible shape. Many of the orthopaedic cases had maggot-infested wounds that posed a health risk in the makeshift wards.

'I did that for a while and then asked for a transfer. By then the commander knew all about my work with the British – London had filled him in. He invited me to his headquarters for tea on several occasions, praising the courage of all those who had risked their lives in the fight for freedom. Of course I couldn't tell him everything and I never mentioned that I had a child. Finally he yielded to my request and offered me a position with the Medical Corps in Normandy. He even gave me a car and had someone drive me there. Two days later I was in Bayeux.'

The waiter came over and asked if they would like to see the dessert menu. They agreed on tarte Tatin. It was one of the few French desserts Claire made at home and it had become a family favourite.

'Tell me something, Mum.'

Claire could tell her daughter was struggling to find the right words.

'One thing puzzles me. If you loved Hoffmann so much, didn't you want to know what happened to him? I mean, after he died. Did Yves bury him along with the dead Maquisards?'

'For a while I thought of nothing else. He consumed me like a cancer. I couldn't believe it was final. But in the end I trusted Yves would have given him a proper burial and I had to get on with my life.'

'When you eventually returned to London, didn't Hugo Manning or anyone at the SOE tell you what happened to everyone?'

She shook her head. 'They said nothing, only that Henri had been killed in an air raid.'

Claire finished the last bite of tarte Tatin and placed her fork and spoon neatly on the plate. 'My darling, I have told you enough for tonight. It's getting rather late and I'm beginning to feel exhausted. We can finish this conversation tomorrow.'

Sarah asked to pay the bill, but the owner said it had been paid. When she asked by whom, he would not say.

Seeing her mother had grown tired, she told her to wait while she fetched the car. She had parked it in the next street and as she put the key in the door, she was aware of someone watching her. Parked nearby was the old green Citroën that she'd seen on her first day at the cottage. Inside someone was watching her, but it was too dark to make out the man's face. She got in her car and as she started to drive towards the restaurant, the green Citroën drove away. Surely it couldn't have been a coincidence, she told herself.

It was the aroma of cooking smells wafting through the open window that roused Sarah from a restless sleep the following morning. As she dressed she could hear voices coming from the kitchen. It was probably Monsieur Leroux delivering another basket of food. Then she distinctly heard a third voice, one she didn't recognise, and they seemed to be having an argument. She pushed open the shutters. There was not a cloud in the sky and in the distance the shimmering sliver of sea across the pale green fields looked inviting for one last swim. Then she saw something that made her catch her breath – the green Citroën was parked by the gate.

When she entered the kitchen everyone stopped talking and looked at her. The two men stood up to greet her. The elderly stranger had unruly grey hair and an olive complexion. Apart from his slight stoop, he looked extremely fit for a man of his age.

It was Monsieur Leroux who spoke first, seemingly anxious to break the awkwardness of the moment.

'When you told me your mother had been ill I thought I would make her something special – *Galette-saucisse*.' He picked up another plate and put one on it for her. 'Pork sausage wrapped in a crêpe. It's a speciality of the region.'

The look on her mother's face told Sarah she had walked in on something important.

Claire said she wanted to introduce someone to her. There was an uncomfortable pause for a few seconds. Monsieur Leroux stood back, coffee percolator in hand and looking uncomfortable, as if waiting to see who would speak next.

'This is Yves,' Claire said, watching Sarah's reaction closely.

The man held out his hand. Sarah looked at him for a few seconds and then shook it. For an old man, he had a strong grip.

'I am very happy to finally meet you,' he said with a smile. 'Your mother has told me so much about you.'

'And I feel I know you already,' Sarah replied. She looked towards the window. 'And I am happy to finally meet the driver of the mysterious green car. But please tell me, why were you watching us last night?'

He waved his hand in the air. 'I knew you had much to discuss and I didn't want to interrupt. Your time together is precious.'

Yves sat down, lit a cigarette and took a sip of his coffee. Sarah was fascinated by this little man. He was everything her mother had described, and even in old age he still bore a touch of bohemian eccentricity.

'My darling,' Claire said, 'when I told you last night that I didn't see Yves again, it was true. Our lives had taken different paths, but after I received the first of his letters just over two years ago, we started to correspond. He had searched high and low for me and eventually located me through an old SOE agent who lives in London.'

'The years had passed and I had something I had to get off my chest,' Yves said. 'When I returned from Brest, I had every intention of catching up with your mother but when I found out she'd left for Normandy, I knew I'd left it too late.'

Claire glanced at her mother, who hung on every word he said.

'I needed to tell her that Jürgen Hoffmann didn't die. We managed to save him. Henri and I discussed what to do with him. I am sorry to say that at the time we couldn't risk telling your mother, and there was no doubt that he would have been executed had he stayed in France. We even thought of killing him ourselves. In the end Henri spoke to London and they gave him an assurance that they would give him political amnesty and protect him from the upcoming trials on the proviso that he agreed to testify against the SS and his superiors. He left France at the same time as Henri and was taken into hiding on landing. It was all secret, you know.

'We were never told a thing but as we followed the trials after the war, we kept a lookout for him. There were many here that would have shot him on sight before he even got into the witness box. His name never came

283

up at the trials and I came to the conclusion that he had done exactly as the British wanted – ratted on his own kind.'

He gave a quick glance towards Claire as he said that.

'And of course, all the intelligence files were classified until a few years ago. A copy of one of those files eventually ended up in the hands of one of our Resistance members.' He looked at Claire again. 'You remember our agent who ran the restaurant in Redon?'

Claire nodded.

'It seems that SS Sturmbannführer Jürgen Marc Hoffmann had been interrogated in private and his testimony brought about the capture and subsequent executions of several high-ranking officials both in France and Germany, including Maximilian Gassner from Avenue Foch. For that he was given diplomatic immunity and a new identity and went to live in Argentina.'

Sarah looked at her mother, who had turned quite pale by now.

'Go on,' Claire said.

'We may never have known anything else, but it seems that he decided to go back to Germany – sometime in the late '60s I believe. His son was still there. He also remarried, a woman who had lost her husband during the war – a wealthy woman from Vienna by the name of Julie.'

Claire covered her face with her hands and let out a gasp. 'Julie Zeidler!'

Yves nodded. 'I'm afraid so. Dr Franz Zeidler died when the car he was being driven in was blown up by Soviet troops during the fall of Berlin.'

Claire turned to her daughter. 'When I received the first of Yves' letters, it was to say Jürgen hadn't died after all but he didn't know where he was. We exchanged a few letters for a while but nothing came up until the *Badische Zeitung* published the death notice. The Black Forest was the last place we expected to find him. We had discussed earlier that he might have been using another name – Jürgen Marc von Rosenkranz. The "Jürgen Marc" seemed plausible to me, but the "von Rosenkranz" – that baffled me. It was only when I saw the photograph in the newspaper that I finally knew for certain it was him. Even in old age I still recognised his face, but it was the scar that finally did it. He could never hide that.'

Sarah thought back to the day she had shown the newspaper cutting to Violette. Now she understood why she had looked so shocked. She *had* recognised him after all. Perhaps for the same reason – the scar! But was Violette aware of what took place after he was supposed to have drowned?

No doubt her mother would tell her when she was ready.

Yves continued. 'He took the name of von Rosenkranz from Julie's father. They came from a long line of Austrian nobility. Titled names were officially abolished after World War I but still remained in use. The home in Schluchsee had once been a hunting lodge belonging to Julie's mother's side and it appears that after he married Julie, they moved there and maintained somewhat of a reclusive existence.'

Throughout all this, Monsieur Leroux had not said a word, but the fact that he was privy to this conversation spoke volumes. It was then that Claire admitted to Sarah that he was none other than Bernard.

'I couldn't tell you until you'd heard my story,' Claire said. 'I hope you will forgive me.'

Sarah smiled. 'It's all fitting into place. I know this hasn't been easy for you but I understand that you needed to resolve the past, especially if you knew Hoffmann hadn't died after all.'

Secretly, Sarah was glad Yves hadn't caught up with her mother earlier; it may have stopped her marrying her father. She reminded her that they had to leave the following day and asked if Bernard would show her the manor. He was only too delighted. She asked Claire if she would like to come with them, but she refused.

'I never want to lay eyes on that place again,' she said adamantly. 'Anyway, I want to spend a few more hours with my dear friend. You two go alone.'

Bernard told Sarah that the manor as it stood today was not the original building. 'Our raid caused a lot of damage,' he said. 'But the final straw came when we arrived in Fougères. Using Didier's radio, your mother contacted London and the RAF finished the job off for us. The Germans never used the manor again.'

When they arrived at the gates, Sarah commented on the gold coat of arms.

'They're the original gates,' Bernard said. 'They date back to the eighteenth century.' He told her he had once been employed as the gamekeeper by the original owners, but after the war when the house lay in ruins, he worked on the farm.

'What happened to the owners?' Claire asked.

'As collaborators and members of the PNB they were executed after de Gaulle came to power. What you see now was reconstructed in the 1950s when the new owners took over. They allowed me to stay on at the farm and today my son is the gamekeeper.'

'Who are the new owners?' asked Sarah.

'Wealthy Americans. The wife's father was one of those who liberated us. They decided to redo the cottage for rent after they'd completed the manor. It was Yves' idea to meet your mother here.'

'Is the manor much different to how it was?' she asked.

'No. The owners had access to the old plans and tried to keep it as it was. They did a good job.'

The owners were not there, but Bernard had a key. When they entered the large reception hall Sarah felt a tingle run down her spine.

'I don't know if I can do this,' she said, a lump rising in her throat. 'I think it's all starting to hit home.' She looked as if she would burst into tears at any moment.

'Come on,' Bernard said. 'You'll be fine. There's pheasant pâté in the fridge. I'll cut you a slice and we'll enjoy it with a glass of Bordeaux.'

She followed him obediently into the kitchen. 'You know, *chérie*,' he said, filling her glass. 'Unlike Yves, I only knew your mother for a few weeks but in that time I came to realise she was one of the bravest women I'd ever known. She had placed herself in a dangerous situation, both in Rennes and here. You cannot imagine how bad this place was. Many people died under torture or were executed. I was there that night when she faced the firing squad. She was fearless. We all had the greatest admiration for her and we never thought she'd survive. The greatest surprise was when Hoffmann turned the gun on his superior. Only later did I come to understand that they really did love each other.'

Whether it was the wine or the pent-up emotions, Sarah didn't know; possibly a combination of both, but she wept like a child.

'We had no idea,' she sobbed.

Bernard gave her his handkerchief. 'Your mother put her life in danger. After the war, women who had cohabited with the Germans had their heads shaved. Some were killed. The fact that she became pregnant was something no one would have accepted.'

Sarah wiped her eyes. 'I know that now,' she replied in a mournful voice.

Bernard cleared away the dishes. 'Come on. I'll show you around.'

Even though she doubted that it had been a good idea to see the manor, Bernard was an excellent guide. The code rooms and interrogation rooms had gone and in their place were beautifully decorated sitting rooms and libraries. More importantly, the cells had been converted back into wine cellars and were filled with fine wines. She smiled to herself. Her mother would have approved of that.

Th
ho
th

be
pa
ho
of

of
an
to
Th
Th
kn

so
th
bu

po
wa

an

It
asl
fri
gl
pr

ca
ga
th

course this is a shock for you. Why do you think I kept it to myself all these years?' Now, my darling, be a good girl and go and get us a drink. The sea air is making me rather thirsty. A nice glass of wine will go down well.'

Sarah got up and walked over to the ship's rail, looking out at the sea to gather her thoughts. After a while she went to the bar, perused the wine list and ordered two glasses of Bordeaux. When she got back, her mother had fallen asleep, a smile of contentment on her face.

'Mum, wake up. I've brought you the wine.'

When Claire didn't wake up, Sarah nudged her.

'Mum!' she said in a louder voice.

Claire's head rolled to the side. Sarah dropped her glass.

'Mum! Mum!'

It was useless. A crowd of onlookers gathered to try and help. Sarah was hysterical. Soon after, the ship's doctor pronounced her dead. This time it was not deemed to be a heart attack: she had died peacefully in her sleep.

St Mary's Church was filled to capacity for Claire Bradshaw's funeral. All her old friends from the various institutes, societies and charities she had belonged to; Violette and their last few remaining Polish friends – airmen who had fought on the side of the Allies. Just as the service was about to start Sarah noticed an old man enter the church. He laid a wreath of red and white carnations next to the others and then sat in the back pew. He wore a stylish overcoat and a trilby and had difficulty walking without the aid of a walking stick.

After the service he came over and offered his condolences to Sarah and Peter before returning to a waiting car. A chauffeur opened the door for him. The only other comment he had made was that their mother was an extraordinary woman and he had been privileged to know her.

Sarah would not have known who he was had it not been for Violette, who had also seen him.

'Who was that?' Sarah asked Violette.

'That, *chérie*,' she replied, leaning closer as if to reveal a big secret, 'is Hugo Manning. During the war he worked for the War Office.'

Sarah watched the car drive away. After all this time, someone had finally acknowledged her mother's courage – rather belatedly in Sarah's eyes, but at least they had acknowledged her.

She turned to Violette. 'You knew all along, didn't you? About Hoffmann, I mean.'

'I thought he had died, but when you showed me his photograph I knew it had to be him. Even in old age he still bore his good looks, and of course the scar. It was quite distinctive. I never knew what your mother did in France before we met up again in Normandy, you have to believe that, but after you left that day, I guessed something had happened. When I went to see her I confronted her. At first she didn't want to talk about it, but then she told me everything.' Violette looked across the churchyard at Peter, who was chatting to some of the guests. 'The thing is, what will *you* do now that you know?'

Sarah let out a deep sigh. 'I don't know. I'm still thinking about it.'

After the service, the guests all returned to Grange House where Mrs P had excelled herself with a fine spread. Everyone wanted to know about the holiday. Sarah assured them that her mother had been the happiest she had been in years — certainly since her father's death.

'She died a happy woman,' she told them. Inside her heart was breaking, but over the past few weeks she had learnt to be strong. She took Peter's hand and squeezed it. Having him there reassured her. 'Our mother loved her family, her friends and life itself,' she continued. 'We can't ask any more of life than that, can we?'

After the guests had gone, Peter joined Sarah in the drawing room.

'How about a glass of port, sis?' he said. 'A nightcap like old times.'

'That would be lovely,' she replied.

He handed her a glass and sat in his father's old chair. 'You never said much about your holiday, you know. What did you do with yourselves?'

Sarah looked across at her brother. After careful consideration she had decided not to tell him her mother's secret. John Bradshaw had loved Peter like his own flesh and blood. He couldn't even tell him he had a half-brother in Schluchsee. It would break Peter's heart if he knew the truth.

'We did lots of sightseeing, went for walks along the beach, ate in lovely restaurants and drank wine. We had a wonderful time,' she said, 'and I was glad that I was there to share those last few weeks with Mum in the country she loved.'

After he retired to bed, Sarah went to the bookshelf and pulled out a book — *The Sorrows of Young Werther*. Inside was the death notice. She took it out, took one long, last look at Hoffmann's face and then lit a match, set fire to it and watched it burn in the empty fireplace.

What was it Violette had said to her a few months ago? 'If I was you, I would let sleeping dogs lie.' Perhaps she was right. Her mother had kept her secret to protect those dearest to her. Sarah would do the same

The Embroiderer

Set against the mosques and minarets of Asia Minor and the ruins of ancient Athens, The Embroiderer is a gripping saga of love and loss, hope and despair, and of the extraordinary courage of women in the face of adversity.

1822: During one of the bloodiest massacres of The Greek War of Independence, a child is born to a woman of legendary beauty in the Byzantine monastery of Nea Moni on the Greek island of Chios. The subsequent decades of bitter struggle between Greeks and Turks simmer to a head when the Greek army invades Turkey in 1919. During this time, Dimitra Lamartine arrives in Smyrna and gains fame and fortune as an embroiderer to the elite of Ottoman society. However it is her grand-daughter, Sophia, who takes the business to great heights only to see their world come crashing down with the outbreak of The Balkan Wars, 1912-13. In 1922, Sophia begins a new life in Athens but the memory of a dire prophecy once told to her grandmother about a girl with flaming red hair begins to haunt her when the Italians and Germans occupy Greece in WWII.

1972: Eleni Stephenson is called to the bedside of her dying aunt in Athens. In a story that rips her world apart, Eleni discovers the chilling truth behind her family's dark past plunging her into the shadowy world of political intrigue, secret societies and espionage where families and friends are torn apart and where a belief in superstition simmers just below the surface.

Made in the USA
Las Vegas, NV
24 April 2023

71023209R00173